STILL NOT LOVE

AN ENEMIES TO LOVERS ROMANCE

NICOLE SNOW

ICE LIPS PRESS

Content copyright © Nicole Snow. All rights reserved.
Published in the United States of America.
First published in February, 2019.

Disclaimer: The following book is a work of fiction. Any resemblance characters in this story may have to real people is only coincidental.

Please respect this author's hard work! No section of this book may be reproduced or copied without permission. Exception for brief quotations used in reviews or promotions. This book is licensed for your personal enjoyment only. Thanks!

Cover Design – CoverLuv. Photo by Rafa G. Catala.

Website: Nicolesnowbooks.com

ABOUT THE BOOK

**Not him. Not now. Not the hell again.
But I need a hero fast...**

I'm about to go nuclear.

Yet I have to smile and pretend I won't slap him into the next century.

James Nobel and I have *history*.

The raging hearts, dueling kisses, nights on fire kind.

A man like him breaks laws with *that* suit and *that* smirk.

So how could I ever forget my first?

Or pelting an Adonis with crumpled love notes in class?

We were young and dumb and lied about forever.

Spoiler alert: he did the lying. Then he disappeared.

Maybe I always wanted to know why, but not like this.

James, my personal bodyguard.

James, my flipping bunkmate in a luxury cabin for newlyweds.

James, who still makes me crave one more night of bad decisions.

Worse, we're snowed in with my very important father and his enemies.

It's a date with chaos. Plus every question I swore I'd never ask again.

What if there's more to us than scalding banter and get-bent glares?

What if there's still - do I really *have* to say it - love?

I: TALE AS OLD AS TIME (FAYE)

*L*et me tell you one thing.

Belle, I most certainly am not. Even if she just so happens to be my favorite fairy-tale heroine.

Don't get me wrong – I love being a librarian. Every book is an entire hidden world waiting to be discovered, one page at a time.

I get the pleasure of endlessly introducing people to new things. My happiest days are when I get to see a kid discover how much they can love reading when I pick the perfect book for them.

What I love most about my job, though, is the smell of old pages, binding, book glue, ink, leather.

Guess what part I hate most?

Just guess.

It's that the scent of a library is *lacking*. It doesn't have the smell of gunpowder and hot, stinging adrenaline that really gets my blood going.

That, plus sometimes, it's too damned *quiet*.

That's how it is today until the glass double doors out front slam open, letting in a hint of crisp Portland air that's half winter, half asphalt, and one hundred percent crunchy granola.

I glance up from checking the condition of a few returns before re-shelving as the commotion starts.

Over a dozen men in black suits rush the room in militant quickness, all of them nearly identical carbon copies of each other: sharp-cut hair, sunglasses, and those little clear coils of earpieces stretching down to their collars. They bark orders to the library patrons as they sweep in, flanking the perimeter, commanding startled, confused people to clear out.

With how they're dressed, the air of authority they give off, no one even questions it – not even the library managers, who find themselves herded out in a flurry of surprised little gasps, tumbling into the crowd streaming toward the exit.

I sigh, grinding the heel of my palm against the bridge of my nose, and set my books down.

God *damn* it, Dad.

Sometimes, the whole Secret Service schtick is a little too extra.

But at least he knows how to make a selfishly dramatic entrance.

And he really pulls off the drama now. Because once the library's clear of everyone but me, two Secret Service agents hold the double doors open like they're announcing the entrance of a king. America may not have royalty, but a U.S. Senator is pretty damn close.

The other agents swarm the single-room space, almost too big for the small, cozy, brick-walled area, an old house that was converted to a library some time during the fifties.

When Dad walks in, I can almost hear the grand fanfare.

Especially when, as he passes, the two agents holding the door salute him with a barked, "Mr. Harris!"

Je-sus.

My father comes gliding across the room like a razor, cutting the space. If the Secret Service agents are black daggers, he's a sword.

All tall, sharp-edged, and PR-ready, his suit the color and hardness of steel, his eyes like polished jade blades. Sometimes I look at this man, with his silvered, backswept hair and stern jaw, wondering who he is and how we're related.

I don't see my father in him, even if I know he loves me and would do anything to protect me.

That's the whole reason I've been squirreled away in this cozy little piece of Portland like a secret waiting to be discovered.

But in him, there's something missing. Like the man who used to carry me around on his shoulders disappeared, leaving behind a skin that some dark, cold, grim thing shrugged on over its tense, bristling shape.

Yet, there's nothing cold about the way he reaches for me when I stand straight with a fond, exasperated sigh and round my desk to approach him. He pulls me into a hug, wrapping me up in his tall frame, resting his scratchy beard on the top of my head as he holds me tightly.

"Faye," he murmurs, his voice as scratchy as his trim beard, deep and raspy and comforting. "You look like you're doing well."

I lean into him, squeezing him tight. "Well, until you barged in with the entourage, I was bored."

"Boredom is good for your health."

"Is that what they're saying in your top secret briefings? Or is it just the latest science fluff piece you read on your way over?" With a laugh, I draw back, looking up at him. "What's with the theatrics? This is pretty heavy, even for you. Feels like you're about to usher me into a panic room. Or pull some kind of Liam Neeson stunt. Look, Dad, if you want me to keep a low profile, you can't do stuff like this at my job. I don't know how I'm going to explain it tomorrow."

"You won't need to," he says, voice firming, and he takes my arm gently in one knobbed, large hand. "This isn't your job anymore."

I blink. "What? But I –"

"Faye, there's no time to explain. Especially not here." His gaze darts around, and I can see his old military training in that look. He's assessing the perimeter, expecting danger, looking for any access holes, points of egress, vulnerabilities.

So, in other words, this is serious.

"We shouldn't be out in the open," he whispers gruffly, giving my arm a light pull. "We'll talk in the car."

Part of me wants to resist, but there's something bothering me. A tension in the air, a sour omen, and my own training kicks into high gear.

Situational awareness is something you never forget. Not even when your Dad drags you out of the FBI not long after you even finish your first field assignments. It's been years, but in the back of my mind, I'm still an agent.

And that agent is saying there's danger in the air, and the time to talk isn't now.

So I keep my mouth shut, for now, as I nod and follow them outside. The Secret Service agents form a cordon around us, flanking us, and I realize they're acting as human shields.

That's *never* a good sign.

Neither is the fact that Dad arrived in a limo flanked by half a dozen black SUVs, and I can tell from the plating and window thickness that every last one of them is bulletproof. This is the kind of gear and protection reserved for a presidential motorcade, not for a Senator.

Holy hell.

This *is* serious.

But I don't realize just how serious until I've allowed myself to be maneuvered into the back of the limo. The doors close, leaving us alone with just the privacy window walling us off from the driver and the agent in the front seat.

I've been in enough of these vehicles to know it's soundproof, double-plated bulletproof glass. So that even if someone tries to take out the driver, they'll never be able to shoot through the front windshield to get a hit in on the people in the back.

I settle in my seat and cross my legs, eyeballing my Dad.

I'm trying to figure out a delicate way to ask while he's gazing out the window with that glaring, brooding look I've seen so often ever since Mom died. That's what changed him, really.

The night she fell asleep behind the wheel on the way home from a charity function and drove her car off a bridge. It's been eight years, but I don't think he's ever grieved properly.

He's still living in that moment. That night he got the brutal phone call and showed up at my college dorm with tears streaming down his face, saying I had to come with him to find Mom.

I still hurt, too.

I still miss her. Miss the way she smiled, the way she smelled, the laughter, the way she *got* me the way moms love to get their daughters, the way she always had paint on her fingertips and her cheeks and all over from one of her latest projects.

Most of all, I miss the way she was a bridge between me and Dad. We're both churning passions and crashing heat while she was this cool, soft touch making the burning air between us safe. She knew just what to say to defuse teenage angst or stop me from saying something to my father I knew

I'd regret. Or to stop him from getting in the way of his little girl growing up.

I'm not like her. I don't know how to be calm and quiet and gentle.

Defusing explosives, not people, is my thing.

And I don't know how to be careful with Dad right now.

But I try. I really do, keeping my voice soft and low as I ask, "Dad? Are you okay? Did someone try to hurt you?"

"Yes," he says, with such bluntness it takes my breath away. "And they've threatened to hurt you, too. That's why I'm here."

I sit up straighter. My heart slams against my ribs and then ricochets back in place.

God. He doesn't even change his pensive gaze out the window, delivering the information with such coldness it's like he doesn't truly care if someone kills him. Or me, though I know he does.

He wouldn't have dragged me out of my job if he didn't.

"I think," I say slowly, "I need a little more. What's going on?"

"I'm not sure how much I should say." He's grinding his knuckles against his chin, the faint light through the blackout windows reflecting off his worn, well-polished wedding ring. "Someone's put a hit out on me, Faye. On us. On anyone connected to us."

"What? Who? *Why?*"

"I don't have answers for that just yet, but I'm looking into it, believe me." Sharp eyes slide to me abruptly, locking on. "I just know they're serious. This isn't your typical anonymous crank calls or talcum powder in an envelope scare. Last night, someone shot out the window of the house. They missed me, but they also got away. Security wasn't able to catch them, and they'd apparently been casing the grounds long enough to find the one blind spot in the CCTV coverage."

Just like that. As casually as talking about going out for drinks. There's this weird detachment in his voice while he's talking about someone who tried to *kill* him.

Right about now, I hate him.

I hate him because I love him, and he didn't call.

He doesn't seem to care that he could've died last night and I wouldn't have even known until he was already a police report, a memory, a nationwide news shocker — and nothing more.

"Jesus Christ, Dad," I gasp, glaring at him. "Why didn't you call me last night? Are you hurt? Are you —"

He stops me with a raised hand. "Listen. I wasn't even close enough to the window to be hit by the flying glass. I didn't have time to call you when I was arranging an investigation and increased security coverage. Everything's under control, but I'd like it to stay that way, Faye — which is why I'm relocating you until the threat is neutralized."

"What? No!" Anything calm and reasonable goes out the window when he tells me so flatly that he's just going to move me around like a chess piece on a board. I clench my fists. "That's not fair. You forced me into this life and now...now that I'm finally settled into it, you're just going to rip me away?"

He grinds his teeth but doesn't react.

Oh, how I *want* him to react, but of course he's got to be Senator Harris and not my Dad and the man who gave me my own explosive temper.

"It's temporary. And it's for your own safety. Please don't be childish."

Stung, I recoil. "So it's 'childish' to want to control my own life? Funny, I thought it was *childish* to let my father order everything for me when I'm twenty-seven years old and I can't even go to the damn Co-Op store without a security escort."

"Please don't exaggerate."

"It's how it feels." I fold my arms over my chest, glowering out the window. "You don't get to do this to me again, Dad. I can handle a little suspense. I used to be a freaking FBI agent. Still would be, if you hadn't been doing this to me my entire life, pulling strings where they don't belong."

"Don't give me that. You know damned well that was for your own good." There it is – that spark of anger, that growl in his voice. "You nearly blew yourself to kingdom come when –"

"Because I was an explosives expert!" I fling back. "Explosives, Dad. Explosives experts deal with bombs – surprise, surprise. What matters is that I know what I'm doing. I wasn't in danger then, and I'm not in danger now. I know how to handle myself."

I have to believe that. *I have to.*

Because I've been holding on to that idea for years, if I'm honest.

I still train, almost every day in my basement with a punching bag, a jump rope, a treadmill.

I still keep up on the latest FBI statutes and changes in surveillance and criminal investigations.

I still re-certify for firearms with a concealed carry license every year.

I still avidly devour info on new developments in explosives tech and neutralization techniques, because as long as I'm doing these things, I don't feel like I'm stagnating, rotting away as this useless little mouse tucked in the corner of a bookshelf.

I'm the deadliest librarian in Portland.

Hiding a skill set that could save lives while I run story time for preschoolers on weekends.

All because Dad decided I wasn't allowed to have a life and tore me away from my job, my world...and the man I thought I loved, until he turned as cold and strange as my father.

And there he goes again – taking a deep breath, pushing down any feeling behind his façade of Senator Harris, looking at me with the same calm, stern command he uses in the office, where he intimidates people into doing his bidding and cutting through the bullshit and politics and red tape every day.

"This is not up for discussion, Faye," he says. "Obviously, I understand you have your feelings, but I didn't ask for your input. And it won't change the outcome. You're my daughter, damn it. It's my obligation to keep you safe. If feelings have to be collateral damage, then so be it."

"Whatever. I might feel better about it if you didn't call me an 'obligation' right after telling me my opinions don't matter."

He sighs, dragging a finger down his chin. "You're too much like your mother."

"I'm *nothing* like Mom, and you know it. That's the problem. I'm too much like you, and that's why I piss you off so much. That's why we –"

"I'm not angry."

"I wish you would be."

I wish you'd feel anything at all for more than half a second. More than the frustration streaming out in his tone because I don't just fold without questions.

I let out a heavy sigh. "Is there anything I can do to change your mind about this?"

"No. And I'd appreciate it if you stopped trying. We'll be coordinating with an external security company. We need the privacy, the secrecy, someone who isn't connected to the Washington insiders."

I suck in a breath, my anger draining, replaced by – okay, I'll admit it – interest. This case smells like conspiracy.

"You think it's an inside job? Someone with connections?"

"I have my reasons to believe so. Which is why I'm turning to an old friend who knows enough about Secret Service protocol to do the job right, especially at the fundraiser event next week."

Oh, no.

Oh, *hell no*.

I know what he's going to say before the rest is out of his mouth. I know because the *only old friend* in security that I know he'd actually trust, when he doesn't trust anyone, is Riker Woods – another Gulf War veteran who was in Dad's unit, a soldier about fifteen years younger who served under Dad's command. Which means...

"We'll be meeting up with Enguard Security at the luxury lodge in Soda Springs," he says, and my stomach sinks. "It's some kind of asinine ski event – I didn't plan it – but apparently it's meant to attract certain types of donors. Good for campaign photo ops. It'll be easier to secure the event than my home or yours, and if anyone tries anything there, they'll be easily caught in a public place. In the meantime, my connections will follow any leads both here and in D.C."

I hardly hear him. Even though every ounce of my training is telling me Dad's holding something back, trying to shelter me by not telling me something, I can't focus on that right now.

Everything recedes into white noise, this blankness settling over the here and now, dragging me back into the hollow, ringing echoes of the past.

That past is James Nobel.

A whirlwind. A sweetness. A sting.

A sunset and a storm of blinding tears so real it still cuts me with a raw, salty edge every day I let myself think about it. And you'd better believe most days, I don't let myself think *anything*.

My heart feels savaged to the core, and for the first time in a good, long while, I want to run. I've disarmed explosives with only a second left on the timer and never felt anything like the dread and cold, sick nervous tremble I feel now.

This is it. This is life post-librarian.

I'm going to be trapped in Soda Springs for at least a week, in close proximity to the only man who ever broke my heart.

And the only man who still holds the pieces.

I'm seeing James for the first time in over five years and there's no way around it.

He's a senior part of Enguard. I'll admit I kept tabs on him.

Just for a little while after I left the FBI. I found out he also left not long after something happened, some disaster that was kept hush-hush but that still shoved him out of the agency.

He never answered my calls after that.

Never spoke to me at all, and it hurt.

It hurt so fucking much, and I want to hate him for it, but I can't.

The fire, the hurt, the loss turning my blood into molten magma for half a freaking decade has to come out one way or another.

And I can't trust what it'll make me do when I finally see him again.

II: SONATA (JAMES)

The only time I ever find peace is at the darkest time of night.

That's when there's nothing but me, the faint moonlight streaming through the window, and the caress of ivory keys beneath my fingers.

Schumann, tonight. *Scenes from Childhood.*

Probably ironic, when I'm in my grandfather's workshop, stealing a minute alone with the sleek, majestic grand piano he's been restoring for at least the past three years. The sound is almost perfect, mellow and sweet.

The keys respond beneath my fingers, flowing with every touch to raise soft, sad notes that wind over the room like they're trying to bleed life into the antiques. They line every shelf, these strange, gilded objects, debris from other people's memories, perched all about like judgmental owls in the night.

Watching over me, asking again and again, *who, who?*

James Nobel, who *the hell are you?*

I haven't known the answer to that fucking question in a long time.

But I feel the most like my true self now. Whenever I can pour myself into each haunting note and for just a few minutes, feel halfway human again.

Feel anything at all, when somehow in the last few years, that's become so very, very hard.

They call me cold at work. Detached. Quiet.

Landon, Gabe, Skylar, Riker – they always say they can count on me *because* I'm cool as ice. To stay in control, while everyone else worries about things that I know will work out one way or another.

They act like I choose to be this way. As if I'm naturally just calm and focused, gracefully in charge of myself like some magic, tortured, half-human thing.

The truth is, I don't have a *self* to be in control of.

Not anymore.

That James was left behind years ago – my ghost, my soul, ripped out of me in a single moment and left behind in that burning, terrible night when I lost everything that ever mattered.

This thing that's moved forward wearing my face for all these years? It isn't me.

I'm gone. Marooned. Missing in action.

But sometimes, when I slip into the music this way, I start to find myself a little.

I start to find the man my mother raised me to be before life tore her away and shattered everything that made me happy.

I manage a faint smile in the darkness, remembering her teaching me to play.

I'd been small, so small, my feet dangling from the bench, unable to even touch the floor. She'd stand behind me with her long, golden hair falling over me, her hands covering mine to show me how to play scales.

Then scales became Chopin, then Beethoven, all the classics up to obscure modern jazz. She'd always delight in finding something new and strange, some gem buried in the lost halls of composition history, something that fit her strange and wild Bohemian spirit that made her everything she was and everything she was never supposed to be.

It's not the mechanical action of pressing keys that does a damn thing for me.

It's memories that *truly* make me feel human again, if only for a second.

They make me feel like there's still something left inside besides whispers.

I'm almost through Schumann, pulling from memory to remember the final fingering, when I hear creaking floorboards in the hall outside the workshop.

Grandpa must already be two fingers in or more with his usual extended nightcap, to be walking so heavily. Either that, or just waking from a blundering sleep and still staggering around.

I let my hands fall still on the keys and glance at the yellow-faced antique wall clock, its bronze hands faintly gleaming in the moonlight through the window. It's nearly two in the morning.

I've been down here for three hours, without even feeling time pass.

Grandpa leans around the doorway. In him, I can see myself in another thirty or forty years, tall and rangy and silver at the temples, blending into pale blond.

But there's a warmth in him, too. Like he was shaped by a kindness and wisdom I'm not sure I'll ever possess.

That warmth shows in his smile now as he settles in the doorway, a half-full glass tumbler dangling from one hand, a whiskey bottle in the other. The smile he offers me is a little fuzzy, but generous, quiet, searching. *Understanding.*

Sometimes I hate how his eyes seem to see me in all my raw glory.

You shouldn't be able to see a ghost.

"You're still good," he murmurs. "For a minute, I thought it was her."

"That would be something." I muster a faint smile, happy a piece of my mother lives on in my fingertips. "I'm sorry if I woke you. Didn't realize how late it was."

"You didn't, son. I keep myself awake. Can't hear a damn thing on the top floor, anyway. But I knew I'd find you down here. I always do." He pushes away from the door and steps into the workshop to deposit the glass on the top of the piano, within my reach, then takes a swig straight from the bottle before nodding toward the smaller player piano in the corner, gleaming and freshly restored and repaired.

I nod, too. Respectfully. This is his pride and joy, bringing these old, forgotten things back to life.

"Feel like putting that pretty girl through her paces? I've got to drop her off at the neighbor's next week, but I don't have your ear for the finer notes. Help me make sure it's perfect before it goes back?"

"Of course." I lift myself from the grand piano's bench, catch the tumbler in my fingertips, and cross the space to the smaller piano, settling on the bench. With a small sip of smoky, stinging whiskey, I run through scales, making the piano sing like rainfall notes, a glissando of escalating delicate plinks.

Grandpa closes his eyes in quiet pleasure, just listening.

It's a moment of communion for us, in a way. A quiet in the space between notes where we can remember we're more alike than we are different, no matter how we may disagree on things.

And I can already feel a disagreement coming, sure as a storm.

Even now, he's weaving his way toward the old filing cabinet tucked behind his cluttered corner desk, just as I finish playing.

I know before he finishes opening the bottom drawer what I'll see. *Fuck, not again.*

The letter.

We call it the letter, but what it really is?

More than three hundred meticulously handwritten, yellowed pages, the ink starting to fade, the pages curling at the corners. It feels like a letter from beyond the grave, and it has since the moment Grandpa found Mom's unfinished manuscript hiding in the attic, tucked away among her old things that we just can't stand to throw away.

It's her novel. A beautifully crafted story of love that's just waiting for one of us to do it justice with an ending that would honor her properly.

The loosely bound pages *thud* against the desk, the wind of their landing making the stacks of invoices and inventory bills rustle. My grandfather's chair creaks almost as loudly as he does as he lowers himself with a groan, then thunks the bottle down next to the stack.

He flicks through the first few pages, then riffles to the end. I've stopped playing without realizing it, my hands resting loose and quiet on the keys as I watch him silently across a cluttered room that still, in this moment, feels too empty.

"It should be you," he says, gruff, raw, his voice thick. He's always been an emotional man, but the whiskey makes it hard to keep it inside. "I can't do this. Every time I look at it, every time I see it cut off like this, I just keep thinking about *her* being cut off and...and I break down like a damn old fool. Can't do it, son. I'll ruin it. I'll ruin it, James."

"Like I'll do any better?" I say, trying to control the sharpness creeping into my tone. "Whatever emotion that story needs...there's nothing in my life that compares. No reference to draw. No inspiration. It would feel inauthentic, shallow, and false if I –"

"If you what?" he flares, smacking his palm down against the desk hard enough to make the books and pencil cup and trinkets scattered all over it jump. "If you stop acting like your life is already over and start to feel something again? Look, I know the accident screwed things up. But it sure didn't kill you. James, you have something left inside. You think you're cold, but that girl –"

"Leave *Faye* out of this," I snarl, almost by reflex.

Just saying her name out loud makes me feel like my lungs have been punctured, but I'm still trying desperately to suck air through the ragged, painful holes anyway.

I can't stand this bullshit lunacy.

I can't stand to feel this, to worry whether or not the old man's right. That's why it's easier to retreat behind an icy wall, push it down, swallow it until it's buried so deep I don't even know where to find it again.

I take a deep breath. Then another and another before smoothing my hand over my shirt and standing. "The piano is fine. Your client should be pleased. I'm going home."

"James..."

"Goodnight, Grandpa."

"*James!*"

I stop. Just stop where I stand, my hands hanging at my sides, while I stare blankly at the door.

It's pure hell, knowing I can't walk away from him when there's so much emotion in his voice.

He's like a vessel filled to bursting. One more tiny drop and he'll shatter and spill all over me. I can't leave him when he's hurting.

"Please," he asks softly while I shake my head. "Finish it for her. You're the only one. If you'd try –"

"I can't. Hire a ghostwriter. Anyone but me."

"It *has* to be you," he growls. "There's more of her left in you than anyone!"

"I'm nothing like my mother."

"Only because you don't want to be." His chair creaks again as he stands, the floorboards groaning under him as he steps closer to me. I can smell the whiskey on his breath, and the old tobacco scent of him, as he stops at my shoulder. "I'm asking you again, James. Just think about it. Please."

Something rustles at my shoulder. I look down.

It's a thick sheaf of pages.

Not the entire book, but what looks like the last chapter with its terrible final, empty page left hanging for so many years. He waits in silence, watching me with his rheumy eyes wet, and I close my eyes with a sigh, then snatch the pages from him. The paper has been so worn by repeated handling that it feels like touching soft skin.

"I'll take a look," I say. "But no promises."

He nods and lets me go without a word.

I walk out into the night, to my car, and to my solitary apartment, which feels much too big for me right now.

I'd barely touched my drink at Grandpa's house. At home, I pour myself a fresh two fingers of bourbon and sink down at my desk, staring at my closed laptop and the pages stacked on top of it.

It's a sick joke.

Who the hell knew I'd be scared by a stack of paper? I deal with bullets, blood, and non-stop danger working for Enguard. I'm sure as fuck not laughing.

I press two fingers to my temples, closing my eyes. I'll try because I told him I would. I'll try, even though I know the outcome.

This won't end well. There's no way.

I've bought myself time, and lately, there's plenty of that.

Things have been fairly quiet at Enguard the past few months, ever since we last tangled with a dangerous crime syndicate called the Pilgrims.

The calm almost defies Riker's superstitions about bad things coming in threes. My friend can't really say the Pilgrims bust ended badly, considering it landed him a wife.

We've spent the last few months protecting easy, predictable clients. Then the tedium of coordinating with the police to provide additional info as they chase the last few Pilgrims out of their ratholes, as well as depositions about using justifiable force during the last operation.

At the moment, there's nothing that requires my complete focus, so I'll take the time to play Hemingway with Mom's magnum opus. Even if I don't have the first clue where a man should start playing editor with a goddamned romance novel.

Is *Gone With the Wind* on Netflix for inspiration?

Still, I have a strange, eerie sensation I might never get the chance. A wicked premonition tingles down my spine.

Maybe it's something in my grandfather's genes. He doesn't trust quiet times any more than Riker does, and always insists things have a way of blowing up.

I'd rather prefer they didn't.

I insist they won't by faith.

That's the problem, though. Faith isn't ironclad.

And life doesn't care what I'd prefer.

Life doesn't slow down to wait for me to be ready to deal with it.

Life operates on its own timeline, its own rules, and in order to keep up, I find my ways to cope.

Healthy or not, they keep me moving and functioning.

They save lives.

They make sure I don't break down when people are depending on me.

That's all that matters in the end. Anything that happens to me as a result is just collateral damage.

I toss my drink down, pursing my lips as the last of it explodes in my guts. The haze of bourbon settles over me in a warm shroud, heating my blood and making that sense of danger, of warning, feel far away.

I sink back in my chair, staring at the ceiling, just letting myself drift.

In a few moments, after the initial burn fades from my blood, I'll go to bed. Tomorrow's another day.

"Just another mundane, ordinary, goddamned day," I whisper out loud.

I have to tell myself it'll blend into the others without changing. No matter what happens, who's missing or hurt or hunted or dead, nothing ever changes for me.

And nothing ever will.

* * *

I REALLY SHOULD HAVE LISTENED to that premonition.

When my phone buzzes at four a.m., I'm awake in a second. Old training makes me ready in an instant, immediate minuteman awareness the moment I open my eyes and hear a noise.

There was a time when the FBI could wake me up in Portland at two o'clock in the morning and have me in Baltimore by seven, and I'd hardly feel the strain.

Now, all I feel are the last dregs of booze leaving my body. Slept away, leaving me clear-headed as I sit up and swipe my phone from the nightstand, reading the text from Landon.

Everyone to HQ. We have a job, and it starts now.

It's a group text, sent to the whole senior staff.

But I still don't have a clue what's waiting for me until I'm dressed in a freshly pressed suit and joining the others at our big board table. This late in the year, there's a lingering darkness by the time I arrive at five.

The only lights are the street lamps over the parking lot and the fluorescent bars inside the office's war room. In the cold, pale, fake morning light, everyone looks, quite frankly, like hell.

Guess we all have our reasons to be exhausted.

Riker's graying brown beard is a mess, dark hollows under his eyes, even when he's smiling. Probably so smitten with his family man blessings he can hardly keep up. With an adorable, creative wife and a brilliant little girl, who could blame him?

Meanwhile, gigantic Gabe looks like he hasn't slept in weeks. The only thing keeping him moving must be the sheer bulk of his muscle. It's possible he really *hasn't* slept, considering his half-asleep, very tired, very pregnant wife is leaning against his side.

Skylar's pale-blue eyes are half-closed and her little pixie-cut bob looks disarrayed. I've never been married, but I've heard the stories with late-term pregnancies. Up at all hours of the night tossing, turning, having hot flashes, going to the bathroom, kicking your spouse, struggling through three a.m. cravings.

I'll deal with my empty bed, thank you very fucking much.

Landon, our fearless leader, he's the only one who looks fresh. Maybe it's because he's the only person in the room who knows why we're here.

He's almost restless with a vibrant, frustrated energy, his blue eyes snapping as he paces back and forth in front of the projector screen, raking a hand through his thick, dark hair. He gives me a sharp look as I settle into my chair, folding my hands over my knee.

That gets my attention.

There's something in his glance that raises a wary intuition under my skin, a voice that wants to whisper into my ear and that I very doggedly ignore. Trouble is, that intuition is highly irrational and illogical. The last time I listened, I got in more trouble than I ever wanted.

But it turns out the intuition's nagging little voice was right.

Too damn right.

Because the first thing Landon says, once he's sure he has our attention as we all settle, is, "We're shipping out within the hour on a protection gig for Senator Paul Harris."

Harris.

Father of Faye Harris. The man who ruined my life, and the man who tore me away from the woman I loved.

I feel numb from head to toe. I'm listening to Landon, processing the information, but I can't really formulate any clear thoughts about it.

I've shut off, switched into robot mode, recording data to be processed later when I think I can actually handle a mountain of preposterous *this-can't-be-happening* bullshit.

"This is a last-minute favor," Landon says. "Apparently Harris is an old friend of Riker's." Riker tiredly raises a hand as if accepting responsibility for this, snorting, before Landon continues, "Someone took a shot at him in his home this week. The place was evacuated, and when the security team returned, someone had been there. They left this."

He flicks the projector on with a remote control, bringing up one of the most grisly images I've seen since my time with the agency: a severed human hand, the stump a meaty congealed red, the fingers folded around a wad of crumpled hundred dollar bills.

It sits in the middle of a marbled counter, next to a message scrawled on the white marble with a fingertip of blood:

GET OUT OF THE WAY OR YOU'RE NEXT.

There's a number written on it. Its structure is quite familiar for a Senator – the labeling for a bill up for a vote in the House and Senate.

And Landon confirms it when he continues. "That number represents a bill currently going to a vote before the Senate Appropriations Committee. A bill our Senator Harris has repeatedly challenged because of the size of the budget allocated to Homeland Security and multiple externally partnered contractors. One of those contractors is our friends over at Pershing Shield."

Riker rolls his eyes. Sky groans, dragging a hand over her face. "Don't do it, boss. Don't you dare mention Hook Hamlin. Don't you *dare.*"

Landon grins. "I'll save my private admiration. But you'll need to deal with him, because Pershing Shield will be working with us on this job. It's high-profile, a little more than either of our firms can handle alone, so we'll be coordinating tightly."

"And you just so happen to get to pick your idol's brain," Riker groans.

"He's the best in the field. Second to us, of course. We have things we can learn from each other. And –" Landon holds up a hand to stave off more ribbing. "They might just be able to let us know a few likely suspects for who'd be pissed about Harris' opposition to the bill. Bipartisan politics, messy as they can be, usually don't warrant assassination attempts. So it's likely someone on the outside. Or one of the many contractors with a dirty underbelly who'd get cut if the budget was trimmed to push the bill through."

"How many they got?" Gabe asks, his Louisiana accent

drawling deep.

"Fourteen total," Landon answers. "If the cuts to the bill go through, that would cut it down to six. Pershing Shield and a few other heavy hitters, while the smaller ones would lose their contract."

"So that's where we start investigating," Riker says with a nod. "I'm assuming we're going to track their movements around the location of this gig?"

"Correct," Landon says. "We'll be going to the resort at Soda Springs. The Senator's hosting a 'sport and ski' fundraiser there for a week-long event to court some big donors for his next election. It's our job to sniff out who's a threat and make sure they don't take advantage of the opportunity to get too close."

"If they had any damn sense they'd just cancel the fundraiser," Sky mutters, tossing back her head. "Who goes courting rich people when someone dumps a hand in their kitchen? Whose hand was it anyway?"

"We don't know. Police took it and forensics are working on that part," Landon answers, before continuing with something else. Something that flies over my head, because the longer they talk, going back and forth, the more I feel shut on the outside.

A normal feeling for me.

I put myself on the outside. I'm a fringe walker, always watching, and I have a habit of making myself so invisible, my friends forget I'm in the room.

Useful for an agent making himself unobtrusive and unnoticed to gather intel.

Not particularly useful for a functioning human being trying to thrive among others.

Especially when I'm clearly not functional enough to realize Landon has been talking to me for the past minute.

Not until Sky elbows me and hisses from the corner of her mouth. "Pay attention."

I blink, shaking myself, refocusing my attention on Landon. They're all staring at me, and I wonder if my mask cracked, when I was sitting here numb and lost in the past. *Can they see it on my face?*

Can they see the plane crash? The night then-Congressman Harris ripped away my soul?

I knew. And I didn't turn him in, for all the wrong reasons.

All because I couldn't stand hurting *her*.

But they're still looking at me, waiting for a response, and I straighten my tie. "Pardon? Could you repeat that?"

Landon eyeballs me, then says, "I'm assigning key targets to key personnel. Shadowing one-on-one. I've got the Senator, with Gabe and Sky for backup. Riker's handling his primary aide. We'll put contractors on the rest of the staffers. I'm assigning you to the daughter, Faye Harris. Can you handle that, James? You'll have to transport her from their current location to Soda Springs. The Senator will provide an armored car."

They're all still staring at me while my boss is asking me to do the impossible.

And I'm not saying a word.

All I can think of are flashing green eyes. Vivid red hair. Curves to all seven heavens that still make my dick way too hard.

Zero sense of her own personal safety, and enough fearless recklessness and bright spirit to not even care. The way she'd laugh, when we were young and innocent, together in training.

And suddenly I'm back there.

* * *

Seven Years Ago

Quantico. A university classroom, a massive projector screen depicting crimes so macabre they'd turn any civilian's stomach, and little scratchy whisper-punches hit the back of my head.

Balls of paper.

I'm trying to pay attention to the instructor, and she's lobbing balls of paper at the back of my head and snickering behind her hand in tiny sounds. I'm trying my damnedest to ignore her.

Is this a fucking high school chemistry class, or where I'll learn to be a federal agent?

Is this what I signed up for after Iraq?

Sometimes, I really wonder.

Here I am, fresh faced and bright eyed and eager to learn...and I've got this silly Tinker Bell creature laughing her sweet little ass off as she lobs another wad.

Then one of her little papers gets stuck in my hair and slips down the back of my suit collar.

I reach back to fish it out before it can fall down and get caught in my belt, scowling as I uncrumple it to see what childishness she's tossing my way now.

I find a little scrap torn from a corner of notebook paper, blue ink scrawled in her little hand.

Hey Nobel,
Made you look.
;P

. . .

THIS GIRL. This girl has no sense of appropriate timing. This girl is –

"Mr. Nobel," the instructor snaps coolly. "Since you have time to pass notes like this is high school, then you have time to do ten extra laps in the morning. Understood?"

I close my eyes. It's on my tongue to protest *it wasn't me*, but no one here wants to hear excuses and I'm not the kind to make them. I tuck the wrinkled bit of paper into my own notebook, pick up my pen, and sit up straighter. "Yes, sir. Got it."

Meanwhile, the entire time, *she* laughs under her breath behind me.

The extra laps can't be worse than what I had in basic training, or running for my life on the narrow streets of Mosul.

Faye Harris, on the other hand, might be a bigger problem.

* * *

Present Day

"JAMES? *JAMES*."

For a second, Landon's voice is the instructor's – the same setup, the projection screen and the dim-lit room and the people all around me. Except, rather than disapproval, Landon stares at me with concern and confusion while I look back blankly at nothing.

"James," he repeats. "You okay?"

"No," I say bluntly. "Sir, I cannot work with Faye Harris. Assign me to the aide. Assign Riker to Ms. Harris instead."

Everyone is staring at me like I've grown a second head. I'm not surprised.

I've *never* directly challenged a company order unless I felt there was a logistical issue that might cause problems. This isn't like me.

I don't *feel* like me. Everything suddenly seems wrong and twisted up, and I wish I'd never opened my mouth, but I can't take it back now.

Almost warily, Landon asks, "Is there a reason why?"

I search for a reason, then admit, "I know her. We have a history."

That much, I can say.

I simply can't tell them why, or when, or how. "I once lived in the Congressman's district. Ms. Harris would attend stump speeches with him, and meet and greet constituents. We grew occasionally friendly. I fear our...familiarity would be a direct conflict of interest. It would hurt my ability to perform my best, plus our client's comfort."

It's a shameful fucking half-lie, but a believable one.

Landon lets out an exasperated sigh. "That's not how conflict of interest works. If anything, since she knows you, she'll be *more* comfortable having you on hand as her personal bodyguard. I'm aware you've got some fancy notions about women and propriety, James, but we're not asking you to follow her into the shower."

More than a few crooked smiles pop up around the room. I'm sitting like a stone, showing nothing, even if there's a small part of me that knows I'll never live this down.

I can't really tell Landon that I've been there, done that with Faye.

Hell, I can't tell Landon anything, or do anything but acquiesce.

Because if my boss knew the truth, it could cost me my job – and the life I've built since I left the FBI.

I've already had one life torn away from me without any choice.

I can't let another one slip through my fingers because I got careless and loose-lipped.

One day, I know, my lies will catch up with me and it'll all be over. I'll lose people's trust. I'll be fired and shut out from this strange little family that I do feel affection for, no matter how distant I may keep myself.

After all, who would want an employee or a friend who covered for a high-level criminal guilty of sabotage?

Sabotage and murder.

III: REUNION (FAYE)

I stare at my phone, reading an article on Enguard Security and the explosive events of a Milah Holly concert over a year ago, where the pop star would've been poisoned to death and several others murdered by a rival security agency if the good people of Enguard hadn't stepped up and brought down the bad guys.

He's there.

Right there, on the front page of the article.

James Nobel looks just like I remember.

No, maybe better.

Dashing, heroic, and ice-cold sexy blond, this man like a shining steel sword transformed into a human being.

There's something dangerous about James and the blade analogy is way too fitting.

He's beautiful to look at, to admire, to crave. That's half of it.

But it's also knowing he can cut so deep, be so deadly, that makes being around him a pure adrenaline rush.

There's just something about men who can be as calm

STILL NOT LOVE

and collected in the middle of a firefight as they are while checking the mail that takes my breath away.

And he leaves me completely breathless in that front-page photo, caught mid-stride by a security camera as he positions himself in front of a half-conscious woman and a beaten man, his Ruger drawn, making himself a human shield with complete and utter fearlessness.

He'd been captured in black and white, but my memories are all the color I need as I look down at that slicked-back, platinum blond hair, those features like a saber's edge, those gleaming grey-blue eyes behind those sternly aloof glasses, the broad set of his shoulders in his perfectly meticulous suit. Even mid-combat, there's not a hair out of place, and in arrested motion he's just...

Graceful.

It's the first and best word.

Graceful, lethal, perfect.

Three fatal qualities far too good at causing heartbreak, fury, longing, and so much confusion. All over questions I've needed answers to for many, many years.

I set down my phone numbly, just staring at his image – and then in a sudden jerk, I make myself look away.

I can't do this again.

I can't look at him like he's the man I once knew. Not anymore.

It hurts too much, and it's not making this miserable situation any better. I've managed to delay having to see him by a little bit, but probably not for long.

Because the second I found out he was assigned as an escort to my father's team, I managed to slip past the Secret Service agents at the hotel where my father stashed me, hooked myself up with a rental car, and skipped down to Soda Springs a day early.

I'd probably have caused a minor national emergency if I

hadn't called my father and left a voicemail once I was an hour out of town, before anyone could really catch up to me. It's not like he isn't already there, departed a few days ahead for site scouting and prep.

I'm only supposed to be there for publicity. Politically calculated optics. All so he can keep me under lock and key.

In fact, keeping our movements separate is part of the protection plan, making it harder to track us when we're operating on different itineraries.

But with James, just waiting around for him, I couldn't.

Couldn't sit there in that hotel room and wait for him to show up.

Couldn't look him in the face and see nothing there while he did his job, shepherding me to the resort.

I mean, can you even imagine *that* car ride?

At least I've got a little time to myself for now. This cabin is small, but I'm used to small.

I've never really wanted the kind of lavish houses or lush penthouse apartments you'd expect a Senator's daughter to have. My rental in Portland is a cute little modern deco cottage fitted out with clean air and water catching tech, solar, even my own little greenhouse atrium in the rear.

I could live off-grid if I wanted. It's one of my daydreams that lets me fantasize about something remotely resembling independence.

Now that I think about it, that's actually kind of pathetic.

But it also means I'm used to the kind of rustic setting in the cabin.

This is one of those resorts where you pay extra to live in conditions a few centuries behind modern times. Or *pretend* to when all the modern conveniences are tucked away behind the raw wood cut siding and hand-carved furniture and fireplace ovens, if you know where to look.

It's just the illusion of roughing it. You don't ask a billionaire donor to actually go to the bathroom in an outhouse and wipe with a pinecone if you want campaign funds.

It's cozy, though. And I'm currently curled up on the plaid-patterned quilt on the bed, sorting through the print books I brought with me along with the books on my Kindle, when I hear a clamor from outside.

It's loud enough to be heard over the howl of the evening wind that's just started kicking up now that the sun is setting over the snow. The light casts bright washes of color, reflecting off glittering fields and hills, throwing spangles of light through the cottage windows.

I'm grateful it's too late in the day to be with the photographers. That particular hell won't start until tomorrow morning. Then my father needs me to appeal to the kind of demographic who'd vote for a single father and widower left to raise his cute, button-nosed, redheaded daughter alone.

He likes me to look *spunky* in these photos. The kind of All-American Girl people would root for in a made-for-TV movie, even if I'm drifting into my late twenties.

Pretend. Fragile. That's what he wants.

Not the kind of woman trained to be at her best in the middle of a terrorist attack, using the skills I've learned to save lives rather than letting them – and myself – molder and go to waste.

Sorry, is my bitter showing?

My curiosity shows, too, and I remember that noise.

Unfolding myself from the bed, I walk over and press myself to the window. The resort is set up like a little village, with the large main lodge for meetings, receptions, and communal dining, as well as saunas and spas and all sorts of other guest services inside, including a freaking mini-mart.

It's a comfortable pace away from the little cabins where couples, singles, and families scatter around with snow-lined paths leading in between and a single central road running down the middle. It's been quiet enough due to the road being covered in a light dusting of snow with no tire tracks in it, but now the snow sprays lightly to the side as two heavy, armored black SUVs come rolling up the hill like gliding leviathans, cutting through the powder.

I don't know if what I'm feeling is a thrill, pure terror, or the thrill I get *from* pure terror.

Because I don't even need to wait for the doors to open to know that James is in one of those beast-cars.

I rub my hand over my aching throat and tell myself to go out there.

Get it done.

I don't like being a coward. If I'd had the life I really wanted – the life I feel like I've half-fallen back into since this entire mess of scares and assassination attempts started – I'd have stared fear in the face every day and refused to back down.

And I can't back down from seeing James again. Especially when this time he can't ignore me.

This time, he can't shut me out.

We'll be together all day, every day, and even if that might kill me inside just a little...

Eventually, I'll get my answers.

I'll get them if I have to annoy them right out of him.

Although after seeing him, after the feel of excitement and danger riding the crisp, snowy air, I don't know.

I don't know how I'm going to go back to my old life. My boss was so confused after I called her from the hotel.

People at the library manage to forget who I am. They let me just be Faye instead of *Senator Harris' daughter*. But she was understanding, at least, and I'll still have a job when I go back, even if I'm not quite sure I'll want it.

I'm still mulling my career prospects when a new shape catches my eye. I suck in a deep, trembling breath.

There. It's *him.*

The driver's side door of the lead SUV opens, and even the way the door *opens* reminds me of those meticulous, careful movements, like he's aware constantly that his own body is a blade and with the slightest wrong movement, he could destroy an innocent bystander.

It's an instant slug to my gut. Something between hate and sad and longing.

Even dressed for the weather in black gloves and a thick jacket over his suit, he's neat and crisp and so perfectly put together. That subtle air of menace around him always reminds me exactly why girls always love those sinister, elegant, wickedly sadistic movie villains.

It's not just that he looks like he could kill a man with his pinky finger.

It's that he looks like he could twist your body up into a million knots without even trying, and then smile in that slow, serpentine way he has as you explode into stars everywhere and completely fall apart. He could be Lucifer himself, fallen angel and master of hell. Or maybe just the quintessential bad boy.

Unfortunately for me, the way my lungs pull tight and the heat in the pit of my belly tells me far too well how true that is.

James Nobel is dangerous in more ways than one.

He's a complete and utter demon in bed, and he'll make you develop kinks you didn't realize were possible. My toes scrunch and I'm instinctively biting my lip.

I had no idea, until one fateful night on a training mission, that I apparently have a thing for lying naked and vulnerable under a fully-dressed man in a three-piece suit, while he strokes every inch of my body, slips his fingers inside me, works me into a fever, and then leaves me breathless and hovering on the edge.

Refusing to bring me over the edge until I admit in broken, gasping whispers that I need him, crave him, can't live another second without his fire.

He's got such sensitive hands, too. Hands that can play a woman's body the same way he plays piano keys...and he used them *ruthlessly.*

Until I came completely undone. Always after I thought I'd gotten under his skin and broken his control.

Instead, I'd only learned he was just as good at controlling my body as he was at controlling his own.

Oh God, I can't be thinking about this right now.

Not while I'm watching that fluid, sexy way he moves.

Not as he opens the back of the SUV and retrieves a simple rectangular black duffel bag.

Even though my body tries to light up with heat, I can't help a fond memory when I see the bag. I recognize it. It's a standard FBI issue field bag, and I guess he's just as bad as I am at letting go of those old bits of the past.

Okay. I'm going to do this. I *can* do this. I have to.

Instead of waiting for him to come to me, I'm going to go to him. I step away from the window and pull on my thick, wool-lined hiking boots and heavy winter coat, then rake my fingers through my hair, tug on my gloves, and head for the door.

By the time I step outside, he's already disappeared.

Damn!

He tends to do that. He moves like a wraith, this ghost who's never where you expect him to be, silent and undetectable until it's too late.

It used to be a game for me when I first met him at Quantico.

He fascinated me then, this silent man in my training class, this handsome mystery man straight out of the Army. He could capture every eye in the room, and then somehow vanish even with so many people watching, completely captivated by him.

He'd been so antisocial, never wanting to talk to anyone. But when he did, there was mischief and elegance in his voice. A rare, refined charm that said he wasn't all street smarts with a college degree.

I'd half thought he'd run ahead of the pack during morning training laps, not just because he was stronger and faster than everybody, but because it let him keep them at a distance.

So I'd become a James hunter.

I tracked the traces he left behind, learned to recognize the tell-tale signs of where he'd been even when he seemed to leave no mark. I'd swear I could catch his scent in a crowded room, his trademark earthy cologne and raw masculinity. Slowly, I developed a sense for where he'd be until I could feel his presence like a prickle raising the fine hairs on my skin.

And I feel it now. Somewhere close by.

I can't see him, but he's here.

I move slowly, careful not to let my steps crunch in the snow.

If he knows I'm on his scent, he'll go to ground like a sleek white fox, elusive and impossible to catch. I'm practically holding my breath, making it all too easy to hear the roar of my own pulse.

God.

I shouldn't be feeling this anticipation, this excitement, but he always brings it out of me. Something about James Nobel makes me want to bat him around like a cat with a toy, even if I'm never sure who's the cat and who's the mouse.

All I know is the moment I saw him, in another life, I knew I'd love to let him sink his teeth into me again.

I turn haltingly, gazing in all directions as I move toward the road and the SUVs.

I'm out in the open, peering at the trees scattered beyond the cabins, no way anyone could sneak up on me.

Which is why I nearly scream when I turn for one more sweep, and find James standing right behind me, practically in the footsteps I've left in the snow.

As it is, I suck in a little squeak and stumble back, nearly falling, before I catch myself and straighten. "Jesus!"

He says nothing.

He's too close. He always smelled like gunmetal without his cologne, and that scent hasn't changed now, carried to me on the cold, nose-stinging winter air.

My breaths puff out in smoky clouds of frost as I stare up at him. He invades my senses without even trying, as if he's taking me over from the inside out.

I'm not sure he's even alive. Unlike me his breaths are nearly invisible, almost like they're the same temperature as the icy air.

And if he's as torn-up inside at seeing me as I am at seeing him, he doesn't show it.

He just studies me with a narrowed gaze, his grey-blue eyes so pale, they're like faceted white diamonds, giving away nothing that could ever be called a *feeling*.

I try to say something. Anything.

Where did you go? Why didn't you call? Why are you here? Why me, why now?

Even a *hello* would do.

Instead, all I have is this wild screaming feeling in my heart and racing blood. It's freezing outside, but I feel so hot, so *hot*.

Until he parts those sensuously stern lips in a smirk, with smooth and almost formal precision, and says, "There are approximately sixteen locations here where a sniper could easily conceal themselves and still maintain an open line of sight for a clear headshot. Why the hell are you outside, Faye?"

There it is.

This man is a flipping *Vulcan*. So logical, it's insane.

And there's my temper, too, deflating that petrified needy-angry-hungry, messed-up, confused feeling inside to just leave me irritated, disgusted, and folding my arms over my chest as I scowl at him. "Hello to you, too, James. Long time no see, James. It's good to see you, James. Now this is the part where you say 'Hello, Faye. Long time no see, Faye. It's good to see you, Faye. I owe you a hell of a lot of explanations, Faye.'"

He tilts his head, eyeing me – then bows briefly, sardonically. "Ms. Harris."

Oh my God.

I'm going to punch this man in the face.

Groaning, I push my hair back with clumsy gloved fingers. "Don't you *ever* Ms. Harris me. And I'm fine. I did my own sweep, and there's no ninja-assassin sniffing after me. You can't expect me to stay locked up for this whole week. The term 'cabin fever' exists for a reason, you know."

"Sure. Reason being a poor understanding of modern mental health and the stressors of a closed environm—"

"Stop." I cut him off with a raised hand. "Just stop, James. If you're going to do that pedantic human dictionary-slash-computer thing this entire time, we're gonna have ourselves a miserable week."

"Fair enough."

I glare so hard, it burns.

So smooth. So impenetrable. So *infuriating.*

Maybe I really am the only one affected by the memories we once had together, a past that never got a happy ending or any kind of ending at all. I can't help staring at him, taking in the sharp-edged contours of his face, the lethal cheekbones and chiseled jaw, the Prince Charming elegance that makes him seem so courtly and just a little dastardly.

James hardly looks a day older than the last time I saw him.

Hardly looks different at all besides being hardened by age like a fine wine, and maybe that's the worst part. It could be just yesterday when I was waking up in his bunk with his tightly crafted body pressed against mine, every inch of naked skin on skin.

I want to reach up, touch his face. Crave it, and I actually catch myself reaching before I pull back, stabbing my fingers into the ends of my hair instead just to keep them busy.

"You don't look burned at all," I murmur, looking for telltale signs of the plane crash, then instantly want to kick myself.

No-Filter Faye. That's me.

But he doesn't react in the slightest.

If I hurt him, if I annoyed him, if I amused him...I can't tell.

He only flicks me over with an unreadable look, before his gaze fixes over my head. "And I see you're as enchanting as ever."

I don't know if he means that – if he's really telling me I could ever be anything beautiful to him again – or if he's being sarcastic about my ever-so-charming personality and complete and utter lack of tact.

But I don't get a chance to ask, to needle the truth out of him when he continues, "I take it you know your way around better than I do. Why don't you show me to our cabin?"

It's like the snow around my ankles turns into ice, grasping my ankles like frozen hands and capturing me there while that chill cuts down to the bone.

What did he say?

Our cabin?

"I...you're...staying with me?" I ask faintly.

"Naturally." He says it slick, calm, utterly unruffled, as if we don't have years of painful history between us, binding us together like stitches in bloodied red. "If I'm going to be a proper guard, I must be in your presence at all times."

"Guard?"

"Yes."

"As in...you've been assigned as my bodyguard..." I'm choked off by my own sour laughter. "Holy hell. You're joking?"

He quirks an eyebrow. "I should think the truth would be obvious."

"Damn it, James!" I explode.

He always did this to me. Forced me to realize I'm *that* girl who falls for men who are just like her father.

Only, where I always manage to whip a reaction out of Dad, with James, he's the one who always pushes me into losing it when I can barely even claw a scratch in his ice-cold façade.

Okay, shock over. This insanity is happening. Time to deal, I tell myself.

Taking a deep breath, I force myself to look away from him and back to my cabin, nodding toward it. "It's over there. Have at it. But you can't stay with me. There's only one bed. I'll talk to Dad, figure out alternative arrangements."

"No need," he says, shouldering his duffel bag and brushing past me. "I'll sleep on the floor, Faye. I'm here to do a job, not steal your damn beauty sleep."

He leaves me standing there, open-mouthed and quietly shattered, hardly able to breathe.

Holy flipping Hannah.

I can't share a cabin with this man. It's one thing to see

him like this, just sparring words in the open and hidden memories. But I can't share a space with him.

Especially when I realize now that there's nothing inside that sleek, polished façade of the James I used to know.

Somehow, since the last time I saw him, that sweetness that made him so redeemable is gone.

The hidden light inside him has gone out.

***

Seven Years Ago

THE REAL WORLD doesn't feel real right now.

Not when I've been living and breathing Quantico for months. Training scenarios, life in the dorms, my every day caught up in the regimen that makes a successful agent. To suddenly be ejected with my badge and full-fledged agent status, already on my way back to Oregon for my first case?

I feel like I'm dreaming.

Like Quantico was real, but this is a dream of life outside the training center, and I'm not quite sure how to wake up.

It's me, five veteran agents...and James.

The only other new graduate on the team, but he looks like he's been doing this his entire life, seasoned and calm and rakish in his tactical gear, seeming to command authority even though he's the second lowest ranked in the SUV.

We've got SWAT with us, too, in another armored car trailing after us, but we're supposed to be the first on the scene. A month ago, one of the local FBI teams caught wind of someone concealing large caches of high-powered rifles and other black market contraband in shipments of tractors.

Farm equipment isn't exactly typical when it comes to smuggling, and the fake farmers embroiled in the scheme might have gotten away with it if not for a mistake during a run from Tacoma to Klamath Falls.

The local agents almost kept it under wraps until they could get the intel they needed to bust the rest of the ring – but somehow something got out.

And we've now got two agents captured, possibly dead. But we're going to try to negotiate them out in a tense standoff with the smugglers who've turned the farm they use for cover into a compound and a very bad hostage situation.

Because they're swearing they have explosives, and if anyone sets foot on the premises, they'll blow it to kingdom come.

Which is where I come in.

This is my specialty.

The plan is that we'll park on the perimeter of the farmland, out of sight, and infiltrate covertly.

Survey the land, figure out who's where, make sure there's no deadman switches or anyone with their hand hovering over the button. SWAT and the senior agents will rush the smugglers, disarm them, get them under control, and rescue our people.

My job is to defuse any explosives on-site immediately, or notify the agents to evacuate right now if it's not possible.

James is here as my cover. My shield. My protector.

While everyone else goes after the smugglers, his job is to shadow me and make sure no one stops me from doing what I need to do.

It's comforting. My blood is somewhere between lit dynamite and a shaken can of soda, my entire body jittering with anticipation and excitement, but James' calm, collected composure is a comfort that reminds me everything's going to be okay.

I know what I'm doing.

He's got my back.

And we'll get in and get out with everyone in one piece.

It's dark when the small convoy of armored vehicles finally pulls up far from the farm's perimeter.

We don't want them to see us coming. It's amazing how a group of heavily armored men and women can move so silently, but we're like a murder of black-winged crows flitting through the dark silhouettes of the trees. The air tastes like autumn and loamy earth and my own nervous sweat.

I fight to ignore it, following the faint green light shining off James' tactical goggles.

There's a square of brilliant white up ahead, through the trees.

A window? No curtain, no shades, easy line of sight in.

Which also means an easy line of sight out, and anyone inside that rickety gray-walled barn could see us if they happen to look up.

A shadow passes in front of the window, a clear silhouette of a man with a rifle.

A signal passes through the team, and we all go to ground, dropping low, finding places to conceal ourselves while tactical does a perimeter scan looking for cameras, traps, any other form of surveillance. When the all-clear comes in whispers, we circle in slow, avoiding line of sight.

I'm moving at a low crouch, my hand at my hip and close to my sidearm, while James is a lithe shadow in front of me, a panther in the night with his carbine at the ready.

There's a moment of frozen silence as everyone takes their position, all of us poised like a whip on the verge of cracking.

Then the signal goes up, and the whole damn night explodes.

SWAT storms the building.

There's a shattered window, tear gas tossed inside, doors kicked in, and suddenly there's shouting and gunshots and my heart racing like a turbo engine as the SWAT lead roars, "HARRIS!"

I know I'm up, so I slide the gas mask down my head to fit over my face. James' hand brushes on my back so we stay locked in tandem as he slips his mask in place and takes off.

We're moving like a single unit, a well-oiled machine. I remember these moments in training when we'd be assigned to each other, and somehow, we'd fall into this wordless, perfect synchronicity where we didn't even need words to communicate.

That synchronicity hits now.

Hits so hard I can almost feel every breath James takes, the power and coordination of his body, as if it's my own – and we're wired with the same impulse as we dive through the door after SWAT.

He's going high, I'm going low, ducking underneath the swinging arm of a smuggler even as James brings the butt of his carbine down on the man's hand with a loud *crack!*

I roll up, take the outstretched hand waiting to lift me to my feet with effortless strength, my gaze sweeping the room before I land on the explosive device. It's a messy tangle of wires positioned right underneath the chairs of the two bound, gagged, coughing agents writhing above it while SWAT and the rest of the FBI team subdue the smugglers amid fading clouds of tear gas.

We bolt forward as one.

But just as I'm about to drop down to cut the agents loose, James has me by my collar, hauling me back and shaking his head as he flicks a finger toward the agents. "Look."

I lift my gas mask, breathing shallowly in the still-fogged air, and peer at them.

That's when I realize James just saved our lives.

I stifle a gasp.

Thread-thin wires, almost invisible, run from underneath the agents' seats down to the explosive device. *Freaking pressure plates.*

There are pressure plates underneath their asses. And if I'd cut them loose, the second they'd have stood up, they'd have blown the entire place sky high.

I'm angry with myself that I missed it – even if I'm new, even if I'm green, even if this is my first mission and this is why they put us in pairs – but I don't have time to be upset when the SWAT team leader shouts, "We've got a detonator!"

I whirl just in time to see one of the smugglers wrestle his arm free from the officer tackling him to smash the button on a small device in his hand. A shrill beep comes from behind me, and both the agents start sobbing against their gags, half-shouting.

The explosive device is armed.

"Agent Harris," James says coolly, "I believe you're up."

"Clear the room!" I cry, slipping into mission mode and dropping to my knees behind the chairs, taking a quick look at the setup.

It's a homebrew bomb. Clip the right wire and it's done and dead, but the timer has thirty seconds and it's not waiting for me to guess which one. *Oh, hell.*

"I'm going to switch the signals for the pressure plates," I say. "So it'll think off is on, and on is off...but that means any pressure *will* trigger a detonation. I need you to untie them, and the second I say go, you get them out of here."

James lifts his mask, eyes dark as he watches me. "What about you?"

"I'll be fine, and we only have twenty seconds left, so don't argue with me. Untie them and be ready to move!"

I'm unrolling my kit with lightning speed, counting the

world's slowest seconds by the beat of my heart. I've lost ten just to give instructions, and we're at *twenty.*

I trace the wires to their source. *Nineteen.*

Rip away the cover to expose the circuit board. *Eighteen.*

Take just a moment to evaluate the connectors. Releasing the pressure would trigger an electrical surge that would toggle the state of a switch wired to the detonation mechanism. *Seventeen.*

Quick switch of wires, lightning-quick, so quick I don't even breathe, and now –

"Go," I gasp, my stomach rising up my throat, my entire body buzzing. "Go, go, go!"

The agents are scrambling away from the chairs, just like that. I don't move, waiting, hoping I did it right. *Sixteen. Fifteen.*

They're gone.

And James, who's supposed to be running with them? He isn't.

Still here. At my side.

He's standing over me, tense, staunch, stalwart, dependable, looking down at me expectantly.

Fourteen. "I told you to go."

Thirteen. "And I am not leaving you."

Twelve. "Then I'd better move fast. Afraid the only death I can handle being responsible for is my own."

Eleven, and a long, lingering look that both tells me how brave he is and reveals how much faith he has in me. For just a split second, his cool façade slips and I see the heat, the brightness, the burning light underneath. "You won't let me die, Faye. You're too damn good."

Then I have *ten* seconds, and a bomb ready to go off.

I don't know if it's the wild rush of my own excited nerves or the bolster of his confidence in me, but I'm lightning in a bottle.

I know which wire to pull, which one to cut, just how to hold it when it's right on the verge.

Eight. Seven. Six.

Five. Four.

Snip.

And everything is quiet.

I slump forward, gasping heavily as my heartbeat reboots, then break into a shaky laugh and drop my clippers, scrubbing my gloved hands over my sweaty face. My heart comes alive again, pulse dialing up to ten.

"Oh my God. *Oh my God.* I did it, James. I actually did it."

"Was there ever any doubt?" James growls.

And for the first time since the very first day I saw him in training, something insane happens.

He smiles, clear and real and genuine, and I know right then and there I'm going to fall head over heels.

I'm not wrong.

Because something forged a connection in those thirty seconds where every scenario became too real, and it was only us. Me and James, knowing we'd live together or die together and nothing in between.

It changes us.

It changes everything.

And even if I rarely see him smile again, it doesn't mean I don't hear the laughter in his voice as the following weeks draw us closer. It doesn't mean I don't suddenly understand the dry humor underneath that aloof mask he wears, until he makes me laugh more often than not, and I feel warmer and warmer in his presence. And it doesn't mean I don't trust him.

Enough to tell him who I really am.

Who my father is, and why I want to prove myself a raving success away from Dad and his choking, oppressive vigilance.

And when he takes my hand and squeezes it and says, "I understand," looking at me with shining silver-blue eyes that don't seem so cold anymore when they glow in the sunlight with an admiration I crave like a flower craves the sun...

Holy crap, I know.

I know. I just know.

This man is going to wreck me.

IV: CLOSE QUARTERS (JAMES)

*I*t shouldn't be such a relief that Faye chooses not to follow me into what will, for at least the next week or longer, be *our* space.

After seeing her face-to-face, standing so close I could almost feel the warmth of her breaths melting the frost on my cheeks...

Fuck.

I don't think I'd be able to handle being shut up in this cabin with her so soon.

Though I'd better get used to it. Orders are orders.

We'll essentially be living underfoot without even separate bedrooms whether I like it or not.

The cabin is a single-room space, with the only separate room being the spa-style bathroom with its elevated, wood-sided square bath and mixture of wax and electric candles. Designed for lovers, which we most certainly aren't.

Not anymore.

Not ever again.

And that's sure to make things awkward in close quarters with only a single bed.

Make that a bed too small to even be a queen, tucked in the corner of the open space and underneath one of the large panoramic windows. The living room area is slightly recessed into the floor, creating something of a fire pit atmosphere in front of the hearth.

The deep, plush L-shaped sofa will be my bed as long as this ordeal lasts. If I turn my back to the bed and face the fire each night, not only will I conserve heat, but I'll be able to pretend that the woman in the bed behind me is anyone besides Faye Harris.

Anyone but the beautiful, brilliant, and all-too-fucking-infuriating whiplash woman I used to call Tink.

She's off looking for her father now.

Probably to blow up on him, ask him what he was thinking hiring Enguard, although the Senator doesn't know my history with Faye.

No more than Faye knows my history with the Senator.

Or the secrets I've struggled to protect her from for all these years.

Now, seeing her still so bright and fiery, her spirit unbroken, I know I've done the right thing, protecting her from the truth about what sort of man her father really is.

He's all she has left. It would fucking gut her, after losing so much else.

Her career. Her mother. *Me.*

It's just a few days. It's just another job. I can get through this.

And I need to stop brooding and go find her.

This *is* my job, after all, and I can't let her out of my sight.

I set my bag down on the foot of the couch. I'll make up a bed later.

For now, I kneel to set a fire in the hearth. The room is cold, chillier than the gas heating should warrant, and if I'm going to protect Faye like any other Enguard client, that means everything – including ensuring her comfort and health.

As much as this resort might fall back on that distasteful thing known as *glamping* to create the illusion of roughing it out, the weather conditions outside are nothing to trifle with.

Ski weather in the Sierra Nevada's can rapidly turn into blizzard conditions. I make a mental note to raid the firewood stores and stock up on extra in case something happens.

I may have medical training as a first responder with the FBI, but there's little I can do for frostbite if we end up trapped here in whiteout conditions with no source of heat.

That familiar, ominous prickle runs down the back of my neck, that premonition.

I shouldn't be thinking about this. It feels like inviting trouble in all the worst ways.

So once I have the fire kindled, glowing orange, and the logs crackling away with a faint smoky smell almost like chicory, I rise, pull my gloves back on, and head for the door to find out where my missing lady has disappeared to now.

Only to pull the door open and nearly walk right into her.

Her hand reaches for the doorknob and instead lands squarely on my stomach.

Fucking hell.

Even through the layers of my coat and my suit, I can feel her. *Faye.*

She's always been that way, this human hotspot generating nonstop warmth even in the coldest weather, until it's possible to feel her coming from dozens of feet away.

It's like her hand is a hot brand taken straight from the forge's fire, scorching through the fabric to imprint that small, delicate palm against my bare skin. It reminds me too much of how good it felt years ago, after she'd torn my shirt open, stroking her splayed fingers over my body like she wanted to learn the shape of a man for the very first time.

I'd taken her innocence. And then I'd taken so much more, wrapping her around me on long, tense nights, fucking soul-to-soul.

She used to whimper when she came. Sometimes, she'd bite my ear, her little teeth the last thing I left her to control as I pinned her down *hard,* owning every inch of her sweetness.

It takes everything in me to hold completely and utterly still. To wall myself away from the instant hot reaction to her touch, raw memory tugging at both my heart and my cock until both are pulsing just a little too hard, a little too hot, and far too angrily.

I arch a brow, sweeping a frustrated hand through the air. Then I step back to make room for her, releasing a slow breath through my nostrils as the firestorm breaks with distance.

"Ms. Harris," I say, schooling my tone to formal politeness.

Faye rolls her eyes. Predictable.

She remains there for several moments, her hand still outstretched, before she flashes a smile that's half sheepishness and half pure irritation.

"You know my name, James. Use it." Her hand drops and she steps inside. "Dad's too busy to talk to me and it's getting dark, so I guess we're stuck with each other for tonight. I'll see about getting reassigned to someone else in the morning. Maybe that big guy with you won't mind putting up with me, but until then...we can deal with each other if we're asleep most of the time, right? And then you won't have to see me for the rest of this stupid stunt of a trip."

My fingers clench into a fist.

Sleep? I'm not ready for that. Hell, not for any of this.

The bitterness in her voice, the active attempt to get away from me. And I have a feeling it's not for her own sake that she took that last step away.

She thinks I hate her, I realize.

Because of the way I cut her off. Because of the way I shut her out of my life.

She thinks I must hate her and must *loathe* being assigned to her when, if anything – despite the pain of it, despite the torture of her proximity, despite the ache of memories and loss and fury attempting to claw their way through my protective armor – the exact opposite is true.

And I can't let a bit of it slip. I have to make her think I'm Mr. Fucking Hyde.

I bite my tongue, holding my peace.

Correcting her assumptions won't make this any easier for her, or for me.

But deep down inside, I rebel at the idea of turning her safety over to anyone else. It's not that I don't trust Gabe. He's a married man, a loyal friend, exceptionally skilled at his job.

It's that at my most secret core, I still think of Faye as *mine*.

I'm stark raving jealous. Even though I gave up my claim years ago.

Fuck, I don't want her in anyone else's hands. I need to see for myself that she's safe for as long as I'm here with her.

This may be the last time in my life I'll ever see her.

I close the door in her wake, and as she begins shrugging out of her coat, I reach to take it. She freezes, tossing a wide-eyed glance over her shoulder, before letting me ease the coat down her arms.

Surely, the flush in her cheeks must be from the cold.

I find my eyes lingering on her red sunbursts even as I hang her coat up on the pegs just inside the door.

She's still a pretty thing like a lit candle, snow in her hair as she pulls her knit cap off and shakes down a vivid tumble of red so deep it's like burgundy and copper and wine, falling around her pale, freckled face and drifting across her delicately impertinent features.

Her eyes are pure witch-fire. A green that snaps with pure heat despite their electric-coolness, flecked in bits of gold like stars reflecting in glass.

She's breathing hard. A shallow, swift, flushed breathing that comes from being out in the cold as she peels her gloves off and rubs her fingers together.

One more sight I *really* don't need.

Because all I can think of, as I watch her chest rising and falling against her pale lavender sweater, is how those rushed breaths sounded against my ear once upon a time.

I can see her as she clung to me, raking her fingers through my hair, clasping my hips between her thighs as she begged *James, James, oh God, James* over and over again.

Double fucking hell.

Do I *honestly* think I can spend the night alone with this woman? And still feign indifference to her presence?

Who knows, but I have to.

Faye's gaze catches mine, her eyes luminous and questioning, and I realize I've been staring. I look away sharply, finishing with her coat, while she clears her throat softly.

"It's freezing in here," she murmurs.

"I've just lit the fire," I answer mechanically, turning to brush past her without fully looking at her. Perhaps if I simply avoid eye contact, I can prevent the rush of vivid memories assaulting my body and mind every time I look at her. "The room will warm shortly. I'll run you a bath if that'll help warm you, though."

"James."

Her voice at my back, low and imploring, stops me.

I halt in place, staring straight ahead without really seeing the rustic log walls of the cabin. Every sense fills with the memory of her taste, her scent, the touch of soft skin beneath my fingertips as I skim over every curve and hollow and swell of her body.

"You're not my servant," she says. It's barely a whisper. "You don't have to act like this, waiting on me hand and –"

"I'm doing my job," I say coolly. "That's the reason I'm here."

"Yeah, sure. I guess that's the only reason, huh?"

I don't answer.

I simply walk away, escaping into the only private space I can find when there's not a single wall in this place that can guard me against the feelings she's awakening inside me.

She doesn't follow me into the bathroom's sanctuary.

I settle on the wooden edge of the large square spa-style tub, the interior gleaming white ceramic. As I lean over to turn on the faucet, it throws my reflection back at me.

I don't like what I see.

My face is troubled, distant, and cold. This hardened mask locked in a constant expression of thinly veiled disapproval and disinterest.

I stare down at my image, even as the water begins washing it out in the polished porcelain, swirling me into nothing but fragments of colors.

Is this who I am now?

Is this all that's left of me, when the rot inside me has slowly been eating away at the soft organic bits of human meat inside this frigid shell?

I tear away from staring down into the water, and busy myself lighting the candles in the room to fill it with a soft golden glow, before laying out towels. There's a separate glass-walled shower that I'll be using later, but for now, I can't help the instinct to want to make her as comfortable as possible, taking care of her in more ways than one.

I clench my jaw, hating every second of this. I'm at war with myself right now.

Everything I say has to keep the wall between us, maintain the appropriate distance.

For her good and mine.

But I can't help the compulsion to give in to these quiet, simple actions that sate my need to look after her.

That say, more than any words, how much I care.

I can't let her get under my skin like this. Not even for a few minutes, and I'm cracking in under an hour.

If I let down my guard, if I get emotional, I'll just endanger her even more.

She makes me lose focus on the world around me.

That's the last thing I can afford to do while there's some unknown actor threatening her life.

Still, I linger until the bath is full, giving myself a little more time to breathe, then shut the water off.

Then I take a deep, fortifying breath, and step out into the main cabin.

She's settled on the bed, one leg swinging over the edge, as she pouts at her phone. When I emerge, she glances up at me, and turns her phone to show me a weather map on the screen.

"Looks like there's a bad one coming in," she says. "I know Dad planned this months ago, but you'd think he'd have called this off when he saw the forecast. I don't think the campaign money's going to keep rolling in after people freeze their toes off and get stranded up here."

"Under the circumstances, your father couldn't cancel the event. Particularly when this gives us a prime opportunity to potentially identify who threatened you."

"It's like Clue, don't you think?" She grins, swinging both

legs now, leaning back to slouch her shoulders against the wall. "Get all the suspects together in one place so you can watch what they do and wait for them to give themselves away. Somewhere isolated where they can't leave."

With an exasperated sigh, I shrug out of my coat, lay it over the back of the sofa, and sink down on the cushions to unzip my bag. "You shouldn't treat this like a game. Nor should you be so excited. Someone's already dead, and you and your father are targets."

"Whatever, James. I've felt dead for years, rotting away in a Portland library. I guess it takes someone trying to kill me to make me feel alive again. Isn't it a riot?"

"I'm hardly amused."

"You never are. Or at least, you pretend not to be."

That girl.

I close my eyes and take a deep breath, praying for patience. Fortitude. Something.

The thing about Faye is she excels in driving me crazy, and somehow manages to annoy me into enjoying it.

"Your bath is ready," I deflect carefully. "You should take it before it cools."

"Sweet, finally some warmth. Want to join me?"

There's that bitterness in her voice, again – that certainty my answer is *no*.

But there's just a touch of hope, too.

A glimmer of soft, sweet, compelling warmth, desire, longing. I ignore it.

I have to ignore it because she can't know how painfully close I am to saying *yes*.

So I hold my silence. Listening to a soft, hurt sound as she stands, just a collection of small noises at my back, but I can track her movements by the rustle of clothing, the soft tread of her boots, the creak of wooden floorboards, the sound of the bathroom door opening and shutting.

Then I'm alone, with nothing but haunting memories and the ache in the pit of my stomach that knows, that just fucking *knows.*

On the other side of that door, wrapped in heat and coils of licking steam against naked flesh, is the one woman in this world who can make me human again.

* * *

I KEEP myself busy by checking the weather report.

Not fucking thinking about the naked, lush woman soaking on the other side of a very thin wooden panel.

Not clenching my jaw to smother the fire in my blood.

Not wanting her under me so bad I could lose every bit of genteel self-control I cling to like a drowning animal.

Faye's right about what's coming. There's a severe winter front heading in overnight.

There's a good chance the mountain will either trap or dilute the coming snowstorm, but there's an equal possibility it'll move in directly over us and stay there. Locked in by seasonal winds and high crags, blanketing us in snow, rabid winds, and plummeting temperatures for days.

It's in the low teens right now, but it's projected to drop below zero overnight.

That tingling on the back of my neck keeps getting worse, though I want to ignore it.

I don't like the feel of this.

Just to be safe, I do another check of the cabin, looking over our stores of food and bottled water, plus the firewood. Cell signal up here isn't the best, but there's wired internet if we get buried enough to need to summon help in some way, as long as the power stays on.

It better.

That's what sends me back out into the lightly drifting

evening snow, wrapped up in my coat and my boots crunching through the top cover as I check the backup generator. The gasoline looks topped up to full, and the rating indicates it can power the cabin at full for up to seventy-two hours on a single tank. There are multiple backup fuel containers, too.

More than enough time, I think, as long as nothing goes catastrophically wrong.

Then again, Murphy's Law can be an absolute bitch and a half.

The moment I think it, I'm struck by an irrational urge to knock on wood.

Just as I'm completing my perimeter scan, I catch a hint of motion in front of the main lodge and pause, looking across the snow-strewn road.

Landon stands before the door, a tall, dark figure, bundled up in sleek, black cold-weather tactical gear. His breaths puff out in thick wisps as he speaks, gesturing with a bulky behemoth of a man with a close military cut of dark hair and an easy, engaging, almost fatherly smile framed in rough, graying stubble.

Hook Hamlin, owner of Pershing Shield.

And apparently, I'm the only one here who's not completely suckered in by his charm, given the excitement in Landon's movements.

But then, I'm the only one here besides Senator Harris who knows who Hook Hamlin truly is, what he does...

And why he may well be responsible for more than one murder.

That he's here, now, is no coincidence.

I'm well aware that hardship makes strange bedfellows, but I sure as hell don't trust his alliance with Senator Harris. Supposedly, they're so deeply entangled, it makes it impossible to conceive of either of them betraying the other.

If one goes down, they both do. Honor among thieves.

Still, someone left that bloodied hand at the Senator's residence, and it's generally those closest to you that you can trust the least.

Or maybe that's my cynicism talking.

It's just as likely some rival contractor wants Harris out of the way. It's also in Hook Hamlin's best interests to protect the goose that constantly delivers him golden eggs.

Fuck. Can it get more complicated?

I can't help feeling I should warn Landon, but I doubt he'll want to listen.

Not when he's got a professional crush on this man.

Even worse, he'll want to know *how* I know these things, and then I'll have to explain more to him than just Hook Hamlin's involvement in some dirty government deals and black market arms trades.

I'll have to explain how I let the man funding it go and covered up the murder of one of my closest friends.

I'll have to expose my soul and send it straight to hell.

I kick at the blowing snow on the ground, angry at the impossible.

Landon will never understand doing something so despicable just to keep from hurting the woman I love, but can't ever have.

That's why I'll keep my lips shut. Teeth in tongue. Grinding every word until it's this bitter, mangled secret I can keep.

"Hey." Gabe's soft Southern drawl startles me, coming up at my shoulder. For such a large man, he moves with remarkable stealth and silence.

I turn to watch him approach, sludging through the snow, his gaze fixed past me and on Landon and Hook. "So that's the big guy, huh? I missed meeting them Pershing folks since they came up in a separate convoy."

"You aren't missing much," I murmur.

"Ouch, James. Thought we were all fans of Hook Hamlin here?"

"That's only Landon."

"Aw, yeah, I don't get the obsession myself, but still..." Gabe's smile vanishes as he scratches his chin. "What's your beef with Hamlin? You sound pretty sore."

"It's personal," I snap, but I can't stop watching him.

On the surface, Hook seems so disarming.

The easy way he moves, laughs, and grins with his whiskey-dark eyes. Most people, you can sense a criminal disposition by the guilt that slowly eats away at them until it either boils out on the surface or swallows the last of their humanity. Most people with something to hide can't help projecting it, one way or another.

Hook Hamlin is a man without guilt, without shame for what he's done.

A man without a conscience.

That's the difference.

And he's as easy and calm as a man who sleeps soundly every night, without a moment's consideration for the lives he's destroyed. He doesn't have to wear a mask to hide who and what he is. He hides in plain sight.

Someone who can commit murder, who profits off illegal weapon trades that *kill* people...

Someone who smiles big and easy as he enjoys a snowy evening beneath the dark mountains and brilliant stars.

"Hey," Gabe muses. "Is that his real name, anyway? Hook."

"No." I shake my head. "It's part of his legend, his mystique in this industry, I suppose. A nickname."

"What, like...Captain Hook?"

"Right," I answer, gritting my teeth.

The fucked up analogy is too apt. Just like the good

captain from Peter Pan, Hook Hamlin is as charming as he is dastardly. He's just missing the infamous claw for a hand.

"If you'll recall, there was an alligator who swallowed the clock in the story, right?" I wait for Gabe to nod. "They say when he's on a target, he's like Captain Hook. Totally obsessed. That's because he's got a reputation to recover."

"Reputation, huh?" Gabe cocks his head, looking so much like a big, overly friendly dog it makes me want to smile.

"His grandfather made a fortune in mining years ago. He came home from the Second World War a hero, saved a whole division in the Philippines from being cut off by a ferocious Japanese attack. Then Hook's old man ruined it. His father had a terrible gambling addiction. He bankrupted them and ran off with some supermodel he met in Vegas on top of it."

"Damn!" Gabe whistles. "If that ain't just a swift mule kick in the balls –"

"Quite," I say, brushing snow off my shoulders. "It shaped who Hook became. A man working against time to undo everything his father ruined. He's done well on the reputation front, but the money...he's a rich man by any measure. But it's not a fraction of the billions the Hamlin North Range Mining Company used to be worth. The steel made from their ore changed whole nations."

Gabe shrugs. "Funny how some boys just can't learn to be happy when they're ahead and winning."

I nod, staring into the night.

He has no clue.

Hook may have his grandfather's frantic drive, but like his father, no moral compass. He'll knock down anyone in his way, whatever it takes to bring the Hamlin name and fortune back to being a household name and a Fortune 100 king.

"No man ever masters time. Hook still isn't where he wants to be, despite his great success. That ticking clock follows him everywhere, inescapable, counting down the moment until he inevitably gets his mark."

Or gets devoured. I keep that last part to myself.

"Huh. I guess that makes sense." Gabe makes an amused sound and nudges my shoulder. "Well, better get inside. You're gonna freeze your britches off out here."

"I'm fine," I murmur, still watching Hook as he turns next to Landon, and then they head inside.

There's a subtle tension in his shoulders that says he knows I'm here, too. That he can feel my eyes cutting into him from afar, and he's pointedly not looking at me.

"I'm just fine," I lie to Gabe again.

* * *

I'M NOT FUCKING FINE.

Not when I walk back into the cabin just as Faye steps out of the bathroom, wrapped in a thin, translucent silk robe that clings to her damp flesh.

The pale, violet fabric slicking over the heavy swell of her breasts and clinging to her hips gives me a deadly view of the lace panties molding between her thighs. The robe's silk chases after it like it's trying to lick and tease at forbidden flesh.

Like it wants to do every filthy touch and taste running through my head.

She freezes with one arm raised, caught in the middle of toweling off damp hair that tangles and pours all over her. It's the reason her robe is so soaked when her hair keeps dripping nonstop, plastering the cloth to her flesh.

I freeze as well, standing stock-still in the doorway.

Her wide eyes lock on mine, pink flushes washing over her cheeks, her lips parted but motionless—before she abruptly stammers, "S-sorry! I heard you leave and I –"

She breaks off with a slight quiver in her voice. A shiver ripples through her body, prickling over her skin, rousing her nipples to hard, straining peaks against her robe.

I can even make out their color, a deep blush pink against cream skin, making darkened discs against the wet silk, and then I'm thoroughly fucked.

Remembering every moment of how they felt against my lips, their sweet texture, how they burned in my mouth as I traced my tongue over their tips and flicked and sucked.

How I kept on until she was owned, writhing under me with her legs clenched together in a pair of pretty little panties just like these, like she could've hidden just how wet she was, how hot, how hungry.

Fuck.

My mouth is torn between watering and going desert dry, but I finally remember to move when I realize the cold wind is gusting in and icing her damp skin. Clearing my throat, I turn away quickly to shut the door, giving her my back and sorely needed space.

"Sorry," I say stiffly. "If I'd realized you were like this, I'd have knocked first."

"Um, I..." Her shaky breath is loud behind me. "I didn't bring anything in with me. This was all they had in the courtesy stuff."

"Then I guess you'd better get dressed."

There's an icy pause full of hurt as loud as a scream, even though she doesn't say a word.

Until I hear her fling "*Asshole*" back in a broken hiss.

I don't turn around.

Not with my dick throbbing so hard in my pants it hurts.

I wait until I hear the *flump* of her suitcase on the bed, then the scrape of denim and the rasp of the zipper on a pair of jeans. Then, and only then, do I open my eyes.

Christ, if I look at her right now...I can't trust what I might do.

This woman is pure medusa – stealing every good sense in my skull and turning every last part of me to stone.

* * *

We spend the rest of the evening in uneasy silence.

Faye curls up to read something on her phone, tucked into the corner of the bed against the wall and huddled there in this small bundle. Sometimes, with the force of her personality, it's hard to remember how delicate and fragile she is.

I watch her out of the corner of my eye, see her fine-boned as a bird and all shivering glass edges.

But right now, it's that fragility whispering how upset she truly is, being forced into this space with me, after I made it damn clear I couldn't stand to look at her too close to naked.

It's too bad doing my job means being a giant asshole to a woman who's taken more than her fair share of it over the years.

Though she's shut off in her own little world, I know she's watching me too when she thinks I'm not looking. No doubt wondering what she did to deserve this special torture.

I wish I knew, Faye. I wish like hell I knew.

I use the time to watch the incoming storm, making contingency plans for an escape route if necessary, using map data showing every possible road, trail, and footpath leading to the resort.

The ski lift is another option, but any scenario requiring transportation down the mountain that quickly would likely disable the power.

I don't like the looks of this storm. I like the idea of being trapped here with a potential assassin even less, although I can't say I'm fond of being snowed in with Senator Harris and Hook Hamlin, either.

So much for being able to pick my poison. I'm having every bad kind rammed down my throat in one go.

I'm still splitting hairs on backup plans an hour later, but it's the distraction I *need* to keep from losing my mind.

Trying to pretend the very woman I've been assigned to protect isn't in this room.

Faye and I even eat dinner separately, heating pre-made gourmet meals that are essentially the wealthy version of a TV dinner. Not exactly haute cuisine, but serviceable.

By the time the night begins to wind on, however, Faye's yawning turns contagious.

I'm more exhausted than I want to let on.

I get up to put a few more logs on the fire, curling my lip when I sense a small draft.

The cold is coming in through the cracks by the bed. I worry about her sleeping beneath that window with frost riming the glass and the chill seeping through. But she seems unconcerned as she climbs off the bed and tosses me an acid look.

"I'm changing for bed, James." She plants her hands on her hips with a challenging twist of her lips that's half smirk, half dare. "You might want to close your eyes so I don't upset your delicate sensibilities."

I sink down onto the sofa again, back to her, and settle my laptop across my knees. "Not looking suffices just as well, Ms. Harris. Thanks for the heads up."

"Faye," she insists. "Use my goddamn name."

"Ms. Harris," I repeat. Unsure whether there's a snarl or a smirk needling my lips.

"*Faye*. Say it."

Of course, I don't. I'm too lost in this fiery game I knew we shouldn't be playing.

I start to glance over my shoulder but stop when she lets out a squeal. "Don't turn around!"

Too late. I glimpse just a few whirlwind hints of naked flesh before she's stumbling back with something clutched over her chest, and I obligingly close my eyes before turning my head away again.

I don't open them again until I'm sure the only thing I'll see in front of me is the weather tracking app.

Not the tempting invitation of slender limbs.

Not the lush little ass that makes my palm itch with wicked memories.

Not the sour scorn on her delicate lips, begging to be bitten.

"You decent now? It's nothing I haven't seen," I mutter under my breath – and that's the pure torture of it.

That I *know* every inch of her body as well as I know my own, and yet I sit here locked inside myself in sheer, terrible denial.

She makes a huffy sound. "What did you say?"

"Not a thing," I reply smoothly, and then, unable to resist, add one more thing I shouldn't say. "Nothing at all, Ms. Harris."

"I hate you," she hisses, then a few moments later, softer, more forlorn, "Good-fucking-night."

I can't help but smile, as long as she can't see me.

This is Faye to the core, even when she's pissed. Maybe *because* she's pissed.

Larger than life and yet so very vulnerable.

All big explosions so you can't get close enough to see the softness and the need all that fire and fury hides. Yet, she let me that close once upon a time.

She let me know her in a way that hadn't seemed possible

at first – and I betrayed it for her own good. But I can't stop the longing inside me that remembers *knowing* her, feeling her, testing the limits of a strange connection we can't forget.

With her, with each other, we could be who we truly were with no masks, no lies, none of the misunderstandings that make human beings these strange ego-machines always reaching and never figuring out how to touch another soul without getting burned.

We did it. We had it. We reached, we touched, we held, we loved.

Before I blew it all to hell, creating these ruins I can't resist exploring half a decade later. Unsure whether I should curse the pain or laugh at the irony of whatever we've become.

We're nothing now.

I see the chasm when we look at each other across a distance we can never cross.

"Goodnight, Faye," I whisper, after I'm sure she can't hear me, and I listen to the sounds of her drifting into sleep.

* * *

THE FIRE BURNS down little by little, leaving the cabin quiet and dark, but cozy with contained warmth.

By the time I let myself look at her, I've been staring at my mother's novel for hours.

Another huge, heaping slice of nothing.

It feels like Mom left a single thread dangling at the end of an unfinished tapestry, and I'm supposed to find a matching thread somewhere inside myself to weave into her design. And to be perfect, that thread has to match precisely in color, in texture, with my fingers insanely skilled in the weave.

I can't find anything in myself with the same brilliant

hues of emotion that my mother gave off, and what little bit I can tease out is just clumsy.

I sigh. Mom always lived in another world – one where the colors were richer, the food more flavorful, the emotions more powerful.

She lived everything with such *intensity*, dismissing the practical for the strange and airy place her imagination took her.

I often wonder, bitterly, if that was why the cancer took her so quickly, so easily.

Because she burned so bright, maybe she burned through life too quickly. Maybe she ran out before it was her time.

Maybe that's why I'm so afraid to be anything like her, too.

She was a child of the air, unconcerned with material things, while I had to nail myself to earth.

That's why I'm the wrong person to finish this story.

My heart just isn't in the same place.

I'm going to break my promise to Grandpa and feel like a fucking tool for doing it.

This book, it's all flights of fancy and daydreams.

Love told by people who still believe in happy endings.

The title, *1000 Love Notes*, fits too well. In it, the heroine tells the hero she won't forgive him for a past transgression until he writes her one thousand love notes. She thinks she'll scare him off with such a daunting task, but rather than give up, he takes it as a chance to prove his devotion.

Suddenly, she's finding love notes damn near everywhere – in her laundry, taped to her fridge, on the hood of her car, written on the side of her cup at Starbucks. At first, she finds it annoying, but over time it grows on her with fondness until finally, she stands on the verge of admitting *maybe* she just might love him, too.

That's the part where I struggle.

I understand the rest all too well because I lived them.

Crumpled bits of paper thrown across the lecture hall, lodging in the back of my shirt.

I never breathed a word about Faye's notes to my mother, but it's like she just knew.

Can't blame the heroine in the book either. Admitting love so easily, so freely, so real seems like nothing but raw fiction.

I set my laptop aside, rubbing my eyes. Then I turn to lean my arm against the back of the sofa, watching Faye as she sleeps.

Even with the winter night breathing through the window, she's kicked the covers off and curled up in a shivering bundle. Her oversized shirt hangs off one shoulder, bunching around her hips to expose bare, shapely legs, her thighs thick and soft but her calves slim and toned.

She's prickling all over with goosebumps.

With a sigh, I push myself off the couch, cross to the bed, and pull the layers of quilts and heavy down blankets up over her.

She'll probably kick them off again, but just to be safe I tuck her in tight and hope it'll keep her warm until morning.

The blankets will have to do the job I can't.

* * *

IT'S WELL after midnight by the time I strip down to boxers and hit the couch, using a throw cushion for a pillow and scrounging up some spare blankets from the emergency supply cache in the closet.

It's warm enough, but I still spend a restless night listening to Faye's every breath.

The slightest creak jerks me awake. It's all too easy to imagine an intruder on the front step, rather than the weight of snow in the eaves and branches coming down in piles.

Still, near dawn, I manage to drift off.

Only to bolt awake at the sound of shouting outside.

I'm up in an instant, Faye a second after, wide-eyed and drowsy but flinging the covers off. In one heartbeat I'm in my suit, in two in my shoes, coat, and gloves.

She starts to get up, fumbling for her jeans, but I point at her firmly.

"Stay," I command.

Her eyes flash, and she scowls. "But –"

"*No*. I'll check on it." I don't have time to argue with her, not when the shouting just grows louder, more urgent.

Checking for my Ruger tucked into its shoulder holster, I stride quickly to the door and fling it open.

There's just a wall of impenetrable white.

Snow sheeting down in huge, frigid waves that make it impossible to see more than an inch in front of my nose.

I'm near-frozen in an instant, icicles accumulating on my eyelashes, and I quickly close the door behind me to keep the heat from escaping before pulling the neck of my coat up high over my face to warm my breath.

Straining, I listen.

A second or two later, I finally catch the sounds of more shouting from my right. Not far from a few of the other cabins where other Enguard members are staying, along with some of Hamlin's crew from Pershing and the photographers that were apparently snowmobiled in last night before dinner.

It's dangerous to move into the white, cold chaos. Wouldn't take much at all to get turned around in this whiteout in an instant and wander into the snow to freeze to death a few feet from the cabin.

But the bellowing voice seems familiar – and after a

moment, I hear another coming from the opposite direction, closer to the main lodge and the larger luxury cabins surrounding it.

"Shitfire, hang on! I'm movin'."

The first voice is definitely Gabe's.

The other, unfamiliar, but I catch a call of, "This way! Follow my voice!"

Then Gabe comes looming out of the white, first a dark silhouette and then color and shape and distinction, ice rimming the fur of the hood on his parka and crusting his scarf.

His eyelashes are all frosted snow. He's shouting at the top of his lungs, from the bottom of that big barrel chest. "Keep talking! I'm almost th—"

He stops just short of plowing into me, then stands in place, huffing out frozen breaths and rubbing his gloved hands together. "James? What's going on?"

"I was about to ask you the same," I answer, muffled through my coat. "Is there an emergency?"

"Emergency? Nah, man, just shift change." I can't see his mouth, but I can hear the smile in his voice and see it in the crinkle around his eyes. "One of the Pershing guys radioed, and we didn't put down guide ropes and stakes last night, so we're playing a little Red Rover."

"Red Rover?"

"Red Rover, Red Rover, send Gabe right over." He laughs, deep and just a little hoarse with the cold. "He's hollerin' his fool head off so I can follow his voice and not get lost."

I sigh, practically deflating, and push my glasses up my nose, dislodging them from the frost that had already started freezing them to my skin.

False alarm. Thank hell.

"Come," I say, reaching for Gabe's arm. "I'll shadow you."

He blinks down at me. "But how're you going to get back on your own?"

"My keen and catlike reflexes," I retort dryly, twisting my head toward the sound of the Pershing guard's raised voice, sounding worried at no response from Gabe. "Let's go join your friend."

Together, we forge through the storm. A total slog.

The cold slaps us in terrible sheets, alternately damp and dry, sucking the moisture from inside my nostrils to leave them crackling and burning. Together, we make a better windbreaker than one person would, allowing us to make a shield of our bodies that clears a path.

We tamp down the snow as we go, making a furrow in knee-high drifts that'll likely cover over our footsteps in less than an hour. Luckily, I only need minutes, and I only need to be able to retrace my steps back to Faye.

Even when I try to keep myself distant, everything always draws me back to Faye.

Once we finally arrive at the lodge, I take a minute to warm up, stepping inside just to let myself breathe before I have to turn around and forge back into pelting snow and needles of ice.

Pushing through the door, I pull my hood back, raking snow and crystals out of my hair and breathing in deep. The air feels so damn warm it's like fire scorching down my throat.

Then I come face-to-face with Senator Paul Harris.

My lip curls into a snarl, watching him.

He's just exiting one of the back rooms, looking far too casual in his knit sweater vest over a crisp shirt, every bit the family man dressed for the holidays, on performance at all times.

His graying hair is swept back. He's cultivated that perfect poker face of the stern but kind older man who'll love you even while doing what's best to keep you safe and happy.

It's all about image with Harris, hiding the cold, bitter, utterly calculating man underneath.

You have to know him to see the glint in his eyes, the sharpness that's quietly seething, constant rage.

There's something dangerous about him.

Something that makes the approachable, fatherly image he's crafted one hell of a lie.

I suppose we all wear masks here.

And his is flawless as he stops in his tracks, looking up from the aide he's speaking with, and locks eyes with me. There's only a second's flash, a pause, before he's all smiles, coming toward me with his hand outstretched.

Oh, hell, here it fucking comes.

"James Nobel," he says cordially, and again I think I'm the only one who catches the cool, threatening edge under the warmth in his voice. "It's been *forever* since I've seen you. How have you been?"

Miserable, I want to tell him.

Fuck, I want to *shout* it at him.

Grind it into his face with my fist.

Miserable, furious, grieving – I want him to know it all with a single sharp blow. The explosion of white-hot rage inside me churns like lava, this wildfire I've tried to cage for years.

Now, it's close to finally breaking past the bars of ice I've locked around it.

Only the measuring, expectant look in the Senator's veiled eyes keep me under control.

He wants a reaction. He'd enjoy it, especially when my job right now is to protect him.

And, of course, if I lose my temper, Landon will be obligated to discipline me. This is chess, and he's just made his move, trying to bait me into exposing myself and giving up the game.

Not today. I've always been good at chess.

It's a game I never lose.

So, I just hold steady, maintain my neutral calm, and reach out to shake the Senator's hand.

There's a certain firmness to his grip, an iron strength, that says he's testing me. I don't waver, holding his eyes as I give his hand a solid shake and let go, tilting my head.

"Senator Harris," I say coolly. "I've been well. And you?"

"Despite recent troubles, I'm quite well." There's something in the inflection there, something that says he's pleased about something I'm sure I don't want to know about. Yet his voice is heavy with mock sympathy, gravity, empathy as he continues, "You've been in my thoughts for some time. Not just because Faye used to talk about you constantly. After the plane crash..."

"What plane crash?" Gabe asks, stepping up behind me and blinking between us. His golden retriever friendliness shatters the building tension between me and the Senator, making more space between us. I tear my gaze from Harris, glancing at Gabe.

"It's nothing," I say. "It happened a long time ago."

"Yeah?" He cocks his head.

I hold in a sigh. Sometimes I wish I could be as easy as Gabe, accepting people and things at face value with pure warmth. "So you two already know each other?"

"We have quite the long history," Harris replies, so smoothly you can almost slip on the words. "In fact, I helped James here get his first job. And he made me proud."

Enough.

No one at Enguard needs to know about my time with the FBI, or how it ended. Even as Gabe stares in puzzlement, I grip his arm with a tight smile for the Senator and steer

Gabe away. "If you'll excuse us," I say, "we'll put coffee on. Won't your guests be arriving soon?"

"They will," the Senator agrees. "If they can get through the snow. I certainly do appreciate your attentiveness, James."

I don't bother with a response, though Gabe is craning back to stare at Harris even as I marshal him away.

And I feel Harris' gaze boring into me, tracking my every move, even as his voice drifts after us, low and ominous and promising.

"You'll take good care of us all, won't you?"

V: UNDER WRAPS (FAYE)

Something about this doesn't feel right.

I've been thinking it all day, ever since James went bolting outside this morning, ordering me to stay in place.

Only to come back with his face set in a forbidding mask, his icy aloofness twisted into a grimness I've rarely seen.

Of course, he wouldn't tell me what's really going on.

Typical James.

Just that the photo shoot's been put off until tomorrow, possibly even until after the guests arrive, due to the inclement weather. We're supposed to hunker down here, keeping an eye on the TV weather bulletins.

But all the cold front warnings in the world can't prepare me for the waves of ice radiating from James whenever I'm 'in his vicinity.'

Obviously his choice, eternal-stick-up-the-ass words.

And when we've been told to lock down and stay put while the wind whips and howls around us, there are few places in the cabin that aren't *in his vicinity*.

Somehow, he still manages to avoid me anyway.

I feel invisible, while he speaks on his phone in a low murmur to the other members of the Enguard team, then switches to a video chat on his laptop, talking through logistics and planning.

He goes strangely quiet when the other security team from Pershing patches into the virtual meeting, though. A big man named Hook dominates the discussion with a few other contributions from a voice I recognize as James' boss, Landon.

I'm stuck messing with the library catalog on my phone, catching up with some digital archiving work while I'm away, feeling like nothing has really changed.

Is it wrong? Once again, I've been shoved into a corner, the little girl told to behave herself and play with her books while the big, brave men handle everything.

Honestly, I'm getting so impatient to be *part* of this drama that I'm ready to set something on fire just for a little excitement.

Possibly James, if he keeps refusing so much as eye contact with me.

I should be nearly clawing his eyes out.

This quiet withdrawal, this retreat, this waiting isn't *like* me.

I tell myself it's because I've grown up and matured. Maybe I'm not the impulsive girl I was when we were lovers.

I'm older and I can sense the danger in the air. Holding back until a more appropriate time just makes sense.

But if I'm being honest with myself, I'm scared. Freaked.

And not because of the storm or the tension or the pointed secrecy.

It's because I told myself I was over James after the shitty way he dropped me.

I'd moved on and left him behind.

Then yesterday happened. The ridiculous way my body

remembers him every time I look at him, the way my gaze can't stop straying in his direction even when he's wholly oblivious to me.

The awful proof it's impossible to keep lying to myself with a pretty little smile on my face.

I'm not over him at all.

I must've dozed off in my rage, though. Because when I wake up it's dark, the evening falling through the windows in shades of blue reflected off deep, still plains of silencing white, snow blanketing everywhere.

James is nowhere to be found. But I can smell food, faintly, and there's the sound of running water from the bathroom.

I glance at the clock on the wall. It's nearly midnight.

Holy time-slip. The endless snowfall must've made me tired, sending me into hibernation.

I follow my nose to the little open kitchen island.

There's a covered dish on the counter, the outside of the metal still warm, and when I lift it away, I'm greeted by the warm scent of spicy chicken, tantalizing my nostrils.

My stomach growls like a grizzly bear.

It might be what heaven itself smells like, even if it's really just one of those fancy prepared meals, arranged neatly like a proper meal, with a little folded note card under the plate.

Please eat. Help yourself, Ms. Harris, the note card says in James' crisp handwriting, the letters slanting and narrow.

Just that, nothing else.

Okay. So, maybe I still want to kick him square in the face, but I can't help but smile.

I fish a fork out of the drawer, then prop my elbows on the counter and lean there to eat right in the kitchen like the etiquette-heathen I am.

The chicken is good, surprisingly, peppered and fried

with broccoli and tomato. A little bit of rice pilaf on the side helps calm my angry stomach.

As I'm happily devouring it, staring out the far window at the shifting night and wondering if the festivities will resume tomorrow, the bathroom door swings open.

I glance up instinctively, drawn by the motion from the corner of my eye.

And immediately wish I hadn't.

Now I know how he felt when I walked out of that bathroom dripping wet.

At least, how I *hope* he felt, when I can't be the only one dealing with this needy ache in the pit of my stomach, this emptiness food can't fill.

No way. Nope. This can't be happening.

I can't be this weak for him when he's impervious to me.

So I need to believe that when he'd seen me half-naked in that bathrobe he felt the same instant jolt of burning, throbbing *hunger* I feel as he walks out in nothing but a pair of loose, light pajama pants, his entire body nearly steaming with heat that practically *dares* the cold to touch him.

When he's like this, James is...he's *raw*.

Feral.

Scary hot.

Almost like how he is in his slick suits with his hair smoothed back, a polished soldier, but when you take away those elegant mannerisms and stylish clothing, he's just a raw, unfinished thing underneath.

Pure jagged maleness no one could try to tame into a proper shape.

His body is powerful and toned and tapered, lightly tanned and marked with scars I know by heart because I've traced every last one of them with my lips.

Though I'm sure he's earned a few new ones since the last time I saw him naked.

He has that kind of Apollo's belt that flares out just a little before dipping inward in that hard cut, arrowing down and pointing to the forbidden.

The shape of his hips makes it hard for anything without a belt to ever stay up around his waist – instead falling down, hanging so low I can see a hint of blond hair tufting above his pajama pants before vanishing.

Just before the point of temptation where his cock begins.

His hair is loose, for once, damp and tousled and tangled, a few strands drifting into his face and teasing at the corners of those cold, sensuous lips.

Lips that are currently parted now, stuck on unspoken words, as he watches me with half-closed silver-blue eyes that glitter.

Completely unreadable. Completely maddening.

All while I'm just hoping it doesn't show on my *face* just how bad I want to lick the last lingering drops of water from his neck and those strong shoulders and those rippling, corded biceps.

Holy hell.

Time to get a grip.

I don't think he has the slightest idea how his monk-like aloofness turns him into pure sex. Makes him this dark and dangerous thing you want to torture you and hurt you as much as you want him to take you every which way and leave you sore and dazed and ruined for any other man for the rest of your life.

That's what I really hate him for. The *ruining* part.

I haven't been able to be with anyone else since him.

And I don't want to know if he's put those long, devious, intimately talented hands on another woman since me.

I definitely can't stand picturing it.

Maybe it's the sobering thought that lets me tear away

from staring at him, sucking in a deep breath and trying to ignore the hellfire in my cheeks.

I fix my gaze on my empty plate. Somehow, while I was busy ogling him, my dinner disappeared.

At last, I clear my throat, busying myself with carrying the dishes to the sink and turning on the water to rinse them off.

"Thanks for dinner," I say weakly. "It was decent."

"Ms. Harris," he acknowledges coolly.

Oh. My. God.

For a second, I'm afraid I'll snap a finger as they curl into a shaky fist.

I sniff so loud I go light-headed.

This man. This horrible, confusing, too-gorgeous-for-life man.

I can only tell he's moving by how the sound of his voice shifts, when his bare feet are silent on the wood. He moves like a huge cat, stalking and lithe, and even though I keep my eyes on my hands, I can picture the writhing muscles slinking under his skin as he prowls through the cabin.

I want to kick him in the teeth just for *existing*, right now.

And for that stupid, formal *Ms. Harris*.

Still, I try to keep my voice mild as I say, "Looks like the storm finally broke. Are Dad's guests still coming?"

"Possibly," he answers. Neutral, factual delivery of information. "Only the first wave of the storm front has passed. This is a lull. Heard the local ranger stations have already issued new advisories about driving on the roads. It's possible the Senator's people might arrive by chopper. Or they may just call off the entire event like sane people."

"Oh." I frown, idly swiping a dish towel over the plate. "Wonderful. So we came up here for nothing?"

He's dead silent.

But he's not ignoring me. His silence is its own language,

James-speak, and one of the rules is it's possible to say everything with nothing. He isn't answering because...why?

If he answers me, will he have to lie?

Will he have to shield me from the ulterior motive for this little getaway, this unspoken thing I can feel skulking around us like a hungry wolf slinking through the snow?

What's really going on at this fundraiser, where everyone here knows someone wants to kill my father – and me?

I don't know what to say into the silence, so I don't say anything at all.

But when I hear him moving again, it's enough to draw my gaze up, watching over the kitchen island as he settles into the couch and draws the blankets over him, eyes closing as he rests his head on the pillow.

"Goodnight, Ms. Harris," he murmurs. "Another early morning tomorrow."

"Yeah," I answer numbly. "Goodnight."

I try to be quiet about finishing up with the dishes in case he's really sleeping and not just pretending so we don't have to talk to each other.

Ugh.

It's hard to tell with him.

He sleeps like an android with an off switch and always has. James just goes completely still, only subtle indicators in the boyish relaxation of his face hinting that he's truly out like a light.

He wakes up the same way, too, that switch turning on and flooding him to full awareness in less than a second, not a moment's drowsiness in between.

It's almost unnerving when he does that, creepy.

Guess I must have something wrong with me because it's one of the things about him that turns my blood so hot, so wild, so needy, so thick.

It's one of those things that's *adorable* about a man who

tries to show the world he doesn't have a sweet bone left in his body.

Changing for bed, I take a risk that he really is asleep.

He's right there in front of me, his back to me but that powerful body *right there.*

God. It's never been harder to strip out of my sweater and jeans, unclasp my bra, and for a moment just...stand there.

Naked except for my panties.

Letting myself *feel* the air touching my skin, teasing that terrible ache that's just gotten worse and worse until it's like an addiction.

And my fix is so close it's pure hell.

I want his hands on me.

I want to remember, *relive* how it feels when he touches me.

When my flesh gives in for him and he strokes every inch of me until I can't do anything but arch and open my legs and gasp out his name.

His lips, his tongue, his fingers, his terrible thrusts...they've never been nearer or had me needier than now.

Shame blossoms on my cheeks.

What the hell is this, anyway?

This hurt? This need?

But I fight to ignore it as I slip on a pair of little jersey shorts and an old faded baseball tee to sleep in.

Hardly sexy, but the way the fabric clings to me and teases against my aching nipples makes me nearly whimper.

I'm so sensitive all over, shivering and unsatisfied and ready to lose it.

Slipping into bed with my teeth sunk in my lip, I burrow under the covers, telling myself to let it go.

But I can't.

It's something about James.

Some crazy, beautiful gravity that's like a force of nature for anything female. Or maybe anything Faye.

Before I met him, I'd always gotten my thrills off that hint of danger as I learned how to defuse explosives and rode the adrenaline rush.

Before that, I'd found it snowboarding, horseback riding, any sport that let me go fast with something only barely in my control, whether it was a straining beast or Mother Nature herself. I'd been curious about sex but not particularly interested in seeking it out.

And then *he* happened.

The day we met at Quantico, something about his aura of menace called to my inner thrill seeker.

Woke something primal.

Something I'd thought died in his absence, but it's wide awake now.

Awake and loud and trying to swallow me in its hot, licking mouth, sucking down my body until I'm a throbbing mess and I can feel the steaming wetness slicking against my folds.

Oh, hell.

Even if I'm in denial, my body knows what I want, what I crave, what I've been deprived of for too long.

It's *right there*, and it's so damn ready and doesn't understand that what it needs will never, ever happen.

Worse, I still remember our last time.

We'd just come back from an operation to assess a bomb threat at a foreign embassy in Kent.

Ever since the black market arms sting that was my first trial by fire, we'd been inseparable.

Together on every mission, tearing each other's clothes off right after.

James, the dangerous and sinister beast in bed.

But after, quiet and sweet while I ran my fingers through

his hair, listening to him talk softly about his sick mom, and how afraid he was of losing her to the disease that was eating her alive.

His unexpected sweetness was just as irresistible as his unpredictable and thrillingly unnerving command in the bedroom...but that night, after that mission, we'd been less sweetness and more a pure firestorm.

Clothing was shed on the floor of our hotel room while we grasped and clawed and kissed so deep it felt like sex incarnate every time our mouths locked.

His tongue sought mine in searching, domineering caresses.

I curl up on my side, pressing my thighs tightly together as I remember too much.

Like how, rather than shoving me down on the bed like he sometimes did, he'd lowered me with masterful control, rendering me completely submissive.

Like how he pinned me down with his body braced over mine, his shirt hanging open over his delicious sculpted chest, one knee pressed between my bare thighs.

Like how his slacks rubbed against my bare pussy.

Oh, I can *feel* it even now.

That sense of sweet, sweet vulnerability when I'm undressed under this predator who wants to devour me, and every cutting look both scares me and takes me even higher.

I bite down on my knuckles to keep from whimpering, my other hand slipping down, cupping myself over the shorts, the panties, then inside.

I can't resist.

Can't even fight when he's *so close* his scent fills the air.

It's like he emits some strange, hypnotic pheromone that completely destroys my mind and leaves me empty of all thoughts but him. As I trace my fingertips over my own wetness, lining the edges of my folds with soft strokes, I curl up tighter, my entire body alert and prickling and aching with the need to be touched by one man.

Every clenching, dripping pulse inside me demands it, and although I know what I want, I need to draw it out a little more and savor it.

Because in the morning, I'll be mortified.

And even though he'll never know, I'll never be able to lie in this bed and enjoy this again when I'll be too afraid of getting caught.

But that's then, and this is now.

So I don't think. I carefully pull my hand away from my mouth and cup my breast, filling my palm with its heaviness and sinking my fingers in.

It feels so good to imagine it's not my own small, cool hand but his.

James' hand is large and rough enough to span the entire swell of my flesh, the strength of him sinking into me and making me soft as he kneads deep and flicks his thumb against my tingling, sensitive nipple.

Mirroring the imaginary James in my head, I flick the tip of my fingernail against my nipple through my shirt, sucking in a sharp gasp as pleasure bolts down to my clit.

I graze a fingertip against the pulsing, screamingly hot little bit of flesh, and have to turn my face into the pillow to muffle a cry.

One little touch ripples through me.

Makes my thighs quiver, spearing up into my stomach and radiating out to my fingertips.

I do it again and again and again, biting the pillowcase harder.

Until my entire body jerks and shivers each time as I set off tiny quakes inside myself, every muscle within me contracted tight and wanting, begging, *pleading* for what I can feel so deep.

It's like James is engraved on me, and my body knows only him.

I can't breathe, and I gasp hoarsely, wetly into the pillow as I let my fingers glide fully along my slit, soaking myself in every blinding throb between my legs.

It's not the same, when I finally give in and slide my two middle fingers into my body, using my index and pinky finger to spread myself open.

Searching for that delicious feeling of being *exposed* as I delve in, seeking to touch that red-hot sweetness that feels like a key to ecstasy.

It's not the same as his cock inside me, his hard body hovering over me, pinning me in place as he slams in deep. Like he can infuse the power in his tense, rock-hard frame into me with every rough, hard thrust.

But my flesh remembers.

My flesh remembers the shape of him too well.

The way his bulk forces my thighs open.

The way I could barely hold him when he was so thick, so *thick*, too big for me.

And yet I opened wide for him anyway and almost *dared* him to tear me apart.

I remember the intensity in his eyes, capturing me with that darkened, stormy silver gaze as he pinned me by my wrists and left me helpless as he took me harder, harder, *harder*.

How I begged for him, how I wept for him, how I lifted my hips into him the same way I lift them now, rocking up into that familiar rhythm, plunging my fingers into his imaginary thrust.

Stroke after stroke after stroke.

Each slip and caress of my fingers evoking the shadow impression of his cock splitting me open, and for a moment I almost forget he's in the room as I arch onto my back, thighs spread, as I circle my clit with my thumb and toss my head back and nearly claw at my breast.

He's *with* me. He's with me so deep I can almost feel his vicious thrust into my belly, surging so deep inside my cunt, it's like he's carving out new places for him to fit.

Not just in my flesh, but in my heart.

And I remember that night how I'd trusted him – how I'd said *forget the condom,* how I'd drawn him down and kissed him and whispered his name with my throat tight and my eyes stinging.

I'm reliving his abs, his hips, his thick ridges and veins, that molten wet *rush* as he arched his back and shuddered his hips and locked us together, snarling so he could come inside me.

I'm gone.

I fall apart, toes curling against the sheets.

My body jerks forward into a taut knot as my pussy tenses around my fingers, gripping and sucking and leaving my entire hand wet, spilling over to soak my panties and my shorts.

I come so hard I lose myself in a muffled shriek on my lips.

James!

By the time the last wave passes, I'm so sensitive I can't even move, afraid to even pull my fingers out when it's going to hurt as my nerve endings sizzle and burn.

But after a shaky, gasping moment, I manage, pulling out quickly and then wiping my hands on the sheets as I curl up on my side to watch what little I can see of him over the back of the couch.

Just one bare shoulder and a hint of moonlight off platinum hair.

I still feel too hot, but this time with a kind of delicious shame.

I can't believe I just *did* that.

With James right here, completely oblivious, and right now I'm such a wet, spent mess I can't bring myself to worry when it felt so good.

I need this delicious afterglow, too.

I'm just lucky he didn't wake up toward the end. I had almost no control over myself or the little gasping sounds I was making in the back of my throat.

Even now, melted and sated, I'm still not fully satisfied.

Even if I made my body sing with memories, it wasn't the same as having him.

It's more than animal lust, this craving.

It's love.

I'm still in love with James flipping Nobel.

And that stupid, walled off asshole can never know it.

* * *

WHEN I WAKE up in the morning, I regret going to sleep without cleaning myself up.

Especially when someone banging cheerfully on the door wakes me up, accentuated by the loud buzz, whirr, and grind of the snow blowers that say the resort staff have come to dig us out of waist-high snowdrifts, clearing a path between the cabins.

It's even worse when the person knocking turns out to be Dad, urging me to get dressed with no time for a shower.

Purely because the photographer's waiting outside and the light is just right for the shot he wants to get.

Shoot me.

That's right. I'm going to have to walk around doing this ridiculous photo op crap all day still feeling last night, making me think about James with every step.

James – who's as coolly indifferent as ever.

A silent, protective shadow trailing along a mere four feet away from everything we do as I bundle myself into my cutest, most photogenic ski gear and let my father drag me outside to pose right on my doorstep with a shovel in my hand, twin to his.

It feels so fake.

Dad makes me uncomfortable when he's like this.

For him, it's second nature, smiling for the camera with his friendly *gonna win some votes* face.

There's still this darkness in him that didn't live there before, that took root and made him its home after Mom died.

I wish he wore that darkness honestly rather than hiding it so effortlessly behind the harmless, friendly politico who just wants your support so he can take care of your best interests.

But this is, unfortunately, part of being a Senator's daughter.

I wonder if Chelsea Clinton ever wanted to smack her own father this badly?

I mean, *probably*.

It's half an hour of different poses and different smiles before the photographer lets us loose for now, promising he wants to get a few other shots of us around the lodge, having staged father-daughter moments. While the photographer packs up his gear, my father catches my arm lightly and pulls me aside, just around the corner and out of James' watchful eye.

"The donors should be arriving today," he says, leaning in closely like I'm one of his aides and he's confiding a secret. "Hook sent a crew from Pershing to fetch them with a helicopter. Driving in these conditions is too dangerous."

"Lovely. Don't you think being here is dangerous, then, too?" I frown. "This is really weird, Dad. Shutting down an *entire* resort so people can be cold and bored. We can't even ski."

His smile is strange and remote. "People do interesting things when you give them idle time to expose themselves."

My eyes widen. "What? You...you think one of your donors is the one who's threatening us? Not another Senator?" I shake my head. "Why? If they're supporting you financially, don't they believe in the same things you do?"

"Some people," he says, something hardening in his voice, "think financial support means total control. They're willing to give me money, but only if they can use me as a puppet they can manipulate and maneuver."

I fold my arms over my chest. It's the kind of cold outside that makes you feel blistery hot, but either way, it's uncomfortable. I'm hugging myself for warmth more than taking a moral stance. "So someone in your PAC has financial interests in that Homeland Security bill and its budget?"

"Very likely."

Just that short answer lets me know there's something he's not telling me. I narrow my eyes, studying him.

"Dad." I curl my hand in the sleeve of his coat, gripping through my thick gloves. "Let me help you for once. Talk to me."

Talk. Very funny.

He doesn't even look at me, his gaze empty, trained somewhere distant. "No, sweetheart. The best way you can help is to stay with James and keep safe, Faye."

"That's *not* helping. That's passively waiting for someone else to fix the problem. Damn it, Dad, I'm an FBI agent –"

"Former FBI agent," he reminds me coolly, as if that isn't entirely his fault. "And you don't have enough field training to handle something like this."

I'd be angry if it wasn't for the fact that at least he's being honest right now.

It's the darkness speaking, not my fake politician Dad, and that darkness is more real than anything he's ever shown the cameras.

What used to be real, though, was my father.

My real Dad, a man of integrity and open warmth, communicative and kind and loving.

I'd wonder where that man went, but I know.

He's buried with my mother.

Deep beneath the earth surrounding her gravestone.

Anything else I might say is cut off by the photographer's voice, calling my father's name. "Senator Harris?" he calls, the sound of slushing snowy footsteps approaching, leaning in so he can talk to Dad privately. "Did you want to go ahead and do the fireside shoot, or wait until dark? We can just curtain the windows, if you want to do it now."

My father's *hello, friend* smile comes back, just like that. "Let's do it now. Whatever you need for the lighting."

And just like that, I'm whisked away again. And I can't help but notice, as we emerge from around the cabin, that James is gone.

It shouldn't bother me as much as it does.

Too bad I feel like James is in on this invisible web of secrets I can feel tangling around me.

I feel trapped in something I can't even touch or understand, and it's making me tense and antsy, more so when he's out of my sight and off doing who knows what.

I'm so restless that the photographer barely stops short of snapping at me.

He has to ask me to hold still for the fiftieth time while Dad and I pose in front of the perfectly staged fireplace in the rustic lounge area of the main lodge.

Faking, of course. Feigning at whatever happy families do when there's a fireplace and bourbon involved.

So ridiculous.

I'm surprised we don't break out board games. When people look at the photos, they'll probably wonder why we look so delighted and stunned by the fir wreath over the hearth.

Real families are *never* like the photos.

Even when you wish they were.

It's not until this leg of the shoot is over and the photographer leans in with my father to discuss other photo ops that James materializes at my side in that way he has.

This time, he doesn't get the jump on me. I felt him coming in that way *I* have, static against my skin, so I'm not at all startled when suddenly he's there, offering me a tall paper cup with steam wisping out of the little hole in the lid.

"Coffee," he says simply, regarding me quietly. "You missed breakfast."

"Oh. Um. Thanks."

It's awkward when our fingers brush.

I feel like he knows that those same fingers still smell faintly of my desperate arousal, and for a moment we both hold still. Both our hands on the cup.

Then with my heart thumping, I turn away quickly, clasping the cup in both hands and inhaling the nutty aroma from within.

Hazelnut. I know the scent before I even taste it. He's flavored it with hazelnut creamer, my favorite.

Maybe his ghost act can't surprise me anymore...but the sweet twist in my stomach when he does things like this still does.

Bastard.

I take a slow, warming sip, letting it burn down inside and chase away the lingering chill better than any fire ever could. As the door opens behind us, though, I glance up, drawn more by the sound than the sudden stab of icy wind that cuts into the room.

Hook Hamlin walks in, all broad shoulders and thick clothing, shaking off like a yeti.

He's a big man. Hell, his whole presence is just imposing, yet there's something bearish about him that says he's probably more likely to hug you than maul you. *Probably.*

Nonetheless, James goes stiff at my side as Hook shuts the door, stomping and clapping the snow and cold out of his hands and feet. Then he crosses over to my father, leaning and murmuring in his ear, his bluntly square-cut face grave.

James is standing straighter. My brows knit together.

There's an eerie, heavy weight in the pit of my gut.

I frown, leaning in close to James. "Jeez. Wonder what that's about?"

He's watching them with a piercing gaze, expression tight, but still he deflects calmly, "Likely security protocol matters. Nothing important. Are you enjoying modeling?"

"Like I enjoy a hole in the head. God, I'm just glad it's almost done. I'm not staying for the rest of this."

That gets his attention. Brows furrowed, his penetrating gaze whips around on me. "You're not?"

"No. I feel like a prisoner. If Dad wants to keep me safe, it's not exactly the best idea to have me locked up here with someone he suspects of trying to *kill* him." I shake my head. "I don't want to play this game anymore. So I'm not. I'm leaving of my own free will and not letting him decide for me."

"Faye –" James starts toward me, one hand outstretched.

He stops mid-stride, drawing himself back like he's pulled on a cord, lifting his chin. "Ms. Harris, listen. While you're right things are far from optimal and perhaps there's more to it than it may seem...I don't think you'd be safer alone, outside of protective custody."

"Well, good thing *you* don't get to decide that, Mr. Nobel," I fling back. "Look, I'm tired of everyone trying so hard to make me happy. If you'd just ease up and –"

"Excuse me, everyone! Lend me your ears." Hook Hamlin's booming, commanding voice echoes over the room. It's not hard to tell he's ex-military with the way he drawls his words with a confidence and authority that immediately draws attention. "I'm afraid we've got bad news."

My stomach sinks. That uneasy feeling I've had is heavier now, weighing on me like lead.

I hate this. I already know I'll hate whatever he has to say even more.

"It looks like the backup crew and our VIP guests won't be coming," Hook says, his hands spreading in open apology. "The storm's far from over and it's about to get worse."

Meanwhile, at his side, my Dad looks quiet and strange, his expression so rigid he almost looks like James. But there's something in his expression I've rarely seen.

It's troubled and almost deferential, as he lets Hook take command.

"And until further notice, we won't be leaving at all," Pershing's head honcho finishes, a firm, but apologetic smile curling his beard. "Settle in. Stay safe. Make yourselves comfortable. Some people call me Captain Hook – all in good fun, I assure you – but I do know how to run a tight ship in a storm. You're in good hands as long as you're with Pershing, and with me." He pauses, assessing several bright-eyed, waiting looks around the room. "And, of course, our friends at Enguard."

Are we?

Somehow, I'm worried I already know the answer.

VI: EVERYTHING WE SHOULDN'T
(JAMES)

I don't like the sound of this.

It's too staged. Too convenient. This entire affair, the threat of being snowed in, only to make it through the other side of the blizzard.

Then the moment we think everything might be going smoothly, here's Hook Hamlin to tell us why we're about to be isolated with each other exactly where he wants us, *when* he wants us.

It's too fucking convenient.

I'm far from the only one disturbed. Several of Harris' aides murmur among themselves in a worried hush.

That's when I notice just how many of Hook's men from Pershing Shield have entered the room, standing spaced along the walls like a regiment with their hands clasped.

Landon and the others from Enguard are nowhere to be found, when they should've been summoned first thing before any kind of operational briefing.

No. This doesn't sit right at all.

And I make a point to stay close by Faye, even though I bite my tongue to keep listening.

"What do you mean?" one of Harris' aides asks. "Why can't we leave?"

"Impassable roads," Hamlin answers easily, smoothly, as if he'd been waiting for the question. "Last night's snowfall created avalanche conditions down the mountainside, and most of the roads leading out are completely buried. The ones that aren't are too steep for large vehicles and aren't safe." As worried, upset murmurs erupt around him, he holds up his hands. "Calm yourselves, ladies and gents. We're absolutely fine. We have power, gas, and all the essentials. Enough food and water to last for weeks. The mini-mart alone is stocked with plenty of rations to support a small village. We have shelter, plus several people trained in emergency medicine. The storm will blow over in a few more days, at which point we'll be airlifted out by chopper if they can't clear the roads."

"Why can't we be airlifted *now?*" It's the same aide, a note of shrill panic in her voice, but other agreeing whispers rise all around us. "You hear that? We have to leave!"

"Sorry, ma'am. The winds are too strong for aircraft. Next to zero visibility. That's why the secondary crew and our political guests aren't coming, either. It's not safe, and the storm will be on us again before we can fly out of it."

"The snowmobiles!" someone else calls. "They can handle the steep roads, right?"

Hamlin shakes his head gravely. "There aren't enough to get everyone out – and the storm would sweep in before we made it down the mountain. Leaving anyone on snowmobiles exposed and trapped. It's a death sentence to try."

I want to ask where Hamlin is getting this info.

If he's been speaking with the local ranger stations. Or if he's just saying what's convenient for an end goal I'm still trying to work out.

"This is weird," Faye whispers at my side. "Really weird. Something's not adding up."

"Ms. Harris," I mutter, "keep it to yourself. Because you're too damn right."

The civilians around us, Harris' team plus a few members of the photography group and skeleton crew of on-site staff, are a riot of uncomfortable, unhappy mutters. They're milling around, growing more restless by the minute, anger and upset simmering off them.

That's when Senator Harris steps forward, ever the statesman, projecting his voice to carry with calm and authority.

"Everyone, please settle down," he says. "I assure you, it's not as dire as it sounds. We're safer here than we could be anywhere else. Just look at it as an extended snow day." He smiles that ever-so-practiced grin. "Frankly, our biggest concern is going to be running out of marshmallows."

I suppose it's the mark of a man with a talent for public speaking that they actually calm down, even if there's still a nervous energy in the air. My teeth pinch together.

It's infuriating, but here, it might be helpful.

They believe in his authority unquestioningly. They want someone to take the lead and tell them it will be all right. The very assurance that makes them trust him is what makes my senses tingle with suspicion.

Whatever reason Hook Hamlin has for us wanting to stay, the Senator knows it.

Which means it can't be anything good.

And every last part of me lights up, warning me of danger as Hamlin and the Senator lean in to murmur into each other's ears.

Less than a second before both their gazes cut to me.

I feign boredom, as if I haven't been watching them.

Glancing at Faye, I say, "Perhaps you should return to your cabin."

She frowns. "Nope, too easy. Besides, I really hate how you and Daddy and everyone with a dick tries to shuffle me off somewhere out of the line of fire at the first sign of danger."

I almost can't resist the urge to smile. "Maybe because we all have a vested interest in keeping you safe."

"That's a really backwards-ass way to say you care, James."

I say nothing.

I can't tell her that I care, not when she wouldn't want me to if she knew the things I kept from her.

About myself.

About her father.

About what happened that fateful night.

And about how her mother died.

I'm saved from having to answer – but it's not a rescue I particularly want, when Senator Harris calls my name, flicking his fingers at me like he's beckoning a puppy.

Biting back a snarl, I balk for several long seconds, pride flaring. I ignore him just long enough to make it clear I'm not a damn pet to be summoned.

But I have to go eventually, see what he wants. With one last nod for Faye, I pull away from her, crossing the room with a sick churn in my guts.

I know what has to happen.

Even if I loathe Harris and blame him for the death of one of my closest friends, there's no escaping this.

For now, I need to play the game.

And a fucking game is what this is when Harris gestures to Hamlin and says, "James. I want you to meet Hook Hamlin, owner of Pershing Shield and one of the most dogged lobbyists for gun reform I've ever met. Hook, James Nobel."

Hamlin sizes me up with a slow, narrow-eyed look, then offers a shark's smile. Wide, but it's all teeth and flat, depthless eyes underneath his warmly authoritative mask.

He extends one thick, meaty hand to me. "I've had a chance to meet Landon, but not the rest of his boys and girls. If you're former FBI, I'm *amazed* we haven't met before. A third of my crew used to be with the Feds, and I'm at every conference the boys from the alphabet agencies love."

Thank God the room is too noisy for anyone to overhear him.

I almost choke. My past is no one's business but mine, and the fact that Harris told Hamlin says something is up. Nonetheless, I force myself to reach out and shake Hamlin's hand.

"I left the FBI some time ago for private security," I say. "And since then I've had little occasion to cross into your line of work. Homeland Security isn't really something Enguard deals with."

He starts to let go of my hand, but pauses on my last words, holding a grip just tight enough to let me know it could be a good deal tighter.

Fuck. Almost challenging me, while I keep my grip firm and steady with no need to show off like him.

I know my own strength. I also know when to use it, and right now I only need enough to make it clear I won't back down while he studies me as if he's wondering just how much I know.

Everything, you asshole, I think to myself. *All your dirty laundry.*

I know *everything*.

Then as Harris leans in and murmurs something I can't quite catch, Hook's grip relaxes, then lets go.

STILL NOT LOVE

That's when it hits me – they're playing a game of cat and mouse.

Not with me, but each other.

Playing at being allies, friends, in bed together on quite a bit of dirty business. Now, the tension seems undeniable.

It's all niceties on the surface, while underneath, it's pistols at dawn, squaring off across sharp-edged smiles and easy words. Only thing I can't figure out is the reason for this game, and I don't like it one bit.

I just have a chance, right now, to make myself a part of it.

Let them *think* I'm willing to be their pawn and wait for my chance.

While they're circling, these jackals vying for territory and blood...

Maybe they won't even notice the lion sneaking in.

"Don't worry," I say, slipping my hands into the pockets of my slacks, giving a thin smile. "Senator Harris can attest to my talent for...confidentiality, shall we say?"

"In short," Senator Harris adds, his tone just a bit too friendly, "James doesn't talk. Never says a word to anybody. This is probably the most he's said in a week."

"That a fact? There's a lot of value in a man who knows when to listen, and when to speak," Hamlin says, his look this time more considering.

Then he offers his hand again, pretending he hadn't just tried to squeeze mine off in an asinine caveman dominance act not thirty seconds ago. Still, I make myself play along, shaking his hand once more.

His grip is warmer this time, that clasp like a binding agreement. "A true pleasure, again, Mr. Hamlin."

"Hook, James. Use the name everybody else does. I look forward to getting to know you, too. Maybe at some point we could even talk about more collaboration between Enguard and Pershing."

Fuck, no.

But I will my eyes to beam back the opposite, even while I swallow bile.

What he means, of course, is that he wants to use me as a lever to pry the doors open and get to Landon.

Landon, who in his hero worship, doesn't even see Hamlin for what he is and would need a great deal of warming up to bring the crew over to Hamlin's side. Riker, Gabe, Sky, they'd all be mighty skeptical hearing it from the boss, but from someone like me backing him up?

Goddamn. It's too devious to contemplate.

Having Enguard under his thumb would let Hamlin expand his eyes and ears. He works mostly on the East Coast now, keeping him close to the political heart of D.C. and the people who line his pockets.

If he could rely on Enguard for his West Coast contacts, he'd have his entire illicit trade locked down on auto-pilot across the continent.

I have no intention of *ever* letting it get that far, but he doesn't need to know that yet.

"It's always possible," I deflect. "Perhaps we should see how well we collaborate on this particular endeavor, first."

"Perhaps we should," Hamlin echoes.

Meanwhile, Harris watches us with narrowed eyes, quietly calculating, but he definitely seems pleased with himself. I wish I knew why.

What's in it for him?

Others might not notice the subtle change when he's stone-faced and impassive...but I know his daughter.

I know those little things that give her away even when she tries to be cool and calm, and she got this mannerism from her old man.

A certain *something* in the eyes, a certain arch of the brows, subtle but undeniable.

STILL NOT LOVE

And suddenly, I want to be back with the woman who taught me those subtleties more than anything, instead of cozying up to the man who betrayed us both.

Before I throw up, I sweep a mocking half-bow and step back.

"If you'll excuse me, gentlemen, duty calls," I say. "I'm sure you're well aware what kind of trouble she can find if I leave Ms. Harris alone too long."

"Oh, I know," Daddy Harris says with a sigh. "I know my daughter. Don't let her burn anything down, James. I'm counting on you."

"No worries. I'll do my best to keep her away from any incendiary devices, but I make no promises."

They both chuckle.

As I'm drifting away, I hear Hook lean toward the Senator and whisper another sickening phrase. "Damn, do I like this guy."

If only they knew I'm hardly joking. Not when it comes to Faye and fire.

Hell, Tinker Bell herself *is* an incendiary device, able to ignite anything in her vicinity with her own special heat. And as I stride back toward her, meeting her wide, curious eyes, I remember last night.

Last night, lying on the sofa in agony for what seemed like hours.

Last night, listening to those soft, hitching sounds from the bed while she thought I was asleep.

Last night, when I thought I'd have to pull myself off just a few feet away from her with my back turned, long after she made her last little muffled whispers.

Pure goddamned torture.

Every little mewl in the back of her throat painted so many vivid pictures in my mind.

Memories of those same sounds rising, gasping in tandem

with my own harsh breaths as I spread her open, wrapped her thighs around my hips, discovered just how deep her heat went as I hurled myself into her body again and again.

I may joke, calling her Tink like she's some fairytale thing, but there's nothing funny about what that woman can do to me between the sheets.

All magic. All fire. All tight, wet, and electric.

And even if I'd kept my back turned last night, even if I'd feigned sleep while she'd touched herself again and again, it didn't help in the slightest.

I'd been awake for every moment, picturing her arching her back in the moonlight, seeing her fingers touching and working her flesh with such demanding need.

I kept my control. Barely.

It's all I have now so I don't breathe her in when I step closer.

Because there's still a faint scent around her, carried on the cold air, creamy-tart and enticing as an aphrodisiac perfume. I can't breathe her in, or I know it won't even be a question. I *will* lose my mind.

Keeping a safe distance, I incline my head. "Ms. Harris. Considering the inclement weather, I think it's best if we retire to your cabin."

She shakes her head, wrapping her arms around herself. "Why? If we're going to be snowed in, isn't it smarter for all of us to remain together here in the lodge?"

"Sure, but there are also practical issues. Let's go. I'll explain on the way to your cabin." It's all I say before I reach out, take her hand, and pull, ignoring her little gasp.

I hope she understands, holding her eyes firmly.

A second later, hers widen, before she nods almost imperceptibly before flashing a flirty smile.

"Oh, whatever. If you wanted to get me alone so bad, James, you just had to ask."

Then she jerks her hand away, saunters past me, curving hips swaying.

Damn it all.

I sigh, exasperated, closing my eyes and pushing my glasses up to press my fingertips to my eyelids.

Some days, I think she loves testing me more than anything.

I pull my coat closer, then follow her out into the snow.

The noon sunlight is almost blinding, reflecting from sparkling plains of white, and the sky is hard and blue and cloudless. But I know the peace won't last. Far off over the mountains, a low, brooding line of clouds makes me worry that Hamlin's projections may be all too accurate.

I rush up to Faye, falling in to walk at her side.

"Apologies," I say. "There are certain things I couldn't say in front of your father's aides or the Pershing staff."

"You think Hamlin's up to something," she says almost gleefully. "Dish."

I smirk, shaking my head. "Tact was never your strong point, Ms. Harris."

"I don't want your tact; I want intel."

"Fair enough." Yet I consider my next words carefully, not wanting to implicate her father, not when she'll likely deny his involvement. And even if she doesn't, I'd rather put off having to destroy her family until I have irrefutable evidence against Harris. "I believe Mr. Hamlin is involved in some rather dirty fucking deals in Washington, particularly with Homeland Security. And I believe he wants us to stay here because he has some end game in mind regarding your father's opposition to the budget bill."

"Jesus." She sucks in a soft breath. "You think he's the one who tried to kill us?"

"I don't know." I shake my head. "The motive isn't there. Not clearly. Even if your father's budget cuts go through,

Pershing Shield is safe. They always get the largest cut of any appropriated funds for top contractors. So I can't imagine what motive he'd have for targeting the Senator – or targeting you."

"But if he wants to keep us isolated," she tells me, tapping her chin, "he'll find a good reason to poop on any ideas about consolidating everyone in the lodge to minimize energy consumption and stretch our resources. Especially when, if everyone's scattered, it's easier to isolate the people he wants."

I lift both brows, glancing at her mildly. "Did you just use the phrase 'poop on' to describe a possible conspiracy to murder your family?"

She smiles brightly and nods, her hair so vivid against the snow, like blood on silk. "I sure as fuck did."

I can't help myself.

I'm laughing, shaking my head. She brings it out in me, even when I feel like there's no reason to ever laugh again.

Even when I feel like the light has gone out in my world forever, she burns so brightly that she chases back the dark, the poison, the bad.

And when I can't stop laughing a second too long, she beams like the sun, looking entirely too pleased with herself. Tink *knows* what she does to me, and this has been her grand plan all along.

At least that's one plan I can figure out.

Pulling myself together, I cast her a mock-stern look. "Your crude words aside, yes. It might make more practical sense to consolidate everyone in the lodge, but we'd also face the difficulty of moving the individual caches of emergency stores to a single depot at the lodge, as well as draining and storing the fuel from each cabin's generators as backup for the lodge's main generator. The logistics would likely be more than we could handle before the storm returns."

She tilts her head, looking up at the sky, her eyes so clear and bright green that they capture the sky, mixing their colors until her gaze glows luminous teal. "But it doesn't look like snow at all."

"Look over the mountains. There." I point.

Frowning, she turns to scan the peaks of the Sierras, marching along the horizon in snow-capped triangles. "But that's...so far away."

"You'd be amazed how quickly strong winter storms can travel."

We stop outside her cabin. All around us, trails of footsteps make patterns in the snowdrifts. Snowy fractals like art and mundane trackings of people's motions to and from their cabins.

She looks up at me with a small smile, her eyes softening, yet her lips ever impudent. "Well. This is me. I'd wait for you to kiss me on the doorstep, but that'll get real awkward when you're staying here too."

Just the thought of kissing her has me torn to pieces.

It's not the right time.

I have things to do, leads to follow, suspicions to confirm, but with just two words, she completely steals my attention and burns everything else out of my mind.

Fuck.

I cannot kiss this woman.

I *cannot* give in to the lure of her scent, the desire to lick her fingers and see if they taste like that scent that's been teasing me all morning.

My cock twitches hotly as I step closer to her, crowding her back against the door.

"Inside," I growl.

She looks up at me, her eyes wide, her lashes trembling subtly.

"You heard me." I nod firmly.

Then she reaches behind herself to twist the doorknob and nearly stumbles backward through the door. I step in after her, snow sheeting down from both of us in cold crumbles on the mat as I close the door behind us.

I swear – and I'll keep swearing until my dying day – that my only intent was to usher her inside, to safety, where at least if Hamlin is attempting to isolate us all from each other, I can be sure she's tucked away somewhere safe.

Somewhere he can't reach her without going through me.

But then her heel catches on a puddle of water that five seconds ago was slush melting in the thick heat of the room. She slips.

Without thinking, I snake my arms out to catch her, wrapping them firmly around her waist and pulling her close even as gravity sends her careening against me.

There's not even time to blink.

Her soft, lusciously curved body molds against mine, and even through the multiple layers of her coat I feel her breasts pressed against my stomach. That special way the round, soft flesh yields and gives as it crushes against the hardness of my body.

She lets out a muffled, sheepish laugh, mumbling against my chest. "Oops."

Yeah. Oops is right.

Because something in me snaps.

Something pure animal.

Faye starts pushing herself upright, lifting her head, leaving her mouth poised like vulnerable prey.

Prey I want to devour, prey I want to savor with every nibble and bite and lick before consuming her whole. And before I can stop myself, before the voice of reason in my mind shouts at me to keep my distance, remember my place, I'm undone.

I'm fucking leaning down, capturing her lips in mine.

There's a moment of startled shock.

An instant when she freezes, her arms curled between us and hands balled against my chest, before she melts with a low purr and becomes the firestorm I remember.

The woman who would let me own her, but only if I won it, worked for it, fought for it.

Faye.

Tinker Bell.

Mine.

She crushes her mouth against me, her lips succulent and burning and ripe. Her slick caresses tease me, combust me, ripping me apart in a whirlwind of heat as she teases with every enticement, every promise that's always caught me and lured me in over and over again.

And I willingly let myself be burned, sinking into her. Taking her teasing moans and giving back bites, raw taunts against the shape of her mouth.

I give it back hard. Wild.

Until her lips go soft and gasping and I can feel how they swell from every abuse as I torment her with sharp edges and delicate licks. She shudders, leaning into me with a moan, this time louder.

My dick jerks. There's instant recognition.

It's that same gasping moan from last night, the one that filled my dreams.

Then she drapes her arms around my neck, slipping her fingers into my hair, opening to me completely as I delve deep to taste her, to relearn her, to rediscover what a sweltering well of madness and beauty and pure, lush desire lives inside those dark, inviting depths.

I'm going to devour this woman.

But when she strokes her fingers along my cheek, that *scent* invades me, and I can't hold back.

Groaning, I tear my mouth from hers, capturing her

fingers. I trace my hot breath over them, drawing them into my mouth to suck, catching those last faint hints of *her* that still linger, that tell me every wicked thing she did to herself last night while I was barely five feet away.

It was shameless and erotic and as wanton as I've always wanted her to be.

I sink my teeth into her flesh, loving how she trembles, gasping with surprise.

Faye tastes like scorching, tart things and just a hint of something hotter. She watches me with startled eyes and flushed cheeks and rapidly shuddering breaths.

All while I taste what makes my cock throb hard against my slacks and drives me fucking mad.

I don't realize I've pushed her up against the door until there's nowhere left to go.

My body is on auto, my senses hazed in lust, everything in me driven by primal compulsion. Frenzied, hot hunger with a mind of its own.

Then suddenly she's trapped against me, and I'm dragging my lips down her throat, ripping at her jeans, flinging the zipper down while she gasps and arches against me, raking her fingers feverishly through my hair.

Fuck yeah, Tink. There you are. And here I am.

I need this.

We need this, too.

I need to remember who I am in every kiss, every scratch, every taste.

So that I can't forget again while I play at showing one face or another to Harris and Hamlin until I can expose and destroy them both.

Right now, when I'm leaving bite marks over the delectable skin of her throat, when I slip my palm down inside her jeans, relishing when she arches against me and pushes the soft flesh of her belly into my hand, her thighs quivering against my fingertips as I delve lower, I remember.

I know.

I feel like I'm being honest for the first time in years, if only through the desperation of my touch.

When I slip my fingers into her panties, she's wet – deliciously sopping wet, and I can't stop myself from stroking my fingers over her smooth skin languidly, taking my time delving lower, flirting with the edge of soft, slick flesh and then away, until she lifts her hips, her dilated eyes flashing dark frustration.

"*James*," she hisses, digging her nails into the back of my neck in bright points of sweet pain. "Don't...don't *tease*."

"No?" I bite down harder on her throat, just to make her gasp and whimper. Just to make her arch her body, her thighs spreading wider for me, baring her to me. Then with a snarl, I slip my fingers deeper into her heat, reclaiming that pussy, running them firmly from the fluttering pink of her entrance up to the tiny, delectable node of her clit. "Is this what you're asking for, Tink? Is this what you need?"

Her mouth pops open in pure swoon.

She doesn't answer with words, but with high, gasping cries that burn me down.

Fuck.

She could scorch this winter straight into summer with the way she writhes, that soft flesh gripping my fingers like she could guide me inside her cunt with nothing but clenching fire.

Lucky for her, I wouldn't be a gentleman if I didn't oblige a lady.

After teasing her a moment more, I slip my fingers through her wetness, coating them.

Then slowly, one stroking fingertip at a time, ease my two middle fingers inside her.

Her reaction is instant and intoxicating.

"James!"

A high, broken call of my name, as she slams her head back against the door, rocking her hips toward me. I devour every hint of passion in her lax features, lingering on her lovely lips, the way her chest rises and falls in swelling gasps, the flutter of her lashes against flushed cheeks.

She's pure siren arousal right now, and she gives herself over with complete and utter wanton willingness as I stroke my fingers in and out of her again and again, circling her clit with my thumb in taunting pressure, pushing deeper every time I fill her.

She's so fucking tight inside, these heavy convulsions gripping, making it hard to pull my fingers free for each new thrust.

Faye's always been like that.

Once she has you, it's almost impossible to break free.

I know I don't want to, either. Not when it's hard for me to breathe.

Not when I'm throbbing with the desire to fill her with more than just my fingers, to take her until we're flesh to flesh and writhing on the floor in a plunging, grasping, hungry mess.

But I still have some sanity left, some last bit of self-control that tells me not to cross that line.

Not today.

I hold myself back by the thinnest thread. For a moment, I feel almost like I'm punishing her for making me want her so much when I add a third finger, stretching her sweetness, searching deeper, twisting inside until she goes stiff with a strangled, needy cry and rakes her fingers through my hair.

"James, fuck – *James!*" she whimpers every syllable.

The only warning before her body bucks harder in a

clenching, shuddering rush. Her hips rock wildly, her flesh locks around my fingers.

She's gorgeous. She's lost. She's pure, raw, undiluted lust captured in the shape of a woman...and I'm privileged to watch her fall apart before my eyes, surrendering to my touch.

She comes real sweet for me.

Head tossed back in pure rapture, red hair flying, lips parted in a tight, endless, straining gasp I want to pull down my throat.

But if I do that, I know I'll lose my last thread of control.

I'll either pop off in my pants, or I'll tear open my fly and fill her wet, calling, irresistible heat.

No, damn it. Not now.

Slowly, I ease my fingers out of her as her tremors soften and she slumps against the door, grasping limply at my shoulders. I try to be careful touching her sensitive flesh, but still she flinches subtly until I've pulled my glistening hand fully free.

I want to lick her taste from my fingers. But something about how she's looking at me, with a dazed, sweet, satisfied smile and her eyes half-closed, throws a sudden icy guilt over me, cooling my desire.

Faye reaches up to touch her fingertips to my lips. "There's the man I missed," she whispers. "It's nice knowing you missed me too."

Fuck.

Fuck me, what have I just done?

All I've done is give her false hope.

Because I was reckless, careless, caught up in a fury of temper and desire, needing something to ground myself, a bitter reminder I'm more than just a pawn in anybody's game.

Hello, unthinkable. The world drops out under me.

I'm quietly cursing myself for letting Faye think we could ever have an *us* again, when that's something I can't give her.

I shake my head, drawing back without words.

I can't even find the right thing to say to apologize. Not when I know everything I've done here is entirely selfish. She stares up at me, that sweet, warm expression crumpling in the most terrible way as she starts to straighten her clothing, drifting away from the door and toward me with one hand outstretched.

"James?"

I can't stay here.

Not with the plea in her voice, begging me to forget my purpose, to forget every reason *why not*.

I take a deep, shaky breath, trying like hell to steady myself.

"I'm sorry for my indiscretion," I tell her tonelessly, and incline forward, wiping my fingers dry on my pants leg. "If you'll excuse me, I have work to do."

It's cold. I know it's pure killing.

But it has the desired effect since she can't even bring herself to say anything.

And her silence haunts me, even after I step around her and pull the door open.

Haunts me, I said, and chases me out into the sub-zero brightness of a day that nonetheless feels like the darkest and coldest of my soul.

* * *

I'm not surprised when Faye doesn't follow me.

What I just did was, to put it in her terms, a *total asshole move*.

It takes the frigid snow to clear my head as I force myself out on a perimeter sweep.

I always keep the cabin in sight, technically doing my duty to protect her, but also making a full and clear assessment of our environment.

For what I'm thinking, I need to know this resort inside and out.

I need to know everywhere Hamlin might stage backup.

I need to know every vantage point a sniper could take advantage of.

I need to know every safe space where I might conceal myself and the woman I've made it my mission to guard, even if I might be the thing she *really* needs protection from.

A plan slowly takes shape in the back of my mind, but I need to know certain things first. Need to be certain what Harris and Hamlin are planning – with each other, and against each other.

Which means I need to get access to Harris' rooms. His laptop.

He's a smart man and wouldn't leave incriminating things in writing. He's been in politics long enough to see dumber, dirtier people burn for their own messy mistakes.

But some things are unavoidable, leaving behind some trace, especially when your self-serving black market plans are tied up in congressional spending bills.

Everything has to be documented and described to death.

It's just a matter of finding the hidden message in all the legalese and determining what it truly means for his future plans.

Maybe, just maybe, whatever I find will give me the opening I need to pry apart Hook Hamlin and find his weak points.

Sure, Harris may be my primary target, the one who makes my blood burn with a quiet but festering need for vengeance. However, there's no love lost for Pershing.

Hamlin is just as tangled up in this, and he deserves to fall just as far, topple just as hard.

I only wish I could confide in someone at Enguard. Landon, Gabe, Riker, anyone.

But telling them what I know about Hamlin's arms deals and black market ops and misappropriation of funds using Harris as a funnel? That means telling them about my past, and covering up for Harris' involvement in the murder of a talented FBI agent.

My mentor, and my friend.

I still hate myself for doing it. And I still question myself every day – *why?*

Did I truly do it to protect Faye from losing the last living parent she had left? Or was it a cowardly choice made in a haze of grief, pain, and loss?

That night I lost my friend, lost my career, lost the love of my life.

And lost my mother when the plane that was carrying me and agent Tanner Egon crashed, nearly killing me.

Leaving me hospitalized, unable to even close the last distance between myself and my mother as she lay dying, that unfinished novel of hers waiting for an ending when she could hardly hold a pen with cancer-riddled hands.

That grief, that loss, are too tangled in my hatred for Senator Harris.

He may not have killed my mother the way he killed Tanner, but he stole her last moments from me.

And that, I can never forgive.

I'm just coming around from checking the large generator array at the back of the lodge when I hear my name echoing across the snow in Hook's ringing, grandfatherly voice.

Damn, now what?

"James, I thought that was you," he calls, raising a hand as he steps out from the lodge and into the snow. His bulk is so large, so monolithic, that even though others have tamped down a path in the snowdrifts leading from the front steps, he still sends snow sluicing out in sheets to either side as he widens the path with his sheer size, forging toward me. "How are things going with patrols?"

I force my rage down. I don't report to anyone but Landon, but we're supposed to be at least pretending to collaborate with Pershing Shield, so I offer a clipped, mock-friendly nod. "Well enough. I was simply assessing the layout of the resort and any problem areas."

He stops in front of me, watching me with those penetrating eyes. He really does remind me of a shark, something flat and empty in eyes that don't reflect the light.

Yet he still smiles, easy and affable, as he asks, "Find anything interesting?"

"Not particularly. I'm concerned about the generator array, however. It seems old. I'm worried that repeated freezing and defrosting has created a questionable safety situation and possible fire hazard."

"I love how you say that like you're talking about what to have for tea." He chuckles. "You're cold as ice, aren't you?"

I cock my head, sizing him up. "More someone who prides himself on self-control."

"Self-control, eh?" Hamlin rubs his chin with one thickly gloved hand, mussing his beard. "I'm a firm believer in discipline. Don't think enough men in this day and age have it."

"Is that so?" Careful, neutral answers. I want to let him guide the conversation, see where it takes me.

"Yup. A man starts to crack, and soon...well, there's no telling how damn far he'll fall."

I pinch my jaw. It isn't hard to sense the reference to his own father, the gambler and womanizer, the man who squandered a fortune and a good name.

Then Hook gives me another of those assessing looks. They're the kind that undoubtedly are meant to put a man in his place and remind him of Hamlin's authority, yet it slides off me like water off glass. "So," he muses. "You're Harris' man, are you?"

"I wouldn't necessarily say that."

"He says he helped you get a job." His eyes narrow. "What kind of job, exactly?"

I shrug, letting my gaze shift away from Hamlin to rove idly over the sun-dotted resort. We're alone outside, save for Gabe in front of the cabin he shares with Sky, looking as though he's actually *enjoying* the effort of digging out a clearer path.

From the fervor with which he sends snow arcing out in glittering sprays, there's very little doubt that he's making the extra effort for his very pregnant wife. Watching Gabe gives me something to do while I consider my response.

"He gave me a reference for a role with the FBI," I answer.

Just enough detail to make him curious. Not enough to leak too much.

A thoughtful, growly sound rumbles in the back of Hamlin's throat. "Wow. So you owe him favors then?"

I flick my gaze back to him, jaw clenching so tight it might fucking pop. "No. I owe Senator Paul Harris *nothing*."

Careful. Not too much, I tell myself. *Bring it home.*

Hook offers me a small smile that I suppose is meant to set me at ease. "Is that a touch of resentment I detect?"

Fuck yes.

Because it's exactly what I want him to perceive.

The mask I'm crafting right now is new, an intricate lie. By the time I'm done, if I've done it right, Hook Hamlin will believe I'd do anything to get to Senator Harris.

While Senator Harris will believe I'll do anything to get to Hook.

STILL NOT LOVE

We're alone in a hostile environment, soon to be cut off from the outside world in dangerous conditions – and conniving men tend to be paranoid men.

When the shit hits the fan, paranoid men need to believe they have the right people on their side.

So I'll let Hamlin's paranoia do the heavy work for me and slowly feed it.

Just enough until he believes I'm the only one who can make it go away.

Hamlin is still considering me, while I give back stony silence, offering nothing.

His lips twist thoughtfully before he asks, "Tell me something, James...are you keeping Harris' secrets, or is he keeping yours?"

"Do you really need an answer?"

"No?" he retorts, deceptively mild, a smile forming on his face. "So you don't want to be free of him? Is that what you're telling me?"

"Forgive me, Mr. Hamlin. I'm lost. I have no idea what you're referring to," I answer coolly, inclining my head. "Please excuse me while I check the maintenance sheds."

I give him what he expects – plausible deniability. And just enough he can ferret out between the lines.

That's how this works, these illicit, tense conversations that shouldn't be happening.

A few minutes later, I walk away, leaving him.

On the hook, as it were – and there's Faye's humor creeping in.

But I can't let myself think about her right now.

The goal is to make Hamlin think that I could be an ally against Harris, but not that I'm disloyal or easily swayed.

I've given him plenty of motive to work with and something to pry at. This game of chess is only just beginning, pawns moving across the board in careful single steps.

Shame Harris and Hamlin don't realize the obvious.

They aren't the only ones playing.

* * *

I DON'T RETURN to the cabin, even after I've finished a meticulous mapping of the grounds, discovering a few interesting things stowed away in the maintenance sheds. Namely, long black canvas duffel bags filled with automatic rifles.

Somehow, I don't think the skeleton crew of resort staff left them there.

You don't need an AK-47 to deal with bears.

Maybe they're worried about the Abominable Snowman, but I don't think so.

After I've finished my rounds, I take up a vantage point on the roof of the lodge.

The interesting thing with people is they never tend to look up.

No one notices me crouched to one side of the chimney, watching the patterns as people drift back and forth. It's mostly worried aides and resort staff, seeking each other out for reassurance and asking if they should huddle up together, including a few trading cabin assignments in the hopes of being trapped with the object of their interest.

Landon and the other members of Enguard, too, walking the perimeter with Pershing staff. They're discussing how to secure the place and ensure communications stay open in the event of an emergency, as well as helping the resort staff with disaster prep.

Storm shutters go up quickly. Buried power cables get checked for insulation. Generator fuel tanks are topped off from the large drums in the storage sheds. Cases of bottled water are redistributed to each cabin with a backup supply at the lodge.

It brings back memories of home.

Of how my grandfather, Dominick, always wanted to be prepared in the event of the "big one" that's supposed to hit the West Coast any time now.

You know, the apocalyptic earthquake that would destroy us all and damn near fling most of the West Coast into the Pacific. He was always stocking up on non-perishables, portable solar panels, batteries, and all other sorts of emergency supplies.

My mother, free spirit that she was, would watch him with fond indulgence, laying her fingers against the piano keys. She'd tell him he worried too much about all the wrong things.

In the end, she was right.

It wasn't a natural disaster, some phenomenon we could predict, that brought disaster to our family.

It was the frailty of the human body, and nothing else.

I track Landon and Hook Hamlin as they disappear into the lodge, catching a bit of their conversation.

Landon discusses how he'd hired several more low-level security team members for this, the screening process, how we more than doubled our staff to be ready for this job.

It's not hard to tell he really wants to impress Hamlin, perhaps even looks up to him as a mentor.

It guts me a little inside, to see someone as honorable and whip-smart as my boss currying favor with a fucking pirate like Hook Hamlin. Whenever the truth comes out, he'll be devastated.

And it'll be my fault.

Maybe that's what's casting doubts over my grand plan.

Will I make the wrong choice again?

Just to protect someone I care for from losing faith in their idols?

It's interesting to me, though, that all of Pershing Shield's personnel have been assigned to the outlying cabins ringing the main resort cluster, leaving Enguard personnel and Faye in the inner ring of cabins.

Harris and Hook are both staying in the two master suites inside the main lodge. The assignments would've been different had Harris' guests been able to make it up the mountain.

They didn't. Now that there's more space to spread out, it's looking like Hook has made some strategic changes.

Almost like he *wants* to box us in.

I see my chance to make a move, though, when I notice Gabe, the setting sun reflecting off his knit cap and parka as he trudges through the paths cut into the snow and toward the main lodge. He must be on shift tonight, guarding Harris' room.

Perfect.

I couldn't pull this off with Riker or any of the more canny members of the Enguard crew, but Gabe is like a big, trusting dog – and he's also too new to our team to know those little tics that give us away when we're lying.

Or planning to deceive someone, even with the best intent.

I drop down from the roof, landing lightly at the lodge's rear, and slip in through the back entrance that most of the staff use.

It lets me cut through the temperature-controlled wine cellar, where I snag a bottle of Domaine Leroy Richebourg Grand Cru.

The name is as impressive as its price tag – over five thousand dollars a bottle, normally.

No one even notices me take it.

I'm sure the Senator won't mind when I put it on his tab.

Stepping out into the main room of the lodge, my timing is impeccable.

STILL NOT LOVE

I show up just as Gabe comes in, blowing on his ungloved fingers, stomping the snow from the treads of his boots in little chunks all over the mat. As he catches sight of me approaching, his eyes light up.

"James," he says jovially, spreading his arms as though he might hug me. "I've hardly seen you around. Where you been hiding?"

I sidestep. I'm not a hugger.

"Pretty busy with Ms. Harris," I say, and then immediately regret my phrasing when it reminds me just how *busy* I was with her a few short hours ago.

She's likely still simmering her way into an explosion that's going to scorch my eyebrows off when I make it back to the cabin. To distract both him and myself, I raise the bottle. "But look what I found in the back."

Gabe falters, wincing. "I..."

I tap the bottle again with one finger. *Come on, big guy, no excuses.*

Glancing over his shoulder, he leans in, dropping his voice to a conspiratorial whisper. "I shouldn't. Sky can't drink right now so...it makes her real mad when I do."

"She'll never have to know. Our little secret." I toss my head toward the seating arrangement in front of the fire. The lodge is empty, at least, all the bustle and preparation to batten down for the coming storm sending people scurrying, but it worries me that Harris has been notably absent.

For now, though, I focus my attention on Gabe, guiding him toward the plush couches and pausing to snag two wine glasses from a concierge cart against the wall.

"James, man, I appreciate the gesture and all but –"

"But we've never had a drink to congratulate you on your first child. Come on. Just one before you start your shift."

Gabe lets out a shaky southern laugh. "Well, don't congratulate me till I survive that baby girl being born."

I raise both brows, sinking down into an upholstered easy chair, carefully using my thumb and precise strength at the right angle to ease the cork out of the bottle with a *pop*. "So it's definitely a girl?"

"Yeah." He flushes with a broad, goofy grin. "Found out right before we came up here. And she's a fighter, just like her Ma. Kicking all the time. Problem is, every time she kicks, I think Sky wants to kick *me*."

"She just might." As I'm talking, I'm pouring. I fill a glass, then push it toward Gabe before filling my own. "Have you discussed names yet?"

"Aw, shitfire, don't get me started on that." And just like that, he's downing half the glass in a heartbeat, while I pretend to sip at mine. "I keep wanting to name her Belle, but she says Belle's a granny name. Then when I get mad 'cause Belle's my mama's name, she's sorry. Then I say it ought to be Martha, my grandma's name. But she ain't sure, naming our kid after her because it's the same name as Clark Kent's mama."

I raise both brows. "Batman's as well, I believe," I point out.

Gabe groans, dropping his face into his palms.

"You're not helping," he mumbles, but all I do is lean forward and refill his glass. "Gotta say, though, this wine's mighty good."

Exactly, big man. I'm helping in my own way.

Both Gabe, the entire team, and myself.

I'll feel guilty for this later.

We talk for nearly an hour while emptying the wine bottle. He empties it, mostly, while I'm very careful to make it look like I'm drinking my fair share when in fact I'm watching the clock.

He's not due on shift just yet.

He came in early so he wouldn't be trudging through the

snow after dark. I need to get him out of the way before he's due on the clock, then report back in to take his place.

Fortunately, Gabe's a lightweight, considering his massive size – and Richebourg Grand Cru is a rather potent red. Twenty minutes before his shift is set to start, he's sliding over to one side.

Then his head hits the throw pillow, and he's out cold, snoring like the big bear he is.

It takes a good amount of my strength to heft him up, draping his arm over my shoulders and supporting his weight as I drag him out into the snow.

The sunset has just finished painting pink and gold on its reflective, glittering canvas of snow. The light show fades to softer hues of violet and blue as twilight sinks in.

It only makes the glow of vividly bright red against Faye's cabin window stand out that much more.

I can feel her watching, beaming daggers that cut holes through me. Just like lasers burning hot against the snowy wind slicing through me right now, but I need to keep my focus just now.

Especially because this wind worries me.

So do the dense, dark clouds it keeps pushing onward.

I manage to haul Gabe back to his cabin, his horse-like breaths puffing against the back of my neck with his snoring the entire time. At least it keeps me warm.

When I thump the door with my elbow, a very pregnant Skylar waddles to answer it, bundled up in no less than three bathrobes and wearing her snow boots inside. She eyes us both shrewdly, her lips pursing. "I thought Gabe was on night shift with Harris?"

"My fault. You have my apologies." As she makes room to let me drag Gabe inside, I step over the threshold and into near-blistering warmth. Gabe's feet thump on the mat, then drag over the doorway and inside. "We settled in for a chat and got a bit carried away. I forgot he can't hold his liquor."

Sky snorts, shutting the door behind us. "And *you* can?"

"Apparently with more fortitude than your dear husband." Trying not to wheeze when Gabe is a veritable *tank*, I haul him toward the rumpled bed. "Here. Let's put him to bed."

Quickly, Sky moves to pull the covers back. I groan again as I haul Gabe over and drop him onto the mattress.

He doesn't even stir, still snoring, sprawled out cold.

Sky gives him a fondly disgusted look, then sighs and helps me tug his boots off, loosening his coat before covering him up again.

"What about Senator Harris?" she asks.

"I'll take Gabe's shift," I answer. "Faye's safe in her cabin, and I have a clear view of it from the window in Harris' suite. It's the least I can do to make up for..." I gesture at Gabe. "*This*."

She folds her arms tightly over her chest. "*This* is going to be a hung over wreck in the morning," she says, before sighing, her gaze softening as she sinks down on the edge of the bed.

Smiling softly, she brushes his hair back from his brow. "He's such an idiot sometimes."

"And yet you love him."

"Yeah. I do. More than anything in the world." Sky cups Gabe's cheek, tracing her thumb gently along the crest of his cheekbone. "That's part of love, I guess. Holding on to someone even when they do stupid things, or aren't their best selves, or something goes wrong."

I don't know what to say to that.

Fuck, I don't know how to *feel* about that.

So I simply take my leave, heading back up to the lodge as night descends.

STILL NOT LOVE

Harris isn't in his suite when I take up my post outside.

He's been oddly absent ever since the photo shoot and panic over the storm, and rather than make me worried for his safety, it makes me wonder what he's doing. Why he can't be seen in the public eye.

His room is locked, but like all other members of the senior security team, I have an all-access keycard for emergencies.

I can justify this as an emergency later, if I get caught.

Glancing around the upstairs hallway, I take a good look before making my move.

It's just a small landing off the stairs with two doors for the luxury suites and a single window at the end of the hall, giving me a clear line of sight to Faye's cabin.

No one's here. No one can see me from outside, and Faye is curled up against the windowsill, tucked into bed in a pair of those damnably tight, short shorts and a t-shirt.

Squinting, I see her nose is buried in a book, her temple resting against a glass pane.

I want to go to her, to tug her gently away from the window to remind her not to sleep there or she'll catch a cold. To bundle her up and keep her safe. To do more of everything I shouldn't have done to her earlier.

But that's not my place anymore, damn it.

And she's perfectly capable of taking care of herself.

She's already wrapped up in blankets, and I remind myself that she's *fine*.

She's not the real target here, anyway.

She's leverage someone might try to use to intimidate the Senator into getting their way.

But she'll be safe, out of my sight for just a few minutes.

I slip my keycard from my pocket and into the slot. The light flashes green, and I catch the doorknob before the automated latch makes its distinctive *click*, instead easing it in silently.

Slowly, I push the door open. I leave it cracked behind me so it doesn't make a sound sliding shut. Then I hold my breath.

Just because Harris didn't answer doesn't mean he isn't in here after all. But the room is dark, with that familiar emptiness that comes when people are distinctly absent, like a body without a soul.

The Senator's suitcases are stacked neatly next to the luxe king-sized bed, completely untouched, the massive and lushly decorated room as pristine as if its occupant had never settled in – except for the desk.

It's noticeably covered in the riot and clutter of a busy, busy man.

Intrigued, I steal one last glance over my shoulder, then step deeper into the room and shut the door behind me. Six steps in and I'm rifling through the desk with gloved hands, looking over printouts, but it's nothing but drafts of campaign speeches, invoices for travel to the lodge, several other mundane documents as incriminating as a grocery list.

It's the laptop that's the real target.

Too bad when I flip it up, I'm greeted by a lock screen asking not for a password, but a biometric fingerprint.

Fuck.

Good thing I came prepared.

Slipping a little kit from my pocket and snapping it open, I lift out a thin sheet of clear polarized film with a light coat of transparent ferrous iron on one side. This baby will do miracles.

Carefully, I press the other side over the fingerprint plate on the corner of the laptop.

A perfect imprint of Harris' thumbprint comes back.

The imprint isn't enough. Next a quick pass with a little

square magnet. Then the coating that imprinted the fingerprint activates, pulling at the iron on the opposite side, until it clusters in lines following the swirls of the Senator's print.

Now I have a raised surface I can work with.

Next comes the little ball of flesh-toned putty in the kit. Rolling it between my hands quickly, I warm it until it's close enough to skin temperature for a biometric reader to sense it as the temperature of skin.

Finally, I press the little die-cut fingerprint into the surface of the putty.

When I pull it away, I have a little round, warmed fake fingertip complete with Harris' print.

And when I gently press it to his laptop, it spins its little wheel, before the screen clears and it greets me with *Welcome back, Paul* in bold white letters.

I smile. My old FBI training is still with me.

I don't have time right now to go through all the documents on Harris' laptop.

I'm not here to copy everything. Just a quick scan tells me he's got nearly a full terabyte of info on here, and I know the SD card in my phone won't be able to handle that much.

Damn. I just need to leave myself a backdoor so I can freely access the intel later without being detected from my own laptop.

I cast another furtive look over my shoulder, my heart racing in a way it hasn't in years.

Call it a clandestine rush. The kind you get working against an intelligent enemy who could catch me at any second.

Quickly, I tuck the fingerprint kit away and replace it with my phone, spooling out a USB cable to connect it to the laptop. I'm just leaving behind a few presents from a little folder I keep tucked away in my phone's files for moments like this.

They won't work on an Android phone, but they're perfectly designed to be undetectable on Windows laptops.

First, a program to capture and transmit all the Senator's keystrokes to a remote server I can check from my own laptop. Then a remote backdoor that'll allow me to log in from another device and either view Harris' screen as though it were my own, or take control of his machine.

Once I'm out of here, I can explore his files at my leisure.

And if there's anything I've learned during my time with the FBI, it's that politicians are notoriously careless with technology.

As soon as the files are done installing, I check the task manager list to make sure the processes are hidden, and I've left no trace. Then I swiftly unhook everything, shove it in my pocket, and shut the laptop down.

I need to be out of this room soon, and by the time Harris comes back, I'll have found someone else to replace me on shift so he'll never even know I was here.

Landon might be willing, if he's not attached to Hook Hamlin again. Landon always likes to keep busy when he's away from Kenna to keep the restlessness at bay.

One last scan to make sure I've left no trace of my presence, not a single paper out of place, before I'm gone, easing the door shut. Not even a print to give me away. I never took off my gloves.

I'm almost reluctant to go. The fresh charge of alertness in my veins demands I do something *now*.

Feels like I've been in limbo for years, but I'm only just now waking up.

Taking action brings something to life in me, all right.

I'm lingering on that as I descend the stairs, brushing past a sleepy-looking housekeeper who's just closing up her cart at the foot of the stairs. She flashes me a worried but warm smile, and I dip my head in a nod.

On I go – only to freeze as I look up to see exactly who's waiting for me.

She's perched on the sofa in the commons room like she knew she'd find me here, her legs crossed and her arms tightly folded and her soft red mouth set in a line that says I'm in more trouble than I would be with the Senator.

Faye.

VII: NO ALIBI (FAYE)

I'm going to murder him.

I'm going to fucking murder James Nobel.

And by the time the snow thaws and they find his body at the bottom of a hill somewhere, I'll be in Bora Bora with a new name and a new life and zero memory of his hands on my body, *in* my body, while he kissed me like he still actually feels something for me.

Right before shutting me out, putting on that fucking android act he uses to keep everyone at a distance.

Including me.

And right now, I'm not having it. I want answers.

Like why I went upstairs looking for my father and found *James* in his darkened room, bent over Dad's laptop, doing something that didn't look entirely on the up-and-up.

I guess I never shook off my training, because he never even heard me, walking on the balls of my feet and making sure the light from the hall wouldn't cast a shadow to alert him to my presence.

I'd watched him for only a minute before jerking away, flattening myself to one side of the wall as he'd glanced over his shoulder. When I'd peeked back, he was looking at the laptop again, so I'd hotfooted it out of there with my heart in my throat.

Then I stopped in the commons room, wondering what the hell I was running from.

I didn't do anything wrong.

It's James who owes me, right now.

He owes me a lot.

Right now, he's standing at the foot of the stairs, one foot still on the bottom step, hand frozen adjusting his cufflink, looking at me with the kind of blank stare that says he knows he's in trouble.

But after a moment he glosses over, face shuttering, and he nods to me briefly. "Ms. Harris," he says smoothly in that oh-so-punchable way. "I was just on my way back to our cabin."

I narrow my eyes, pursing my lips.

Nope. No freaking way.

My temper is *boiling.* He's lucky I'm keeping myself in one place, or I'd be at his throat.

I'd probably punch him, if I'm being honest. "Uh-huh. Our cabin. Was that before or after you finished messing with Dad's laptop?"

I'd hoped to get a reaction out of him, but he's ready this time, not even blinking, batting it back at me with, "Laptop? I have no idea what the hell you're talking about."

"Don't lie to me. Not to *me*, James." It hurts that he'd try, even if I knew he would.

He's still Agent Nobel all the way. Everything hidden behind that perfect gloss, dissembling his way through everything.

Hostile situations. Conflicts. *Commitments.*

"Don't even." I push to my feet, glaring at him, my throat

tight. "I saw you, James. I came upstairs and saw you tampering with Dad's laptop."

He closes his eyes, taking a deep breath, shoulders squaring, before he steps closer.

"Lower your voice, please," he says tightly, looking down at me with pale eyes like sleet. "If you insist on discussing it...fine. Not here."

I scowl at him. I'm hardly ready to roll over just yet, especially not when I'm basically being told to be a good girl and shut up. "So there's an *it* to talk about? Wow."

He arches a brow, cool as ever. "Depends on which 'it' you're referring to."

"*Both!*" I hiss, but still drop my voice. "You did two bad things tonight, James. Two really, really shitty bad things."

A silvery-blue glance like a razor blade slides over me from head to toe, leaving too much behind.

First shivers, then heat in its wake. I hate how he does that to me, even when I'm ready to take his head off.

Especially when he glides right past, heading for the door with a final quip. "Interesting choice of words, Ms. Harris. You didn't seem to mind one 'shitty bad thing.'"

I whip around, glaring at the back of his head, my cheeks in flames.

God Almighty. If I had something, anything heavy enough close by right now, he'd be suffering from blunt force trauma to the skull.

I hate how he makes me want to kiss him and kill him at the same time.

Yeah. *Hate.*

That's the thing I'm feeling most.

But I turn to follow him – only we don't get very far at all.

Not when the second he opens the door, people come pouring in, shouting and trading panicked whispers. My father is with them.

And from the way James looks at my Dad, there's something going on here I probably don't want to know about, but *need* to.

Dammit all.

When I said I missed the excitement of the FBI, I didn't mean I wanted conspiracies and messes with my own family.

Before I realize it, James is back at my side, standing like a knight protecting his queen.

I can't miss the way he angles himself to block the line of sight to me. My father speaks, trying to get the panicking mob under control, and I strain to listen while he gets everyone quiet, gathering them around him like a flock of trembling baby birds.

"Calm down," he says firmly, pitching his voice with an orator's practiced ease. "I know you've all seen the troubling news, but there's nothing to worry about. This is, hands down, the safest place we could possibly be."

"What news?" I hiss to James, and he shakes his head.

"I don't know," he answers.

For once, I believe him.

"For those of you who haven't heard," my father continues, casting a glance my way. "One of my closest aides in D.C. was shot this afternoon. The news is just reaching us here. I know you've all been patient with heightened security here, but I'm asking for a little more. The fact that the cowards targeting me took aim at my dear friend, Manny Price, in D.C. says they haven't traced us here. We're safe. And you'd better believe I'll work like a dog to get answers and drag them to justice."

I don't believe it.

He's my own father, and I don't believe it.

Something just rings false.

Despite the emotional pitch in his voice, it's like he *knows* why this happened. Like there aren't more answers to uncover.

And I have an ugly feeling that even after we leave here, going back to a normal life won't be possible. Not as long as people are still trying to kill us.

I turn to ask James another question, but he's gone again, forging across the room toward Dad. I sigh, pressing my fingers to the bridge of my nose.

God *damn* it, James.

I've heard enough. I don't want to be here for this, and I double don't want to stand around feeling this doubt, watching my father bald-faced lie to people with those hints only I can read.

I don't want to stand here while James ignores me, with all these questions hanging between us and more coming by the second.

So while no one's looking at me, I slip through the crowd, out of the lodge and into the night, back to my own cabin.

* * *

Five years Ago

I'm worried about James.

He's normally not like this. Maybe he'll always be a rock, but there's a warmth in him, a kindness, a gentleness I've come to love.

That stony shell just can't hide the man underneath forever.

But lately, he's been closed off. Withdrawn. Cold.

Locking his emotions away even after he told me why: his mom's cancer took a turn for the worse.

She's dying, and he's doing everything he can for her while also dealing with an unexpected house guest. His friend, Agent Egon, ended up couch surfing at James' place after life gave him a big swift kick in the balls.

Tanner's house is being foreclosed. He's dealing with a pending divorce and two kids.

And James has a lot on his plate right now, a lot on his mind, but he still couldn't resist helping a friend.

Something about that touches me so deeply I hurt for him.

I'm scared for him, too. Frightened like never before.

James shouldn't be on this mission.

But we're already here, poised with the SWAT team, ready to go in on a raid. We're positioned in close formation on the streets around a seemingly abandoned warehouse on the south side of Portland, where months of tracking have uncovered a secret contraband weapon distribution hub.

Whoever they are, they're using this warehouse as a meeting point.

The directors are worried the ringleader doesn't just have guns in there. They're worried he has incendiary devices, and that's why I'm here.

Because someone's holed up in the warehouse, armed and ready, and after a standoff with local police, it's the Feds' turn.

I'm going in first. It's equal parts terrifying and exhilarating, but it's on me.

As the explosives expert, I'm just supposed to talk to him, find out what he's sitting on, maybe defuse him as much as I'm able to defuse a human being instead of a bomb. Disarming explosives is as much about knowing how to handle the people wielding them as it is knowing how to handle the deadly weapons.

James has my back, at least. I know that.

He's with me as I separate out from my hiding place around the corner of an old mall, my flak jacket on, half an inch of Kevlar between me and a bullet, my hands up to show that even if I'm not unarmed, I'm not brandishing a weapon right now.

"Mr. Keuhler?" I call toward the open slit of a narrow window where he's been spotted watching us through a sniper rifle. I tilt my head back, looking up, but the glass is covered in some kind of reflective yellow film and I can barely make out a shape, movement. "My name's Faye Harris. I'm with the FBI. I'm here to talk."

There's a long pause, a hesitation, and then a sullen growl. "Not talking to any Feds. Fuck off."

"I can understand your frustration, Mr. Keuhler," I answer soothingly. Just like the negotiator told me. "But right now, the FBI is the closest thing you have to an ally. The local cops want to send in SWAT to shoot first, ask questions later. Me and my fellow agents, we just want to talk. And we've got the power to do what the police can't."

Again, more silence, hesitant, suspicious, then, "Yeah? What's that?"

"Cut you a deal without anyone having to get hurt." I slowly start to lower my arms. "Now I'm going to lower my arms, you're going to lower your weapon, and maybe we can have a nice talk –"

"Faye!" James snarls, half a second before I hear the gunshot go off.

It's possible I wouldn't have died.

Not with the Kevlar vest, but if Keuhler had aimed for my head, I'd be a goner anyway.

I'll never know.

Not when suddenly James is there like lightning, shoving me aside, shielding me with his body. The bullet zings between us, hits the wall, then everything is chaos.

My service pistol appears in my hands, drawn by instinct. Then there's James' carbine discharging loudly. Muzzle flashes and shouts explode everywhere as SWAT storms the building, hoping there's nothing rigged to blow up inside.

Only Keuhler's not alone in the warehouse.

It's my first real firefight since I graduated Quantico as a true agent, and it's nothing like what I expect.

The movies show you people being mowed down in waves by scattered, desperate shots. In reality, it's a lot of ducking, peering, taking precisely aimed shots at opportune moments, breath racing and heart pounding and veins throbbing against your throat while you can taste gunpowder in the air and you don't know how to feel when you fire a bullet. Or when you hear that *thunck* sound of it striking flesh, when you smell blood and you may hate to kill, but you don't want to die.

All I have is in my training. My instinct. And James.

And I don't know how to feel when every time I catch movement out of the corner of my eye, it's the gorgeous man I'm in love with, picking people off with icy precision, standing over me like he would keep the world from me with his body and take a thousand bullets so I'll never have to feel one.

It's so scary and sad and sweet, I'm numb.

Yet somehow, even when a bullet grazes so close to my head, I feel the burn of its velocity and heat against the upper curve of my ear...

I've never felt more alive.

There's barely a moment to collect ourselves once the gunshots die down and suddenly everything is quiet. Still.

We have a moment to search the premises. I do a thorough check for explosives. SWAT searches for more men hiding, but neither of us find anything.

We wait for the field specialist to give the all clear.

That's when I remember how to breathe. The entire time James and I are locked on each other, hot-eyed and wordless, every glance sizzling with the adrenaline that's still surging inside me.

It's like the battle heat never quite died, never quite calmed.

My body still thinks it's fight or flight time.

Part of me wants a fight. Just not the kind where anyone bleeds.

And the second no one's looking...somehow James and I are in a dark crevice in an alley, tearing at each other's clothes, kissing hot and deep and with a wild desperation.

God, if we weren't in public, if we were alone...

But that kiss is enough to keep my battle-hunger going, stoking the fire high until we're dismissed and can slip away.

His place is closer. Even with his friend on the couch, we're as quiet as possible as we burst in tangled up in each other and locked in mid-kiss, whispering and stumbling around the man sleeping on the couch until we can tumble into James' bedroom and onto the bed.

It's as wild as the first time.

Hell, maybe *wilder* – something new awakening between us, something primal and animalistic.

He's a shadow with burning quicksilver eyes, moving over me.

Intense, fierce, silent, keeping me totally in his thrall as his hands shape my body and I arch to his touch. His mouth sears me everywhere, devouring me from head to toe, leaving my body tingling, singing, screaming with need.

My pussy feels so good underneath his tongue.

Then good becomes amazing, and a few licks more makes amazing *oh-my-Gawd.*

Every last bit of me is scrunched. I'm so close to coming I can hear my own heartbeat whispering *O* in my ears.

James knows it, too. He rears up, gives me this dark, wildfire look, his tongue sweeping across my slickness on his lips.

"Please," I whimper. "So close."

"Fucking bite your wrist," he growls, just before a loud whimper ignites off my lips. "Bite it, Tink, and I'll bring you off so hard you see stars."

So that's exactly what I do.

It's ridiculous and crazy and kinda hot, but I do it just for him, just like he asked.

I hold up my wrist and sink my teeth in. Bite down so hard it adds an extra wicked brushfire to my nerves when his face returns beneath my legs, bringing back the delicious heat of his tongue.

Oh, hell!

James pushes his licks faster, deeper, so deep, setting off an explosive release and a need for more, more, oh God, *more.*

Thankfully, he's happy to oblige.

I feel so exposed, so naked, so open, but I've never felt safer in anyone's hands.

I give myself over completely as he touches me until I writhe, until my wrist is hardly enough and I'm biting the soft part of my palm to keep from screaming loud enough to wake his friend.

He wrings my flesh until I'm nearly sobbing, dripping with pleasure as he toys with me some more with his fingers, his tongue, slipping in and out of me again and again, licking and tasting, nibbling gently on my clit before biting my inner thigh.

That crisp love bite of his brings every sensitive, sultry nerve alive with a sharp, sweet shock of pain.

Oh.

Oh. Holy. Hell.

I'm already coming apart again before he's even in me, panting and spent and shaking.

Then he's perched neatly between my legs, a devilish silver-blue glint in his eye.

If you've never had sex with a man who just saved your life, let me tell you one thing.

Nothing else compares.

Absolutely nothing.

No drug, no joy, no money could ever take me higher than I get when James Nobel fucks me that night.

He nudges the head of his cock against me and the string of my body snaps tight. I'm biting my lip, whimpering wordlessly, begging because I need him in me now.

Not want. *Need.*

In one burning thrust he plunges into me, and I arch back on the bed, wrapping my legs around his hard waist, digging my heels into the small of his back, pulling him deeper.

He's all raw heat inside me, pounding pleasure against my flesh over and over again as he takes me, claims me, makes me his. It's a friction I'll never forget. A steady, rising burn in every nerve, starting near my womb, entangling my mind, finishing my soul.

His cock does honest freaking miracles.

And some that are far too dirty to be honest at all.

I'm adrift in his beastliness, caught in a tempest of pleasure and muscle and grunting, thrusting, painfully gorgeous man.

James slams himself into me. I see his teeth appear behind his lips, feel his hips quicken. Then he's in me to the hilt, growling this sweet madness, the swell of his cock one fiery pulse away from the inevitable.

There's no such thing as pretending I could take his come without it setting me off.

And I burn hotter and hotter by the second, winding ever

tighter, letting the wild liquid friction of every last thrust from his erupting cock carry me with him to a dizzying peak.

Coming!

I'm crying when I shatter. Crying in wordless, moaning, gasping overload.

And maybe something more.

I want to say his name. I want to say it so much, but I'm afraid if I do, it'll sound like the one thing I've been afraid to say to him all this time, especially when so many heavy things weigh on his shoulders right now.

I love you.

And when we crash, we crash together, and I know I'll never, ever love anyone else again.

* * *

Present Day

EVERYTHING after that is a haze in my memory.

I remember drifting off to sleep in James' arms, and waking up to find him and Egon talking about the case...and a name that seems familiar now.

Pershing Shield. *Oh my God.*

Now, I remember where I heard the name. A former employee of Pershing was behind the black market weapons hub, and it was far from over after that man, Keuhler, died.

They'd found copied checks, the secondary imprints used as receipts.

I'm waking up for real even as I realize I'm dreaming, reliving a memory in my sleep, but before I can fully register the hand on my shoulder and the voice calling my name, I remember that night.

Tanner Egon waking up, talking to James about the checks long into the night. The names on them.

And that one of them was made out to a Senate exploratory committee.

Was it Dad's?

I feel sick even as I flutter my eyes open, taking in my unfamiliar surroundings, only to realize I'm still in the cabin at the lodge, and someone's leaning over me.

Someone's saying my name softly in a way that turns me inside out and makes me feel too weak.

James.

VIII: ACE OF HEARTS (JAMES)

Watching Faye sleep does something to me, soothing the turmoil in my soul.

She must've fallen asleep waiting for me to come back from the lodge after a rather fruitless conversation with Harris. Her father danced around my subtle leading questions, implying he might or might not be aware of any plans to isolate us up here.

The situation left me uneasy. Getting back to Faye was more important than prying at the Senator for nothing, especially when I don't want to make him suspicious.

Besides, I owe *her* answers. She caught me red-handed.

It's time to face the music.

I pause for a second next to the bed, staring down at her. Fuck, she's beautiful.

Whatever else she became over our years apart, and whatever I turned into, nothing changed what happens when she's caught in my eyes.

Phoenix red hair. Curves to tomorrow. Delicate snowy skin.

The demon in my slacks starts to throb, hounding me to

make another big mistake. Clenching my jaw, I try like hell to ignore my own lust. Sobering up for a hard talk instead.

I grip her shoulder and shake gently, whispering, "Faye. It's me. Wake up."

She stirs with a sleepy whine.

Then rolls away from me, giving me her back, burying her face sullenly into the pillows, shoulders hunched.

I hold back my smile, nudging her again. "*Tink.*"

This time she comes more alert, yawning and opening her eyes, glancing over her shoulder.

"What?" she mumbles drowsily. Her features sharpen as her gaze focuses on me.

I look at her firmly and nod.

Then she's on fire in half a second, eyes alight as she pulls herself up, twists around, and promptly shoves me in the chest. "You *asshole!*"

I rock back a couple inches but don't lose my seat on the edge of the bed. "I deserved that."

"You *think?*"

"My apolo—"

"*No.*" She sets her jaw, folding her arms over her chest and plumping up her breasts in a way I can't help but find distracting, even as I keep my gaze on her snapping green eyes and the furious line of her mouth. "Just don't. Every time you say, 'my apologies,' it sounds like sarcasm. I want a real apology, James. Be a normal person and say *I'm sorry.*"

I give her a long, aching look. *It's fucked up because she's right.*

She'll never know how sorry I really am for what happened, but I can at least give her this. I nod, then offer a whisper, "I'm sorry, Faye."

"*Hmph.*" Her cheeks color, and she looks away from me, turning her nose up. "It's a start." Then she unfolds her arms, thumping my shoulder, *hard*. "But it's not enough. You don't get to walk out of my life, then come gliding back in and treat me like a stranger only to fucking pin me up against a wall and kiss me and *finger* me before snooping around on my *Dad*."

"When you put it that way, I suppose the past twenty-four hours have been a touch extreme," I say wryly. The hot death in her eyes tells me she's not amused. "I know I fucked up. Went too far after someone kept me awake last night, and I wasn't acting like myself."

"Kept you awake? How did I—" Her eyes widen, the flush in her cheeks turning furiously red, and she lets out a mortified groan, burying her face into her palms. "Shit. You heard me...oh, *God*. You *heard* me."

"I did. And it was nothing to be ashamed of, Faye."

Saying her name this often instead of the formal *Ms. Harris* seems too intimate, but this is a moment for intimacies when she knows that I heard her.

Knows she drove me so wild I lost control in a flash of frustration and passion and pure raw need for her. She peeks over her fingers at me, her eyes dark.

"I'm so confused," she whispers.

"I know," I say. "And that's my fault. I'll own it. Unfortunately, I'd gotten so used to keeping secrets that it's second nature, even if they might fare better spilling out." I smile faintly. "Two minds are better than one. We've always done well when we combine our intellects."

She takes a sharp breath. It's amazing how all I ever have to do is give her an implication for that sharp mind of hers to click every piece together.

"Pershing," she breathes out. "You really do think Pershing's dirty, and my father might be tangled up in it?"

I eyeball her quietly. Even now, I don't have the heart to tell her I think her father might be more than a victim tangled in Hook Hamlin's web. Or that I *know* her father is simply the other side of a coin with two faces, and both of them belong in a damn mug shot. So I only ask, "How'd you work that out so quickly?"

"I remembered that stakeout, years ago. The arms warehouse in Portland. The main guy was a former Pershing employee, remember?" she says, her eyes lighting again with breathless interest as she lets her hands drop. "So, obviously, most of the time you can't blame *former* employers for the actions of the people they fired...but what if they only fired him as cover? So he could work for their *other* business interests..."

"Just like I've suspected," I say with a nod. "But you should absolutely keep that information to yourself, for now."

Or you could meet the same fate as your mother.

Or, God forbid, Tanner.

Faye practically bounces like a kitten who's caught a toy.

She's sitting on her knees with her thighs spread, her little shirt barely falling down to conceal that warm, soft mound of flesh pressing against the tight clinging shorts that have bunched up. She leans toward me with her hands braced between her legs, tits straining against her shirt, caged between her upper arms.

Sweet fuck. I adore how carefree this woman can be when she's excited.

I just wish she knew how distracting she can be. But when she speaks, I drag my attention back to her face, her mouth...fuck. No. The words she's saying.

"I can keep a secret, James," she says breathlessly. "So come on. What's going on? You'd be fired if anyone else knew you were tampering with Dad's computer. Not to mention up for a felony charge. You wouldn't risk it if it wasn't really important."

"I believe Hook Hamlin has other motives for keeping us here," I tell her slowly. "You saw the same thing I did. His whole damn grandstanding performance? It was staged, with your father backing him up."

The excitement goes out of her eyes, replaced with something else. *Fear.*

"So, what? You think Dad's being...blackmailed?"

"It's possible," I answer carefully. "That part, I'm not certain. His cuts to the appropriations bill for securing contracting wouldn't harm Pershing Shield very much, if at all, so I don't see a clear motive if they're really in bed together. However, Pershing collaborates with many smaller contractors who *would* lose out if funds dried up. What if those 'collaborations' are actually part of Hook's black market trade? And without funding, he can't move his contraband without getting caught?"

"Jesus. Meaning...he'd go all assassin-like to threaten my Dad without actually letting Dad know it was him." Faye shakes her head. A small gasp escapes her lips before she scowls. "Talk about a real dick move. Playing all nice and friendly, even to the point of guarding everyone, when he really wants to kill us, get us out of his way."

"Hook's no fucking gentleman," I counter, angry but amused. "But it seems like your father is more aware of Hamlin's schemes than he lets on. He may have an ace up his sleeve."

She frowns. "I know Dad can take care of himself, but –"

"He's in over his head. He's still a politician, never trained in espionage or counter-surveillance."

Her eyes glitter. "But we are."

"Trained, yes. Technically, no longer licensed to conduct either of those activities. *Former* FBI agents don't have the same latitude."

"Yeah, but *current* security contractors do, and you're an Enguard officer. So. What'd you do to Dad's computer?"

"Logging his keystrokes," I answer. "And I gave him a

packet sniffer, as well as a backdoor I control. I can capture any data from his machine as long as it's online, and even log in to view his activities in real-time or take control of the device."

"What are you hoping to find?"

"Incriminating emails, mostly. Possibly documents in private folders that may contain information he wouldn't save anywhere else. I want to know what he knows about Pershing Shield, and if any of it qualifies as evidence."

She frowns, knitting her brow. "Why not tell him you know so you can work together if you're after the same guy?"

I can't answer that honestly. I just fucking can't.

This honesty is new, and there are limits. I can't just up and tell her, *Because I'm after your father, too.*

Because I want to take down the man who murdered my friend and the man who killed your mother in one fell swoop.

Your father will pay for Tanner, for your mother, for my mother.

And Hook Hamlin will pay for every unknown life he's ever claimed.

Faye still doesn't know.

She still doesn't know how her mother died, or she'd have already tried to take her father's head off – and possibly succeeded. I can't be the one to break the truth to her.

It's not my place.

So I only shake my head, offering, "The less your father knows, the better. He's not equipped for handling a big career criminal like Hook and Pershing."

"That's a lame excuse." She sighs, pouting and slumping a little. "Jesus, James. If you're going to lie to me, at least come up with something *interesting*."

Fuck. I tighten my lip, staring her down, pulling every bit of acting I have.

"I'm not lying, Tink."

"Yes, you are." Her smile is weary, shaking off the nickname I thought would soften her like nothing. "Your left eye always twitches just a little bit when you lie. It's the worst poker tell ever."

I scowl. "I don't have poker tells."

"Everyone does." She's smirking. "And you're just sulking because I know yours better than my own."

Little brat. Little monster. Little *minx*.

A low growl in the back of my throat pushes pointedly out. "You're missing the point, Faye. Hook has a reason for keeping us here, and it involves your father. Last I checked, our reports estimate we'll be stuck here a week or more, considering the storm. Plenty of time to do Hook's dirty work."

"So he's that type? The ones who take *forever* to just bring it?" She frowns, tapping her finger to her lower lip. "I don't like the slow ones. The teases. They take their time, plan ahead, and cover contingencies. It makes them harder to catch. That's no fun."

I almost smile. It's fascinating watching her work, dissecting and breaking down people's motivations. "He's forgotten one thing, though," I tell her.

"What's that?"

"We're not trapped here with him," I point out. "He's trapped here with us."

"Oh my God." She bursts out laughing. "You stole that from *Watchmen*, nerd."

I frown. "*Watchmen?*"

"Rorschach? The prison scene?" When I just stare at her blankly, her laughter redoubles. "Holy hell. You actually said that seriously. Somehow, that's even worse than ripping off movie quotes."

"I have no idea what you're talking about."

"No, you usually don't. For someone so attractive, you're

clueless with women, James." She arches a brow pointedly. "So now since I know why you were snooping on Dad...maybe we need to talk about the other thing."

"No time," I say, rising to my feet. "I took over guard shift for your father, but still haven't found someone to take my place."

She stares after me, her eyes wide. "You're really going to do this again?"

I have to.

I can't let her close, and I can't let myself break again.

What I did this morning was not only a *dick move* – her words – but a mistake that'll get us both hurt, no matter how willing she might've been. "Good evening, Ms. Harris," I say, heading for the door. "I'll be back later to make sure you're sleeping safe and sound."

Her wounded silence chases me long after I'm gone.

Reminds me what a terrible fucking thing I've become.

* * *

NEARLY MIDNIGHT.

I'm back at the lodge, ostensibly to keep an eye out for Hamlin, Harris, or anything interesting.

Truly, I'm avoiding going back to that cabin. I can feel fairly certain Faye is safe right now, when Hamlin is still in the setup phase of his plan and the storm hasn't yet fully rolled over us, the clouds a black smudge on the horizon. He'll make his move once we've been snowed in, people trapped in their cabins, unable to summon help.

Faye isn't a target, for now. I've kept her safe in the world's most ham-fisted, fucked up way.

But I just can't go back and face her when I can't trust what I might do.

What she'll *let* me do, willingly and wholeheartedly.

It's not my touch she hates. Even though she should.

It's when I stop and walk away. That's what guts her.

Better, then, not to start at all.

So I give my attention to the piano in the commons room.

I need something to ground myself, a healthier indulgence than a red-haired woman who's nothing but trouble. I need to clear my head, too.

Chopin comes out of my fingertips. Familiar, easy, delicate melodies that wrap around me, quietly calming my thoughts as if washing them away with rainfall patters of sound.

Until a voice at my back pulls me from my trance, interrupting with, "You're quite skilled. A man of many talents, it would seem."

Hook.

I glance over my shoulder. He's leaning against the wall, watching me shrewdly, that insufferably pleasant smile of his locked in place.

Fuck. I should pretend to be flattered, but the most I can manage is a nod. "I learned from a very young age and kept up the habit."

"Your mother, I'm guessing?" When I sit up straighter, arching a brow, Hook offers an almost self-deprecating smile. "Boys who learn piano at their mothers' knees grow up to be quite the refined gentlemen, I've learned."

It's maddening that he knows me so well. Or *thinks* he does.

Hook's little psychological profile that's supposed to impress me isn't me at all.

I wear the gentleman's mask to reconcile a past born in low roots, poverty. My father nowhere to be found, my mother too gentle and strange to survive this world, left leaning on my grandfather for support and barely struggling through.

Grandpa's stories used to embarrass me when I was young. I'd hear them when he dragged me out fishing with his buddies, anecdotes about faces full of trench mud and rescuing stray dogs from burning buildings outside Saigon.

They were always too happy, too sweet, too glamorous to reflect the realities of war.

I didn't realize until I was sixteen how he hid behind masks, too. Not until the day one of Grandpa's stories turned into a tale of how him and his buddies spent two days of hell trying to get the dog tags off a fallen friend. And two more good men died doing it.

I realized it then. Grandpa's grit, his jokes, his bawdy laughter, they weren't there to hide the reality of war. They were meant to paper over what it did to him, how it made him the rough-as-nails man he still is in hellfire and grief. And maybe, having a part of him in me wasn't so bad after all.

It wasn't until long after Mom died that I fully learned not to be ashamed of that person.

Grandpa was never more shocked the day I said I'd follow his footsteps into the U.S. Army. That's where, just like him, I began finding my soul.

His old war stories were all I had to cling to in active battle. Two dozen hellish firefights in Baghdad and Mosul that killed half the men who rushed into the storm next to me.

House to house. Bullet to bullet. Blood to blood.

There was fucking nothing genteel or civilized about the fighting.

There was no room to be a gentleman in an active combat zone.

A hero, maybe, but not a gentleman.

I didn't get that privilege again until after I was discharged honorably and went to Quantico for FBI training.

Hook thinks he has me figured out? *Is he fucking joking?*

Maybe. And I'll let him think I'm exactly what he sees – a slick, refined sneak who moves in the shadows and is too good to ever get his hands bloody. Because then, if I'm lucky, he'll never see the rest of me coming, the part I inherited from Grandpa Dominick and grandfather war.

"James? You hear me?"

I look up from staring down at my hands, resting lifelessly against the keys. "Yes, good guess. I did learn from my mother," I answer, offering nothing more than what he's already assumed.

Let him think he's found his insight into me.

Let him think he's getting under my skin, finding a way to make this personal, until I'll confide in him.

He steps closer, pushing away from the wall, settling to lean on the piano instead, bending over it with his arms folded against the glossy wood. He tilts his head, eyeballing me closely.

"You're a lucky man," he says. "All I learned from my mother was how to hide."

I arch a brow. "Hide?"

"Yeah." His smile is bitter, grim, self-mocking. "Can't be found, can't be hit."

I say nothing.

This is the frustrating part about real life: the villains are never as clearly defined as they are in stories.

Never as easy to hate – especially when every last one of them has a touch of humanity at their core, and it's often that last shred that drives them to horrors when it's the last bit of themselves they can protect.

You also never know when they're lying.

Did Hook really have an abusive mother on top of his reckless gambling addict father? Or is it just another lie manufactured to win me over?

Regardless, even knowing this *maybe* human thing about Hamlin, I can't offer him sympathy.

I can't offer him forgiveness. The words die cold on my tongue when I murmur an obligatory, "I'm sorry."

"Don't be. Another life, another time." His unfocused gaze clears, lingering on me. "I guess I just start remembering, tucked away up here in a place like this. I'm from up north. Juno. Used to live in a world of winter, and I guess this takes me back there."

I thought you were from Boston, asshole, I think, but don't say it. I remember what I dug up on him. He didn't move to Alaska until he was older, out of the military, a full grown man.

"Do you ever visit home?"

"Nah. No reason to." He shrugs, smiling. "I think this is the most snow I'd ever like to experience again. It's nice to be on familiar turf, but I'll be damn glad to get out of here and find warmer waters."

There's something unspoken here.

He's asking me something, but I can't quite figure out what. "Do you think we'll actually be here for an entire week?"

"Depends how long it takes the storm to blow out. Honestly, we probably could've made it out by car by the skin of our teeth during the break in the storm, but Harris insisted on staying for safety's sake. The Senator's a cautious man."

I have trouble believing that.

It also contradicts his grandstanding speech, where he made it ever-so-clear the roads were totally impassable.

Another goddamned lie.

Still, it's interesting that he's maneuvering to blame Harris already. "Do you not think we're safe here?" I ask.

"Oh, we're plenty safe," he answers. "Safest place in the

world. I can just imagine a lot of people who'd rather be home, snug in their beds, versus freezing off their unmentionables here."

"I don't see how anyone is any safer here than they would be in their secured homes."

"No?" His laugh is quiet, but hearty. "Then I guess you aren't as sick of politics as I am, my friend. No lobbyists here. Even Harris' donors and pack of fellow Senators couldn't make it. It's just us and the snow, peace and quiet. Not even a two-term Senator can turn that into a stump speech."

He's laying out more of his animosity toward Harris, carefully waiting to see if I'll bite.

I look away from him, back down at the piano keys, and play a soft scale. "I suppose he does have a tendency to argue his point. Loud and often."

"You can say that again!" Hook gives a rough snort. "Damn, you get it. Thought you might. You don't seem like a man who's overly political, James. Neither does your boss, Landon."

My hands fall still on the keys.

I don't like this.

Not how he's fishing about Landon, and what it could mean for his plans to lure Enguard into his sickening machine.

I won't let it happen.

I won't let this fucking pirate destroy my colleagues. My company. My *friends.*

Before I get a chance to brush him off, the door to the lodge flings open.

Several shivering Pershing men step inside, laughing among themselves and stomping snow off their feet, rubbing their hands together. Hook straightens, watching them with narrowed eyes, while I close the cover over the piano keys and stand.

"Perhaps," I say, "you should ask Landon about his feelings. Not me."

Then I just turn and walk away, leaving Hook Hamlin alone with his loyal men.

* * *

There's a brief meeting in Landon's cabin, the entire crew – minus Gabe – gathered to discuss logistics. He wants to go over our individual assignments in Hamlin's emergency plan.

I'm silent, watching through the window as the first warning wave of snow begins drifting down outside, igniting an urgency beneath my skin. This kind of snowfall starts off gentle but avalanches quickly into a blizzard.

And I don't want to be trapped somewhere without Faye, leaving her alone in the cabin, whenever it hits full force.

Once the debriefing is done, I'm the first out the door.

I can't stand being shut in this little cabin with its flickering fire that reminds me too much of burning, catastrophic flames.

It's more than just wanting to trade one confined space for another. I can't explain this urgency when I'm running hot and cold, giving mixed signals even to myself.

But the scent of snow in the air worries me, metallic and heavy and promising something bad. The night sky overhead is black, not a single star in sight.

All clouds and drifting flakes of white so cold they nearly burn every time they find a patch of naked skin.

Back at the cabin, I'm relieved to find Faye asleep.

She looks so small, so peaceful, curled up in bed and bundled under the blankets.

She looks so alone.

Settling on the edge of the bed, just watching her for God knows how long, I feel it.

This is my last chance to imprint her on my memory.

My last chance to lock these little moments in my mind like pages in a book.

Like the thousand little notes she left me over the years. Everything from a cheery *Good morning, Mr. Smirky-Smirk!* to the more dire *Can we talk?*

That one led to her telling me that treating this, *us*, like an on again-off again fling wasn't enough. I'd promised her we'd talk as soon as I came back from witnessing my mother's final moments.

But that never happened, the path of my life shattering off course in a single night.

I trace the curve of her nose, the bow of her heart-shaped lips, the way her lashes rest against her cheeks with a lingering eye.

Then I make myself pull away, slipping into the bathroom to change before settling on the couch with my laptop. The first thing I do is check the remote server I've set up to capture the data transmitted by the spy goods I left on the Senator's machine.

Nothing.

Damn.

I frown, trying to pull up the remote login screen to activate the snooping app, but it flashes *Cannot connect to host device.*

No matter how many times I enter the masked IP, the app should have assigned to Harris' laptop.

Something's wrong.

Either Harris cut his laptop offline immediately after I installed the apps, or he's more tech-savvy than I thought, and some advanced firewall detected and blocked the ports I'd left open for easy access.

Or maybe it's just the lodge's wi-fi going dead.

Except with the entire resort on a shared connection, it

seems oddly specific that *only* the main lodge would lose its connection.

Unless someone was blocking it.

Fuck.

There's no time to dwell on it, though.

Not when a sound behind me warns me Faye's woken up, and she's already locked on my screen with a bright, curious question. "Hey, James Bond. Find anything good?"

IX: SMOKE TO FLAME (FAYE)

I'm so disappointed in myself right now.

I keep letting James jerk me around and I still find it in me to smile. He won't *talk* to me, won't give me the answers I know I damn well deserve.

And I just let him walk away from me again and again because I'm almost afraid to hear what he has to say. He never really wholly ended us all those years ago. He never really started us as a real, proper couple either.

He just cut me off.

And some naïve, lovesick, sucker-for-punishment part of me apparently clings to the idea of rekindling the flame.

If he outright tells me no, that's not possible, not now, not ever like I expect...

It'll hurt too much.

But it'll hurt even worse to walk away forever.

How's that for complicated? Considering someone at this resort may be trying to put a bullet in my skull, I really can't afford to be distracted. Or turn into a curled-up ball of heartbreak mush when I need to be alert.

So when I wake up to find James back, sprawled on the

couch in an effortless stretch of washboard abs and wicked masculinity with the faint moonlight painting his bare chest silver, I force my feelings down into a little box and tuck them away.

The pang of heartache.

The rage at his indifference and mood swings.

The fear, knowing how easily he could crush me. All of them, compacted into a knot so I can smile as I stretch, then bounce across the bed and make my way over to the couch to lean over the back, peering over his shoulder at his laptop.

I recognize the program he's looking at. It's a remote infiltration app used for tapping someone's computer.

"Hey, James Bond," I say. "Find anything good?"

He stiffens, eyeing me warily from the corner of his eye.

"No," he says slowly. "I have wi-fi signal, but I can't connect. It's almost like...something's blocking the connection from that side."

With a frown, I lean in closer to peer at the screen. "Maybe Dad turned the laptop off. Or let the battery die."

"Or you pulled the battery, Faye." His eyes narrow. His speech is slow, measured, every word as emotionless as the words of a stranger. "I'm beginning to wonder how far you would go to protect your father."

That stings – that stings more than it should, hurt striking hard and cutting deep, but it's nothing compared to the sudden realization what those words mean.

James has been lying to me.

He's not using my father to spy on Hook Hamlin at all.

He's spying on my Dad himself.

That asshole.

My heart is a flaming stone, as I stare at him. "You think my father's up to something," I whisper. "My father. My *Dad*. The man who even helped you start your fucking career."

"Then ended it," he points out tonelessly. "Just as he ended yours. The man you call Dad now isn't the man we knew then, Faye. Tell me I'm not right."

"Of course he's not!" I flare.

The worst part is, it's true, and I hate it. I don't need another reminder how different Dad is since Mom died from this lying, conniving beast-man who I keep letting tear up my heart.

My throat goes tight.

I hate how my anger always makes me want to cry, when I want to be fierce and proud and full of righteous rage. "Grief changes people, James. Big surprise. It changed *you*. He lost his wife. My mother. That's no reason to think he's behind some kind of sick plot. Next you'll say he's faking the assassination attempt, won't you? Why? Why would he ever do that?"

I'm so offended I could punch him. But I can't move a muscle when the way James looks at me with his silver-blue eyes says my question isn't insane at all.

"A number of reasons," he whispers.

God.

Right now, I hate James Nobel more than I've ever hated anyone.

Hate how calm he is, like this information means nothing.

Hate the way he looks at me without blinking, like he's not completely shattering my world.

Hate that he trusts me so little he couldn't talk to me about this so I could tell him how insanely, hellishly stupid it is.

And I hate that some small part of me is *terrified* he may be right.

Because I don't know my Dad anymore. I haven't really known him in years.

Or what he's capable of.

While I hate-stare him down, sucking in shaking breaths,

my stone heart fighting to beat again, James continues, "Faye, I don't think your father orchestrated or in any way staged the assassination plot. He'd never put you in danger. The threat is very real, both to you and him. But it's the motive that makes him suspect. If your Dad has been dealing with the wrong people for his own gain, they may well use violence to push him into place once he steps out of line."

I shake my head. I don't understand. "What kind of wrong people?"

"The very same people who use Homeland Security funds to operate black market gunrunning rings."

Holy hell. I feel like I can't take another hit, but I have to understand this.

"You think...you think Hook Hamlin is misappropriating funds for illegal weapons deals? And Dad's helping him?" I shake my head. "*Why?* My...my Dad's a good man. A freaking Senator. He'd never, what does he even get from this?"

"I'm still trying to figure that out," James says with a growly sigh, and some of his icy façade defrosts. His bright eyes turn almost regretful as they flick over my face. "I didn't want to tell you, Faye. Not until I was certain. I didn't want to hurt you like this."

"No, but you could hurt me by accusing me of sabotaging your investigation?"

"I'm sorry. That was a knee-jerk reaction, and it was cruel of me. But..." His eyes lower, then flick away, fixing on the window. "I wanted to be wrong. I truly did."

"You *are* wrong," I force out around my knotting throat, my chest tightening. "Is the rest of Enguard behind this, too? Are you all fucking spying?"

"Hell no. This is my baby, an independent investigation. All mine."

"Why?"

He says nothing.

"Why?" I demand again, banging my fist against his shoulder. This human wall doesn't even flinch. "What did my father *ever* do to you?"

"More than I can ever stand to tell you." His gaze slides back to me, dark and haunted, old hurts, things I can't stand to think my father caused. His hand rises to cover my clenched fist, trapping it against his shoulder. "Let it go, Faye. I never wanted you to get so involved in this."

"No." I yank my hand free from his and step back, shaking my head fiercely, my eyes burning, welling. "I'm telling Landon. You want to accuse Dad, then you'd damned well better be able to prove it to your boss."

I turn, stalking toward the door, barefoot in my little cami and shorts sleep set.

I'll march out into the snow just like this.

My fury will keep me warm against hypothermia, if it means putting an end to this insanity – but James doesn't even try to stop me. He just sets his laptop aside and rises smoothly, crossing to the small liquor cabinet next to the open kitchen and pulling down a bottle of scotch.

While he begins to pour with almost fatalistic calm, setting out two tumblers, I yank the door open and let in a whooshing gust of air so freezing it slices through my skin with a razor's touch.

And I barely stumble backward in time as the ice spears forming along the edge of the roof come crashing down like daggers. Dislodged by me yanking the door open. I watch them fall, breaking apart like heavy glass on the step right where I'd been.

Oh, God.

As I stare, heart hammering, an avalanche of snow comes sheeting down in its wake. It cascades off the roof in a frozen waterfall, piling up in a matter of seconds, almost fully blocking the door.

All I can see over the heap is maybe a foot of open space, but even that isn't much when there's nothing but white whipping beyond, snow piling higher and higher against the walls, the windows.

The storm is here.

And we're not going anywhere.

"You're welcome to try burrowing your way to the lodge," James says mildly. "I'd suggest warmer clothing. And a flashlight so I can find you and bring you back before you freeze to death."

I whirl back on him, slamming the door again before the wind can blow any more snow inside.

Asshole. I want to open it and try again just to spite him.

But the internal temperature of the cabin plunged just from my first attempt, and I can't stop shivering. I wrap my arms around myself, trapped, suddenly feeling pathetic and forlorn.

I'm locked in place and helpless and *cold*. I stare at James miserably.

I hate this feeling, conflicted and confused and doubting.

Doubting everyone from him to my father to myself.

"What now?" I ask as he steps away from the counter toward me, moving with that sinuous grace that's always made him so hypnotic, until he's so close I can feel his annoyingly perfect five o'clock shadow grazing my cheek.

"Now," he whispers in my ear, pressing one of the tumblers of scotch into my hands, "we wait. We stay warm."

X: WAX DOLL (JAMES)

I'm sure there are a number of ways that conversation could've gone worse, but I'm not sure how.

We're firmly into colossal fucking disaster territory.

I never speak off the cuff.

Yet, I had to go and accuse Faye of sabotaging my work on her father's laptop like an imbecile.

It's not that I don't trust her. It's not even that I think she's treacherous or deceitful or two-faced.

It's certainly not that I think she's in *any way* involved in her father's bad business.

It's that I know how unbelievably loyal she is, and right now, she has more reason to be loyal to her father than she has to be loyal to me.

Still. I've hurt her with both the truth and with half-truths.

I don't know what the hell to do with that as we sit in awkward, almost eerie silence, both sipping our drinks to chase the warmth back into our bodies.

The fireplace helps, burning the cold from the room and

bringing it back to a safe, comfortable temperature. At least I'd been right to get back to the cabin as fast as possible, making sure Faye stays safe enough to wait this out.

We'll be trapped here for days, whatever Hook says. I hate that it limits my mobility.

Then again, if I'm stuck in one place, so are Hamlin and Harris.

Unfortunately, with both of them occupying the master suites at the lodge, they're stuck together. Away from me.

I'm worried what I'll find when the snow clears enough for me to move on them.

I feel like hours pass before Faye finally breaks the silence filled with nothing but our own thoughts and the crackling fire.

She leans forward, setting her empty tumbler on the table, and casts me a mournful look before rising, unfolding those long, lovely bare legs and smoothing her little camisole top over her body.

"I'm going to bed," she says softly. "I don't know what to think right now, but if we're going to be stuck here for days, I need rest." She shakes her head. A tired ghost of a smile flits across her lips. "We can fight more when we have the freedom to storm out without dying."

"Okay." Fuck, I ache at the idea that we'll have to fight at all. "Sleep well."

She gives me a long look, lips parted as if she might say something else, before she only shakes her head a second time and walks away.

I turn my head to watch her as she climbs back into the rumpled bed, wrapping herself up into a little bundle in the blankets.

Only after I'm certain she's asleep do I move.

The scotch has done just enough to warm my blood without making me fuzzy. My thoughts are racing as I get up to pile a few more logs on the fire, then dig out a few of the smaller spare quilts from the closet and circle the room, tacking them up over the windows.

I have to winter-proof this place.

Whoever designed these cabins clearly did it for the view, not for practicality.

The windows aren't curtained or insulated enough to stop cold like this from seeping in through the glass and leeching hard-won heat from the room. The electric heater chugs along quietly in the background to complement the radiant heat from the hearth, but I don't want to wake up in the morning to find the power out, the fire dead, and all our heat escaped through badly insulated glass.

When I cover the window over Faye's bed, though, I can't help stopping.

Looking down at her, at the spill of red-rose hair, tumbling across the pillow.

Gently, I brush back a few locks falling to tickle the tip of her nose.

I hesitate for another second. Then I say *fuck it.*

Bending low, I brush my lips against her cheek, the fine peach fuzz of her skin caressing my mouth like velvet.

I know I shouldn't. I *know*.

But at least right now, damn it, she's not awake for me to confuse her more.

Only myself.

Because for some unholy reason, I can't keep myself under control around her.

But I force myself away after the lightest kiss, returning to the sofa to try my laptop again.

Outside, the wind howls, a lonely and mournful sound that seems to echo my own desolation.

Tonight, there'll be no solace. No answers. Nothing to ease this tension save for the sweet escape of sleep.

And since sleep won't find me, I can at least get something useful done.

The laptop still screws me over, though.

No connection – and the wi-fi in the cabin is beginning to flicker as well.

Even if I could get an outbound connection, it wouldn't hold for more than a few seconds. *Damn.*

I check my phone. There's no signal. When I try a call out to Landon, then another to Riker, it confirms my worst suspicions.

There's absolutely nothing. The phone won't even dial a line, the 3G and 4G icons grayed out, even wi-fi calling not working. There's an ethernet outlet in the kitchen, but when I plug the laptop in, the LAN icon shows a red X.

That means the landline internet isn't connecting, and since the wi-fi runs off the landline, that outlet is completely fucked.

The portable radio is my last resort. I'm not worried about waking anyone when no doubt the others with Enguard are as restless as I am, awake and planning for every contingency.

What I'm worried about, though, is this storm disrupting communications so bad I can't raise a single person on any channel.

Of course, that's exactly what happens.

Right now, there's nothing I can do until morning. The sense of building tension hasn't broken yet, and I don't think there's anything to worry about tonight.

I doubt the storm will break with the dawn, but there'll at least be enough visibility so if I need to go outside, I'll have some hope of finding my way back.

Finding my way back to Faye, some part of me whispers, when it's a lie.

It's a bitter lie, a false hope, a dream that can't come true, and that's my own damn fault.

So with one last look at her, I push it away and stretch out on the sofa to pull the layered blankets over me, letting my real dreams draw me into the dark.

***

Five Years Ago

I WASN'T THERE.

I wasn't fucking there for her final breath, and now the first I'm seeing of my mother since I left for a long-term assignment in Washington is this wax doll.

Painted up to make her look like she's still alive. Like she might open her eyes any second and smile at me and tell me it's all right, she was just exploring other worlds for a little while, learning new things for her book, but now she's back.

Only she won't be.

She won't ever open her eyes again. The details are just wrong enough on her face to be sickening.

Her skin is too tight and waxy, the laugh lines around her eyes puttied over, too smooth, her lips artificially plumped as if asking death for a kiss.

This isn't my mother anymore. It's just a shell that used to hold her, but the vibrancy that made her so wonderful is gone forever. Blown out.

Other people are lined up to see her, waiting to file past her casket and cry, but I can't move from my spot. I suddenly want to reach in, to shake her awake, and I stretch my hand out, unable to stop myself, my body like a zombie's, taking complete control of my will with no choice.

Grandpa's hand settles on my back. "We'll get through this, son. It's a miracle you're here at all. Let's not forget that."

His words are completely lost on me, even if they're true.

Yes, I survived a fucking plane crash. But this, missing her and seeing her dead...how the fuck could anyone ever survive it?

With hands shaking, I touch the back of her hand, find it cool and stiff.

Only, where I touch her, flame bursts to life. A flame that smells like burning engine oil and machinery. A flame that swirls out in a firestorm from that point of contact until it envelops the funeral parlor in hellish orange, flickering everywhere.

Breathing shallowly, sweating, heart racing, I stagger backward.

"James? What's wrong?" Grandpa's just a silhouette, words calling, fading, echoing after me.

I turn around swiftly, but the funeral parlor is gone. There's only the wreckage of an airplane, the mournful sobs of the dying pilot, Tanner's screams.

And my mother's casket in the center of the wreckage, burning and burning and burning away.

* * *

Present Day

I SNAP AWAKE SHARPLY, my heart trying to punch through my chest.

"A fucking nightmare," I mutter to myself, wiping a rough hand over my face.

Christ. The furious sweat of my body chills on my skin,

sinking in like ice. It's the cold that hits me more than anything, chasing away the sick, dark horror haunting my dreams, trying to work its way into my bloodstream to turn my blood to black poison.

It's too cold in the cabin. I sit up, wrapping the blankets tighter around my shoulders. The fire has died down, but that's not why I'm freezing, my teeth chattering helplessly.

The bed is empty.

The bed is *empty*, and the front door is wedged open by an avalanche of ice and snow with the clear shape of a body churned through it, pushing the snow aside, only to send it collapsing back so heavily it was impossible to close the door.

Faye's gone.

She's gone, into a predawn night that's as black as the gates of hell, completely eclipsed by whiteout snow.

The horror of my dreams becomes a real stabbing terror that sinks into me.

I'm on my feet in an instant, bolting into my clothes, dragging layers on as quickly as I can. I know where she's going. To the lodge, to her father, to find her answers.

But if I can't find her in the snow, Faye may never make it there at all.

XI: WINTER MAZE (FAYE)

Okay. This was a very, very bad idea.

I realize it thirty seconds in, wading through snow that comes up to the center of my chest.

But the path I forged has already collapsed behind me, until I'm a single island in a sea of white.

Snow everywhere.

Up, down, left, right. I can't tell where the ground ends and the sky starts when everything is a terrible colorless swirl.

It's cold, so cold, like I've been plunged in liquid nitrogen...but there's something almost comforting about it, too. And that's the part that scares me.

Because as I trudge on toward where I know the lodge should be – barely a couple of blocks along a road that I know is buried under here somewhere, even if I can't feel the difference between earth and pavement under my boots – there's a part of me that knows it'd be easy to give in to winter's embrace.

The cold is like a lover. Always reaching for me, promising that if I just stop struggling against the icy particles stinging my eyes and slashing my cheeks, if I just stop resisting the deep freeze sinking into my bones until I hurt down to the roots of my teeth...

Then I'll finally be warm again.

It'll be so warm, if I just lie down and give up.

I could close my heavy eyes and rest.

But I *know* that's the exhaustion talking. Panic trying to set in when I don't know which way I'm going, and I can't even see the trees, the lodge, or the other cabins through the white.

I can't see anything at all.

I think I'm going in a straight line. That's why I couldn't turn back once I started and realized the snow was filling in behind me. I'd pointed myself in the direction I knew the lodge would be.

If I turn back and go even one degree off course, I could wander off into the wilderness after passing within a foot of the cabin and die out here in the cold.

So straight forward it is.

I'll have to hit something. Eventually. *Anything.*

And later, when I'm safe in front of a fire and asking Dad what the hell is going on, anyone who wants to yell at me for being stupid enough to go storming out into the cold like this can call me every variant of dumbass they want.

I'd be calling myself a dumbass, too, if I could move my frozen lips.

I'm scared.

Won't pretend I'm not, but if I'm scared, it means I'm still okay.

Fear gets my heart rate up, gets my pulse moving, keeps me alert and on point. Fear raises my body temperature even if I don't really feel any warmer.

The fact that my limbs are still moving is something, even

with every step fighting through the snow making them heavier and heavier.

It's so weird how it's so dark and so light when everything is stark raving white.

But there's no sunlight here. It's like there's no time, and I don't know how long I've really been out here.

Too long.

Too freaking long, when I should've smashed nose-first into a cabin wall or the lodge by now.

That fear spikes up a little too high, shrilling down the back of my neck, but I force it down, bow forward, and hunch into myself to conserve body heat and give the wind a smaller surface to hit.

My legs ache from slogging through the snowdrifts. My body hurts from fighting the wind.

What little skin I have exposed between my hat, scarf, and the hood of my coat is chapped and burning.

I can't stop moving, or I'll die.

My eyes sting, but I blink the promise of tears away. The last thing I need is icicles stuck to my eyelashes.

My whole body nearly sings with relief as I bump into something hard.

I'll take it.

A car, a cabin, anything. I know how to pick locks and hot-wire vehicles to get the engine going and the heater running. But this is rough, catching on my clothes. It's...

A tree trunk.

Lovely.

And scary as hell.

Because the area around the lodge and cabins was cleared of trees for easy walking along the footpaths and the main road. The first trees start farther away, as the plateau where the resort was built begins to slope off in either direction.

Fuck. *Fuck.*

I have to stop now. Before I have a full-blown panic attack.

Slumping against the tree, I press my hand to my scarf to trap heat so breathing doesn't feel like swallowing icicles, panting into my palm.

If I've made it to the trees, then I overshot somewhere. And I've got to find some way to get my bearings, or I'm royally screwed.

I won't need an assassin to kill me if Mother Nature does the job.

Closing my eyes, I swallow against the tightness in my throat and tilt my head back.

This was really just so *dumb*, but I wasn't thinking straight.

I was scared.

Scared to be alone with James after finding out what he's been hiding from me.

Scared of my father and how far away he might've fallen.

Scared *for* my father, if Hook Hamlin really does want him dead.

Even now, Dad's alone with that man and snowed under.

No one can help him except Enguard...assuming they haven't been compromised too.

I don't know what I think I'm going to do.

Here, I'm not Faye the explosives expert, or Agent Faye Harris, or Faye the fearless spy.

I'm Faye the librarian, and I feel so hammer-on-the-head stupid that I ever thought I could protect Dad and sort this out when he's been controlling my life for so long.

I've never done anything on my own after the FBI.

I've practically signed my own death sentence trying this time.

Bad, bad timing.

I must be the fucking queen of bad timing.

And I can't help but laugh, as I huddle against the tree to keep it between me and the wind, and wonder how the hell I'll ever get out of this.

* * *

Five Years Ago

"Absolutely not, Faye," Dad snaps into the phone. His voice is hard, dead, commanding in a way I've never heard before. But ever since Mom died in that accident, there've been a lot of unsettling firsts where he's concerned. "I don't know what gave you the idea this was a request. You *will* turn in your resignation. I'm not standing around until you get yourself killed."

"What makes you so sure I'm going to die?" I snap back. "I've been doing this for two years now. I've handled explosives that could've blown the entire city to kingdom come and survived with hardly a scratch. Why now? What's with this whole protector act?"

"It's not an act," he bites off, low and grim. "Two agents and their pilot just died in a plane crash, and one barely walked away alive. That could be you next."

Those words punch the breath out of me with hurt, with fury.

He's practically thrown James in my face.

James, the sole survivor of that crash, and although I know he's alive out there somewhere...the fact that I haven't heard from him since ignites this terror in my heart.

What if he really did die, and my father's just keeping it from me? Telling me he didn't like some kind of sick carrot offering?

But a bitter part of me says Dad doesn't really care about my life, or James'.

This is about political grandstanding, and it's hard to be a family-first Senator when your daughter's disarming explosives and shacking up with a hot agent and possibly dying disarming a terrorist bomb.

If both your daughter and wife are dead, it's hard to present the image of a caring family man, and he can't crack.

It's unfair of me.

I know it's unfair, and it's just my frustration talking when he's charging in and taking over my life, ordering me to end the job I love, giving me no choice in the matter.

And I know if I refuse, he'll have me dragged off by Secret Service agents. Probably squirreled away in a virtual prison of a safe house for the sake of 'national security' or whatever stupid crap he'll use as an excuse.

I don't know this man barking orders. He's not my father, not the Dad I remember.

And there's no one I can even turn to for a safe place to run, to hide, to talk about it, when James is out of my reach.

According to a few of my coworkers, a resignation in his name showed up yesterday...but no one saw him.

He hasn't answered a single phone call or text. He wasn't even in the hospital when I went to see him, discharged without a trace.

It's like he never existed in my life.

Like the past two years were nothing, a figment of my imagination.

And the fight goes out of me as I realize I don't think I can go back to the field office every day without James there at my back.

"Yeah," I say numbly, wondering why I ever thought I could do this. Or if James Nobel ever cared for me. "Sure, Dad. Fine. I'll turn in my resignation tomorrow."

* * *

Present Day

I shouldn't have given up so easily.

It's the one thought I cling to as I'm falling asleep.

Wait. When did I start to fall asleep?

I feel warm, at least.

Warm, receding, safe. Away from the biting cold, from the feeling of my body freezing in place and the blood slowing in my veins.

Everything goes numb and then hot again. But it's a pleasant, distant warmth.

Maybe if I just take a small nap, I'll wake up and the storm will have blown over. I could just...

"Faye," James says urgently out of nowhere. *"Faye!"*

But that can't be James.

I must be dreaming.

James doesn't care enough about me to be out here in the cold.

He doesn't care enough to say my name *that* way, with such harsh, raw emotion. Such fear.

He doesn't care to be touching me the way he does now, his hands stroking over my body and kneading some of the feeling back into it.

In the back of my mind, the logical part of me knows he's checking for hypothermia. But my fogged, exhausted brain can only dredge up an almost hysterical smile.

He's touching me like I'm the most precious thing he'll ever lay hands on.

And even after all this – all the hate and words and ugly secrets – I kind of like it.

I try mumbling something about him feeling me up, but my lips don't want to move.

Yet suddenly, somehow, *I'm* moving.

I crack my eyes open, even if it takes all my fading strength when my lashes are frozen together, my vision rimmed in uneven frost.

James is there.

He's really *there*, picking me up, lifting me against his chest.

I can barely see past his cold weather tactical gear. Even his eyes are covered with goggles.

But behind the clear plastic, his silver-blue gaze turns from hard, cold edges into soft, liquid quicksilver, gleaming with emotion.

I don't have to see him fully to know he's beautiful right now.

I know his expressions so well that I can read his relieved smile in the subtle creases around his eyes, his fear in the pinch of his brows.

It's got to be a dream. I'm hallucinating.

Because the real James Nobel would *never* look at me this way. The real James cut me out of his life and moved on.

This must be a ghost, some last little bit of comfort sent to make it easier as I slip away.

But damn if I don't fall in love with the fantasy.

"James," I sigh, finding it in me to force a hand up to curl in the front of his jacket, clinging limply.

A strong hand folds over mine, squeezing like it'll be okay, and always will be, as he holds me tighter.

So I let go, falling into the darkness with a smile.

XII: TRUTH TO FLAME (JAMES)

For the second time in my life, I've nearly lost Faye Harris.

Even when I pushed her away, closed her out, I still knew she was safe, *alive*.

Then the fear that gripped me when I realized my secrets, my duplicity, had chased her out into the killing storm...

Fuck.

I thought I'd known hell before. I had no clue.

Everything I've ever suffered up to this point was only purgatory compared to the thought of her dead.

I can't hold her tight enough. Even as I bundle her in thick blankets on the couch, I have to remind myself she's truly safe now.

She's alive and breathing. Just sleeping. Recuperating after the cold took a vicious toll on her body. I've stripped her down to just a shirt and panties, and for once, it's not because I'm thinking with my dick.

It's because everything else clinging to her was soaked in half-melted snow. Far more dangerous for hypothermia than bare skin now that she's inside, close to the fire and the cabin's heat cranked up as high as it'll go. I'm sweating my ass off, but I don't care.

Nothing matters except keeping her safe.

I'm like a man possessed, moving all over. I check her pulse, her temperature, gently moving between massaging her hands and feet. Fighting to restore circulation and stave off permanent nerve damage.

I was close to several medics in the Army. Their words whip up from the back of my mind now, every bit of advice they ever gave for saving lives.

I'm trying to stay calm. To remember my own field training in the military and FBI alike, and remind myself that she's in good hands when I can do as much as nearly any EMT – but the panic inside me, that blind animal thing, lost all reason when I saw her crumpled, lifeless, barely breathing against that tree.

What if I'm not enough, damn it? I want ambulances, sirens, trained medical professionals, the safety of a hospital.

Everything we don't have here.

Sure, I'm overreacting, and it's not like me.

Or maybe it's too much like the man I become around Faye, and I'd forgotten for the longest time what he felt like.

Reluctantly, I draw away from her and try to get Landon on the radio again, then try my phone, the wireless, anything.

Still nothing. Just useless white noise and dead calls that won't connect.

I need to update my boss on our status in case Faye's condition worsens, but I'm not getting out to anything with a pulse any time soon. The storm still whips wild, and the only sounds I can make out that even tell me it's dawn are the whistling wind and the distant, growling sound of the generators at the lodge kicking up, probably drawing power to run the kitchen as the staff wake up for the day.

Wait.

If the generators are starting at the lodge, that means one thing.

I thrust to my feet and rush to the wall panel in the kitchen, where the generator power indicator is fading from green to yellow. I've been running the heater trying to keep Faye's body temperature from dropping dangerously low, but I shut it off now. Then I'm quickly piling more logs on the fire before checking the windows and stuffing the blankets tighter into the cracks.

I don't know how long the power's been out.

All I know for sure is we only have two spare gas canisters, and those will run out fast if we're not careful.

I need to get Faye the hell out of here.

The situation escalates from bad to worse. We're snowed in with a man who may want to murder her and the Senator. The power's out, and there's no way to call for help.

I'm sure there's a damn horror movie director out there somewhere smiling in amusement.

Here we are, surrounded by evil. It might be dangerous out in the snow, but I'm beginning to feel it's far more dangerous to stay. I know Faye will never leave without her father.

But maybe if I can find Harris, talk some sense into him, I can convince him to abandon this game of cat and mouse with Captain Hook.

For his daughter's sake, if ours won't do.

Once I'm sure I've sealed in as much heat as possible, I return to her side. Gathering her in my arms, we settle on the floor closer to the fire, cushioning her from the hard stone flooring with my body.

I want to let her rest a while longer, but the sooner she's conscious and ready to move, the better.

Still, this moment will haunt me forever.

The crackling fireplace, the gold and orange light dancing

off her skin, her parted lips, the way she subtly shivers and shifts to press close to me. Even pale and half-frozen, she's gorgeous, her hair damp with melted snow and slowly drying in the warmth, her body soft and curving even through the blankets.

Too beautiful. Too fragile. Too mine.

I don't know how much time flits by simply studying each and every last one of her freckles, listening to the reassuring sigh of her breaths, following the flicker of firelight as it glides like honey over the stubborn slope of her jaw. But as her eyes begin to open, I snap my gaze to hers, watching her lashes flutter as her brows knit together. She shifts weakly, restlessly against me.

"Faye," I whisper. "Can you hear me?"

She makes a low, protesting noise – and something inside me nearly combusts as she curls up and burrows into me so sweetly.

But it's not her last drowsy mumble. She sighs a few more and opens her eyes fully, peering up at me.

I know she's about to pull away, to shout at me, to possibly hurt herself demanding I finally break my silence and talk to her. She wouldn't be wrong.

Still, I don't want to see her hurt herself more just for the satisfaction of taking me down a notch. So I stop her the only way I know how, before her drowsy expression can melt into a scowl and mean words.

I kiss her.

Take her lips and chase her tongue and pull her open, hoping some of the fire I breathe into her will give her back life.

It's an impulse, wild fuckery, the sort of recklessness she'd do.

I can't regret it, though.

Not when her mouth goes soft and luxuriant and sighing

against mine. Not when I feel like I'm bringing her home from the brink with every pull of my teeth, chasing the cold from her, replacing it with my own warmth.

For just a moment, she's pliable against me, sweet and giving and leaning in with a low sigh of my name. A sigh that cuts at my heart, a sound that reminds the blood to move again in my veins, as if she's spoken me into existence.

Until she gives it back, biting down on my lower lip hard enough to make me hiss, thrusting back enough to glare up at me with snapping green eyes.

I wince, touching my fingertips to my lower lip. It's not bleeding, but it's stinging enough to tell me she's furious.

"All right," I say. "I deserved that."

"You're damn right you did. I'm not your sleeping beauty," she growls, thrashing weakly against the blankets, trying to shove back. "Now get me out of this freaking *burrito!*"

I sigh and just gather her closer.

I don't want to force her, but right now it's a matter of holding her still until she stops trying to hurt herself. "Please go easy," I whisper. "You're suffering from exposure, Tink. And while I'm glad I found you before you could be hurt any more, you're still not well."

Faye pauses, biting her lip, her eyes flicking over me searchingly.

"You came looking for me, idiot," she says wonderingly.

"Yeah. I did," I say, nodding. "I couldn't leave you to the mercy of the storm, Faye."

"That's why I don't *get* you," she bites off, frustration sharpening her tone. "You keep cutting me off, lying to me, icing me out, keeping vital info from me, and you're after my *father*, but then you just..."

"Kiss you. Protect you. Risk life and limb hunting you down," I finish. "Believe me, I know. I'm well aware my behavior is a bit frustrating, Ms. Harris."

"James. If you call me Ms. Harris one more time, I *will* dislocate my own arm to slap you."

I can't help the low chuckle that slips out before I clear my throat. "Duly noted, *Faye*."

"Right there." Her voice is puzzled, aching, *longing*. "Right there...I see you again. Not the mask. Just you. But you keep throwing it back up...and you keep *lying*, James."

"No," I sigh. "I'm less lying and more obfuscating certain truths."

"But *why?*"

"Because sometimes those truths can be used as a weapon." I tuck her hair back gently. "And I never want to use those weapons to harm you."

"But you're doing it anyway!" she flings back. "You keep jerking me around. Hot one minute, cold the next, and you actually think my Dad – my *Dad* –" Her voice cracks with all the grim, unspoken suspicions about the Senator. "How could you?"

Good fucking question.

"I have my reasons," I say, the only answer I can pull.

"Reasons. Great. And you won't just tell me what they are," she snaps bitterly.

"Not yet, Faye. Give me time." I shake my head. "Time, woman."

Any more right now and I'll give away things she doesn't need to know unless it's absolutely necessary, when they have such power to hurt.

She isn't looking at me anymore.

I reach out, gripping her hand, until I've got her eyes. "I need you to trust me, Faye. I know it's fucking maddening, but soon, once we're safe, you'll understand. I swear."

"No. You haven't given me any reason to trust."

"A leap of faith, then." I feel like I'm asking for something

I have no right to as my gaze deepens. "You trusted me with everything, once upon a time."

She holds her silence for a long time before she looks away, fixing her glare on the fire. "Yeah. And I was a total idiot because you walked away from all that."

I have nothing to say to that. How can I argue with bald-faced honesty?

So I don't. I just hold her closer.

It's not hard to see the conversation has exhausted her. She doesn't fight me and just goes limp in my arms, her head resting on my chest.

I wish like hell I could offer her more than this. I wish I could offer her a truth that won't hurt her, destroy her, rip the last of her family apart, but it's not possible.

I can't tell her that her Senator father is the reason I left her behind.

The reason my friend and two other people were killed. Possibly the reason her mother died, too, and still he's flinging himself on this reckless headlong charge into the dark, not seeming to care that it could get Faye killed, too.

All I can give her right now is the warmth of someone who cares about her and wants nothing more than to protect her – even if I can't tell her what I'm protecting her from.

Hell, *especially* if I can't say that.

But I'm realizing something now, as I settle to rest my back against the bottom of the couch, stretching to keep her against me and hold her close while the fire bathes us in its yellow warmth.

I can't do this alone.

Not anymore.

Maybe it's time to stop hiding from the only people who *can* help. My team. Maybe it's time to finally come clean to Landon and hope it doesn't blow up in my face.

I let out a long, tense sigh, knowing I've stumped on my only sane choice.

Fuck it. Fine.

As soon as I can reach him, I'll tell him everything I know about Pershing Shield. About Senator Harris, too.

I've isolated myself so much I've forgotten what it can feel like to have friends to turn to, when you're desperately in need of guidance and a steady hand. I just hope once Landon knows the truth about me, about the things I've hidden, that he doesn't want to kill me where I stand.

That he'll still have enough faith in me to trust me and to take action. And once I've told Landon, once I know I have Enguard at my back...

Then I'll tell the exhausted woman falling asleep in my arms.

I'll tell her everything.

Every last sordid detail about the night her mother died, about the night a plane crashed out of the sky and ripped my life apart, about her asshole father and the web of darkness he and Hook Hamlin have woven together, one that threatens far too many lives.

About how much I love, and always have loved her, even if I'm not sure if there's a man left for her to love in return.

Or just a hollow shell.

XIII: HEAVIER THAN WINTER (FAYE)

This wasn't how I imagined falling asleep in James' arms again: frozen, heavy as lead, just reeling back from death's door.

And so, so hurt that he could look at me like he still has feelings for me but refuses to just tell me a few simple truths that would fix this entire mess.

Ugh.

But I'm too exhausted to dwell on it. Too exhausted to push myself through more mental gymnastics.

I let myself lean into the breadth and solidity and warmth of his chest, allowing his body heat to soak into me and chase away the chill.

I don't even know what I was thinking, honestly. If I'd gone storming into the lodge, if I'd made it through the storm...what would I have done?

Confronted Dad with James' vague suspicions? Hoped he'd tell me the truth? Or would I have tried to protect him from Hook Hamlin somehow?

I'm not thinking straight. Maybe that's the reason James

won't come clean, even if he's a real rat bastard for keeping those furiously kissable lips sealed.

I'm pulled from my frustrated, sleepy half-thoughts when I notice I'm suddenly alone in the cabin.

James is gone?

Why? Has the storm broken?

I can still hear the wind howling, a soft hiss blowing against the blankets he put up around the windows. A sick feeling starts in the pit of my stomach.

God. What if something went wrong, and he went out in the snow...and there was no one to save him the way he saved me?

A thump on the front step makes me sit up straighter, clutching the blankets to myself, hoping.

Praying it's James, just coming in from scraping ice off the roof or checking the generators. But my hopes are dashed when the door swings open.

There's a wall of white snow coming down nonstop, piled so high it must have buried the cabin up to the roof.

There's also my father.

Dad's on the doorstep with a chain of shivering aides behind him, all of them strung together with safety ropes, each of them carrying a high-powered Coleman lantern. The lights create beacons through the snow, marking a path back the way they came.

I've never seen a group of people so miserable, and I wonder why people follow my father so loyally.

But aren't I doing the same? Denying James' suspicions without even thinking?

I'm too confused to sort it out now – and too worried.

"Dad?" I gasp. "Where did James go? Is he with you?"

My father stomps his boots on the mat and gestures to two other aides, murmuring, "His, too."

I don't understand what he means until the two scramble to start packing up not just my things, but James' stuff, too. Plus all the blankets, food, water, and other emergency supplies.

"Thank God you're okay," Dad says, fixing his gaze on me. "James is at the lodge. The power's out through the resort. He came to find me to let me know so I could get you and anyone else safely into the lodge so we can conserve generator fuel and avoid emergencies."

It would've avoided a lot more if we'd done this to start with, I think, but unfold my body from the blankets and stand. I'm a bit wobbly, but I can move better than before, so it should be enough.

"Let me get dressed," I say.

I'm not sure how I feel about this. I feel like I'm being maneuvered, still.

But I can't deny it's practical for our safety, and I just don't have the strength left to fight.

I also can't spit on the fact that James made his way through the blinding snow *again.*

Alone and directionless, to make sure someone could get to me safely.

And I can't ignore the fact Dad came for me, either. In person.

He didn't send someone else. He didn't ignore the possible danger and settle in to wait it out, rolling the dice to see if I'd still be all right on the other side. He *came* for me, came to make sure I was safe and protected, just like any father should do.

It eats at me fiercely, this reminder that underneath the dark layer shrouding him, he's there.

He's still my father.

How can I possibly believe he'd do the things James keeps implying?

It takes me longer than I'd like to get dressed. Both

because I'm weak and because I'm trying not to give Dad's aides a peep show.

By the time I'm done, they've carried all of my stuff outside, but there's no sign of James' duffel bag – or his laptop.

Oh, boy.

He must've taken them when he left. And if he brought his laptop along, knowing what it can do, I wonder if help was the only reason he stormed off to the lodge?

I don't know why I keep my mouth shut.

It just seems like something I shouldn't mention.

As I zip my coat with half-numb, glove-thickened fingers, I stop in front of my father and look up at him with a wistful smile. "Guess I'm ready to build a snowman."

He doesn't answer my smile.

The father I remember years ago would've laughed and made a terrible joke about *letting it go.* This one doesn't say anything at all.

I guess I hoped for too much, too soon.

But he dips down and catches me up, lifting me against his chest, holding me close before he turns to forge our way through the snow.

My heart thumps with a sense of bittersweet homesickness.

And even as the storm swirls around us, a curtain of lethal white, Dad protects me with his body as a human shield.

Almost the same way James did.

God.

Apparently, there are *two* men who'd hurt themselves to save me, to protect me.

But I'm supposed to believe one is good, and one is bad. One's wrong, and one's right.

I'm supposed to choose a side.

Like hell.

I *can't.* I love them both in different ways, and I need them both in my life.

So I huddle against my father and close my eyes, anticipating a long, grueling trek back to the lodge...but suddenly the wind cuts, and I open my eyes.

There's a car blocking off the driving wall of snow. It's one of the security team's black SUVs, but it's been outfitted with a sharp metal nose – a snow plow.

My father did this the smart way. He came with ropes and lanterns, and even now the aides who'd staked out our path with lights from the car to the cabin are reeling everything in, bundling it up, climbing in.

Dad settles me in the front passenger seat, where blankets are already waiting. He lingers for just a moment too long. One that tells me he's not as detached as he pretends, and I catch his hand.

"Dad." I squeeze his fingers, looking up at my father with his normally perfect hair whipped into a frenzy by the wind, snow in his eyebrows. "Thank you. For coming for me."

"You're my daughter, Faye," he says, but it's soft and quiet and lacks the inherent edge that seems to live in his voice lately. "And I'm glad James came to me for you."

There's a touch of warm approval in his words. It guts me even more, the contradiction.

Dad almost seems *impressed* by James.

Meanwhile, my snarly, smirky walking secret thinks my Dad is dirty.

Can it get more complicated?

Shaken, I hold my tongue, burrowing into the blankets while Dad shuts the passenger door and then trudges around the front of the SUV to the driver's side, always keeping one hand on the hood.

Then he's at the steering wheel, blowing out clouds of

dragon breath as he slams the door shut, brushes snow off, and reaches over to turn the heat up to peak.

"Buckle up," he says. "This is going to get rough."

No kidding. It's over an hour traveling less than a mile, moving in start-and-stop jerks while the chains on the snow tires grapple with the road.

My father wrestles with the wheel and limited visibility.

Other lanterns dropped in the snow light up like sentinels, outlining the road in eerie ghost-glows beckoning us onward. Through the whirlwind sheet of white, I can make out other dark shapes heading toward the lodge.

Looks like...Pershing staff?

Out there with lanterns, collecting everyone from their cabins and bringing them in.

What now? A chill that has nothing to do with the cold drifts up my spine.

James and I worked out that Hamlin must have a reason for wanting us all separated. But now they're bringing us together.

Did the power outage change his plans?

Or is something worse coming?

Seeing people in the snow worries me, makes me wonder for James, that he'd charge out into this weather but not come back with my father to fetch me.

Until, as we slowly grind past, I see him.

He's there, standing tall against the dagger wind and driving snow.

Too proud to let it cut him down.

He's stern and strong and firm with his feet planted wide and those broad shoulders practically holding up the world.

And he's playing human shield, moving one step at a time to help shelter a pregnant woman, Gabe's wife Skylar, while Gabe himself carries her against his chest and curls around her protectively.

That idiot. That gorgeous, reckless *idiot*, hurting himself to save people like this.

He's going to get frostbite. Even through the snow I can tell his strong jawline glows red, wind-chapped. He's thrown off his heavy thermal coat for extra dexterity, carrying Skylar's things with a lantern in another hand.

I press my fingers to the window, loving him and cursing him under my breath.

It's like he feels my touch, lifting his head, and although I can't see much in the dark, I can tell he's looking at the SUV.

Looking at me.

And I don't know what to do, when I love my father and want to trust him.

But I can't deny my faith in a man as heroic and noble as James, either.

By the time we get to the lodge, the SUV sputters, coughing and threatening to die. My father doesn't even bother parking properly.

He just whips to a stop outside the lodge, and that old military wit of his returns. He's out of the car in quick, tactical jerks, gesturing to his aides, barking *go, go, go!*

The aides are already moving, gathering things up and diving inside, while Pershing and Enguard employees stand in snow-crusted huddles. Right outside the lodge's front door, helping relieve people of their luggage and ushering them inside.

Dad yanks the passenger side door open, and the cold and wind assault me again before he's picking me up and charging through the snow to the lodge.

Finally.

We nearly spill inside – and it's nothing like how it looked earlier.

The main room with the grand piano and grander fireplace looks like a refugee center.

STILL NOT LOVE

There are people bedded down on pallets made of folded blankets, supplies stacked everywhere, lanterns glowing on shelves and in corners, a few people being checked over with first aid kits for blue-tinted fingers and rough scrapes on snow-abraded skin.

"Dad?" I murmur as we stand outside the threshold. "What...what happened?"

"Looks like the grid here isn't as reliable as we thought," he sighs.

The door shuts behind us, then opens again as a few more people come stumbling through. We move to one side, both of us rubbing the feeling back into our numb fingers.

I look at him while he shakes his head like it's suddenly a hundred pounds.

"We miscalculated. Thought everybody could stay safe and ride out the storm in their cabins, but with the power going out so quickly..." His shoulders tense and he looks down. "There's not enough generator fuel at each cabin. This storm won't blow out for at least a week. People would die. So we're bringing everyone in, consolidating the fuel so we still have one big generator running."

My heart skips a beat. I've never heard my slick-talking Senator Dad sound so ominous, so lost, so *unsure*.

That's when I notice the huge canisters of gasoline stacked along one wall, too.

Everything in me goes tense at *that*. The very idea of an open flame in a room full of highly combustible accelerant makes my inner explosives' expert insanely twitchy. But I bite my tongue.

There's no sense in adding to the worry.

I also bite my tongue on the fact that people wouldn't be risking themselves in the snow like this *at all* if my Dad hadn't brushed off their concerns and just did this from the *start*.

And if Hook hadn't made his big speech, telling us to stay.

Holy hell.

James is right.

We're all being manipulated. Everyone here.

I'm just not sure by who.

* * *

THE NEXT FEW hours are a blur.

I'm burned out, and Dad wants to take me up to his suite to rest, but I'd rather be down here where the action is. Even if I'm so tired I could collapse.

I stake out a corner on one of the couches and curl up with a blanket snug around me. Despite the growing noise of dozens of people in the room, I manage to fall asleep again and again as exposure and exhaustion overtake me.

Every time the door opens, though, I jerk awake.

I won't lie to myself.

I'm watching for James.

Gabe and Skylar are here. Skylar ensconced in a plush recliner while someone with a first aid kit runs a stethoscope over her pregnant belly...he shouldn't be far behind.

But I barely caught a flash of James before he was back in the storm, resolute and tireless, the grim determination on his face making my heart do strange, wild things.

In ones and twos, the stragglers come in, escorted by Pershing or Enguard staff.

But without James my blood feels too thin, watery with a slow growing fear.

I'm ready to *demand* someone go out looking for him, *anyone.*

Until the door bursts open one more time.

James comes staggering in, skewed to one side by the weight of a rather thick-set man.

I recognize the stranger. He's one of the resort chefs, and he looks barely conscious, one of his legs twisted at an odd angle from mid-calf down. The leg of his pants is dark with what looks like...

Oh.

Oh, no.

Frozen blood.

James must've dragged him half-conscious from the snow, nearly carried him here with his broken leg.

He saved his life from the storm, but I'm worried.

Scared for that poor chef when freezing blood may be one way to cauterize a wound, but it's also a good way to lose a limb. And while I watch with my heart in my throat, James lays the man down on a free pallet with careful hands.

Then he goes to work with that intent and utter focus that's *so* James.

No matter the situation, he always seems to know what to do to save a life.

He's already snapping off sharp directions to aides and staff to fetch this or that while he produces a knife from inside his coat and slits the chef's pants leg up, exposing the bulge of bone pushing against muscle, threatening to burst free.

I can't take it anymore.

Tumbling off the sofa, I straighten my wobbly legs and rush over, dropping to my knees across from him. "Is there anything I can do?" I ask breathlessly.

James snaps a silvery-blue look up at me over the groaning man's body. He may be cool as ever in this situation, but there's no masking his urgency, the demon drive telling me he really *cares* about this man's life.

"I'll have to set his leg. You can hold his head, Faye. Make sure he doesn't bite or swallow his tongue from the pain."

"Of course!" I quickly shift around to kneel at the man's head, coaxing him to rest it in my lap.

I fumble around the supplies for a minute until I find a gauze pad, roll it up into a compacted tube, and urge the chef to open his mouth so I can get it between his teeth.

"Bite down on this," I tell him gently. "It's okay if you need to scream."

There's fear in his pain-hazed eyes, but no doubt he trusts us. And he manages to force one hand up to curl against my forearm as an anchor as he nods slowly.

I look up, catching James' eye again.

A silent signal passes between us.

Let's do this. Save him.

Then James abruptly yanks the man's leg, stretching the muscle tissue out while he snaps the broken bone back in place with the heel of his palm. The chef roars, his fingers digging into my arm.

I don't blame him one bit, even if it's the only morbid sound.

A hush falls over the room. Everyone staring. Waiting to see if we can pull this off.

But James doesn't let the pressure stop him, working quickly to lay a wooden slat from the first aid kit along the side of the man's leg, then beginning to wrap it swiftly in gauze.

Slowly, the man's moans soften...but the hush in the room as James finishes working makes the noise sound like a jet engine.

It's nothing when there's a *thud* like a gunshot.

One of the first-floor conference room doors bangs open sharply, bouncing off the wall.

Out comes Hook Hamlin, trailed by a few Pershing staff. His face is the kind of crimson that can only come from rage, his jaw a steely lump.

He doesn't even look at anyone in the room, just sweeps upstairs, disappearing around the bend of the landing.

Dad emerges a few seconds later.

He looks less livid and more grim, even a touch darkly satisfied, as he straightens his tie. His small entourage of staffers is another story.

All of them are pale and shaking and giving each other wide-eyed glances, asking without words if what they just saw was *real*.

My heart jumps into my throat. Somehow, what's happening here is worse than the man writhing in agony with a busted leg.

But my father seems calm. So whatever just happened in that room can't be the end of the world.

Right?

I can't focus on it right now, though, not even when my father starts moving among people to offer quiet reassurance. There's a sobbing, gasping man in my lap who needs me.

And so does James.

It takes me back to a time when it used to be this way all the time, the two of us able to do anything.

As long as we worked together.

In love, we were indestructible.

* * *

By the time everyone is accounted for, I'm ready to collapse again.

I'm still recovering from my own near-death experience in the snow. Yet here I am, whirlwinding between one frozen or injured person and the next.

James and I move in tandem. Nothing's critical, at least – as long as we get out of here in the next few days.

There are a few more broken bones and a couple people we've got to keep on close watch for frostbite.

But everyone's safe and warm. No one missing. Every break splinted.

We just have to keep alert for possible infections.

That's what scares me, too, cooped up in here.

Technically, yes, everyone may be safer consolidating resources and staying tight to keep warm and conserve power.

That also means just one nasty flu bug let loose in this confined space could become an epidemic.

Without hospital services, real doctors, or medication, that could be deadly.

Sometimes, we forget that things like the flu used to be more than just seasonal nuisances and a few ugly days.

I want to ask James if he's heard anything about the forecast. My phone can't get a signal and the wi-fi looks to be down.

But he's gone again.

Disappeared the minute I looked up from rummaging around for those neat little hand-warmer heat packs for a few freezing people. He couldn't have gone out into the storm again.

We've brought everyone inside, and there's no reason for him to risk himself out there.

The room is dim, quiet, most people bedding down on their pallets or whatever furniture they've claimed to sleep on. Only a few left awake, sorting through the perishables from the mini coolers and freezers to determine what needs to be cooked and eaten first.

We can't have heavy-duty appliances draining power.

More disturbing, there's no sign of Hook, either. I'm guessing he's retreated to his suite and left the peasants to fend for themselves in the commons areas.

I see Dad, standing over the receptionist station, speaking urgently with a few of his aides, maps unfolded while they lean their heads together with Landon and Riker from the Enguard crew.

It looks like they're doing something proactive to get us out of here, but...

I'm not ready to talk to him yet.

Not until James answers my questions.

The only person who looks even a tiny bit approachable is Skylar Barin.

She's perched at the bar, sipping a hot steaming mug of something that looks like tea. If I'm being honest, "approachable" is a stretch with her.

There's something downright scary about this woman. Something that says she could eviscerate you with a single word and she has no time for nonsense, but her smile is polite enough as I settle down on a barstool with one between us so I'm not crowding her.

I can only imagine what it's like when you're carrying around another human being inside you.

You definitely don't want people cramping your space.

For a second, I wonder if I'll ever know what having a baby feels like. I'm pushing thirty, and no one's touched me since James.

I couldn't stand it. I don't know how I'll stand it again after he's done confusing the hell out of me and disappears from my life.

Ha. Looks like I'm set for spinster-librarian with secret ninja skills.

I'd find that funnier if my heart didn't ache so much.

But I push the thought aside and lean over the bar to snag a clean tumbler and a bottle of Wild Turkey, before lifting it with a wry smile for Skylar. "I'd offer you a drink too, but..."

I'm joking, of course.

She chuckles tiredly and pats her swollen belly. "Yeah, let's not get this one started on a habit that soon. With my luck, she'll be a lightweight like her father."

"Just trying to be polite. You need more tea or something?" I pour a couple of fingers for myself as she shakes her head, but I'm not sure I actually want to drink it. The atmosphere of danger here says I need to keep a clear head. No matter what.

So I only nurse my whiskey, tipping its strong taste against my lips without actually swallowing much, and glance at Skylar sidelong. "Heard any updates? I've been a bit busy playing Nurse Nancy, so I'm out of the loop."

"Not a damn thing." She grimaces and takes another sip of her tea. "If I go into labor here, I'm going to be *pissed*."

My eyes widen. "Are you really that far along?"

"Not quite, but conditions like this can trigger contractions from stress."

"Oh...crap." I sigh heavily. "That makes this even worse. Gotta be too much to force our way out?"

"Not in these whiteout conditions." She shakes her head. "With all communications down, I haven't seen anything in hours. The last time I saw the weather map, it showed this storm trapped between two mountain ranges. No wind to push it anywhere. If we weren't at this elevation, maybe we could hope for it to move on by tomorrow, but seeing how it's parked right over us..." Skylar frowns, more than a hint of worry in her eyes. "We'll just have to wait for it to blow out."

"Damn. And with how heavy those clouds are –"

"It could take more than a week," she finishes for me.

"Oh," I say faintly. "Fuck."

That wins a smile.

"Exactly."

"My Dad has really crappy timing."

Skylar smiles wider, grimly. "Well, no surprise. Politicians don't check weather reports when they're looking for money."

I nod. She's too right. Or I wish she was, so this whole strange thing could be explained away by Dad's clumsiness.

But the rest eats at me. The fact that Dad even *tried* to hold a fundraiser at a ski lodge right after a haphazard attempt on his life...it's just weird.

He usually does charity galas, dinners, conventions, even the occasional fun run.

Whisking donors away to this private, isolated place in unpredictable weather? It's not like him.

Not like him at all, even with the whole woodsy family man vibe he was going for in the photo shoots. We could've done the shoots without the donors, without this huge mess of people carted up here – a mess that's smaller than it would've been if the others had made it.

"At least the plumbing still works," I mutter, taking a deep sip of my whiskey.

Because now?

Right now, with the confusion in my head, I really, *really* need it.

Heck, I'm sure she does too, and I'm drinking for both of us.

Sky lets out a dry chuckle. "It'd better. I pee practically every ten minutes."

I can't help laughing. "God, I'm not looking forward to being pregnant."

"You say that like it's definitely going to happen." She arches a brow. "You and James sort your shit out, then?"

I splutter on my next sip, nearly choking on the sharp burn before I set the tumbler down, coughing and wiping at my mouth.

"Sort *what?*" I shake my head quickly. "There's nothing to sort out!"

"Look, girl, I've been around James Nobel long enough to know he has two modes: Broody and Super Broody. He's gone up a level from Super Broody to Mega-ass-tastic Broody ever since he found out he's been assigned to you. You two clearly know each other." Her pale, sharp gaze skewers me. "And you've got history."

"I, uh..." I shrug uncomfortably and pretend to check my shirt for stray whiskey drips. "It's just that. History. He's barely even talking to me right now. I'd think he talks to you guys a whole lot more."

"For James, one extra word is 'a whole lot more.'"

I crack a shaky smile. "That's too true. He told you about his issues with Pershing, though, right? How they were involved with him leaving the FBI? It just seems weird that knowing it, Landon would be all over Hook Hamlin like that."

Skylar sits up straighter, her round belly sticking out, giving me a strange look. "I think you have a very skewed idea how much James says to anyone, considering this is the first I've ever heard of him being in the FBI. You *sure* about that?"

I cringe. Fuck. *Fuck.*

With how secretive James can be, I hope I didn't just spill something he wanted to hide.

I smile thinly and pull a page from James' book.

"History," I tell her. Just one word, vague and uninformative.

Before I get up with a quick *excuse me* and take me and my whiskey mouth toward the stairs.

God, I need sleep.

But really, I'm just going to hide away in Dad's suite. Maybe claim the couch for myself so Skylar can't ask me the questions hovering in the sharp gaze that trails me from the room.

Honestly, I don't blame her. I've got a few loaded questions myself.

From what I've seen, these people aren't just James' coworkers.

They're his *friends*. Yet, for some reason, he kept his old job from them?

Why?

What's James so determined to hide that he can't even tell the people closest to him the smallest things?

XIV: LAVA TALK (JAMES)

The only thing keeping me moving right now is the hot, raw burn of bourbon spreading through my chest.

I shouldn't even be out here, damn it.

But after quizzing a few resort staff and checking the rosters for duty shifts, no one's sure if there should be twenty personnel on-site or twenty-two.

Not after there were a few last-minute shift changes before the storm blew in. No one knows if two of the waitresses, roommates who live down the mountain, made it in before everything shut down. With phones out of commission – even the landlines refusing to connect, which worries me – no one can even call them to be sure.

So here I am, tied to my friend Riker by a rope around the waist, more rope trailing behind us to the main lodge as we forge through the snow. Out on one last unholy perimeter check of the cabins.

Riker takes another swig off the canteen and passes it back to me, pulling the insulated mask stitched into the hood of his coat back up over his mouth.

His voice is a muffled shout through the fabric, pitched over the wind. "When I get back home," he says, "I don't know if my daughter and wife are going to kill me for getting into this, or kill me for leaving them out of it."

I can't help a faint smile as I shove my own mask down for another hot sip of liquid courage. It helps chase away the tired, sore ache in my body straining to fight this never-ending storm.

The last cabin we haven't checked is a distant shadow in the white wall ahead, just a smudge of brown that disappears and reappears as the snow swirls on, glittering in the light of our high-powered lanterns. "Young Olivia hasn't gotten over her thrill-seeker phase yet, I take it?"

"Nah, not even close. I'm under orders to take her skydiving for our wedding anniversary. Fucking *sky diving*. It's like she's trying to make up for all her sheltered years at once. Living every rush she can."

"Hardly sounds like a bad way to live with your wife," I point out. "As long as you're all happy."

"Absolutely," he says, his voice softening, almost inaudible in the shriek of the wind. Even in the snow and the dark, though, I see the warmth in his eyes. "And Em is, too. Even if Liv's starting to turn her into a little daredevil."

"Glad to hear they get along without friction."

"Yeah. Two brainy peas in our family pod. I'm damn happy my little girl loves Liv as much as I do." He lifts a hand to shade his eyes, peering through the snow. "Speaking of friction..."

"I know," I say grimly. "Things have grown rather strained between the Senator's staff and the Pershing team. Looked like a real altercation earlier. I hope it doesn't get worse while we're all stuck in close quarters."

"That's not what I meant, James."

We're at the cabin now, and Riker shifts around to the

side. It only gives us a little shelter with the wind blowing so hard, but there's a tiny corridor of calm under the eaves.

He stomps his feet, rubbing his gloved hands together as he eyes me. I settle in next to him, glancing through the window, searching for a distraction.

I have a wicked feeling I know where this conversation is going, and it's not happening.

The glass is fogged over, frosted, but the cabin seems clearly empty.

Still, we'll do one more thorough check soon. I'd like another second to regain feeling in my nose, and I take another sip from the flask.

Only to nearly spit it out as Riker continues, "Man, I wasn't talking about the words with the Senator's people and Pershing. I mean the friction between you and the Senator's *daughter*."

Oh, fuck. Not now.

Snarling, I glug down a sip that suddenly burns like fiery judgment, then give him a flat look. "You're mistaken. There's no friction between me and Senator Harris' anything."

He arches both brows. "Bull. Come the hell on. You usually have a better poker face than this."

"I don't *need* a poker face. Nor do I need a bluff. There's zero friction between me and Ms. Harris."

"Dude. The fact that you can't lie as smoothly as you usually do says there's plenty." He elbows me. "You can tell me, James. I'll keep it a secret. What gives?"

I thin my lips. *Secrets* at Enguard tend to stay within Enguard, yes, but are often freely passed around between the team, who gossip like nosy siblings because to them, they *are* family.

To them, *I* am family, too.

They just don't need to know I agree.

That I've always held myself apart, because if they truly knew me, they'd disown me all too fast.

And I damn sure can't stand disappointing them that way.

Then again, if anyone would honestly keep a secret, it's Riker.

Older. Dependable. Wiser. To me, world's best and most annoying friend.

From the impatient way he watches me, he's not letting me out of this any time soon.

Fuck.

I sigh, then shrug tightly. "Look...it's true we're old friends, Ms. Harris and I. We once knew each other in what feels like another life."

"Yeah?" Riker's gaze is shrewd, penetrating. "Interesting. Though somehow, I've got a funny feeling 'friends' is a heaping understatement."

"It doesn't matter," I snap, my blood lighting up.

"I think it does, buddy." He claps my shoulder. "But you'll tell me when you're ready. Tell *us* when you're ready. I know how it works for you. And Lord knows I've had plenty of secrets to work through of my own." His mask still covers his nose and mouth, but I can see the movement, the outline of his smile. "C'mon. Let's have one last look for those girls, and then head in and get some rest. We earned it."

* * *

WE CHECK THE CABIN, but it's empty.

Cleaned out. All water, food, blankets, and emergency supplies taken.

It's likely the girls just never made it up the mountain and are safe at home. So Riker and I turn to retrace our steps, following the rope we'd staked out toward the lodge.

I'm ready to drop, aching down to my bones, the searing cold reaching through my clothing to nearly devour me.

We don't hear the faint, tired shouts until we're closer.

And turn toward the noise to see the smallest glimmers of light down the road, on the slope leading up the mountain to the lodge.

Headlights.

Riker and I exchange glances.

There's hope in me, a flare of relief in my chest. Maybe heavy-duty rescue vehicles made it here after all.

Together, we wind up the ropes and forge down the road. It's at once easier going downhill and much worse in the open spaces, when there's nothing to act as a windbreaker. It's just us against the driving force of the storm, moving toward those headlights, hoping beyond hope that –

Nothing.

No hope at all.

Because all we have are two girls in a car that stalled on the mountain just a few hundred yards from the lodge.

The missing waitresses are half-frozen, struggling to stay warm. Their car battery dying from the heater draining it. They're crying and terrified, thinking no one would find them until they saw our lanterns moving up on the peak.

We're quick to bundle them up, raiding their car for anything we can use, including draining the tank into the emergency gas can in the trunk. We've got to think about survival right now, and we've just added two more liabilities to our roster.

Of course, I'm real fucking glad we found them now, rather than leaving them to freeze to death in the cold.

Their names are Becca and Amanda.

I remember that, as I carry Amanda up the slope. She's too cold and weak to walk by herself, Becca clutched firmly in Riker's arms behind me. Becca and Amanda might be a living, breathing miracle.

I feel like death follows me.

When I actually get to help someone cling to life, just like the chef who's leg I fixed, I can't help it.

I want to remember them.

I don't realize how truly late it is until we slog our way back to the lodge with our scared, shaking cargo and let ourselves into the commons room.

It's dark. Almost everyone has bedded down, the fire crackling and dim and the shared body heat combining with the generator's to make the place toasty.

Amanda actually makes a pained sound in my arms as we walk into the wall of heat – and that worries me.

For people with frostbite, the cold can make a sudden heat blast seem painful.

Together, Riker and I find a free space for the girls, bundling them up in blankets.

Skylar, still awake, mutters something about pregnancy and restlessness. She's quick to share the hot pot of tea she's kept brewing – between giving me bizarre looks I don't have time to focus on right now.

We work at finding the girls dry clothes and check their fingers and toes for frostbite. I'm relieved to see the pink flush in their fingertips as blood rushes back where it belongs.

It'll hurt for a bit, as their bodies try to restore equilibrium. They're crying, flinching from the heat of the mugs, but also clinging to them desperately.

But they'll be all right. They're safe. That's all that matters.

Me, though, I'm not so damn sure of.

I haven't been this exhausted, this battered, since the

night I pried myself out of the wreckage of a shattered plane with my friend's dead body in my arms.

I should get some rest so I can be ready to tackle tomorrow.

As an Enguard officer, it's on me to help keep these people safe and handle disaster management until rescue arrives. I need to be on point. But as I pull away with one last reassuring murmur for Amanda, Riker catches my arm.

"Hey," he says softly, something meaningful in his gaze as he studies me intently. "Landon's probably still up. I think he stole an empty pantry for a private bedroom and office."

I smile dryly. "Are you trying to hint at something, Riker?"

"Less hint and more sledgehammer. If there are things Landon needs to know..."

"My personal life has no impact on our work, if that's what you're implying."

"Doesn't it?"

I can't answer. Not when, if I'm honest with myself, I knew the moment we stepped inside that Faye isn't here. I feel her absence keenly.

Her presence makes me biased. Makes me weak. Makes me insane.

And in close quarters, over the length of this storm, it could cause problems.

I swallow a growl, pulling away from Riker with a nod.

Goddamn it, fine.

If I have to do this, I might as well do it tonight, when I'm so tired that no matter what old demons are eating me, I'll be able to pass out and sleep off the aftermath of whatever hurt fury Landon sends my way.

I don't know if I've braced myself so much as I don't have anything left in me to feel dread.

I head back toward the kitchen to find this pantry Landon's made into his own little bunker.

Before I even reach the kitchen, the sound of laughter draws me up short. I recognize those voices.

One is Landon's.

The other is Hook Hamlin's.

Damnation.

Slipping to one side of the kitchen doorway, I instinctively conceal myself beyond the wall and risk a glance around the frame before pulling back. Landon and Hamlin are leaning against the stainless steel prep counter, the room dark save for one of the small power lanterns.

In the glimpse I'd gotten, Hook was in the middle of topping up a tumbler of scotch for Landon, the two of them companionable and relaxed.

What a fucking mess this is.

It tears me apart to see it. To see Landon so enamored with this vile man, fully ensnared by his grandfatherly-mentor act, starstruck by his many achievements.

That's the real danger with Hook Hamlin. He's made deception an art form.

He's every man you've ever known who's done great things, only to mask what a rotten snake he really is. Only, Hook has managed to keep his crimes hidden so deep – more buried than my own past rushing up to explode in my face – that Landon has no clue the man he's so glibly trading stories with, idolizing, possibly even confiding in is a horror of a man.

A hand in the deaths of thousands. Hell, maybe even tens of thousands, when he's almost singlehandedly responsible for a quarter of every illegal arms deal funneling out of this country and into brutal wars abroad.

And I have no fucking proof.

Nothing but my own memories, hearsay, that sense of brimming intuition that promises I'm right.

Captain Asshole Hook is up to no good.

Right now, though, there's no way to get between them.

I can't even try, especially not for this conversation I don't even want to have.

Landon's too distracted, his hero worship too strong, and I'll need something more concrete before I bring my problems to him and possibly trust him with them.

There's only one way I can actually gain solid intelligence on Hamlin.

It's from the only man who knows more about him than anyone else.

The one man who's made all of Hook Hamlin's illegal activities possible.

I need to corner Senator Harris and force him to talk.

* * *

I KNOW where I'll find him.

In his suite, hiding away where he doesn't have to deal with the little people, all huddled below in misery while he's ensconced in his own cozy private space. What else is new?

I pull away from the kitchen and head up the stairs, having every intention of knocking on his door and confronting him on his own turf.

But I catch him just as he's stepping out, moving with a careful quiet, easing the door closed behind him.

Harris stops as he sees me, the door still half-open.

He blinks for a moment, then holds a finger to his lips. "Shh," he says softly. I'm not expecting the almost familiar warmth in his voice, as if something in his attitude magically changed toward me.

Fuck, like something in *him* changed, when I'm accustomed to cold, hard-driven, focused distance or the smarmy fake smiles of a Senator. "Faye just fell asleep. She's worn out."

"Ah," I say tightly.

In that one sound is every last conflicted emotion Faye's name brings.

The storm and the turmoil that makes it hard for me to think.

Harder for me to process my feelings toward this man in front of me when for once – for *once* – he's saying Faye's name with love.

It barely computes in my head. I still remember the look of worried panic on his face when I fought through the snow to tell him Faye had nearly gotten lost in the snow and needed an evac to the lodge immediately.

Harris looks at me oddly, then offers a tired smile. "You know, I never got the chance to thank you, James. I don't know what I would've done if I hadn't been able to get to Faye, or known she was safe. I'll make sure you're compensated, somehow. Even if it's just putting in a good word for Enguard with the boys back in D.C. I assure you..."

Compensated? *Compensated?*

I'm not even fucking listening anymore.

He thinks I want to be *paid* for ensuring his daughter's safety?

Of course.

Of-godddamn-course he does. That's how men like Harris think. Everything has a price tag.

And everyone has a price.

Something inside me snaps.

Something that's been building for years, this tension coiling inside me until I finally hit the last inch on my extremely long fuse.

My voice feels like thunder pouring out of me, words like

lightning, striking hard as I snap, "Keep your fucking bribes to yourself, Senator."

He blinks back shock.

I'm too angry to find any satisfaction in Harris' startled, widening eyes. "The only reason I even had to save Faye was because *you* put us in this situation. You're engineering something, and I don't know what – but after everything you've done, I won't be surprised if even more people wind up dead by the end of it. You murdered three good men, and probably more. Who's next?"

He blinks at me again, this time more blankly.

Gone is the mask of the Senator. I'm waiting for the dark, calculating thing hiding underneath.

Except it doesn't come.

He's genuinely confused, his shoulders going stiff, a touch of offense in his voice. "I haven't murdered anyone. I don't know what the hell you've been concocting –"

"*Don't lie.*"

"James..."

I take a step back so I don't send my fist into his chin and wreck everything.

He has to be lying – *has to be*. Because I can't stand the thought that after all these years, my hatred was misdirected. I can't believe this bullshit bewilderment is honest, not feigned.

"I nearly died the night that plane crashed, asshole. Tanner Egon *did* die. So did the pilot, and another agent. How can you sleep, knowing that?"

Harris' face goes white. "The crash? You think...you think I?" He shakes his head quickly. "No, James, no. Jesus. Now isn't the time to tell you everything, but I can promise –"

"Save it," I fling back. "I know you're in bed with Pershing. And I know you'd do anything to keep those connections buried. The two of you throw just enough busts to the authorities so nobody ever suspects your little illegal gunrunning business. You play world's best gun reform lobbyist in Congress, while Pershing Shield cleans up as heroes and everyone's favorite Homeland Security darlings. Meanwhile, the weapons you ship all over the world just go to the highest bidders. Blood money for fucking guns." I practically spit the last words.

"James," Harris says tightly, his voice oddly hollow, "you need to stop. Now. This isn't –"

"Why?" Fuck. I mean it, *why?*

It's like every word I've refused to say for years is barreling out of me, impossible to stop, this torrent of fury and hatred coming like lava now that I've cracked wide open.

I can't stop this lava-talk for anything. Not to save my own life.

"I covered for you once, for Faye's sake, Senator. It was the biggest mistake of my life. She needs to know the truth about who you are. Everyone does. You nearly *killed* me. You murdered three men. You fund and facilitate Pershings' black market weapons operation. And I wouldn't be surprised if *you* killed your wife when she found out about it."

Silence. Dead silence, while Harris stares past me, somewhere over my shoulder.

But I can't turn around. Can't look.

Because the door to Harris' suite is swinging open, revealing Faye.

Standing there, white-faced, her eyes wide and wet, her mouth trembling.

And accusation and horror in every line of her sweet face.

XV: GOOD INTENTIONS (FAYE)

I don't know what hurts more right now.

Hearing the man I love completely eviscerate my father?

Discovering Dad is dirty? So darkly flipping dirty he *could* be responsible for so much evil, if James is to be believed.

Or is it finding out that Mom didn't die in an accident? She was murdered.

Or the sick, ominous sense of fear I get as two men from Pershing Shield emerge from Hook Hamlin's suite across the hall?

And they've clearly heard everything James said, too.

I can't.

I can't breathe, because if I inhale then I'll have to exhale, and if I exhale, I'm going to burst out sobbing. This is officially too much.

Sure, we were already in mortal danger with this storm and the power outage and the generator only able to last so long, but the elements? I know how to fight them.

What I don't know is how to fight my own father, or the

peril he's put us in by bringing us up here with that horrible *man* from Pershing.

I still don't know what's going on.

But I'm more and more certain we came here for all the wrong reasons.

And I'm terrified none of us will leave alive.

I only have a second to stare into James' stricken face.

For once there's real emotion in his cutting silver-blue eyes.

There's surprise, sorrow, regret.

His lips work soundlessly like he's trying to find the right thing to say to erase all of this.

But he can't.

No one can.

I feel like a rubber doll, moving numbly, just as Dad – his expression strained, his voice grim – grasps my arm, drags me back into the room, and slams the door firmly in James' face.

At first, I think Dad is angry. Furious.

Then I numbly take in the strain lines around his eyes and realize he's not angry at all.

He's *afraid*.

Oh, God.

Nothing makes it more evident than when he bolts the door, and then shoves a chair up against the handle to barricade it shut.

He stops. Looks at me grimly, breathing heavy, the mask of that cold dark man back in place. Slowly, he steps toward me.

I flinch back instinctively, retreating, shaking my head.

Can it get any more messed up? I don't want to be afraid of my own father.

But I am.

I'm angry, too, and that's what's working away the numbness, burning it off to let me function, let me process, let me move, let me speak – even if my first words are a croak, broken and wounded.

"Dad? What the *hell* was that? You...and Pershing...and *Mom*..."

"It was the truth, Faye," he says calmly, and every word hits me like a bullet. "But it's not the truth James thinks it is."

I make a strangled noise. Here it comes – the tears, my throat closing, but if I'm sobbing with anything, I'm sobbing with sheer raw fury. *"Explain,"* I demand. "Now."

My father just looks at me, then sighs and crosses the room to sink down on the couch, brushing aside the blankets I'd used to make it my bed.

At least we're alone. The aides who were staying with him moved downstairs for now, although the room's adjoining bathroom was supposed to be for public use until we get out of this. Right now, though, I'm grateful there was no one else here to overhear this mess.

A mess nobody ever should've had to hear.

Especially not me.

Because it shouldn't freaking exist.

Leaning forward, my father braces his elbows on his knees, laces his hands together, and presses his mouth to his knuckles. A troubled expression crosses his face.

He remains silent for an eternity before beginning to speak in slow, halting whispers. "James Nobel is right about one thing: I've been collaborating with Pershing. Your mother was murdered, Faye, but not by me. God, *never!* And someone did engineer the plane crash that nearly killed James, but it wasn't me either."

My legs drop out under me. My pulse roars in my ears.

I tilt into one of the easy chairs, nearly falling off it before

I curl forward and bury my face in my hands. "But why? *Why*, Dad?"

"Because," he says, so flatly it's like he feels nothing at all. "Hook Hamlin killed your mother. And he's the one who ordered the hit on me...and on you."

My chest feels like it's inverting, my ribs digging spears into my lungs and heart.

And I just cry again – deep, hoarse, gasping, hurting things.

Every memory of Mom floods through me, then cuts off. Maybe that's what hurts so fucking much.

That in one night, one awful instant, I lost every chance to ever make new memories with her.

And every day that passes, I risk losing the old ones to time. Mom fades into a ghost of vague impressions of warmth and cheeriness and dark cherry-red hair like mine.

And someone took her away from me, for evil reasons I don't even understand.

And Dad sounds like he doesn't care at all.

It's only when I scrub at my eyes, clearing my blurring vision, forcing myself to look at him with my breath rasping and my chest heaving, I realize I'm *wrong*.

Even if his voice was dead and toneless, his face gives him away.

His eyes are wet. His trembling mouth is racked, ravaged, and I understand the past years so much more now.

My father is hurting. Has *been* hurting, this constant raw wound that will never heal or scar, and the only way he can stop the bleeding is to feel nothing at all. To shut himself away.

I shake my head, scrubbing at my nose. "I don't...I don't understand anything right now."

"Let me start at the beginning," he says gravely. "You remember what your mother used to do?"

I nod. "She was a clerk for Senate Appropriations."

"Yes." He pauses, then continues, "She was auditing records one night when she noticed something wasn't right. Numbers didn't add up. The notations on what the spending was for led to initiatives that didn't exist, or ones that died on the House floor and never should've had funds allocated to them. She didn't tell me, not for a long time. Not until she was sure. She dug through years and years of records for months, following lies, paper trails...and uncovering the heart of Hook Hamlin's operation. Pershing Shield's work with Homeland Security is just a cover for what he really does: illegal arms deals, much of it funded by the Department of Defense itself, even if most of them don't know it. And the ones who do are too powerful to even think about taking down. It's the perfect cover. Pershing gets to play at being the good guys, working for pennies in the name of justice, while really they're making billions off gunrunning."

I feel like I'm going to throw up. I stare at him. "Then...the accident?"

"She was run off the road, Faye," he says wearily. "It took me a long time to find proof, but I did. I don't know how Hamlin realized she knew, but her car was forced over the bridge. I saw the traffic cam footage before it mysteriously disappeared. And I had to pretend I knew nothing about it and believed it was an accident."

"*Why?*" I flare. "Jesus, why didn't you tell the truth? Why didn't you –"

"Because Hamlin would have *killed you*," he snaps off, eyes flaring. "And if not Hamlin, then his DOD contacts. Men with the world's deadliest skills, compromised by bribes. I couldn't fight him from the outside. So I had to get him from within."

"So you've...shit." My voice chokes again, my throat closing. "You've been working the long game, trying to take him down by pretending to collaborate with him?"

My father nods. His voice drops, and he casts a wary glance toward the door before looking at me again. "I've been trying to get the information, the proof, I need to destroy Hamlin in ways not even his high-level friends can prevent without outing themselves. And take them down, too, if I can. But to do that –"

"You had to get your hands dirty," I finish weakly. "How dirty, Dad?"

He regards me solemnly for long moments, before dropping his gaze. "You don't want to know."

"Tell me."

"I can't. I hate it."

"Tell me!" I cry, clenching my fists. "You've kept so much from me for so long – you can at least tell me this."

"I'm sorry, my dearest Faye," he whispers. "I can't tell you that part. Not for anything. But I can tell you I wasn't the one who engineered James' plane crash. It was Hamlin, after his friend Tanner uncovered damning information about Hamlin and Pershing Shield on your very last case."

My eyes widen. "That's...that's why you wanted me to quit. Why you *made* me quit."

"Yes." He exhales heavily. "He nearly killed your friend James. I couldn't bear the thought of him killing you, as well. And if he knew you were on the case..."

I hate it.

I hate that it makes a sick sort of sense.

All I want to do is shout. Scream up and down how I could've protected myself, could've handled it as an agent if I'd gone to my seniors and we'd worked out a plan, but I can't deny it.

James is the best agent I ever knew. I admired him, learned from him, looked up to him.

If Hook Hamlin could come that close to killing James so easily...

He'd have squashed my rookie ass like a bug.

"Fuck," I breathe blankly, and my father actually cracks a smile.

"Yeah. Exactly." He leans back against the sofa, watching me worriedly. "You can't say a word, Faye. Let me deal with those two goons who overheard James, and deal with James as well."

I stiffen. "What do you mean, 'deal with' James?"

"I'll talk to him. Bring him into the loop. Work together. He's a fine man." He smiles sadly, and I get a glimpse of my real Dad once more. "A better man than me. I don't know if I'll ever be clean again. Not even if we take Hamlin down. That's what this entire trip was about. Cornering him where he couldn't run, then getting rid of him if it came down to it, with as few witnesses as possible. Trouble is, it seems he's worked out the same plan for me."

I want to say I understand. I want to say I forgive him.

But I don't.

I know some men can be driven to extremes when grief and loss are at play.

But if I've even half guessed at how far the gun operation runs, not to mention the fact that arms dealing often supports drug production and distribution, and sometimes human trafficking...

I can't look at my father the same way, knowing he was *helping* with that.

The ends don't always justify the means.

And I wonder how many lives have been destroyed by my father's actions.

How many lives are being wrecked now?

We're all in danger thanks to Dad, Hook Hamlin, and their stupid fucking games.

That's why they wanted us to wait out the storm in the cabins.

So when someone's dead body was found at the lodge later, there'd be no witnesses to counter the story of how it happened.

I can't say that right now, though. I can't really organize my feelings at all, or my thoughts.

I only shake my head, and for a moment his brow wrinkles before his expression smooths and he looks away.

"I understand if you're disappointed in me," he says. "The past years have been sickening. I had no idea how deep Pershing's connections went. It's like an infection spreading its way through every limb, following the bloodstream down to the tiniest capillary. I thought I could get in, get out, get done. But it's not that simple, Faye. That's why I set up this fundraiser."

"To get him alone."

He nods stiffly. "I think Hamlin's onto me, which is why I'm not worried about those men. I wanted to give him a chance to act on it, so I could enact my own plans. Either I'll get something solid from him that I can take to the DOJ, or else..."

He doesn't say it.

I don't need him to.

Because I realize now that the man Dad has become is capable of things I'd never imagined, even in his cold and quiet withdrawal that left me shivering and alone without an actual family.

My father is willing to kill Hook Hamlin here.

And honestly, right now, thinking about my mother – about her car crashing over the bridge, how she must've felt as it fell, as it sank, as the water rushed in on her and pulled her into the cold – so am I.

I could wrap my hands around Hamlin's thick throat and squeeze until he just goes blank and stops breathing.

And I can't deal with that feeling.

I can't deal with this searing grief over Mom, or the new grief over the loss of any hope of recovering the Dad I knew. Fury over what Hamlin did to my family, what he's taken away from me.

And I can't look Dad in the face right now.

I shove to my feet and grab my jeans, yanking them on over my pajamas. My father stares at me. "What are you doing?"

"Leaving," I bite off, pulling a sweater on over my pajama top, then going for my coat. "I just...I can't be here with you right now. I need some fucking air."

He's up in an instant, ducking in front of me, blocking my way as I head for the door and my shoes. "You can't, Faye. I can't let you go out there alone. Can't let you be unguarded around Hook's men."

For a second, I look up at him.

Then I do something I've never done in my life.

I shove my father.

Hard.

I shove him with all the fury and hurt and loss pent up inside me.

All the feelings of frustration.

All the times I reached for him and he didn't reach back and left me hurting and cold and scared because he thought that was *protecting* me.

I'm sick of men doing this to me.

My father, and James, even if I love them both. And I pour it all into my hands, into my arms, as I plant my palms against my father's chest and *push*.

He's still so much larger than I am that even with combat training, I can only make him stagger and stumble backward, catching him off guard. He stares at me while I sweep past, ducking to grab my boots and then yanking the chair from in front of the door.

"You can't stop me," I throw back, ripping the door open to storm out into the hall.

It slams shut behind me.

And he doesn't follow, thank God.

I stalk to the head of the stairs and drop down to sit on the top step and pull my shoes on.

But what I really end up doing is burying my face in my hands and crying.

I feel like I've spilled more tears in the past few days than I have in years, but every time I think I understand why, my world rips open and shifts itself back together again in a new ugly shape.

I'm ripped apart and reshaped, all these pieces of my heart inside me broken and tumbled around like bits of sharp-edged red glass in a jar.

And stupid me, stupid, stupid me...

I still want James right now.

I want James so bad for the comfort, when he's been just as bad as my father about keeping secrets and shutting me out.

But at least James never turned himself into a black market kingpin, not caring who he hurt as long as he got his revenge, his mission.

I sniff, wiping my eyes, and that's when I hear the commotion below.

I yank my boots on, then lean over the rail, watching, listening.

No one knows I'm here. I'm grateful for that as Hook Hamlin and several of his men pass below the upstairs railing, murmuring urgently about James.

I catch words like *perimeter sweep* and *wide area search*.

My heart thumps painfully – and harder still when I see Landon Strauss with them – listening intently and nodding as Hook murmurs *rogue agent*.

No, damn it!

Landon is James' friend, his trusted boss, isn't he? He can't believe Hook's lies. He *can't*.

Riker and Gabe are next, hanging back from the others...and speaking so low I can hardly hear them, but what I do hear eases the ache in my chest just a little.

There's no way and *he wouldn't go AWOL* and *if he did something, it's gotta be for a good reason.*

Both of them are looking at the back of Landon's head with troubled expressions.

Good. Good that *someone* still has faith in James.

The same faith I do.

I can't go down there right now, though. Not when they probably think I'm locked away in Dad's room, and they can find me whenever they want.

It's easy to paint James as a rogue agent, but I'd be trickier. So Pershing is probably saving me for later when there's not really anywhere I can go.

I shouldn't stay here, either. I'm too exposed.

There might be more of Hamlin's men in his room, and if one comes out in the hall and catches me...I'm cooked.

I can't go back to my father, either. I back up away from the bannister railing, out of the line of sight from downstairs, and stop when my shoulders hit the cold-frosted window. I glance over my shoulder – and freeze as I see something written in the frost on the glass, left there with a fingertip.

Come down.

That's when I realize there's a light outside.

A single lantern glowing in the snow, and a shrouded figure standing against a tree, watching, waiting.

James!

I don't even hesitate. I pry the window open, letting in a gust of cold wind. It's two stories down, and I don't care.

I squeeze myself through the opening, just as James tilts his head back to look up at me. And even as he spreads his arms, I do it.

I jump.

XVI: SLOW MOTION (JAMES)

Five Years Ago

I DON'T KNOW how many times Grandpa can call to tell me it's ending.

I don't want to fucking hear it anymore. *I know.*

I know the way I know the sound of my own voice, the way I know the feel of cool white piano keys beneath my fingertips, the way I know the dull beat of my own heart.

It's burned into my flesh, into my bones, and I can't escape it.

My mother's dying.

There's nothing anyone can do.

And soon she'll be gone forever.

That's why I'm on my way home, coming as fast as I can.

Right now, it feels like I'm on my way nowhere, when the plane is still sitting on the runway and the clock is ticking down. I thought I'd have more time.

Just yesterday she'd seemed better. No hope for the

cancer to go into remission, of course, but it's the little things that buy her days, hours, minutes to enjoy what life she has left while it's still hers.

I thought I'd be able to go home and at least spend a few days with her and Grandpa.

Maybe take her for a walk through the daffodil gardens she so lovingly cultivated in the backyard.

Play music for her, her old favorites from Rachmaninov.

I don't like to think those songs could be a funeral dirge, serenading her to the other side, but I'd have played them anyway. For her and the way every boy should love his mother.

I'd just hoped for *a little longer.*

But Grandpa's phone call says I have hours. Not days.

Goddamn *hours* to get from the Seattle field office and back to Portland.

I'd meant to take a commercial flight. I couldn't justify pulling FBI strings for a private plane, but Tanner had to go and be the good friend and call in favors with Congressman Harris for his daughter's "special" friend.

So here I am, sitting in a private jet, Tanner strapped in at my side, reading something on his phone, while I stare blankly out the window as the baggage handlers load up our things.

Baggage.

Fuck.

Isn't that just it?

I'm carrying too much baggage, including the guilt that I didn't fly home sooner. I'd been too wrapped up in work.

Too hellbent on cracking the Pershing Shield thing, gathering a brutal litany of evidence.

Surveillance photos of shipments coming into Tacoma ports. Mysteriously unmarked containers of unknown origin. Shipments that somehow managed to avoid passing through customs while men from Pershing Shield stood guard, waving them through.

The almost militaristic Pershing security presence around several large shipping containers bound for Portland, too.

Last I checked, Pershing wasn't in the business of freight and logistics.

And such a high-profile company doesn't hire out on small warehouse gigs.

It's also bizarre Senator Harris' signature is on funding for many Pershing Shield projects that don't seem to have an actual purpose.

I'd been too wrapped up in that, and too wrapped up in Faye.

There's something between us, something I can't name just yet, something I've promised her we'll talk about once all this is over.

I've known it for a long time, but my last mission drove it home. I'd been sent without her because the recon team didn't need an explosives expert. But the way she'd looked at me with those lovely green eyes, begging me to come back safe, fuck.

That image stayed with me the entire op, reminding me why I had to go in smart, go in strong, go in fast, and get out safe.

"You're brooding again," Tanner says.

I don't look away from the window. "Yeah. Pondering the many ways to kill you for arranging this."

"I'm partial to strangulation. Just ask my ex-wife. And you don't mean that."

"Don't I?"

Not really.

I'm grateful to him, but I'm too embarrassed to admit it.

But I don't realize, in this moment, how much I'll come to regret those words.

Tanner, at least, lets me brood on as the plane finally gets moving, taxiing down the runway and taking off. He loves giving me a hard time for being so serious, but he's more sensitive than he seems – and he gives me my space to work through my thoughts as the plane soars over the West Coast.

I don't know how to prepare myself for Mom truly dying. I've never lost anyone before.

My grandmother died before I was born, and my father was never in the picture.

I don't know if he's dead or alive and have zero emotional investment in him.

As an only child, I've always just been alone with my grandpa and my mother.

When I think of Mom, I always think of light. She's like a butterfly in summer, energized by sun, always gravitating to the rooms with the most windows when she's not outside soaking it up. Every memory of her is wreathed in gold and warmth, gleaming off her pale-blonde hair, dwelling in the laughter in her eyes.

Sometimes I think it's not the cancer that's killing her.

It's those cold, windowless rooms in the hospital and the cancer treatment center, where the only light is sterile and white and cold.

That's why she asked to spend her last days at home, too.

Our house is filled with light, floor-to-ceiling windows in every room. It's almost a house of glass. Her bedroom looks right out on the garden, with tall French doors leading to the patio and the waving daffodil heads.

I hope it can make her happy one more time, that those flowers will be the last thing she sees.

That, and her family, my grandfather and me, gathered around her to see her home.

Only I won't make it.

Because I'm so sunk in my thoughts that I don't realize

the plane is shaking until Tanner catches my arm, looking around with alarm as the lights flicker, and the other agent on the plane, a transfer hitching a ride, lets out a nervous yelp.

I look up as the pilot's voice comes over the intercom.

"We're experiencing a little trouble with one of our engines, guys, but we've got backups and should be able to get over these mountains just fine before we make an emergency landing on the other si—"

He never finishes.

There's a flash of light, a burst of smoke, a loud explosion from outside the window. The wing disappears in a cloud of billowing black.

And then we're dropping out of the sky.

The other agent screams, but Tanner and I are silent, stiff, clutching at each other's arms. Hoping our friendship would somehow hold us stable, get us through this, save us from the shrill adrenaline and tension as the plane plummets.

It's so fast. Over in seconds, and I must've passed out from cabin depressurization because I don't even remember the crash.

Just the shrieking whine of descent growing louder and louder, a voice – I'm not even sure whose, maybe not even Tanner's – whispering *James.*

The awful realization I'm not going to make it, I'm going to fail the people I love.

Faye. Grandpa. Mom.

Faye!

And then it's all black.

Black nothing, dead and gone.

I don't know how long I'm out. I only know it's the smell of burning fuel that wakes me up, tinged with something else.

A thought, tickling in the back of my mind. *Shit.*

If I'm close enough to smell it burning, then I'm close enough to die if that fuel explodes.

The sense of danger drags me awake, back to full awareness of my aching, sore, torn body.

I'm caught underneath a crushing weight, my nostrils seared, and I can't see until I blink several times and rub the blood from my face with one shaking hand. The other is pinned down, and it hits me.

I'm *trapped* under the debris.

I try to move and end up coughing as I inhale smoke in a scouring rush down my throat. I can taste my own blood, harsh and metallic.

Even worse, I hear a voice calling from the wreckage somewhere.

It sinks in that it's Tanner before it sinks in that we've actually fucking crashed.

Suddenly, everything zeros in on his voice, and I have to get to him.

I'm not sure how I'm moving, what I'm doing. I don't have any recollection of twisting and fighting my way free from the crumpled metal on top of me, or struggling my way out of the charred, torn-up seat I'm still strapped into.

I must have at least two or three broken bones, but I don't feel them. I don't care.

All I care about is finding my friend.

I stumble through the flaming piles of wreckage, dodging mini fires everywhere, searching through the cold, wind-torn night. We've hit somewhere in the mountains, no roads or civilization in sight, just rocky slopes and trees and snow at greater altitudes.

I stumble over the body of the pilot first. His eyes are dead and blank, the arm I trip over like rubber.

I linger only long enough to close his eyes out of respect before forging on toward the sound of that weakening voice.

When I find Tanner...I know there's little hope.

He was flung free from the wreckage but slammed hard into a tumble of sharp, cragged rocks. He's bleeding everywhere. So much blood I can hardly tell where it's coming from. Not when he's this lacerated, his clothing shredded, deep cuts torn in his flesh over every surface of his body, contusions on his temples. I don't know how he's conscious, or alive.

Or how he smiles at me when I drop down to my knees next to him, reaching for him and then drawing back, almost afraid to touch him.

"H-hey," he rasps weakly. "Fuck. I th-thought you stood me up. Bad first date etiquette, y'know."

"Stop talking," I gasp. "You're straining yourself."

It takes a second for my medical training to kick in.

I'm supposed to be neutral and detached in these situations, but first responder training never really overrides the shock of seeing your best friend bleeding out on the ground and most certainly about to die.

But then something takes over. I search around quickly, finding a few blankets in the wreckage and bringing them back to make him more comfortable.

I fold one up behind his head to elevate it and manage to roll him onto a couple others, layered to form a pallet that gets him off the hard, cold ground. Then I peel his ruined shirt open to get a better look.

I suck in a sharp breath, my stomach sinking with pure and utter dread, horror, sorrow.

It's not just the way his leg dangles, clearly broken. It's his entire abdomen, nearly black with bruises, and swollen outward, firm and unyielding. Tanner's a lean man, and that's not his belly.

That's severe internal bleeding, building up under his skin.

That's proof he's going to die.

He's going to die as surely as my mother's going to die, and I can only be there for *one* of them.

Even though I know it's useless, I still try to make him comfortable. And the entire time I'm working, he's still smiling.

His eyes are wet, pained, but he's smiling with a sort of fatalistic acceptance, refusing to go out broken and afraid.

"Hey," he says again. "N-no one told you it was okay to f-feel me up."

"You're not funny," I rasp, my throat thick.

"I know it, Nobel." His smile widens. "S-smile for me anyway."

And I do. I do because this man is my friend.

Because we've worked together through so many missions.

Because he'd do anything for me, and the least I can do when I can't save him is fucking smile like he asks.

I feel like I'm letting him down. But the dice was rolled by someone other than me, maybe God, and I'm not the one who crashed that plane.

Fuck, even now, I know no plane should *ever* go up in midair like that. Not with even the most basic pre-flight checks and preparation.

Which makes me think the plane was sabotaged. The crash was staged.

Someone wanted to get me and Tanner out of the way because of what we knew.

About Pershing Shield.

And about Congressman Paul Harris, the man who chartered this flight.

In that moment, something black and hateful is born.

Something that knows only loss, only pain, only emptiness, as the night wears on and Tanner's ridiculous jokes devolve into groans of pain and soft pleas.

He wants me to make sure his ex-wife and kids are taken care of.

I hold his hand until morning, promising they will be. I hold his hand longer still, even as he slips into unconsciousness and I don't think he'll wake up again.

It's a distant thing, when the rescue chopper finds us hours later. I can't feel relief, when I know that as they cart my friend's near-dead body away, it's over.

I'll never see him again.

Just like I'll never see Mom.

And somehow, it's numb, when they tend to my own injuries and ferry me to the hospital.

I can't feel it. I can't feel anything.

Because the only way to cope with the hideous and murderous rage inside me is to go blank, go dark, and swear that someday, I'll make this right.

I'll make it right if I never feel anything again.

* * *

Present Day

When I gave Hamlin's men the slip and left that note for Faye in the fog on the window, I never expected she'd take *come down* quite so literally.

But she's wild-eyed and wet-faced, the tracks of tears running down her cheeks. I know what she's like when her emotions are high and she's upset, ready to set everything on fire.

She's impulsive, reckless, spitfire incarnate, and I think I know before she does that she's going to jump, when she shoves the window open and squeezes herself out with one foot braced on the sill.

She looks down at me almost defiantly for a moment. Almost *daring* me to break her trust, as I have so many times before.

Then – fearlessly, beautifully, wildly, madly – she leaps.

I'm moving before I'm thinking, but there's no time for anything else.

Faye comes sailing down through the snow with her hair a brilliant red like flame. I drop the lantern and dart forward, positioning myself under her with my arms open.

She's a small, slight thing.

Damn if she doesn't hit me like a cannonball, though, gravity giving her weight and sending her crashing down into me.

I'm barely able to wrap my arms around her before we're tumbling back into the snow, hitting a soft drift so hard it plumes up around us like a crashing tsunami, flinging snow that's just fallen down in the biting, tearing wind right back up to be swirled away again.

For a moment, we just lie there, her on top of me, the cold soaking in, the duffel bag strapped to my back digging at my bones. She's wheezing, and I can't tell if she's struggling to breathe in the icy air or struggling not to cry.

But soon she pushes herself up with her hands braced against my chest. The cool blue-white light of the Coleman lantern teases against the fiery strands of her hair, making glowing copper filaments that seem to shine with their own light.

"If you wanted to kill me, Tink," I say, "there are easier ways to do it."

Her mouth trembles, and she glares. "That's not funny. We need to talk, James."

I arch a brow. "If you want to gloat, I'm in no mood."

Faye sits up, straddling me, glaring down.

Then she promptly picks up a double handful of snow and grinds it into my face, whomping it down in a big pillowy handful.

I almost don't even feel it. But I do feel a smile coming on.

So fucking ridiculous.

It's so Faye.

Here I am, lying on the freezing ground in the middle of a blizzard, danger everywhere, bundled up far more than she is while she pummels and pelts me with snow over and over again, half-sobbing, half-shouting, and it's only the howl of the wind that keeps us from being discovered.

"You jerk," she cries. "You jerk, you jerk, you *jerk!* I hate you. Hate how you never tell me anything, hate how cynical you are, hate you for being right. Hate you for being *wrong...*"

The only way to stop her – and by now she's pounding my chest, dull thuds I barely feel through my layered coat – is to catch her wrists. Hold her in place.

She fights me for several more seconds. Then she goes still, looking down at me with her face a mask of misery, her nose flushed red and her mouth swollen pink and lush from crying, her hair whipped everywhere, and her lashes dotted with snowflakes.

"Faye," I say softly. "Slow down. Tell me what's going on."

She swallows thickly, glowering.

"You're right. That's what," she rasps. "Dad's dirty. But you've got it all wrong."

Wrong? I frown, looking up at her framed against the darkness and the swirling snow. "Not now. We should find somewhere safe where you can explain, before Hamlin's men notice the open window –"

"No!" she hisses, scrunching up her face. "You're going to listen, and you're going to listen right now, James Nobel."

I sigh, then loosen my grip on her wrists. "Then stop trying to hit me."

"I make no fucking promises."

But after a moment she climbs off me, plopping back into the snow and rubbing at her nose, before shivering and pulling her coat up around herself.

Even with the lodge blocking some of the wind, she's not wearing nearly enough.

I sit up, peel out of my outer coat, and settle next to her, wrapping it around her shoulders.

"Here," I murmur.

She eyes me mistrustfully, then sniffs and scoots into the coat. And into the circle of my arm, tucking against my side. I blink, and she scowls at me.

"I almost froze to death out here *once* already," she bites off. "I'm not doing it again. Body heat. Doesn't mean we're good."

I don't point out we could find somewhere warmer and safer to have this conversation.

Faye wants me to listen, so I intend to do it.

Even if I have to freeze a few fingers and toes off in the process.

I wait in silence. She watches me hesitantly, curling her fingers in the edges of my coat and pulling it closer. It dwarfs her, makes her look so small and vulnerable that I can't help tightening my arm around her.

For body heat, of course.

What else?

After a few hesitant moments, she says, "Hook Hamlin killed my Mom."

Her voice sounds small, hurt, still so shocked and disbelieving that it's not hard to tell this knowledge is new to her, and it shakes her very soul. "It wasn't an accident, James. Dad didn't kill her. She figured out what Hamlin was doing with the arms deals, how he was misappropriating government funds with the help of some insiders, and he killed her. She didn't fall asleep behind the wheel. Hamlin ran her off the road."

"Faye. I'm sorry."

She shakes her head fiercely. "He tried to kill you, too. That's where you're wrong. It wasn't my Dad, never. He got in bed with Hook, trying to find revenge, but he got in too deep. He's...he's done things. Things I don't even know if I can ever forgive. Things I don't know if *he* can ever forgive himself for." Her lips tremble, then tighten, and she glares like she can intimidate me into believing her. "But he didn't arrange your plane crash. I know he didn't. It's not his fault your friend died."

My raging, snarling instinct is to deny it. Tell her how fucking wrong she is.

Christ. I've been carrying this grudge around like a lit torch for five long years, the flame of my anger keeping alive, my rage and my hatred for one man.

Yeah, those emotions were the only things I could feel forever. The only things that reminded me I was still alive, not a ghost.

And now, to be told it's been misdirected all this time...

I don't know if it's my own self-denial that makes me hate to believe it, or my cynicism.

What if Senator Harris is lying again? Anything to stay in his daughter's good graces?

I shake my head. It's all I can give her.

"I don't know," I say. "Damn it, I –"

"*Don't*," she hisses. "Don't, James. Don't make this worse. Don't tell me it's not true. I haven't had a father for years. And now I finally get why. I saw *him* again tonight, the real man. Not this obsessed monster I've been living with forever." She swallows hard. Tears form in her eyes, gather on her lashes, and freeze into tiny glittering ice crystals. "I know what he said. I know what I believe. You can believe what you want to, but I can't fight you over this."

I don't know what the hell to say.

I'm still skeptical – but I also *trust* her.

I've *always* trusted her, and while we're all victims of our own biases, Faye is no fool.

Even this upset, she's smart enough to separate her feelings about her father from the facts.

The question is...am I?

I don't have time to wonder right now. Not when voices drift in from the open window behind us, and I stiffen, shifting into a low crouch, positioning myself between her and the wall of the lodge.

She feels it too. Without being told, she scrambles over and douses the lantern, breathlessly clutching at it like some kind of safety object, watching me with wide eyes.

I look up at the window, watching for someone to move toward it and spot us, but it's only voices retreating.

Until I hear the closest door to the lodge open.

I rise quickly, offering her my hand. "We have to go. Now."

She takes my hand and pulls herself up. "They're looking for you. Hamlin's telling everyone you went rogue and did something awful, but he won't say what."

"Because he knows it won't hold water if he tries to convince any of my team. Landon won't come down on me without a fair trial. The only recourse is to turn it into something top secret and leave them guessing and working with him to find me so they can get some answers."

I grip her hand tightly, glancing over my shoulder, then turn to lead her around the other side of the lodge, forging through the snow. Using my body to break the packed ground cover and make a path, while also shielding her from the blowing sheets of white.

We've got maybe ten more minutes out in this cold before we have to worry, but I don't intend to take that long. I need to get her somewhere safe.

I've already lost everything.

I'm damn sure not losing her again.

And once we're somewhere out of danger, we're going to sort this out – and I'm going to figure out what to do about this mess.

And about the feelings I can't deny.

After all, my first instinct the moment I knew I was compromised was one thing, crystal clear.

Find Faye.

Take her away from this horrible place.

Always keep her with me.

* * *

FAYE DOESN'T protest when I lift her up in my arms.

We've reached the far back corner of the lodge. She's shivering deeper and deeper now, and I'm worried not even my coat will help her for long.

Just a few minutes longer. That's all we need.

I lean around the lodge's wall, peering through the blinding curtain of snow toward the faint dark shapes I can barely make out farther away.

Pershing men. They're moving away from the building in tight formation, fanning out as they go.

Bastard fucker. Hamlin must be real worried, if he'll risk his men's lives in this to come after me.

He's either scared or all too aware that I know exactly what I'm doing, and he can't just leave the storm to finish me off.

The moment I'm sure the snow gives enough cover so we won't be seen, I clutch Faye closer and dash toward the side lot between the lodge and several cabins. One of the reinforced SUVs is parked there, a snowplow fixed to its fender, tires wrapped in chains.

Perfection.

I set Faye down next to the driver's side door, fishing in my pocket until I come up with a small spool of wire. It's an old habit to always keep certain little things on me so I can MacGyver situations if I need to.

That wire makes it easy to slip the lock on the SUV when I unspool a stiff length of it, make a hook out of the tip, and slip it down the window well to hook the lock.

"Can you still hot-wire a car?" I ask, as I swing the driver's door open, glancing over my shoulder nervously as the interior lights come on, making a beacon out of us in the dark.

"Please," she scoffs, ducking under my arm, squeezing between me and the car door to squirm under the steering wheel, already ripping at the plastic casing and digging at wires inside. "Thirty seconds!"

"You have fifteen."

"I'll be done in ten."

She's done in eight.

I'm just slinging my duffel bag down from my back to stuff it in the back seat when the SUV comes on with a loud grumble. She makes a triumphant sound and wriggles out. "Told ya. Who's driving?"

"I am. Get in, Faye, they'll have heard the noise."

I can already hear the shouts.

Then there's lights bobbing toward us, the dark, distant figures growing more solid. She tosses a wide-eyed look over her shoulder before scrambling in through the driver's side to reach the passenger seat. I dive in after her, slam the door shut, check the fuel gauges, and then fix my gaze on the rear-view mirror before backing the SUV out of its slot.

Right into a snowbank, sending white plumes up in sprays.

Real smooth, I think to myself with a snarl.

Faye eyes me, smirking. "Drive much?"

"Save your impertinence, please," I say flatly.

But I'm almost smiling.

Because Faye flushed with adrenaline and excitement, saw me relying on skill and instinct to get us out of a tricky situation.

Just like old times. *Almost.*

When we were partners, near-lovers, instead of just lost, bitter memories.

I flick the heater on to flood the car with warmth, then shift gears and grind the engine. The chains on the tires churn, digging down through the snow to find traction.

A second later, we're chugging forward, cutting a tight arc in the lot and surging toward the subtle dip in the endless plains of snow that mark the road. I catch one glimpse of Hook Hamlin himself, bundled up to his eyes.

But those eyes are cold and dark and certain, before they vanish behind the wall of white that surges up on either side of us, burying our pursuers as we blaze past.

Perhaps *blaze* is an exaggeration.

We're doing thirty miles per hour tops, but we're still moving faster than men on foot can manage in this onslaught, and that's what matters.

By the time they get to any of the other few vehicles that might be able to manage this storm without stalling out after five feet, we'll be too far away for them to ferret us out.

The snow is coming down hard enough, fast enough, to bury our tracks as quickly as we make them.

Good for concealment.

Bad for safety. Because if we stall out halfway down the mountain, we'll end up buried in snow and rapidly running out of what little air is trapped in the vehicle with us.

I check the rear-view mirror. No sign of pursuit, and the SUV is holding up.

Faye has her gloves off, and she's holding her hands in front of the heater vents with a blissful expression on her face, teeth chattering.

"My bag," I murmur. "There's a hot thermos of tea and a map."

She flashes me a quick smile, the tension and animosity left behind for the moment, eclipsed by the synchronicity when we found our connection again. Then she's twisting into the back seat to drag my bag into the front and across her lap.

Last, she retrieves my thermos and takes a deep sip, before gasping and wiping at her mouth. "*Blech!* This stuff *burns.*"

"It's meant for sipping, Tink. Not guzzling."

"Yeah? Should've told me that before I scorched my tastebuds off." She drops the thermos in the cup holder between us and fishes out the folding brochure map I'd grabbed from the reception station, then spreads it out carefully against the dash on her side. "So...where are we going?"

"Away," I say grimly. "Unfortunately, every escape route I'd plotted earlier is now null due to the storm. Right now, my only interest is finding a safe way down this mountain and to clear highways out of this blizzard, before we get back to civilization and contact the authorities."

She smiles faintly. "Old friends at the FBI?"

"It pays to have connections."

She digs in her pocket and fishes out her phone – then frowns. "Weird. My phone's got 4G again. No bars, though. I can get internet, but not make a call."

"Weird is right. More like...fascinating that technology starts working when we're away from Hamlin and his crew."

She stares at me. "Holy hell. You think he was jamming wireless signals?"

"With him, anything is possible. I bugged your father's laptop, and yet I barely had a chance to get a quick data dump before the internet crashed, even before the power went out. Both the landline and the wireless were out like lights."

Faye frowns. "But couldn't that just be the storm disrupting things?"

"Could be, but doubtful. The storm would be less likely to impact buried cables," I say. "Or it could be a convenient excuse to keep people from questioning."

She goes pale. "So Hamlin has...he's basically got everyone *hostage* there with no way to call for help? Including my father."

"Exactly," I say grimly.

She takes a shaky breath, then diverts her gaze back to the map. "Drive faster," she says, tapping into her phone and looking between the map on screen and the map on the page. "I'll find us a clear route from local ranger reports."

It's Faye who navigates us down the mountain using the map, her phone, and the dashboard satellite GPS – why doesn't this thing have OnStar? – one grueling stop-and-start mile at a time, pushing through heaps of snow.

We force a trail that fills in behind us almost immediately, until it feels more like driving through water than snow, flowing to fill the lowest space.

During a few slower stretches, I try calling Landon on my cell, but this time it really *is* the storm and not any suspicious business blocking the signal. I can't get 9-11, either.

But we're not even halfway to the main highway when we run into another obstacle that's not on the real-time danger maps updated by the local ranger stations, and that we can't drive around.

A narrow rock passage, cliffs and forest high on both sides, and an *avalanche* piled in the middle of the road. So big it fills the miniature canyon from wall to wall.

Fucking great.

It's taller than the SUV, packed gravel and snow and boulders, and there's no good way we can plow through it. I have a brief thought of shoveling it out, but this time I don't have the right tools. And we'd damn near freeze to death trying to literally move mountains.

I slam my hand against the steering wheel, closing my eyes and swearing.

"We can back up," Faye whispers. "I think...there was a turn-off on a smaller feeder road about half a mile back. I ignored it as I thought bigger roads would be clearer, but there might still be a way around."

I shake my head. "No. We're too low on fuel. I don't trust it."

"What other options do we have?"

"Finding somewhere safe to shelter." I brace an arm on the passenger seat and twist to look behind me, at the blank white canvas where a road should be. Then with a snarl, I jack the SUV into reverse. "Even if we have to stay in the car, we'll be better off down that feeder road, finding somewhere sheltered from the wind and any future avalanches. If we can even find a good stable rock face, maybe we can avoid being buried in snow dunes and wait the storm out."

Faye looks troubled, folding her arms over her chest and shivering. "Won't we run the battery down trying to stay warm?"

"There's a recharge and jumpstart kit in my bag."

She lifts a brow. "Really. And food?"

"Look in the back."

"No freaking way. You didn't stock the car...did you? You couldn't have. You didn't plan for this."

I don't say anything. I just wait for her to twist around to squeeze between the passenger and driver's seat, craning around to look over the back, into the storage area.

She swears, then plunks back down in her seat and glares at me.

"*How?* You are not really James Bond. You don't get to pull crap like that. There's like...six cases of water and a ton of soup packets and stuff back there. Blankets. What the fuck, James?"

I hold back my smirk. "We used the SUVs to bring in supplies from the cabins before the snow got too bad. Not everything was brought inside."

Faye lets out an exasperated sigh. "Don't look so smug, then. This isn't your super-secret agent planning. It's just a happy accident."

"Operative word being 'happy,'" I say, then shift the SUV back into drive as I manage to get it turned back around and pointed the way we came.

It's another grueling ten minutes until I catch the faint green flash of the half-buried road sign for the turnoff in the headlights. I manage to grind the SUV down a narrow road that I can only make out by the trees lining it.

The going is steeper, slower, and I'm worried about the snow tires losing traction. Faye stays tense and quiet in the passenger seat, watching her phone intently, only to look out the window as if she's checking for familiar landmarks.

"It says there's a ranger's station somewhere here," she murmurs. "But I don't see it."

I glance at her sidelong, keeping my eyes on the road. "Is that why you wanted to go this way?"

"You're not the only planner. Even if the power and signal's down at the lodge, the ranger station's got to be working, right? Assuming it's still manned." She bites her lip. "I hope there's someone there."

"As do I."

Then I see it – tucked between the trees a little ways off the road, a break in the guardrail hinting there might be a driveway under the snow. For a moment, hope flares.

Until I really process what I'm seeing, and my stomach sinks.

There'll be no one at this ranger station. No power, no signal, no help, no anything.

It's abandoned, one wall collapsing inward, the roof sagging under the weight of the snow and accumulated debris piled on top. Possibly years' worth of pine needles and bark and other seasonal flotsam.

Hell, I wouldn't be surprised if the roof is completely rotted through. I bring the SUV to a halt. It's eerily silent, the car cutting the sound of the wind until it's just us, the headlamps, and the sense of rising dismay building between us.

"Crap," she says.

I nod.

"What now? I mean, it's a mess. Can we use this?"

I sigh. "It's possible. We might be able to make it airtight, or at least steal one of the rooms away from the collapsed room and seal it off."

"Ugh. Wouldn't we be better off staying in the car?"

"I don't think so. The jumpstart kit is a contingency, not a survival plan. We don't want to have to rely on it only for it to let us down. We're better off leaving the car for our getaway and burrowing down here to wait out the storm until morning."

She grimaces. "It looks *terrible*."

"I know," I say, reaching back for my bag. "But we've had worse. Remember some of the hotels in D.C.? The FBI's dime didn't exactly buy glamorous. We'll make do here, and in the morning, we'll reassess."

She says nothing, but she's already bundling up, climbing into the back to start sorting through everything to bring with us. I didn't even have to ask.

It's just how we work.

When we're together, we always know what we need to do without being told, this quiet understanding that makes us a single machine working together.

It's something.

Even if tonight is hell, we'll at least have shelter away from Hamlin and his schemes.

We'll have each other.

XVII: IT ACHES LIKE WINTER (FAYE)

This was supposed to be a relaxing resort getaway, despite the irritation of playing Dad's photogenic little doll and pandering to his constituents.

Instead, I've been trapped in a cabin with my ex-lover, caught fingering myself thinking about him, been slammed up against the wall and fingered *by* him, only to almost die in the snow, get rescued *twice*, discover my father's a double agent who's gone too dark, find out Hook Hamlin killed my mother and is trying to kill again, and run away with the very same ex-lover to get stuck in the most dangerous blizzard I've ever seen, leaving us camping outside in a dilapidated ranger station that's only fit for squirrels.

Lordy.

I'm pretty sure there's a dozen squirrels hibernating in the rafters, along with a few other little creatures – but the fact that they feel safe and warm and sheltered here is actually a pretty good sign.

The station isn't as bad as it seems from the outside.

Mainly because it's separated into five rooms – a front lobby, a commons room, a bedroom with bunks, a kitchen, and a bathroom. Wonder of wonders, there's running water in the kitchen and bathroom, though we can't get any power to the appliances.

I don't trust the gas stove not to explode if we try to turn it on – though it may be a last resort if we end up getting too cold. The front lobby and commons room are open to the elements, filled with snow and debris, the right wall caved in.

Luckily, the kitchen, bathroom, and bedroom are on the left side with their own shielding walls. One window in the bedroom is cracked. Sure it's a little drafty, but when I ball up a blanket and stuff it in the broken pane, the place turns downright cozy.

Okay. Maybe not *quite* cozy.

But we're less likely to freeze to death in here, and we can actually build a fire.

Though any hope of sleeping in a bed is doused by the fact that the only wood we have to burn right now is the furniture. That includes the frames of the bunk bed, which are so dry-rotted they'd have broken under us anyway.

That also means they're so dry-rotted they'll burn too fast if we're not careful.

James and I exchange worried, tired glances as we finish piling up the debris of everything we've broken down against the bedroom wall.

It's not looking good.

"Do you think it'll last all night?" I ask.

"If we're strategic about it," he says. "The chair seats are dense hardwood and haven't degraded nearly as much as the other pieces. We can scrape one out to get it going and put the other wood inside it to burn. The seat itself will eventually catch and hold a flame longer."

"So we won't die."

"Possibly."

"I'd like a yes, James."

He lifts his head from studying the pile of wood, that intense concentration on his face clearing as he looks at me solemnly, intently, then says firmly, "I won't let anything happen to you, Faye."

I can't help how my heart skips – with warmth, with longing.

But also with fear. Because I know far too well the extremes James goes to in order to protect someone close, and I can't stand the idea of him hurting himself for me.

I don't say anything.

I'm exhausted, hungry, cranky, tense, and frankly, I think I'm going to need a month of therapy once this entire clusterfuck is over. Honestly, I just want to eat, sleep, and hope things look more hopeful in the morning, especially since I'm worried what Hook might do to my father.

All I want is to get the police and FBI up there to sort everything out.

James and I set to work quickly. The heat we'd absorbed in the car is already dissipating, the cold creeping in, and the sooner we get a fire going, the better.

We pull the old mattresses from the broken-down bunks into the least drafty corner, sheltered against the interior wall, and cover them over with many of the blankets we'd brought from the car to create a single large pallet.

An old cookie sheet from the kitchen becomes our hearth, keeping us from setting the floor ablaze as we build our fire on top of it. James uses a kitchen knife to hack out a little hollow in a wooden chair seat, then uses the chips he cut out to start a crackling fire.

It's small at first, but even that bit of heat makes me feel better, loosening my frozen limbs and making it easier to work as I scavenge in the kitchen. Soon I'm rigging up a little camp stove using the racks from inside the oven and a few inverted pots.

James keeps feeding more wood into the fire until it's roaring, then frowns and gets up, turning his head slowly, looking around.

I tense, instantly alert. "What is it? What's wrong?"

"Nothing," he murmurs. "I just think we could do a better job conserving heat."

The next time I look back, he's gone. I catch a gust of wind, the creak of the front door, and I realize he's outside again.

That *idiot*.

I pick myself up from sitting on the edge of the pallet – which is actually pretty comfy, four twin mattresses stacked two side by side and two on top – and push to the window.

I can barely see James in the snow, but he's trudging toward the vehicle, not even a lantern in his hand. He's quick, though, opening the back of the SUV and rummaging inside, then gathering up an armful of something before turning and quickly heading back, head down.

The instant he's back inside, shutting the bedroom door to close off the wind whistling in from the front, I fling myself against him and smack his shoulder.

"*Stupid*," I growl, glaring. "You didn't even have a guide rope!"

He lifts both brows mildly. "It was less than a dozen feet to the car."

"People have gone off course and *died* traveling five feet in storms like this." And my heart races at the thought, fear hot inside me, far more shrill and tense than it should be.

But this is *James freaking Nobel* and he flays my emotions too raw.

I rub at my aching throat, looking away, looking down at the bundle in his arms. "What is that, anyway?"

"A little more insulation." He shakes the bundle out,

revealing several nylon emergency tarps and multiple hook-ended bungee cords. I frown, shaking my head.

"What are you going to do with those?"

"Give me a minute, and you'll see."

I stand back, feeling a touch helpless, but also grateful to stop clawing for survival and let someone else do things for a bit when I'm so *tired*.

I still don't get what James is doing when he uses the hooks in the bungee cords to stretch a sort of latticework around the mattress and the fire. Not until he drapes the tarps over them.

Suddenly, it's a tent, another layer locking out the cold and trapping in the heat. I can't help laughing a little when it reminds me of building forts out of sheets and couch cushions as a little girl, then crawling inside with my friends to tell secrets over flashlights and big bowls of popcorn.

That image hardens as James sets the lit lantern inside, its cool radiance mixing with the warm flicker of the fire to make our little tent glow. He pulls one flap aside, then sweeps a near-mocking bow.

"Right this way, love," he teases, "your chamber awaits."

"Lame." I roll my eyes, but laugh anyway, ducking to crawl inside. Then I tuck myself into a corner to start rummaging through the water bottles, supplies, and dishes I'd scavenged. "It's not the Hilton but...it's actually pretty nice for a cold night."

James settles down next to me, draping his elbows on his knees and looking into the fire. He's quiet, firelight reflecting in his eyes to turn them from silver-blue into flame, gilding all his gorgeous edges.

"Will you be all right sharing the bed with me?" he asks softly. "We should try to conserve body heat so the fire won't have to work so hard."

O-oh. *Oh.*

I shouldn't feel this hot, nervous flush snap through me.

It's hardly a setup for sexy time.

We're in mortal peril, camped out in a squirrel shack, relying on a little bonfire and a few tarps to keep us alive...and I'm a grown-ass woman who used to know what it felt like to fall asleep next to this man with our bodies tangled and naked and slick.

I'm no blushing virgin. He made sure of that. And I'm no stranger to the feel of his muscles, his hips, his tongue.

But maybe that's why everything in me is so twisted and tight and breathless.

Because I have to lie here, fully clothed, cradled against him, remembering how it feels to have his touch over every inch of my flesh while he's only holding me for warmth.

"I'll be fine," I manage faintly, focusing my attention on stirring the bubbling pot of chicken noodle soup filling our little tent space with its aroma.

I glance at the other pot of water I've started boiling for tea. Anything to get heat in us, even with the tent helping insulate, it's still *freezing* outside our little fire. But I can't look at James as I smile and say, "I'm a big girl. I've seen boy parts before."

"Have you?" he asks tightly, and I can feel the stiffness and tension radiating off him. I steal a glance at him sidelong, but he's glaring into the fire, his mouth tight.

"Yours," I clarify, even if the word feels like a lump in my throat, and his expression goes so deliberately blank I want to shake him.

I suppose the only thing worse than imagining another man's hands on me is remembering when they were his.

"So." I clear my throat, changing the subject as I ladle out a paper cup full of soup and another of tea for him, then for myself. "What's the game plan?"

"For once, I didn't think that far ahead, Tink," he says

with a touch of grim self-deprecation. "My main goal was getting you out of there. Safety first."

"Yeah," I answer faintly. "But my Dad's still back there with Hamlin. We have no idea what's going on. And this isn't exactly safe."

"Faye..." I can already tell before he says it that I won't like what he has to say. "I understand your concern for your father. And I'd like to see him extracted from this situation as well, especially if what you've said is true –"

"It *is!*"

He raises a hand. "I'm not arguing. Just speculating on possibilities. The point is, we can do more away from the lodge than we can trapped with them and equally vulnerable. In the morning, we'll get down the mountain, make contact with the FBI – and not even this hell-storm will stop specialized sweeper teams in military helicopters. They'll put an end to this and make sure everyone goes home."

I bite my lip, sipping at my soup.

It burns, but right now I'm so hungry and cold that the reconstituted freeze-dried noodles and chicken bits and thick, chunky broth are the best things I've ever tasted. "And you?" I ask softly. "What about you, after this?"

He pauses, staring into the fire over his tea, barely touching it. "I don't know," he admits. "I disappeared once. Started over. Depending on how my team at Enguard responds to the news of my past, and the secrets I've kept from them regarding Hamlin, I may need to do it again. This might not be over and done for a good, long while."

"They're your friends, James," I point out. "Do you really think they'll reject you?"

"Are they? Will they be after they hear –"

"I think they are." I smile faintly. "You should hear them when they talk about you. They know all your grumpy, broody habits. Hell, they adore you for them."

NICOLE SNOW

"What they 'adore' is surface only," he says flatly. "The man they *think* I am."

"If you say so." I shrug.

God, he's so stubborn.

I can't help feeling the same fondness that the Enguard crew display when they talk about James being *exactly like this*. He's such an idiot, and I love him for it. "Hey, if you go...if you disappear...please take me with you?"

I don't realize what I'm saying until it's out. It wasn't even scary when the words first came, but now that they're hanging in the air between us, they feel downright terrifying, my heart thumping.

James frowns, glancing at me.

"It's not safe around me, Faye."

"You're wrong. After this, *especially* if Hamlin gets away – God forbid – it might not be safe for me anywhere *but* with you." I bite my lip. "Stop pushing me away, will you? Do you even know how bad I wanted to go with the night you got on that plane, James?"

"Do you know what would've happened if I hadn't refused?" he flares, cold eyes going hot, crackling.

I do.

I might be dead.

And even knowing what I do now, it doesn't change my mind.

I look at him, my throat tight. "You can't spend your entire life living in fear of what-ifs. And you can't keep pushing people away for those what-ifs, either."

He just looks at me, something naked and harsh and scared on his face. I don't understand that fear, not when I've never seen James Nobel so afraid in my life.

Until I realize what he's afraid of.

It's hurting *me*.

I realize he's not going to say anything. Not one damn

word one way or the other, so I do the only thing I know how.

I shift over closer to him, tuck my legs up against my side, leaning against him and resting my head on his shoulder.

Sometimes, when words are hard, warmth will do better.

Sometimes it's easier to share the depths of a soul through touch.

And he lets me, this once.

He lets me lean on him, and subtly leans back, giving me the quiet understanding that he's not shutting me out, not entirely.

He's just not quite there yet, and while he takes the time to get where he needs to be, I'll wait. Just like this.

It's okay to be close.

We stay like this for a while, both of us nursing our soup and tea, until it's almost gone.

James moves to feed a few more heavier bits of wood into the fire until it's burning stronger and not chewing through the softer decayed bits as fast. Wow, between our shared body heat and the insulation of the makeshift walls, it's almost downright cozy in here.

My eyes are starting to droop. I've hardly slept since we came to the resort, and since then, it's been a whirlwind of stress and upset and near-death experiences and medical emergencies.

I'm exhausted, and there's nowhere I'd rather fall asleep than tucked up against him like this.

But then in the silence, out of nowhere, he suddenly murmurs something that stops my heart. "I'm trying to finish my mother's book."

I stir with a drowsy sound, realizing I'd drifted off still clutching my near-empty tea cup to me like a squirrel with a particularly fascinating nut. I blink sleepily, trying to process what he just said, while I drink down the last of the cooling tea before it loses its warmth. Yawning, I rest my head back on his shoulder, nuzzling in.

"Her book?"

"She was writing a romance novel when she died. It's a long book, basically finished, everything except the ending."

He says it so coolly, so flatly.

That right there's a dead giveaway that he's trying not to let the words hurt him, like razors on his tongue.

I lift my head again, coming fully awake, watching how the firelight paints those stern features in soft colors that smooth them out and make them less harsh, less forbidding, even if the light can't wash away the pain lingering in those reflective silver-blue eyes.

Curling my hand against his arm, I lean in close, as if I can somehow offer warmth and comfort with my body heat.

"I never got the chance to tell you I'm sorry. For the way you lost her."

His jaw tightens, the handsome lines on his face straining. "No need. I don't think I deserve *sorry*. It's my own fault, Faye."

"No, James! No, it isn't."

His fists clench, arms braced against his knees. "I wasn't *there*."

"And that isn't your fault either." I push myself up to fully face him, setting my empty cup aside so I can touch his cheek.

He flinches, but then lets me stroke his skin, the first hints of stubble marring his perfect smoothness under my fingertips, like a great beast reluctantly accepting a taming hand. He stares at me, waiting for the words at the tip of my tongue.

"James, neither was her disease. Cancer isn't your fault. It's not anyone's fault. It's cruel and unpredictable and it just *happens*. You can't blame yourself." I smile sadly. "But I know it won't stop you. Blaming yourself is what you do. I just wish sometimes you'd stop."

"Faye..." My name comes out ragged, hoarse on his lips, and he closes his eyes as he presses his cheek into my palm.

"Hush. Come here." I can't help myself. My heart is bleeding out of me in an invisible, molten pool, every bit of it pulled by this beautiful, damaged man.

I curl my hand against the back of his neck, tugging, drawing him in.

He's hesitant, but then lets me coax him down to lean against me, resting his head to my shoulder. "It's okay," I whisper as I slip my arms around his shoulders, curling my hands against his back, and taking the fullness of his weight leaning so heavily into me. "It's okay. Is that why you're trying to finish her novel? To atone somehow?"

"I don't know." His voice is muffled, his face hidden against my shoulder, his breaths warm even through the layers of clothing shrouding me. "I didn't even want to know, at first. But fuck, Grandpa insisted it *had* to be me. I have to play goddamn Nicholas Sparks with a romance novel I don't know the first thing about."

"Tell me about it," I whisper, reaching for his hand. His fingers come around mine, clenching like we're on course for the end of the world.

Oh, James.

"It's about what you'd expect. This ridiculous flight of fancy." He sounds both bitter and amused...and totally freaking lost. "A small town hero and heroine. Set in some place called Heart's Edge. The hero loved the heroine her entire life, but he made a mistake, betrayed her trust when they were teenagers. They're older and have put it behind them, but she says she won't date him because of what he did. He asks if there's anything he can do to convince her, to win her back. She says maybe if he writes her a thousand love notes."

I chuckle, gently playing my fingertips through the soft hair at the nape of James' neck. "That sounds sweet. But kinda difficult."

"I suppose her aim is to discourage him. Of course, he doesn't go down without a fight. He begins finding more and more creative ways to leave her notes. She finds them everywhere – pinned to her front door, written on her lawn in flowers, drawn across the sky in smoke. He even enlists the townsfolk, who bring her notes when they're paying at the register where she works."

"So instead of giving up, he sets out to prove she's worth the effort? And he's willing to do it?" I can't help smiling. "Sounds a lot more romantic than my strategy. Remember Quantico? Pelting you with balls of notebook paper until you finally paid attention?"

Whatever I expect, it's not his strong arms slowly creeping around my waist, wrapping around me as tentatively as if asking for permission. It makes something click inside me.

Something that feels like coming home.

Something that soothes all the hurts of the past few days in ways I need so desperately.

Something like – *oh, God.*

Love.

I swear my eyes aren't burning as I lean into him, taking that vast embrace for as long as it lasts.

But it's hard to breathe right now, and my chest is so very tight.

"It worked, didn't it?" he whispers hoarsely.

"Yeah." It comes out thickly, my throat knotted, and I curl forward, resting my brow to the top of his head. "What happened to us, James?"

"I did." It's hurt, condemning, entirely directed at himself. "I happened to us, Faye. I ruined us."

"Not ruined!" I shake my head fiercely. "Just...cut off. Delayed, maybe. You shut me out so much, James, and I didn't even have any warning. You put me out in the cold and left me to freeze."

"I'm sorry." His shoulders are shaking. "So fucking *sorry.*"

Three simple words shouldn't mean so much, but it's the *way* he says them.

Hard, cold, slick James Nobel, the icy, detached agent, fully calm and in control...it's not him.

This man's voice is breaking. Ragged. Rough with emotion, fervent and raw.

So real no one on earth could mistake what he means.

Wow.

Sometimes, *I'm sorry* isn't shit if the other person doesn't mean it.

But sometimes it's everything, when they rip open and bare their heart and soul to say it.

"James, I...I..."

I want to say it. I want to say *I still love you.* I want to ask *can we start over? Do we have a chance?*

But I'm more afraid than I've ever been in my life.

Because I know this prickly, stubborn, stupid, overly noble man far too well, and I know just how far he'll push me away because he thinks it's for my own good.

I can't stand to let him break my heart.

Not for a second time.

This time, it might just break for good.

There's a silence between us, before he takes a shaky breath and pulls back, looking down at me. His eyes are red-rimmed but dry, pale silver searching me, as if looking for something – but I don't know what.

It makes my heart turn over, when those eyes aren't closed, aren't cold, aren't shielded and walled off.

They're just *wondering*.

And as afraid as I feel. Like he's just as worried that I'll crush him and say *no, we can't do this again.*

"I need to show you something," he whispers, twisting away from me to retrieve his duffel bag from the foot of the pallet, dragging it up to rest at his hip. "I'm not even sure why I brought this with me. I suppose it seemed appropriate, when I knew I'd be seeing you."

He unzips the bag. Inside, everything is so militantly folded into perfect squares, but past the clothing and a disturbing array of weapons and tactical supplies is a small, worn wooden box.

It's plain, unvarnished, clearly old – and obviously it's been handled a lot. It's got that certain weathering to it that only comes to wood that's been held and opened and cradled by loving hands again and again. It closes with a simple little swinging bronze latch, and he flips the latch open before offering the box to me without a word.

Confused, I take the box. It's as warm as skin, as if it's been absorbing the heat from the fire.

With a glance at him for permission, I lift the lid delicately.

The entire box is filled with...bits of paper?

All of them beginning to take on that slight faded softness of age.

Yellow slips of folded paper from mini legal pads. Scraps from a notebook, torn off and crumpled, then smoothed out again. Folded up entire sheaves of note paper, and printer paper.

I catch glimpses of handwriting on them, but there are so many pages layered on top of each other. I can't make out the words overlapping. But when I finally realize what it is, my heart stops mid-beat.

Wait. Holy hell.

That's my handwriting.

On every last paper.

I stare into the box and have to clutch it tighter when my fingers begin trembling and my breaths come short, my entire body lit up. "What...what is this, James?" I whisper, darting a nervous glance up at him.

He's watching me so strangely.

I've never seen James Nobel look fragile. He's bold, courageous, powerful, and handsome to his core.

But if he ever has, it's right now, when he looks at me with that odd mixture of open vulnerability, naked longing, and careful withdrawal, as if holding his hand out for a wild thing, ready to pull back if he's bitten. He takes a slow breath, then says the unbelievable.

"Every last note you've ever written me." The words are husky, soft, as if he truly cherishes each one. "Even the ones that fell down the back of my shirt in training."

Oh. My. God.

Wonder rolls through me.

Wonder, and a flush of heat, of shock, of sweetness, of *love*.

I can't stop smiling, but I feel like I'm going to cry, too, as I pick up one after the other.

Made you look. :P one says.

And *Hey hey guess what crankyface? I'm thinkin' 'bout you.*

I want to laugh at my younger self because she was so stupidly, beautifully in love.

P.F. Chang's in the fridge. Don't forget to eat and *I cleaned your Ruger, you owe me* and *I hope you know the more you scowl, the more I like you.*

Yeah.

That girl was in love. So in love.

But so am I.

And it chokes in my throat as I let the box fall, old notes, old memories spilling everywhere as I fling myself at him with a whisper of, *"James."*

We tumble back together, half-mad with emotion.

The heat of the fire becomes the heat of the moment.

Pure sugary combustion between us in a wildfire kiss.

There's no hesitation as our lips lock together and James Nobel storms over me.

All the heat and passion I've missed. The man I'd remembered rising from the ashes of the icy rock he'd become to wrap me up in his arms and hold me tight. *So tight.*

I'm only on top of him for a couple seconds before he's tumbling me back, pinning me beneath his heat, his weight, his muscle and his smile.

Yes, he's smiling.

He's finally flipping smiling.

Then the smile fades, replaced by something feral, the same bright spark in his silver-blue eyes.

He pushes himself up with one last scorching kiss, one bite to my lower lip that's like a trigger, turning my whole body electric. My nipples press against his chest, pulsing.

Racing the hot, wet throb between my legs for attention.

Holy, holy hell.

Before I can even blink, he's not touching me anymore.

Now he's looking down at me with that keen, searching stare I know too well, making the trembling start in the pit of my stomach.

When I know he's looking at me the way a hunter looks at his prey, searching for the most vulnerable places to make me scream.

I'm already keyed up so tight just from missing him, wanting him, aching for him for so long...but as those razor-sharp eyes slide over my body, touching me like a raw, cold edge tracing over my skin and leaving goosebumps, I press my thighs together. I beg for sweet mercy with my eyes.

I bite my lip on a sound when I can feel my heart pounding, sense how bad I want it in the fireball building in my belly. It's already rising hot inside me, tickling my pussy like no tomorrow.

"Fuck, Tink. You need this bad, don't you?"

Haven't I always?

He hasn't even touched me save for one kiss, and I'm already ready to explode, my breaths coming shallower and shallower. My heart beats louder and louder the longer he just *looks* at me in the building silence.

I don't need the fire to keep me warm.

One look, heavy with almost sinister intent, has me so hot I could set the walls on fire.

And when he pushes my jacket open and grazes his fingertips along the hem of my shirt, just barely touching naked skin underneath, I suck my stomach in with a gasp as the touch of rough fingers sends shivers throughout my entire body.

He makes me feel so vulnerable.

So helpless, with the way he can take control of the sizzling air between us with a single look. Any other time, being helpless would piss me off. I don't like being at anyone else's mercy.

But there's something about James.

Something that makes me want to arch my neck and bare my throat to this beast-man's teeth.

And as he slips his hand under my shirt, pressing his broad, weathered palm to my skin, I feel so completely captured. So in thrall.

With just one hand he holds me motionless, and I watch

him with my lips parted and my eyes wide as he slowly strokes his way up over my stomach, my ribs.

I feel like he's shaping me with his touch. Burning, branding me, the skin where his heated palm passes forever changed, every nerve fine-tuned to his frequency.

God. I'm as responsive to his touch as his piano keys and their quivering strings.

I suck my lip harder as his fingertips skim beneath my breasts, just barely hooking on the thin strap of lace joining the cups of my bra. My tongue catches between my teeth, silencing a soft whimper.

James stops, watching me with an arched brow, cocking his head. "Something you want to say, Faye? Something you want to tell me before we go *hard?*" he asks softly, his rough voice stroking over me with seductive menace.

I shake my head quickly. *Oh, no. Not today.*

I know him too well.

I know if I plead, if I beg, if I snap, if I demand, he'll just make me suffer more. But he only smiles slowly, shifting his body to nudge his knee between my legs, settling to kneel between them and keeping me spread open by his sheer bulk alone. My thighs already ache, and the tension in the muscles pulls deep between my legs, making my breaths shallower.

The stretch and pull on my jeans rubs my panties up against my clit, making me feel like he's touching me when he's barely done a thing.

And his smile turns downright wicked as he tugs the strap of my bra just enough to make my breasts bounce, before hooking his finger underneath one cup of the bra and delicately tracing the edge of his nail along the sensitive underside of my breast.

"Are you sure about this silent treatment, Tink?" he nearly purrs. "Normally you'd be cursing me raw right now."

I shouldn't say anything.

The words on the tip of my tongue might scare him away, just after I've gotten him back, even if it might be only for tonight. But I can't lie, either.

Can't deny the trembling ache in my chest, the longing, the need, or the sweet insanity.

"Normally, I haven't been missing you for five years," I whisper.

He stops cold, just looking down at me.

Crap.

I brace for him to pull away, shut down, put that distance back between us. Shatter my heart all over again.

But there's something strange in his eyes as they dilate to near-black.

Something not cold, but burning-hot. He slips his hand from inside my shirt.

Then he leans down to kiss me.

So very deep.

So very wild.

So very *claiming.*

Sweet, sharp agony comes in the perfect crush of his lips on mine and the weight of his body pressing down. And I realize it might just be heaven in the chase of his tongue, the heat of his teeth on my lips, the fury in those quicksilver eyes.

I swear we're going to burst into flames as I wrap my arms around his neck and twine my fingers in his hair.

I rip at him, dragging my fingers tighter through his thick, blond hair, down the back of his neck and into his clothing, tearing at it as fiercely as he tears at mine.

As fiercely as he devours my mouth, kissing me so hard my lips ache, throb, pulsing and sensitized to every touch as we collide. We're dueling bites and lashing tongues, punishment in the form of pleasure, trading sting after sting of hungry, consuming, claiming kisses, dragging at each other's clothing wildly until bits fling everywhere, kicked off to the floor in our haste to tangle flesh on naked flesh.

Okay. So I'm dying.

Dying of hope, of love, of longing, when he's not pulling away from me.

He's not going anywhere. He's as desperate as me, his voice rising in low growling groans between us as he bites at my jaw, my throat, my shoulders, the upper curves of my breasts. Each bite blooms pure heat on my skin, marking patterns, making me feel like a human garden of little rosettes.

Just pain and pleasure and gently reddened flowers painted on my skin with teeth and tongue and soft, soothing kisses.

James strips me naked, but worse is that he leaves me bare. My heart, my soul, every part of me exposed to him, when all he has to do is graze his lips over the contour of my body to make me need him more than I need breath.

I'd never be this reactive, this responsive, for anyone else.

And when his mouth dips over the curve of my belly, licking along my inner thighs before it skirts around my aching, needy pussy...I tangle my fingers in his hair, press gently, lift myself up to him shamelessly, and beg, "James. James, *please!*"

His answer comes in a raw, bestial growl, closing his eyes as he leans up into my touch like a wild animal being stroked.

"Careful. Don't say my name that way," he grinds out through his teeth.

I don't understand, but something about the feral edge of hunger in his tone makes me shiver. "Wh-why?"

"Because." Glowing silver-blue eyes lock on me, hot with frantic need. "Because when you fucking do....I can't control myself, Tink. And I think you know it."

One more moment to tremble, pinned under his gaze.

Before he dips his head and shows me what it means to be utterly *consumed*.

His tongue is more than clever, more than fire.

It's devious, wicked, devilish, pure *torture*, and he finds every sensitive fold.

Every little aching bit of flesh, every secret crevice and he licks in long, dragging strokes with the roughly textured flat of his tongue. Only to counter with teasing flicks from the very tip, driving me *insane* with friction and denial and those sharp little shocks that make me see fireworks.

I buck my hips, twisting, but he catches my thighs, hooks them over his shoulders, and holds me trapped as he teases me open one long, probing caress at a time.

His tongue works in and out of me in a shock rhythm. I never know if he's going to slide deep with a slow, lingering taste, or dart in quickly, stinging me with a scorpion's barb of pleasure. Or if he's about to push up, take my tongue between his teeth, and bring me off so hard I scream.

I'm undone.

Fighting his grip, thrashing, dragging a handful of his hair, tossing my head back against the mat.

My blood roars so loud in my ears I can hardly hear my own breathy cries, but I can't hold them back either when he's ripping me apart, making me feel like I'm going to come out of my skin if he doesn't either let me come or let me come *down*.

I'm shaking. Clutching my thighs against his shoulders. Convulsing inside. The pleasure is so good it *hurts*, and as I feel it building up inside, I gasp, "*James!*"

And he stops.

The bastard *stops*.

But before I can curse him, call him every name in the book, he's surging up to meet me once more.

He's capturing my lips, and this time I taste myself on his kiss and it's heady, intoxicating.

Oh, hell. I'm so close to the edge, but I need more, need *him*, and I clutch at his hips, digging my fingers in, pulling him into me.

There's just a moment of skin sliding to skin, slick and wet and so very hot, deliciously intimate, as our bodies lock together and find all the perfect places where softness meets hardness and we're poised, trembling, his breaths heaving, the tension waiting to snap like a falling blade.

Then just the slightest arch of his hips, tightly controlled, shuddering, his head falling to rest against my breasts.

And he slips inside me like coming home, filling an emptiness that's been hounding him for five long years.

"Fuck!" he snarls, his voice raw. At last, the beast overwhelms the civilized man.

It's better than I remember.

So much more real, so much more passionate, when I can feel how much he missed me in every tremor rippling over his body, every moment when he starts to lose his prized control because I'm driving him as crazy as he's driving me.

Start and stop. Slow, deep strokes and then sharp, furious shudders of uncontrolled lust working hard and rough inside me, stirring me into a frenzy. I'm only soothed in every gliding movement of his body over mine. There's no rhythm, only a raging storm, crashing in cataclysm, and yet somehow, we find each other.

Somehow, we meet just right each time, as my flesh parts around him, grips him, molds against him like I can keep him deep inside me, always holding fast to that feeling when his cock licks at my insides with deep, relentless thrusts.

His mouth is everywhere, too.

Pulling at my breasts, sucking at my nipples, kissing over

my throat, searching past my lips, taking my tongue places I can't even describe.

I can't stop touching him, tracing every scar, every ripple of hardened muscle, memorizing him with my fingertips. He moves faster, arching over me, and every time he pierces into me, it's this perfect fire, making me toss my head and strain and dig my nails against his back.

Oh, shit! I can feel it coming, feel it like an inferno moving in a quickening wave with every thrust.

Just a little more.

Just a little more of that sweet, sweet pressure to make me lose it, but I fight it.

I fight it *so hard* when I want to hold and keep this moment forever.

But I can't.

I'm breaking.

I'm shattering.

I'm wrapped up in James, completely consumed, destroyed by the pleasure only he can give. My soul a storm of flame.

One only he can kindle, until I burn hotter and hotter for him, and him alone.

His breath hitches and his thrusts go manic. "Now, Tink. Now, fuck. Come for me. Come with me."

Oh.

His cock swells inside me and his head snaps back half a second before I'm in ecstasy. He's snarling and grunting and spilling himself in me, and yes, he's still fucking. Going so hard and deep it makes my eyes roll.

And when I come, locked around him, drawing him deep until he touches that perfect quivering place inside me that makes everything see stars...

I know there'll never be another man's name on my lips, ever again.

I need James Nobel like I need air.

And this time, I won't *ever* let him run away.

* * *

Oh, *God*, I needed that.

I feel like I've been pent up for years, only for someone to finally burst my bubble.

And that bubble became an explosion.

I'm still feeling it the morning after, when I'm waking up in James' arms with my body warm and my toes frozen and the tip of my nose buried against his chest, the bits of notepaper scattered around us like rose petals on a honeymoon bed.

I've managed to kick one foot outside the blankets, and the fire has died down to just embers, and if not for the lingering heat trapped inside the nylon tarps and insulated in our little space, I'd be saying goodbye to the toes on that foot.

With a drowsy mumble, I pull my foot back underneath the covers, snuggling deeper into James for warmth. He lets out a sleepy grunt – and I smile.

Damn. I'm so awkwardly head over heels all over again, but I can't help it when I've never seen him like this.

He's not doing the android thing now.

The on switch-off switch thing, where he's either fully charged or totally dead. He's sleepy, grumbling, mussed, *adorable*. And he's embracing me, dragging me in closer like he's trying to get me to hold still with the world's biggest bear hug.

I insinuate my frozen foot between his calves and burrow closer. We should probably get up, especially when this isn't exactly the best place for a love nest. Even with the blankets over them, the lumpy mattresses are weirdly noticeable.

But I don't want him to let me go.

I never want this to end.

I don't want reality to come rushing between us again, pushing us apart.

James twitches, though, opening one eye. The silver-blue hue is hazed to a soft, misty gray as he peers at me grouchily. "Your toes are *freezing*, Tink," he mutters sleepily.

"Well, we're kind of buried in a snowstorm," I tease, peeking up at him with a shy smile. "But you did a pretty good job of keeping every other part of me warm last night."

He comes more alert, looking down at me intently – and I hold my breath.

But not coldly. Thank God not coldly.

Just a sort of quiet regard, thoughtful and deep, before he brushes his lips to my brow in a touch of warming sweetness. I close my eyes and snuggle against him, while he tangles his legs with mine.

"It sounds like the storm blew out," he says. "I don't hear anything. No wind."

I lift my head enough to peer over his shoulder toward the window. "I see light. A bit of sky. And snow piled up almost to the top of the window. Jeez."

"So we'll have to dig our way out."

"Great. Morning exercise." I can't stop rolling my eyes.

He chuckles. "Why don't you check the forecast and see how much time we have?"

"But...that requires moving."

"The sooner you do, the easier it'll be." He leans in again, this time to kiss my lips. It's quick, ferocious, deep, just rough enough to make my toes curl and get them warmed right up, and I moan in disappointment when he pulls back. "Motivation, beautiful. The sooner you get up, the sooner we can put this mess behind us and find a proper bed."

Whoa.

Mama.

My heart stumbles in the best giddy way. I can only stare at him for another maddening second before looking away quickly.

I don't want to ask if there's hope for us now. If there could ever *be* an us again. Not because I'm afraid of the response, but because now just isn't the time.

Once we're out of this, though, things might be different.

We're going to talk.

Really talk.

No deflections, no avoidance, no bolting away in fear.

Because he's making it sound like we could be *us* again, and I want to hear it straight from his lips with none of that trademark James Nobel diversion and caution and excuses.

For now, I reluctantly snake an arm out into the cold to feel for my coat and the phone in my pocket.

Only, I squeal as he dares to *get up*, letting a rush of freezing air in under the blankets.

He moves around stark naked like he doesn't even feel it, this glorious bastard Adonis made for thumbing his nose at Mother Nature.

With his body so hard-cut and tapered, he bends to put fresh wood chips in the little fire dish we made and light them up with a little camping torch from the supplies. While I tap at my phone, fighting to get at least a 3G signal while it's stuttering in and out, he kindles the fire again and puts water and soup on to boil.

I drag myself from watching the narrow, tight curves of his ass and instead focus on my screen as the weather app finally opens.

That's the moment our little piece of heaven crashes to hell.

What I see makes dread glaze the pit of my stomach. Not even the blankets draped over me can chase it away.

"We've got an hour, maybe," I say. "And then the storm's

coming back. Even worse than before. They're anticipating another six feet, easily."

"Fuck. That'll be enough to bury us with no hope of being dug out until spring," he says dryly, and settles down next to me, his hip resting against my thigh. He casts me a warm look, raking over my shape under the blankets. "As much as I regret saying so, you should get dressed, and we should get moving."

I nod, shaking off the fear.

It's more than a little scary, thinking we have such a narrow window of time.

I'm quick to wriggle into my clothes, dressing under the blankets. Not because I'm modest but because I'm so blazing *cold*.

But by the time I come squirming out, fully clad, the fire has warmed our little space up again.

We're quick to eat breakfast, then carefully retrieve and store every little note in the box, and set to work dismantling the space, gathering our supplies and hauling them back out into the SUV.

Of course we have to dig the SUV out first. That takes more time.

It's just a white lump under the snow dune, almost indistinguishable from the other hills of piled white fluff. We sweep snow away underneath a clear, bright blue sky.

It looks like a strange hole opened in the blackness of the clouds, just a single tear of azure and then pillowy, brooding, angrily threatening darkness on all sides.

It's enough to make us move faster. But we can't help stopping to steal little kisses, too, as we move in and out, tamping down the snow into an easy path.

It's so strange. It's like those five years have never passed, yet we can't ignore them, either.

We're not the same people we were then. Not by a

long shot.

But there's still something there between us. I can feel it like an electric tether, stretching from James to me.

And it shocks me in the most delicious ways, every time our hands brush.

I try my phone one more time before we leave. It still won't make a call, can barely get enough data to slowly update the weather app.

James' phone is no better. No signal and no 3G or 4G or any-G. We're still on our own.

But we've got a clear path, open sky, and hope.

It's hope that keeps me warm as we bundle up in the SUV and make our way along the feeder road, but something isn't right. The road's clear.

Well, not quite clear, but it looks like someone's driven through the snow ahead, making an easier path for us.

Maybe it was just someone else on the mountain – a camper or a homesteader – making their great escape while they could. But James and I glance at each other, a sense of unease brewing between us.

Without a word, he slows the SUV, both of us on high alert.

We're not quite ready to round the bend of the mountain path when we see a car blocking our way.

A big, black truck, one that was in the convoy, fitted with a snowplow. Except now it's firmly stuck in a snowbank, skewed so it's blocking the road.

And I recognize the man exiting the driver's seat, even if he won't be as familiar to me as he is to James. My stomach leaps and my flesh chills just as James goes stock-still in his seat.

Waiting for us, his expression set in a black scowl, his arms folded over his chest, is none other than Landon Strauss.

XVIII: RED-HANDED (JAMES)

Fuck.

Talk about an unexpected turn of events.

I suppose this is the part where I pull over, get out of the SUV, and approach my boss with my hands up.

I should be more freaked out, but last night with Faye calmed and centered me in a way nothing else could. Gave me a new outlook on life, hope for the future, possibly a chance at something *more*.

Maybe that's why I'm not scared, and I'm damn sure not ready to surrender.

If Landon wants to be upset for chasing what's right against these odds, in the face of the danger we've been in from his very own hero, Captain goddamned Hook, then screw it.

He's not the man I think he is.

Still, I want to believe my smart, courageous boss wouldn't throw away *years* of work we've done together without hearing me out. I tell myself he won't toss the trust we've built, all over a past that even I didn't understand until

Faye peeled the blinders from my eyes and showed me the stark raving truth.

I ease the SUV to a halt a few feet away from his parked truck.

He watches me flatly through the windshield, then his mouth moves in an annoyed, gruff snarl I can't hear but can easily imagine as he trudges through the snow between his truck and our SUV.

Now I know why the road was already cleared by someone else's passage. He must've driven past the ranger station looking for us and missed the SUV when it was just another snow hill among many.

It catches me off guard when Faye reaches over and squeezes my hand reassuringly. After a startled hesitation, I squeeze back, before rolling the window down to face the music.

Landon leans in, resting his arms on the window frame and eyeing me with blue eyes as chill as the sky overhead. "There something you want to talk to me about, James?" he rumbles. "Like maybe, why you're playing fugitive with the Senator's daughter? The same Senator you've been investigating? Since you worked for the *FB-fucking-I?*"

I arch a brow. "It does seem as if you're already quite well informed, sir. So what would I need to tell you?"

"Don't." He thumps a fist against the window's edge. "Don't you pull that slick dick smartass thing with me. You worried the fuck out of me, James. Why the hell didn't you tell me about all this?"

I blink.

Of all the questions I expected, this isn't one. "Pardon? I...I suppose I didn't think it was relevant. Not while Pershing was safely on the other side of the country, away from Enguard."

"You didn't think it was *relevant* that you used to be FBI?

That Hook Hamlin is dirty? That he tried to kill you years ago, tried to kill the Senator, and basically the only reason we're up here is so those two can figure out who's going to murder who first." He glares at me, and I blink again.

"When you put it like that...no."

Tink breaks the tension with a loud laugh next to me, burying it in her hands.

Landon groans, dragging a gloved hand over his snow-dotted face. "You're impossible, man. We could've been helping you all this time, but you had to go and –"

"Be James?" Faye cuts in ever so helpfully through her laughter.

I shoot her a flat look.

"Exactly!" Landon growls.

I sigh. I seem to be caught in the peanut gallery, but I ask, "And just who informed you of all these particularly pertinent details?"

"Senator Harris himself." Landon's brows knit. "Things went to hell last night, James. Hamlin had a long-winded story about you going rogue and being a threat, but he wouldn't give details. He thought I actually believed it. *Idiot.*" He snorts. "I know you better than that. You've been on my payroll for years. But I didn't get clear intel until this morning when Hook and his men took off on the snowmobiles while Harris took me aside and told me everything."

"So much for that man understanding confidentiality."

"He was worried about you. And about his daughter." He glances past me at Faye. "The two of you could've died out here. What were you thinking?"

"The police would be a start," Faye says. "And the FBI. We were trying to get help. Hell, get military helicopters, get everyone airlifted out of here, get Hook arrested."

"With what evidence?" Landon asks. "Right now, it's all hearsay."

"Not necessarily," I point out. "I bugged Harris' laptop. I didn't get a chance to see much before I lost connectivity, but I did get a mirror image of his hard drive uploaded to a cloud server. I just can't access it out here with no internet."

"Fat lot of good that does us," Landon says.

He's right in his always blunt, typical Landon style.

"Wait. There's another way," Faye whispers, and we both look at her.

"What's that?" Landon asks.

Faye shrugs, her smile bright. "Just ask my Dad to tell us what he knows."

She's right. It's the simplest solution.

If Harris is willing to come clean to Landon, on record, then maybe he'll step out from the shadows and bring the evidence he's collected into the light.

I don't know. The man I once knew, Congressman Harris, might.

The man he's become now, Senator Harris, that's another story. One I don't know how to read.

He might be too obsessed with his endgame, with revenge.

"We can only ask," I say. "Which means we have to go back."

"Not much choice," Landon says. "We managed to pull up the National Weather Service, and we've got maybe under an hour to turn this thing back around before it hits again. I want to get back in before Hamlin does, too, so I can pull together our staff and have a strike team ready. I want them briefed without him breathing down the back of our necks. Plus..." He gestures sheepishly toward the truck. "I don't think that's going anywhere, and you're not getting around it."

"You're just a terrible driver," I say dryly. "Get your things and get in."

Landon just snorts, then rolls his eyes and pulls away, trudging back to the truck to begin unloading what few supplies he packed, mostly emergency road gear. While we watch him, Faye leans over and rests her head on my shoulder.

"No leaving me out this time, okay?" she asks softly. "He's my father. And I'm invested in this. I'm part of it. Let me help."

"You might be the only one he'll listen to." I squeeze her hand. "We'll do this together."

It's quiet in the SUV on the way back to the resort. Landon sits in the back seat, fiddling with his phone, trying again and again to raise a signal. No luck even with a few amplifiers and other devices.

He's growling under his breath, muttering about setting up an emergency military satphone, which may indeed be an option if we can get it to connect, when we pull back into the resort.

Instantly, I stiffen.

People are outside, moving around, going back to the cabins to retrieve the belongings they left behind during the rush to migrate to the main lodge.

Something feels wrong.

Something that makes all of us quiet as we park and step out.

None of Hamlin's men are in sight, or no doubt they'd be rushing to take me into custody immediately. A few people give us odd looks, likely after picking up on last night's chatter with the search for me, but no one interrupts us as we go inside and upstairs to the suites in search of Harris.

His door is open, something that already makes my hackles stand on end and my body go chill and sharp and quiet.

Landon, Faye, and I exchange glances before I hold a

NICOLE SNOW

finger to my lips, edge to one side of the door, and carefully nudge it open.

"Really, James," Harris says, "there's no need for such pomp and ceremony. You could've just knocked."

The pleasant tone of his voice is almost menacing. It's certainly damn bizarre.

It makes me uncomfortable, keyed up on high alert, and both Landon and Faye are stiff as stones, looking at the door warily as it swings open on the Senator. He's standing in the middle of the room with his professional politician's smile on his face, but it's his body language that tunes me in to something very wrong.

His body language, and the fact that he's carrying his laptop under his arm, drumming the nails of his other hand against it slowly, rhythmically, almost ominously.

What the hell is going on here?

While we eye him silently, his gaze flicks between us before he makes an amused sound. "I knew you'd come crawling back. There's no getting out of here right now. Smart. All of you. Especially you, dearest." His gaze locks on Faye for a moment, before shifting to me, drilling into me. "You, though..."

We lock eyes.

Then he cocks his head, letting his fingers fall to rest possessively on the laptop. "You're not as smart as I'd hoped, James. Or maybe you'd have noticed that my computer is set to turn the webcam on whenever it's activated, until I shut it off. Funny, it captured you fiddling around. Did you find what you wanted? Is this what you came back for? You should *run away* again like the craven coward you are, before I have you brought up on charges."

What. The. Fuck?

Something isn't right here.

The Senator isn't the type to gloat like a mustache twirling villain.

These grandstanding speeches, taunting, toying with us – with me. Something is off in his tone, in his stance, and in the fact that suddenly he's turned on us, when he's the whole reason Landon came out to bring us back.

He wanted us to help with the strike against Hamlin before the storm traps us once again. My sense of unease only grows as the Senator holds my eyes firmly.

Then I hear it.

A slow, rhythmic clap coming from the suite's sitting room.

I stiffen, whirling around, just as the door in the hall opens at my back.

I hear the stomp of boots emerging from Hamlin's suite, the *click* of safeties sliding off.

Shit. I don't even have to turn around to know Hamlin's men are in the hall, boxing us in. I can't take my eyes off the man emerging from the sitting room, anyway.

Hook Hamlin, larger than life. Standing with a knowing smirk on his lips and an AK-47 in his hands, trained right at Senator Harris.

Now, I understand.

Harris' only job in this was diversion. To keep us occupied until Hamlin could flank us – unless he wanted to get shot.

Yet, still, he tried to warn us.

Run away.

It's too late now.

I swear softly under my breath – but don't resist as we're herded inside the room, the Pershing men shoving us roughly, barking at us to get our hands up.

Fuck, I can't fight just yet. We can't have a shootout here.

It'll endanger Faye and her father. Plus, I need a plan. One that prevents Hamlin from doing his worst.

He's still got collateral.

One wrong move, and he'll be using all those defenseless people downstairs as hostages to get what he wants.

And what he wants is deadly clear as he flicks us over with a look before gesturing to his men to tie us up.

"Now, now," he says with a grin. "Now, boys and girls, we're gonna have a little fun."

The door bangs open again. In comes a tied, cuffed Riker, then Gabe and Skylar are pushed into the room, along with a few of the new hires we'd brought on.

My friends are snarling, stumbling, cursing, but just as helpless as we are. I've never seen anything so fucking terrifying in my life.

Hook's eyes are burning black caverns as he looks me dead in the eye. "First, you're going to sit tight while I figure out *exactly* what I'm going to do with you. What you say next – especially you, James Nobel – will be a very, very important factor in how this turns out."

XIX: INCENDIARY (FAYE)

It's almost an insult that they didn't bother tying me up.

They searched, disarmed, and bound everyone else. Even Sky's been tied, and what's she going to do? Beat them with her pregnant belly?

But not me.

Not the helpless little Senator's daughter.

Not the fragile thing expected to collapse in shock and useless whimpers, trembling with fear before the big, strong, armed men ringing the room, keeping us all hemmed in the center, clustered on the floor and crammed together.

Just because I'm pissed doesn't mean I'm not afraid.

This is seriously chilling. We've walked into an ambush, and right now, there's no clear way out.

Even Dad's been bound, shoved in with the rest of us, sitting shoulder to shoulder with me. His head is bowed. He's glaring at his thighs with an odd mix of resignation and fury on his face, defeat and determination. I don't want to think about what stupid, heroic thing he's going to try to do.

This is on me.

I'm the only one with the slightest advantage here, having my hands free.

And I'm going to have to use it soon, I realize, as one of the men grabs Riker by the arm and hustles him to his feet. He moves slow, flashing them a defiant look.

"Move, asshole!" one of the Pershing goons snaps.

Then Riker resists, snarling, and he gets an AK-47 butt slammed in his face with an audible *crunch*. He reels back, staggering, blood spraying from his nose.

Several members of the Enguard crew swear in horror, struggling, before freezing over as the mouths of guns swing toward them. I don't move. I don't dare.

But I can't help wincing. Or worrying as I watch Riker being led from the main room of my father's suite into the sitting room.

I have all the reason in the world to worry.

Especially when one of the men follows the others into the room with a camera, and I hear the vicious, terrible sound of fists, rifle butts, and God only knows what else striking flesh.

The sound of Riker's knees hitting the floor.

And his restrained snarls, rising with each blow only to trail off. I can picture him gritting his teeth.

A proud man, a husband and a father from everything James has told me. Too proud to cry out or beg them to stop, while they film him.

It's fucking horrific.

My heart feels sick with it. My stomach, completely hollowed out.

And I don't know who I'm more disgusted with.

Hamlin for playing these games? Or Dad for playing right into them?

No one says anything. The Enguard crew are so tense, it's

likely they don't trust themselves not to snap and endanger Riker even more.

Meanwhile, Dad is withdrawn, off in his strange, quiet place. Fine then.

Fine.

If no one will say anything, I guess it's on me.

I lift my chin, looking at Hook Hamlin dead-on, who's preoccupied watching something on his phone with an eyebrow quirked like it's nothing more than a baseball game. From the low sounds, I know it's the live video feed from the other room.

What kind of fucking coward orders a man tortured in the next room but can't stand to see it up close?

"You don't have to do this," I say, quiet but steady. I'm trained in negotiations.

Maybe I can talk him through this. Maybe, even though I know there's no FBI team at our back, ready to bust in and save the day.

"What's the purpose of hurting Riker? Just because he's my father's friend?"

The look Hamlin gives me is patronizing, almost pitying. "Oh, my dear, do you really think I care about your father's friendships? No wonder you weren't fit for the FBI."

There. He's doing exactly what I want him to, gloating.

He's rubbing my nose in his plan because I've just proven that to him, I'm some stupid witless little girl begging him, *don't hurt my daddy's friends*.

He turns the phone toward me, letting me see as a knee crashes into Riker's jaw, sending his head snapping to the side.

I flinch, lowering my eyes, while at my back James swears softly under his breath.

It's killing him one piece at a time to see his friend destroyed like this.

I can't let it.

"Once I send this to the family of your father's *friend*," Hook scoffs, "no one will question why we came back to the lodge to find all of you slaughtered with none the wiser. Your *friend* has made quite an enemy out of the last of that drug cartel, and they do enjoy going for the soft underbelly, destroying families. There's a lot of grief ahead for a happy wife and a little girl watching daddy dearest get torn apart. The rest of you were just collateral, we'll tell the Feds. A little neat revenge tale based on that operation you pulled off against the Pilgrims."

I don't know these people he's talking about – the Pilgrims, even if I vaguely remember old records on local drug operations, the name possibly among rising street gangs.

It doesn't matter. I grasp what he's getting at.

He'll kill us all. Then stage his men as if they're responding to the sound of gunfire and come rushing in.

They'll "discover" our bodies. There'll be a manhunt for criminals who'll never show up, before the storm conveniently cuts off all efforts at searching and leaves the last of the civilians here forced to accept it, or face off against Hamlin with nowhere to run.

Then by the time the storm clears the optimal window for investigation will have passed, bodies cooling for days – probably tossed out into the snow and frozen, the fictional perpetrators long gone.

God, it's devious.

He'll trot out that line about a revenge killing, the video will back him up, and so will the family's testimony. And Hook's hideous reputation means people will *believe* him.

Son of a bitch.

I don't say anything. He wants to see me afraid, or wants

me to ask more insipid questions so he can gloat in his brilliance. He's not getting it.

At least, not out loud.

I feel James' hands against my back, tied behind him.

Mine may be free, but I let them slip around behind me as if assuming the position to be cuffed, under the guise of getting more comfortable in the close-packed bodies.

Instead, I slip my fingers into James' and nudge his palm into uncurling.

Okay. Now for the moment of truth.

Very, very slowly, I begin tracing letters on his palm. Slow, delicate, as neat as I can make them. Writing him notes just like we used to. Only this time it's skin, instead of ink and paper.

You read me? Tap.

It's so incredibly slow, it has to be slow not to risk being noticed and to make sure James understands what I'm doing, and I hold my breath, hoping, waiting.

Then it comes. Just one gentle tap, right with his middle finger against the edge of my thumb.

Thank God.

Will untie you, I spell. *Keep secret. Okay?*

Another tap, quick, sharp, almost eager.

Then I run. You make noise. Distract.

Have plan. Will return. Wait for me.

One more tap, so firm it's almost like he's shaken my hand in agreement. Then I can feel his resolution, his determination. James has my back right now.

Just like he used to. Just like I had his.

We'll figure this out, Lord willing.

Together.

And we're going to get everyone out of here alive.

I push my hand into his and spell one more thing. *Love you.*

The last tap I get back is so fierce it's like lightning.

Then I settle, leaning my back against James' shoulders as if I'm tired, so tired, and just need to rest against the big strong man while I await my inevitable doom.

Actually, I really am dog tired, and leaning against James is a comfort...but what I'm really doing is masking my movements as I slowly work at the ropes around his wrists.

They're nylon safety cords, small and slick, but that's good because I have small fingers. It makes me quick and efficient, working at the knots one at a time.

The entire time I'm scanning the room from under my lashes, the mess of my tangled hair.

One man is stationed in each corner, armed and ready. At least three others are in the other room, still working over Riker in horrible, slow rhythm.

Hamlin with another armed man at the desk, Dad's laptop open and logged in while they're poring through data, occasionally glancing at us, muttering demon whispers.

I hear something about starting on the pregnant one first.

They don't even try to hide it, which has Gabe straining like a rabid bull on a tether, only to be shoved back by the barrel of an AK-47 pushed between his eyes, while Skylar hisses, spits, *dares* anyone to touch her.

"Try it! I'll snap your dicks off," she snarls.

I halfway think that fierce Mama bear would take someone out with her teeth, if they threatened her baby.

But I don't want to give them the chance.

There's a casement window over the desk. The very same desk Hamlin stands by now.

If I bolt for it, he won't be expecting me to run straight at him and won't be able to react quickly enough. Especially if James can give me a good diversion.

I'm fast. I'm small. I'm slippery as a damned eel.

If I'm smart and quick, I can get past Hamlin and out the

window before he has a chance to grab at me. He won't be able to risk chasing me with his entire crew, not when he'll have a ton of panicked civilians to deal with if his men go charging out after me with live guns.

And he definitely won't have a convenient alibi for why so many innocents were found riddled with bullet holes, but somehow, he and all his men miraculously escaped.

He'll have to let me go and only hope I'll have the decency to die in the snow.

I won't go down easy.

Soon? I trace against James' palm. Just one more note; one he won't be able to put in his keepsake box, but that I hope we'll have forever to remember. He taps again.

My turn. I write out, *Distract them. Now!*

He's silent a moment.

Then he sticks one leg out, shoving his foot against the calf of the man menacing Gabe and Sky.

"Hey, fuckface," James says, and I almost want to *laugh* because it sounds so bizarre in that cultured, yet growling accent. I don't think James Nobel has ever said *fuckface* in his life. "Are you so pathetic you can only get off by threatening a bound pregnant woman?"

"Save it! I'll kick his ass even tied up," Sky spits back, her shoulders twitching, but James has the man's attention now.

He pulls away from Sky, stalking toward James, sneering down at him. "You rather I get off on you?"

James curls his upper lip. "So crass."

"Fuck your crass," the man snaps, flipping the rifle over his head to invert it and drive it down toward James' skull.

Three things happen at once.

James rocks forward, still keeping his hands behind his back, and slams his head into the man's gut.

The man doubles over, gasping, grunting, the butt of the

rifle coming down in a glancing blow on James' back instead of his head.

But that pulls the trigger. Everyone ducks, shouting and swearing as the bullet zings toward the ceiling. Screams rise from below.

And I launch myself right out, surging to my feet, making a running dive for the window.

While everyone else is dropping to the floor at the gunshot, I'm rising up, racing past the bound Enguard crew and my father's startled look, surging past Hamlin.

I hit the desk.

Grab my father's laptop – leverage, all the data and all the proof – and clutch it against my chest as I bound up the desk, sending papers scattering everywhere.

I kick the casement window open, sending the pane slamming outward like a loose door. Holding my breath, I leap up to the windowsill, bracing my free hand against the frame as the cold wind scours in, stealing my panting breath.

It's a long drop down.

Two stories, but the snow dunes are thick.

There's no James to catch me this time.

And there's no time to wait.

I start tilting forward – only to yelp as pain slices through me.

There's something in my hair. Ripping at my scalp as a cruel hand tangles, dragging me back.

Hook Hamlin snarls, yanking me so hard I drop down on my ass on the desk.

"You sly little bitch!" he hisses, shaking me by my hair like a scruffed cat, nearly ripping it out at the roots. "What are you trying to pull?"

"This," I bite off.

Then I bite *him*.

Right on the sliver of bare wrist exposed between his

glove and the sleeve of his jacket, the only place I can reach. Sink my teeth in *hard*.

It's honestly jarring when I slam against the stark wrist bones under his skin, getting a mouthful of muscle and brittle hair for half a second.

He's yelping, cursing, and calling me a few more things I never need to hear again, before he jerks backward.

Several men around the Enguard crew go running, trying to protect their boss. Hook holds his good hand up with a snarl, waving them on. "Get her, assholes! Go, go, go!"

There's my window of opportunity.

My last chance.

I clutch my father's laptop to my chest and scramble into a crouch, not even stopping to look down again.

And jump.

* * *

I'M PRETTY sure I blacked out halfway down as a preemptive measure.

Just in case hitting hurts more than I expect it to.

It's a jarring thud and a whoosh of snow all around me, almost like doing a cannonball in water. I rocket into a snow dune, sinking so deep the snow collapses on top of me, burying me completely.

Holy crap.

Sputtering, my entire body jarred like a slammed door, I flail my way out. My head comes up first, thankfully, spitting snow out of my mouth and swiping it out of my face.

I can barely stand for a moment, wobbling on aching legs, but adrenaline surges through me with the strength I need. I'm standing out here, still in the pajamas I was wearing when I ran away from Dad, covered over in clumsy layers of clothing and outerwear instead of the tactical gear I'd have on a mission.

Too bad. There's no time for it to matter.

I'm going to save my Dad. I'm going to save Enguard.

And I'm going to save James.

I tilt my head back to look up at the window and catch the only glimpse I need.

Hamlin, looking down at me, wide-eyed and teeth clenched. Jesus.

Not all of the chill is from the cold and the snow seeping down the back of my neck. He doesn't shout. Doesn't bluster. Doesn't command anyone to chase me.

He only looks at me with dire, grim certainty that promises I've earned nothing but pain for everyone I love.

And if I know what's good for me, I'll come back this instant so he won't have to hurt them.

Like hell I will.

I just hope James and Dad will forgive me for leaving them to a few minutes of pain so I can spare them a quick, untimely death.

In something close to a dark salute, an answering promise, I lift the laptop to Hamlin. A reminder that I have leverage of my own.

When it rips out of me, it's so unexpected, the full force of the words scare me.

"Harm one hair on their heads, you freak! I'll find a way to get this out there, internet or no internet, phone or no phone. Even if I have to shout it from the goddamned mountains!"

I'm roaring into the night, lungs totally spent and exhausted when I finally open my eyes.

We hold eye contact for a blistering moment, dark challenge sizzling between us.

Death wishes. Agonies. Souls.

One light. One dark. And only one can win.
Finally, I turn my back on him and walk away.
I have work to do.

* * *

I WAS RIGHT about Hamlin not sending anyone after me, but I'm quick and elusive anyway as I scout the grounds. I'm not quite sure what I'm looking for just yet, something that will let me single-handedly rescue everyone, I guess. I'll know it when I see it.

It's too bad I can't rely on the small army of people at the lodge, but they're innocent bystanders. Civilians. Nervous, twitchy congressional aides and resort staff who probably don't have a mean bone in their bodies.

Even if I'm no longer a registered agent, I'm still sworn to protect.

I can't get them involved.

What I find as I snoop around, though, is disturbing. Sections where the packed snow is disturbed, and at the lowest layers toward the ground, it's mixed with freshly dug up earth.

The holes are easy to miss in the driving snow. Easy to hope the snowfall will cover the tracks until it's too late.

The buried power and internet lines have been dug up. The phone line, too.

Predictably cut, severing all electricity and communications to the resort.

James was right. Those outages were no coincidence at all.

Hamlin planned ahead.

In more ways than one, I realize, as further sniffing around reveals the gas lines to the main generators have been cut, the fuel leaking all over the ground as the generators try to pump it and fail, wasting precious fuel as it soaks into the earth. Creating one hell of a fire hazard.

It takes temperatures minus forty or fifty for gasoline to freeze, and we're not quite there yet.

But those people in the lodge must be freezing.

I check the cabins. The generators there are just fine, hooked up and waiting to be started. I need to get everyone out of the lodge and into separate cabins again before the snow starts coming down again, trapping them with no heat but their own and one paltry fireplace.

But as I step in through the front door, raising my hands, following in my father's footsteps to use that calm, authoritative *voice* to calm everyone, to reassure them it will be all right, to explain the gunshot as an accident, to get them moving, to tell them *why*...

I realize something else.

I need them out of the lodge.

Because my eyes keep drifting to the dwindling stack of gas canisters against the wall.

It hits me in a rush that's almost blinding.

I actually manage a smile.

This is either sweet perfection, or the *worst* idea in the world.

While everyone else is busy packing and preparing to move the wounded, I steal several of the canisters and squirrel them away behind the reception desk. Near-empty ones.

I don't want to take fuel away from people who might desperately need it if we can't get out before the storm breaks its lull. Plus it's the near-empty canisters that interest me most.

That's where the *boom-boom* is.

Thanks to air pressure and the nature of gasoline, the last

of the fuel in the sealed containers will begin to evaporate, creating a highly flammable explosive gas.

Ever wonder why they tell you to be careful of an empty gas tank? That's why.

The last trace bits of gasoline in the tank can, in a sealed vacuum, release a vapor that'll explode at the slightest spark. People have blown up their cars this way, completely by accident.

But I'm not trying to wreck some junker at a demolition derby for the applause.

I'm going to blow up a freaking building.

Entirely on purpose.

I don't have much time. Not even with the laptop stuffed down inside my parka buying maybe a little immunity for Dad and James. But I should be able to rig something up, especially when there should also be propane tanks in the kitchen for the grills.

I'm going to get these people out of here first, hunkered down safe, away from not just the powerless lodge, but the danger that a desperate, cornered Hamlin and his men represent.

And then...

Oh, *then* I'm going to have a little fun like I haven't for years.

I'm going to make Captain Hook Hamlin sorry he ever fucked with my family. With James. With Tink.

They don't call redheads fiery for nothing.

Welcome to Faye Harris' patented hell.

XX: LIKE VELVETEEN (JAMES)

If I didn't love Faye already, I most certainly do now.

Not just for her daring escapades, or for her foresight to steal her father's laptop on the way out.

Not even for the fact that my hands are free thanks to her, and I'm slowly working at Gabe's bonds. He's the closest person to me, though the ropes around his huge wrists are particularly thick and tight, and I'm having little luck making headway.

My love for Faye isn't even due to her bravery in the face of danger.

My love is in the look of sheer panicked confusion slowly turning into simmering rage as Hook Hamlin cocks his head, listening to the commotion below, and realizes Faye's shepherding his potential hostages to safety.

And he can't do a bloody damn thing about it.

Not without creating even more witnesses to dispose of so they can't testify against him in court.

Hamlin listens for a few moments longer – then moves like a tornado.

He whips around abruptly for a man his size, and backhands poor Skylar across the face with one massive paw.

Flesh meets flesh with a mighty *crack* that sends her sprawling over on her side.

Fuck.

The room stills like a heart in cardiac arrest, all tension and pain and shock, my own breath catching in my lungs because I know what's coming next.

There's barely a half-second of frozen, stunned anger before he fucking *snaps.*

And suddenly, giant Gabe is out of my reach as he charges like a raging bull – and Hamlin just waved a red flag in front of his face with the backhanded attack on his pregnant wife.

Gabe surges at Hamlin like an unstoppable force of nature, hands still tied behind his back, this massive goliath of a man enraged over his wife and unborn child, and even as I'm silently praying *no, Gabe, don't do it, this isn't the time!*, he lowers his head and slams himself at Hamlin.

But he's too emotional, too blind with fury, not thinking straight, not reacting quickly.

Hamlin has just a split second to sidestep him, sending Gabe blundering past.

Then Hamlin brings the butt of his AK-47 down on Gabe's skull, right at the nape, with enough force to send him spinning down across the floor in an unconscious heap.

Hamlin looks up slowly and sniffs. "Pathetic."

With a disgusted gesture, he signals for two of his goons to catch Gabe by the arms, dragging his bulk back to the cluster we've formed in the center of the room. They drop him down in a heap at my back.

A place where I can't reach his wrists anymore. Fuck.

And I can't maneuver to get closer to anyone else, either, without being obvious that I'm untied and working to get the others free.

It can't get worse than this.

Until, predictably, it does.

The door to the sitting room flies open and two more men enter, carrying a limp, battered, but still conscious Riker between them. My heartbeat becomes a dull, angry roar in my ears when I see my friend.

He's silent, deathly so, but the look on his face, in his bruised and swollen emerald eyes, speaks the promise of murder. Of revenge. Of savagery.

He's bleeding all over, covered in bruises and scrapes.

Just like Tanner, fuck. He looks just like Tanner before he died.

Only, Riker doesn't look as weak. There's a fiery resolve in his gaze that says he's not down yet, he's not dying, but a human body has its limits and he's so close to his.

I have to look down. I can't fucking meet his eyes, or I'll wind up just like Gabe.

Instead, I bite my cheek so hard I taste blood.

Captain Hook Hamlin *will* pay.

My eyes flit around the room, and everyone is thinking the same thing. No doubt. No hesitation. No second-guessing.

Good. We'll need that resolve.

All of us, if we're going to work together to get out of this.

For some unholy reason, I can't help thinking of my mother's book right now.

Of the happy ending I keep failing to write.

Maybe it's because I've never believed in happy endings. Never believed that much joy could just be spontaneously generated and given to people for no good reason other than that it can happen, so it does. Happy endings never just happen.

You have to work yourself to the bone for them.

I'm no stranger to hard work.

And maybe this isn't a romance, this moment with our lives hanging on the whims of a madman, the woman I love frantically trying to help with so much stacked against her. Against all of us.

Still, I'm going to make sure this story has a happy ending, nonetheless.

For everyone. For my team. My *friends*.

And for Faye.

The Pershing animals drop Riker in a pile with the rest of us, his wrists and ankles bound.

Now I've got something to do. Now I've got something to keep me busy, when his feet are close to my back and I need him to be able to run when Faye gives the signal for whatever she's planning so we can react and do our part.

I shift a little like I'm trying to get comfortable, making sure my body hides my fingers as I start working on the ropes around Riker's ankles.

Only to freeze as Hamlin paces slowly toward me, watching me with a sort of cold avarice.

"I'm disappointed in you, James," he says in a mockery of grandfatherly concern.

Asshole. I know what real grandfatherly concern is, and it's waiting for me back in San Francisco, with a man who understands what love and family truly are.

"I thought we understood each other," Hook whispers. "You're nothing like them, and yet here you are. Pissing your last moments on earth away for a band of children."

"Don't." I'm not giving him any part of me, let alone any reaction, and I meet his eyes stonily. "I'm *nothing* like you."

"I can see that now. You aren't smart enough to recognize an opportunity when you see one, and you're most certainly not smart enough to pick a winning side. Shame, shame, terrible shame." He paces past me toward Landon, looking down at him with something almost like fondness. "You, though. I've really enjoyed our talks, Landon. I've almost felt like you're a son to me."

"Sorry," Landon bites off. "I've already worked through my daddy issues. That angle won't work with me."

Hamlin lets out an irritated sigh. "Ah, yes. Your little issue with Crown Security, protecting that pop star whore, Milah Holly. That was almost as ridiculous as everything else you people have been involved with – like bringing the Bay Area Kidnapper to justice." Hook's eyes go to Gabe, then Skylar, who sits in a heap, quietly seething. "I honestly expected more from a crew who's been in the national spotlight as heroes. Several times. But perhaps you're ready for big league press and none of the consequences."

I'm almost foaming at the mouth.

This fuck is like Lucifer, waltzing around the room, taunting us. Crown, Milah Holly, the kidnapper who took Skylar's baby niece for months, taking down the Pilgrims...it's all streaming back like some sick slideshow of Enguard's life flashing before its eyes.

Worse, he's not done. My teeth grind together like sandpaper when I hear Hook's voice again.

"Tell me one thing...why is it you people have no common sense?" He sinks down into a crouch in front of Landon, AK-47 across his thighs, and looks at my boss eye to eye, still exuding that grandfatherly air paired with pure menace. "Nothing, huh?"

Landon's gaze is icy silence. A death wish in scalding deep blue eyes.

Hamlin just smiles.

"Fine then. I'm going to spell this out for you. With or without you, Landon, I'm going to stage the death of a U.S. Senator and his daughter. It's almost too easy. We'll blame it on rival competitors who managed to sneak up here under the cover of the storm, of course. But your next answer, and you are going to give me one, tells me whether or not you'll walk away from here whole with your crew intact..." He gestures at us – Gabe unconscious, Riker broken and bleeding, Skylar's jaw an angry, swollen purple. "...or if your merry little group of miscreants heroically died trying to protect Harris. Answer carefully."

"Don't," Harris bites off. "You want to kill me, then kill me, Hamlin! But leave Faye alone and don't make these people collateral damage. They had no idea what they were getting into."

Hook smirks. "If they die then that's your fault, isn't it, Senator? Because you knew. And you dragged them in anyway without telling them."

"I would've come even if I'd known," Landon says, low and deathly serious, that quiet seething that says when he gets out of those ropes, Hook is dead. "Because I'd have chosen to protect the Senator. Just like I'm choosing now. And I'm choosing to protect my people." He stares Hamlin down fearlessly. "Take me. Let them go. I'll be your sacrifice. They'll keep quiet on my order. No police, no testimony, no sign they were ever here."

Fuck.

It takes everything in me to remember I'm supposed to pretend to still be bound. That's not easy when every part of me that's loyal to Landon wants to thrust myself between him, Hook, and the rifle that's suddenly pressed right between his unblinking, challenging eyes. I take a deep breath, restraining myself, and continue to work at the ropes around Riker's ankles.

Hook's bluffing. He *has* to be, testing our reaction.

I don't believe for a second there's any scenario where he lets any of us go alive.

And I'm the first to speak as I bite off, "That's not happening." Even as I lock eyes with Hamlin, I'm slipping one of the coils of rope free from Riker's ankles, working busily behind my back. "You kill Landon, you'll have to kill us all. Because we won't stop coming for you. We live together, we die together. Enguard, to the bitter end."

Snarls of assent rise all around, furious and quietly seething but resolute. We're of one mind.

If this is meant to be our last stand, then so fucking be it.

We won't let Landon sacrifice himself for us alone.

And we won't live dirty at the cost of his life.

Hamlin sweeps us all with a patient, tired look, patronizing as ever. "You're all agreed, then?"

No one speaks.

We don't have to.

Our resolution speaks for us, every last dagger's edge in our eyes. We aren't playing his game.

Hamlin stands with an annoyed click in the back of his throat. "How touching. I'd hoped I wouldn't have to stoop to these levels, but since you're refusing to be at all reasonable and cooperate..." He slips his phone from his pocket.

Of course *his* phone is working.

Of fucking *course*.

It's more proof he's behind the dead signals here, but I can't think about that right now when he's pulling up what looks like a live video feed.

And I recognize the woman in the video.

Kenna. McKenna Strauss.

Landon's wife.

She's sitting on a barstool at the kitchen island in their airy beachfront home, the French doors and broad windows giving a clear vantage point as she jots in a notebook while one of their blue cats naps in her lap, and the other suns himself in a cat bed under the window. She's humming to herself.

Innocent. Oblivious. Endangered.

I swear softly under my breath. It's nothing compared to the litany of curses Landon spits, his face going red, muscles in his neck straining as he starts to shove himself up, fighting against his bonds.

Only to go completely still as Hook shakes his head in warning, holding up a hand.

"I wouldn't test your luck with heroics," he says, then pitches his voice a little louder. "Carlo, can you hear me?"

A few moments later, another man's voice pipes through the phone's speaker. "Aye-aye, Chief. Waiting for you to call the shot. I've got a clear line on her pretty little head."

Hook's smirk deepens, ugly. "That, my friends, is Carlo. And the view you're enjoying right now is down the barrel of his sniper rifle. One shot, and pretty Kenna is dead. Someone will have to write an obituary for a bestselling author. Don't worry, it'll be painless. She'll never know what hit her. No fear. No reason to make her suffer. Of course...she'll be gone from your life forever, Landon. Just ask Harris how that feels – nothing you do, no petty little act of vengeance, will ever bring her back."

Harris snarls, low and deep and threatening. "You goddamned coward."

But Landon goes pale. Bone-white.

It's no secret how deeply he loves Kenna. Reuniting, falling in love, marrying her changed him in ways so true we all saw it, saw how he grew and matured until we only respected him even more than we already did.

It's part of why we'd follow him anywhere. Even into death.

And I realize now that if Hook goes through with this...

We might have to follow Landon to even darker places.

Landon stares at the video numbly, his jaw tight, his voice strained. "What the fuck do you want from me? Why are you doing this?"

"Because I really don't want to have to kill you, Landon," Hook answers in mock conciliation. "You're more useful to me alive than dead – all of you. Your little crew just needs the proper motivation."

Skylar loses it then. "Go shove your motivation up your –"

"Now, now. Quiet, girl. The boys are talking," Hook snarls. "Landon, Enguard could be a very useful asset to me in extending my operations to achieve complete dominance, coast to coast. It could be very lucrative for you, too, but you're continuing to be stubborn. So. Either you – and your entire team – cooperate, or you find out just how long my reach is. And how deadly. I know what's valuable to each and every one of you. I know your families and your dreams." His gaze flicks to us, one by one, even to Gabe, who's slowly starting to stir to consciousness. "Cross me, continue playing rebel, and I'll take it all without the slightest hesitation. Or you could finally open your eyes. Think this through and realize we could all make each other very rich men." His smile for Skylar is oily. "And women, I suppose."

"I don't want your money," she bites off. "A fucking creep like you can only buy loyalty with threats for so long. Force us into this, and we'll come for you. We'll find a way to destroy you, even if we have to get dirty to do it."

"Ah, yes. *Dirty*. Ask the good Senator how well that worked for him," Hamlin replies, and that flat shark's smile is back, those dead, killing eyes. "All the evidence he's gathered? Everything his pretty little runaway daughter took that she thinks will give her a bargaining chip? It's just as damning for him. He can't torpedo me without sinking himself. You'll end up just the same way."

Unbe-fucking-lievable.

He has us backed into a corner like a bottomless abyss.

"I'll give you boys and girls a minute or two to think. Let's have some music." Hamlin snaps his fingers and paces the room.

A song comes on over the room's speakers that's far too upbeat and too ironic for this mess.

It's Milah Holly's new hit single, *Mew for Me Like Velveteen!*

The music video has only played in our office about a thousand times since it came out. Gabe and Sky thought it'd be funny to torment Landon regularly with a song inspired by his cats, Velvet and Mews, courtesy of the most outrageous and (in)famous client Enguard has ever dealt with.

It's just as ridiculous as it sounds. The lyrics wash over us like some gut-wrenching anthem, and I can't stop picturing Ms. Holly herself jumping around the stage, whiskers drawn on her face, blowing kisses to the camera as a stampede of blue cats of every kind come galloping around her feet at the end.

Won't you mew, mew, mew for love?

Won't you mew, mew, mew for me real sweet?

Won't you mew for me like Velveteen – tonight!

Apparently, the devil has a sense of humor. I always liked to think the last song I'd ever hear would be something by Handel or Brahms – not this outrageous pop song that's become a background track for the end of our lives.

Think, damn it.

I don't see any good options.

With Kenna at the other end of that sniper rifle, I'm just as helpless to do anything as I was to save my mother, or Tanner.

If I take advantage of my untied hands to jump Hamlin, the man on the other end of that video will shoot her the second Hamlin gives the order.

I have to think of something else. Some alternative. I have to –

Wait. There's something in the air. A strange, stark odor that wasn't there a minute ago.

Do I smell...gasoline?

I only have half a second to think about it.

Milah Holly sings one more line – *mew for me like velveteen, you precious thing!* – before everything goes white.

Then a violent explosion rips up from below, this concussive blast of force and heat that punches up so hard it's like the floor lifts underneath us, rattling like a game board to send chess pieces flying everywhere.

And we *do* go flying, as flame and smoke billow out of nowhere, as the back wall of the room blows out in a jagged-edged, smoking hole and the shock wave flings us around like ping pong balls.

The whole world tumbles end over end.

It's like the plane crash all over again, falling out of the sky, into a hellish chasm.

Only this time, I'm plummeting toward the snow in a tangle of both Enguard and Pershing Shield men, weapons fire going wild, and there's only a half-second of gut-dropping freefall before I hit hard amid tumbling bodies and plumes of flaming wreckage that come sailing down from the sky only to extinguish themselves in the snow.

My head is ringing.

I hurt all over, dizzy and aching with the raw impact both from the explosion and from the subsequent fall, but I can't miss this opportunity.

Because if anything is Faye's signal?

It's the giant damned fireball that took out the entire back wall of the lodge.

Everything's quiet for a moment.

A stunned quiet, full of blinding white, everyone reeling and dizzy and trying to collect themselves, assessing the situation. Then a slim, triumphant figure steps forward, standing in the massive hole exploded out of the wall and looking at us with a smirk.

"Hello, boys," Faye says. "Miss me?"

Hook comes charging out of the snow like a bull, flinging himself at her. "You psycho *bi—*"

He doesn't get to finish the word.

Not when I'm up a second later, leaping after him, locking my arms around his neck from behind.

Hamlin's huge, but I'm stronger, and I've got the advantage.

I keep both arms tight around his thick neck, squeezing with all my might, while he roars and thrashes, snapping his fists back, and beating at me with frantic blows.

I still won't let go, even as he spins us around and around. I barely have a second to yell out to her.

"*Faye!*" I call, hoping she understands.

She does. I see her from the corner of my eye, going for the other fallen Enguard crew, a knife coming from her boot that she uses to saw through their ropes. They're up in an instant and tackling the other Pershing Shield men, wresting their guns away, knocking them out cold.

Hook staggers, an angry behemoth. My arms are aching, going numb, but I'm going to choke this bastard out if it's the last thing I do.

Gasping, wheezing, he raises his voice.

"*Carlo!*" he shouts. "Carlo, take the –"

No. Fuck your shot.

I stiffen, whipping my head around, looking for his phone.

And that's when he turns the tables.

His elbow crashes into my gut. Pain explodes. I'm winded.

My arms loosen, and he throws me off, flinging me back into a snowbank. In a single breath, he's on me, pinning me down, one hand choking down on my throat, the other fist smashing into my face in an explosion of blackout pain.

My vision goes dark, but I can still hear him – still *feel* him as the impact of his knuckles strikes my face again and again, pushing me closer and closer to the edge of gone.

I have to stay conscious. I have to keep fighting, keep him distracted, keep the only opportunity we're going to get open.

Surging up with the last of my strength, I slam my forehead into his chin. There's a sickening *crack*, a dizzying blur, his hateful, gnashing teeth caught in pain.

For a second, he's stunned and I'm ready to hurl myself at him again.

Until there's a click. The familiar sound of a safety lever.

The frenzy stops, leaving me groaning, struggling to open my eyes as the darkness tries to resolve into shapes, color, light.

And I see Faye standing over us both, an AK-47 in her hands, the muzzle pressed against Hamlin's temple while he's frozen, a monstrous snarl on his face as he looks at her sidelong with murder and violence in his gaze.

"I'd stop, if I were you," she says almost too mildly. "I'll put a bullet in your skull and not think twice."

"Shoot me then," Hamlin snarls, "and Carlo kills your friend's wife."

"N-no."

Another voice. It's the Senator who interrupts this time. He's wheezing, gasping, struggling to push himself up out of a snow pile that's stained red with blood. His blood, pouring from what looks like a bullet hole in his shoulder, dangerously close to his heart. He's pale, shaking.

And holding Hamlin's phone.

"Dad?" Faye whispers, going white. *"Dad!"*

Harris manages to hold up a hand. "Stay back, Faye," he

chokes out, his voice gurgling. He needs medical attention, but we're caught in a stalemate, everyone frozen, lives in the balance.

Somehow, we're the ones armed, and Hamlin still has the ultimate weapon if he's able to give an order to that fucking sniper.

Until Harris begins to speak.

Not to us.

Into the phone.

"Can you hear me, C-Carlo?" he forces out.

Carlo lets out an awkward snarl through the phone. "Who's this? Listen, I don't know who the hell you are, but if you've hurt the boss, I'm going to put a hole in this woman's skull."

"Think twice." Even weak, bleeding out, the Senator's voice is one of command. But more than that, too.

It's resolve. And he's looking at Faye the entire time, something almost desperate in his eyes.

Something I recognize as love, a father's. Because it's almost the same kind of love I feel that would make me do anything to save her.

And Harris continues, "This is Senator Paul Harris. I don't doubt you know who I am and what I know about your operation, Carlo. I'm willing to fully testify even if it means jail time for me. One of two things will happen here today. We'll kill Hook. You might kill that woman, but it won't change a thing. Your entire organization will fall apart and you'll end up on the FBI's most wanted list. You'll be dragged in sooner or later for murder. The other option is, we'll *apprehend* Hook, and he'll go on trial...and every last name of every last person who's ever worked for him will come out. Including yours. But you have a third choice, Carlo."

Hamlin interrupts with a snarl, his face a mask of bitter hate. "Don't fucking listen to him!"

Faye prods the tip of the AK-47 against his temple. "Shut up, you creep."

There's a long silence before Carlo asks warily through the phone, "Yeah? What's that?"

Somehow, even though his face is turning white, Harris keeps going. "You can run. Walk away right now and disappear. Take whatever Hamlin paid you for this job, and start over somewhere you'll never be found."

Carlo scoffs. "Bullshit. Hook'll find me."

"The hell he will," Harris answers with a grim smile, his hard, flinty gaze boring right into Hamlin. "He won't be finding anyone from a maximum security cell. I'll make sure he serves life in the strictest federal prison outside Guantanamo, Carlo. You have my word on that, as long as you leave that woman alone and walk away."

There's a long pause. A soft click from the other side of the phone.

Everyone sucks in a breath, including me.

Then the camera view swings around on a masked man's face. He pulls apart his sniper rifle, watching through the screen distrustfully. "Anybody finds me," he says, "I'll make you pay."

"Go," Harris orders.

The screen goes dark.

Landon collapses to his knees, burying his face in his hands with hoarse, relieved breaths. The Senator slumps into the snow, his eyes closing.

And I shove myself up again, plowing my fist as hard as I can into Hamlin's big face. It feels like the sheer force shatters my fingers, but I don't even feel it.

He reels backward, his nose bloody and twisted, and crashes to the ground, out cold.

Knockout.

I linger over him, triumphant, wondering when I'll ever have a moment as satisfying.

Riker and Landon aren't through. I wonder how my friend is even standing when he has so many bruises and he's limping on one leg, but *nothing* will keep him from this.

They practically tackle Hamlin, shoving him down, grabbing for the ropes used to bind them to start tying him up. Gabe dives for Skylar, helping his pregnant wife out of the snow, stroking her belly, nearly sobbing as he presses his face to her stomach as if listening for a heartbeat. She needs medical attention, immediately.

But so does Riker.

And the Senator, more than anyone.

With a soft, hurting cry, Faye drops the rifle and dives for her father. "Dad!"

He's face-down in the snow, not moving. She rolls him over, and he comes alert with a cry of pain.

She echoes that cry as he slumps once more, tears springing from her eyes as she grasps at him helplessly, the bravery she'd held onto to fight for everyone dropping away to leave a young woman so very afraid of losing her father just when he'd stepped up to *be* her father again.

I can't let that happen.

Even if I hurt everywhere, even if I think my nose may be nearly as broken as Hook's, I shove myself up to my feet and stumble over to the Senator's side.

Dropping down on my knees, I gently push her hands away and apply pressure to the wound to slow the bleeding. I couldn't save Tanner half a decade ago. The Senator, maybe.

"Hamlin's phone," I tell her quickly. "It works. Call 911, tell them we need a medevac, and damn the storm – a Senator's about to die. Get them to dispatch a heavy lift from the nearest military base if they have to." I'm ripping out of my coat, tearing it up, creating a bandage to at least keep as much of the Senator's blood inside his body as possible.

The irony isn't lost on me. I came here with an urge to kill this man for what I thought he'd done. Now, I'm working like the devil to save his life.

Because he may have helped save us all.

And one way or another, for Faye's sake above all, I know I won't let that good deed go unpaid.

I will *not* let this man die.

XXI: MOVE THE EARTH (FAYE)

This must be the living definition of what it means to be in shock.

It's been *three days*.

Three days in San Francisco, and I still feel like everything that happened wasn't real.

Maybe because I've barely had a second to regroup. If I haven't been collapsed in an exhausted heap recovering from minor injuries and fatigue, I've either been in the hospital with Dad or else in the San Francisco FBI field office, making yet *another* statement. Or going through yet another debriefing.

I know it's proper procedure. I know it like the back of my hand.

But I'm tired.

So damn tired.

And I've hardly seen James since I started my stay.

Sure, I could just pick up the phone and call him, but I can't help being afraid.

Considering past history, he might not answer, or he won't want to hear what I have to say.

These are words better said in person, anyway...but nailing him down in the flesh hasn't been easy.

I don't think he's been avoiding me. Not intentionally.

He has a home here in San Francisco, while I've been staying in a hotel under FBI protection.

We're still not quite out of the woods yet. Some of Hook Hamlin's higher-level friends may decide to take me out before I say anything that could lead to massive government takedowns and loss of a significant amount of power.

It's possible. Hamlin had his claws in deep everywhere, and my father's been tracking him for a long time.

I handed his laptop over to the Feds with all of the evidence he's been gathering.

The digital forensics analyst I gave it to nearly *squealed*, her eyes lighting up with fiendish delight.

Yeah. It's like that when you really love the job.

And all of this is making me realize how much I miss it.

I have a lot to get in order with my life, though, before I can even think about what's next with my career.

Dad will make a full recovery thanks to James' swift response time. His medical attention saved his life while we waited for the airlift, no question. The Enguard crew is mostly okay, too, except for poor Riker who suffered several broken bones and bleeding. He'll be here for at least another week, with his family by his side, his sweet wife Liv and that adorable, whip-sharp little girl, Em, his daughter.

Still, I want to keep a close eye on my father – well, as close as I can through the cordon of Secret Service agents surrounding his hospital room at all times. I want to sit down and take a long, hard look at myself. Maybe think about what *I* really want for once without other people pushing and prodding and pulling.

And right now, I want to talk to James.

I want to sit down and have a real, human conversation.

Not one overseen by government specialists and Federal agents and grim faced attorneys dedicated to making sure Hook Hamlin and his entire crew rot behind bars.

I have little doubt about that. It's not even clear if Hamlin will make it to trial. He's already been attacked once while he was being transported. Apparently, Dad and Enguard were hardly his only enemies. Every rival cartel and motorcycle gang he ever pissed off stealing their black market gunrunning business wants a piece of him. Or to silence him before he can squeal.

Thankfully, Dad and his evidence can help fill in the gaps. There's no doubt whatsoever something will make Hamlin sing sooner or later. And if he doesn't, we've got plenty to make sure Pershing and friends, and all the king's horses and all the king's men, never ever put this lethal bad egg back together again.

I only wish our lives didn't revolve around the Hamlin case.

James is what I need, just a moment alone, more than anything. I want more than legalese and horror stories.

I want to be with him for more than a few fleeting seconds. Mostly, we've been ships in the night, just passing by each other at the FBI office, giving our depositions, and now and then stopping to look at each other across the room.

A brush of hands in the hallway.

A murmured *are you all right?* and a soft *I'm managing* passed between us.

A lingering look at his healing bruises and the cast over the bridge of his nose. But this last time, this morning, as I was on my way in and he was on his way out, he pressed something into my hand without even looking at me.

A note.

Just a crumpled little bit of notepaper with an address.

And I don't need to be told that if I want to see him again...that's where I'll find him.

It still takes all of my nerve to work myself up to *go* there. Not to mention all of my best negotiation skills to talk my FBI guards into letting me out of their sight.

Going to visit a friend doesn't really fly well with the people trying to protect you from a long-range headshot, but I promise them I'll be all right and then slip into my rental car and escape before their skeptical looks can turn into outright refusal.

Even when I'm supposed to be recovering, I can't resist the urge to make a grand getaway.

It's not far to the address James gave me.

Whatever I'm expecting, it's not anything like what I find.

I can't believe this small, charming, light-filled house at the end of a wooded lane, tucked away in a little forested waterfront suburb of San Francisco with its many windows shining.

Private, cozy, the cottage sits in a sunlit glade like something out of a fairy tale, surrounded by an overflowing garden of fresh-bursting daffodils. They give off a healthy glow even in the chilly San Francisco winter, their yellow beaming like they've absorbed too much of the sun's own radiance and want to give some back.

The cottage even has its own freaking mini clock tower, and I don't understand why until I see the attached workshop with the store front window. Then the Victorian hand-lettering proclaiming *Nobel's Noble Antiques*, the inside a riot of strange and gorgeous things that make it look like some kind of steampunk dream.

No way. This can't be James' shop. His home. Can it?

Can the cold, icy man I've always known really live somewhere this warm, this magical, that he's been keeping locked away like a secret in his heart?

STILL NOT LOVE

All of a sudden, I know it.

Because every bit of light I've ever loved in James came from this place.

I can see it was born here. I can see it still *lives* here, and it feels like it's been waiting for him to be ready to reclaim it again.

I have to be brave. I have to tell him *I love him.*

And that I want him to run away with me, to live a life less ordinary, but just as sweet and magical and happy as this place.

When I park the car in the front lane and step out, I can hear it – piano music.

The music James has always loved. Part of that secret heart that made me love him in the first place.

My own heart trills in pattering rhythm with the keys as I step up the walk and follow the sound not to the front door of the house, but to the door of the shop. Tentatively, I push the door open.

Although a little bell overhead jingles, the man seated at the piano doesn't stop playing. Icy blond hair. Firm shoulders.

My entire body comes alive with breathless anticipation at the sight of James.

Until I step closer, reaching for him...

And realize it's not him at all.

It's an older man. One who tells me who James will be in many years, from the sharply similar features to the kindness around his eyes, the smile lines around his mouth.

God, I want to be there for that.

I want to be there to see James grow into this kind, weathered man with a hundred thousand memories engraved into his flesh.

I want to grow old with him. Together.

But I also feel immensely awkward standing here with

my hand outstretched while the older man doesn't even seem to realize I'm here. So I start to turn away.

Only to squeak, yelping, heart stuttering, as I realize James is *right behind me.*

That sneaky, stealthy freaking *snake-man.*

He looks down at me mildly, his lips quirked subtly. "Were you looking for someone, Tink?"

"Oh, you *ass!*" Laughing, I shove at his chest.

He rocks back lightly, steadying the two wine glasses in his hand without spilling so much as a single drop.

"Easy now," he teases softly. "A good red does stain."

Then that quirk of his lips softens. So do his eyes. They both become a real honest-to-God smile as he looks down at me, and everything I've been scared of, telling him how I feel, evaporates.

"Hello, Faye," he whispers.

"Hi," I answer quietly, while the old man keeps playing at my back – and also snorts in amusement. I chuckle. "Your place?"

"His." He lifts his chin toward the old man. "My Grandpa's. But I grew up here. Just me, Mom, and my grandfather. I visit often so he can yell at me about the book –"

"He *still hasn't finished it,*" the old man rumbles mid-song.

James takes the interruption in stride, clearing his throat. "And so I can tune the pianos he repairs."

As he speaks, he tosses his head toward the front window of the shop and offers me one of the wine glasses. "Come with me."

I take it, follow him to stand there, looking out over the golden daffodils. Just a little more privacy away from his grandfather until he melts into soft, soothing background noise, delicate piano notes plinking away.

It feels good like this.

Standing at James' side, shoulder to shoulder, his warmth

so close to mine. I smile, watching the wind make the daffodil heads bow in waves. "I can see it. Feel it."

"Feel it?"

I turn to face him, looking up into those stern features that don't seem so stern anymore.

Not when I know every little thing that gives him away.

He's just elegant. Handsome. Strong.

Perfect.

Even if there still *are* two little strips of white tape over his fractured nose, that once razor-sharp straightness now forever just a tiny bit crooked. Charmingly askew.

"Faye? Care to fill me in on this 'it' you're talking about?" he asks, taking a pull off his wine.

"Sure. First, tell me one thing – do you think I love you because you're cold and ruthless and sadistic?" I ask softly, then grin. "I want to fuck you because of those things, maybe. Ah, don't. I'm not finished." Before he can open his mouth, I press a finger to it.

He's grinning. James freaking Nobel is *grinning*, and even if I made sure to drop my voice enough to keep his grandfather from overhearing, it's just adorable to see him like this in front of his family.

"Faye."

"Don't. Not yet. I know I'm being crude, but..." I turn that silencing finger into a caress, tracing the line of his lips. "I love you because there's this secret heart of brightness in you. And it feels like this place. This *place* is like the living source of all you are, and I was so scared you'd lost it forever."

He stares at me with something like wonder, uncertainty.

And I realize then, with every unfolding moment showing me a deeper understanding of who James is, that it's not that he doesn't want to be loved.

It's that he believes he's not worthy. He walls himself off

behind his icy mask of smooth confidence so it won't hurt when people he trusts to care for him end up proving him right, rejecting him for the smallest failure.

That's why he tries so hard to be there for the people he loves, to do everything just perfect.

And why he torments himself over the slightest perceived inadequacy.

I love him for it. I do. And it almost breaks my heart when he asks quietly, "You truly love me?"

"Does it sound less believable if I'm not punching you and shouting it at you? Or writing it on your palm?" I ask, tilting my head with a wistful smile. "It's okay if you don't trust it. It's okay if you don't love me back. But if you'd like to try, maybe we could get away somewhere, take a vacation, see the world, be a little irresponsible for a while and –"

I don't get the chance to finish. Not when James – somehow without spilling a drop of our wine – hooks an arm around my waist, drags me in close, and seizes my mouth in a deep, breathless kiss.

Oh, God. It's a kiss so *different* from any way he's ever kissed me before.

No dominance games, no control, no taunting and tormenting and teasing this time.

Just pure, raw passion. More overwhelming than any command, a firestorm so potent it seems impossible from such an icy man.

He's melting me, melting *for* me, and *oh,* I'm dying to finally be able to touch the raw, sweet warmth at the heart of James Nobel.

I'm dying and coming alive again to have it bared for me in every lingering, deep stroke of his lips. They warm me from head to toe, leaving my knees weak and trembling.

And I can barely breathe by the time he parts our lips and

leans into me, brow to brow, those intense silver-blue eyes consuming me.

"Drink your wine, Tink," he whispers.

I'm left blinking, confused, my head spinning. "Huh?"

His lips quirk, reddened and damp from our kiss. "Just trust me. Drink."

"Okay." I swallow thickly, my heart going a mile a minute, and he watches me closely as I take a tentative sip, only to make a surprised sound. It's sweet. I recognize this flavor. "Il Duca Cardinal," I murmur.

"Your favorite."

"Yeah." I love that he remembers things like this.

Smiling, I take another, deeper sip – only to pause as something in the glass clinks against my teeth.

Something hard but not heavy.

Something that shouldn't be there unless...

Holy hell.

I freeze, straightening, pulling free from his arms so I can look down into the glass, frowning.

"Something's in there."

James lifts both brows in mock surprise. "Is there now?"

I give him an odd look. I don't dare think what it might be.

What's this about, really? Surely James wouldn't do something insane and impulsive and totally this sweet.

But my curiosity can't be ignored.

Slipping a finger into the long-stemmed glass, I swirl it around until I come up against something cool and metallic. Something...round. Something my fingertip slips neatly into, letting me hook its loop and draw it out, dripping wine from smooth gold curves and sharp diamond edges, into the light.

A ring.

A fricking *engagement ring*.

My stomach drops out to my knees. My heart rises up in

my throat. I just stare at it, then at him, then at it again, my lips numb. "J-James?"

He only smiles, his eyes crinkling at the corners, a warmth in those silvery depths like nothing I've ever seen. "I suppose it's a good thing you came here to tell me you love me," he says. "Since I asked you here to tell you I love you too. I love you, Faye, and I never should've turned my back on you. I made that mistake once. Never, ever again."

Then he's coaxing the ring out of my trembling fingers.

Sinking down to one knee, and I...I can't breathe.

My head is a whirlwind and it's got nothing to do with the wine. I'm completely lost and yet at the same time completely anchored in place by the certainty in his eyes, in his touch, as he clasps one of my hands in both of his, looking up at me with that quiet earnestness that's so James.

He's so *serious* about everything. But that's how I know he means it.

How I know he means it when he says he loves me as calmly as this. Like those words aren't the needles stitching my heartstrings together to make it whole.

How I know he means it when he stands there on one knee before me, smiling, reaching up for my hands.

And how I know he means it when he finally says, "Faye Harris, will you do me the honor of becoming my wife?"

The world's loudest *yes!* is out of my mouth almost before I realize I'm speaking.

Speaking, laughing, crying, clapping my hands over my mouth, only to realize he still needs them.

There's so much love in the warm, genuine smile this once-frozen man gives me, as he gently wipes the ring clean and reclaims my hand to slip it on my finger.

And when that ring slides home, I know what it means.

It's a promise.

A promise between us.

One that we'll always have each other's backs.

In every firefight, in every moment, in every day of our lives.

Now I belong to James Nobel.

And he sweeps me up, pulling me into an incandescent kiss while his grandfather laughs fondly and welcomes me to the family.

With every touch of our lips, with every kiss, I'm also reminded that James Nobel belongs to *me*.

We've almost died together too many times.

But now...

Now, we get to start a new life.

XXII: WITH THIS RING (JAMES)

"*F*or the last time," I tell Riker icily, "'Groomzilla' is *not* a word, and I'm not *being* one."

Riker gives me a skeptical look as he straightens my collar and boutonniere. We're standing in my old childhood bedroom in our tuxedos.

It's right across the hall from what was once my mother's workroom. Fitting, in a way.

Kenna and Olivia and Skylar are presumably busy tormenting my bride-to-be into her dress – apparently with much pricking and sticking of needles and pins involved, assuming the squeals and yelps of pain drifting through the doors are any indication.

Perhaps planning a wedding at my childhood home, in such close quarters, wasn't such a good idea.

But I wanted it to be here, in the garden of daffodils that my mother loved so much.

And Faye gave her input, too.

Faye said it *should* be here, in this place where she can easily see the heart I hide so much.

I'd like to think, over the last few months, that I've learned not to hide so much.

That I've shown her, every day, how much I love her.

How much her happiness matters to me.

How much I want to be with her, even if we've had a few minor hair-pulling fights over picking out a house that turned into wild hair-pulling sex as we snarled it out.

We ended up buying the beachside cottage where we defiled the kitchen counter while the realtor was out in her car looking for papers.

The sale was the proper thing to do, after all, after we'd marked the place.

I'm honestly amazed we haven't grown tired of each other yet, considering we're together every hour of every day – even at work.

And even though she's now my direct equal in company rank, it amuses me greatly to see the glitter in her eyes when I call her "Ma'am."

Because she knows, once we're alone at home, tumbled into bed, she won't be the one giving any orders.

Not when she begs for me so sweetly, while I take pleasure in denying her until she's ready to snap and fall apart.

Still. She's settled in well at Enguard.

After that display of explosives expertise at the resort and a little briefing with Landon about her work history, the boss abruptly decided that with the scale of increasingly complex, high-security jobs we've been taking on, we needed someone to coordinate bomb sweeps, detection, and disarmament for public security gigs.

And my fiancée just happened to be perfect for the job.

Riker, Landon, and Gabe give me a little good-natured ribbing over it, about being henpecked in the office and at home – though Gabe goes suspiciously quiet at even a glance from Skylar, leaving me smirking.

Damn if I mind.

I'm *proud* to see Faye so happy, blooming now that she's back to doing something that values her expertise rather than shoving her into a corner. Even though she's done being a librarian, she still sorts books some weekends, too, becoming a well known face in every charity reading program around the Bay. She doesn't need a watchful eye on her at all times to be protected.

My girl is perfectly capable of protecting herself. Of protecting me, even.

It doesn't mean I don't want to do whatever I can to keep her safe – and to make everything perfect.

Including our wedding.

I eyeball Riker, then bat his hands away and lean forward to adjust the boutonniere myself. He'd been doing it wrong, disarraying the spray of baby's breath cradling the crisp golden daffodil. "I told the florist I wanted yellow jonquils for Faye's bouquet," I say firmly. "Just like the ones in the garden. He shouldn't have waited until the day before the wedding to tell me he could only get petticoat daffodils."

"Uh-huh." Riker folds his arms over his chest, eyeing me with his lips twitching. "And the cake?"

"Buttercream is cloying and foul."

"...and the music."

"Anything more than a string quartet would run the risk of trampling the entire grounds and leaving a mountain of cleaning, so –" I stop, scowling at his reflection in the mirror, and straighten, smoothing the coat of my tux. "The point is, wanting things to be done to my specifications is *not* being a 'groomzilla.'"

"God, I don't know how Faye lives with you, man." Riker takes my shoulders and draws me around to face him. "Now listen to me very closely, Nobel."

"Obviously. I can't listen to you any other way. You're standing right in front of me."

"First, stop that pedantic shit, or I'm going to drop you off a cliff." But then he laughs, clapping my shoulder firmly. "Look. I know you're only being this much of an anal-retentive asshole because you care. It's a big day. You're trying to hide how nervous you are because you're about to walk out there and marry the most amazing woman you've ever met, and deep down you don't quite understand what she sees in you."

Everything inside me goes still.

Still and aching and quiet because he's too damn right.

Riker knows. He's done this before.

And it scares me a little that he's right. Not because there's anything wrong with being nervous on your wedding day, but because, fuck.

Riker *sees* me.

The way a true friend sees someone, and it makes me realize that all the years that I've thought I concealed myself so cleverly behind my walls, these people at Enguard have been learning me, knowing me, *loving* me as part of their family.

I'd thought I was just a ghost, a shadow.

It's unnerving to know they could see me all this time, yet the feeling is also wonderful.

Covering his hand on my shoulder with a firm clasp, I lower my eyes. "I know. And I know in the end she'll be happy even if the flowers are the wrong type."

"She'll be *happy* because she's marrying you. Just like you'll be happy because you're marrying her." He squeezes my shoulder. "You won't even notice the details, once you set eyes on each other. Everything else is incidental."

He's right. I know he's right.

For now, Faye is all that matters. I want to see her so badly, but I can't.

Not yet. No seeing the bride before she walks down the aisle.

She'd threatened to put my eyes out if I saw her in her wedding gown before the perfect moment. I don't even know what she'll be wearing. Hell, it doesn't matter.

She'll be beautiful to me. She'll be gorgeous. She'll be perfection, no matter what.

Gabe knocks on the door, then pushes it open enough to peek in. "Everybody's ready and waiting on you," he says. "If you wanna get in position, we can start this rodeo."

"Of course. Thanks, Gabe." I straighten my collar one more time, glance at Riker, and step outside into the hall.

The wedding is staged out back in the most lush, overgrown part of the daffodil garden, with Faye's father, a few cousins, and Senator Harris' security entourage in the folding chairs to one side.

Grandpa and my extended family are on the other, alongside the whole senior Enguard team.

Kenna, Skylar, Olivia, and Riker's daughter Em are bridesmaids. Landon, Gabe, and Riker are my groomsmen.

The bridesmaids' dresses are pale yellow, pretty A-line things with their hems flared and fluttered just like a daffodil's bell. Every groomsman wears a boutonniere with a daffodil in the center. Maybe I'm overdoing the motif a little.

But I'd like to think it would've made my mother happy.

And I think I finally know how I want her novel to end.

There's going to be a swirl of love notes coming full circle again, back where they began. I'll have the hero hunt them down, bring them together, and present them to the love of his life one more time. All simultaneously. A dramatic, fictional swan song to love and its ability to move mountains, hearts, and time.

Because for once, I'm living a life worthy of inspiring art.

I'm standing here, focused on taking my place at the altar, where the priest waits under an arch of interwoven flowers. As I move up the aisle, Senator Harris catches my eye and nods in approval.

I return the gesture and even manage to smile faintly. We haven't quite warmed up to each other yet, but give it time. He's my father-in-law now, and he seems to be *trying*.

Trying to treat Faye like family again, instead of like an object.

Then everyone's at attention as the music starts.

An adorable little girl named Jessie – Landon and Kenna's niece – comes traipsing up the silk-carpeted aisle, scattering flower petals everywhere. Followed by an even smaller toddler girl, Joannie, Skylar and Gabe's niece. She's so small she can barely focus enough to hold the ring box in her hand, let alone stumble up the aisle with her eyes wide, darting everywhere before landing on her mother, Sky's sister Monika, as she coaxes her on with little whispers of *come on, baby, come to Mama* while the small crowd *aahs* with delight.

I see Gabe and Skylar lock eyes. They know it won't be long before their own baby daughter catches right up to her older niece. That's the way it always is with children – something I know little about – but hope to one day with Faye.

And she's the very reason why every eye darts to the back as the door there opens, and Faye steps out.

I inhale a shaky breath. Just like a boy on his first prom date.

Goddamn, she's glorious. Beautiful in white and deep red hair like embers.

Every last bit of perfection I could imagine in a woman is here. From her simple white silk sheath dress with its pearl bodice to the short, yet elegant train.

Her shoulders are bare above the embroidery, pale and

subtly dusted in shimmering gold. Her hair, bound up into a coil of ringlets woven through with gold daffodils and white baby's breath against the fiery strands.

She's moving like time itself turns to mud, and it's still going far too fast.

This holy moment when I know I'm about to claim my wife is over too fast.

Soon, she stops just at the foot of the aisle, clutching her bouquet in nervous hands, frozen.

Until our eyes meet and she blooms into the most radiant smile I've ever seen.

Now, I understand what Riker meant.

Because suddenly the entire world falls away, and it's only me, Faye, and the space between us as she walks slowly up the aisle in time with the processional music.

She'd refused to allow her father or anyone else to give her away, wanting to walk the aisle alone after Harris overshadowed so much of her life already. But even if she were surrounded by a dozen people, I wouldn't be able to see anyone but her.

My heart is on fire. My world is ablaze.

And I hope my love will always burn this bright, this mad, every day this wonderful woman graces me with the beauty of her presence.

Time stops as she steps up the aisle toward me – and then she's there.

Standing in front of me, looking up at me with that smile that's at once shy and wicked, her heart-shaped face alight and glowing from within.

"Hi," she whispers.

"Hello, beautiful," I answer, before the priest raises his voice to get our attention.

The words he says don't matter.

This is just a formality. I don't need a ceremony to tell me I'll be with Faye for the rest of my life.

We're putting on pageantry for the sake of our loved ones and tradition, letting them join in this joyous feeling we share, but this? This crazy silver cord between us?

This has been real, solid, from the moment she said *yes* and I put that ring on her finger.

We've fought through hell together. Escaped the unthinkable. Not even the threat of death could keep us apart.

And time?

Time will only bring us closer.

I draw myself away from gazing into her brilliant green eyes, though, as the priest asks us to exchange our custom vows. Her smile grows merrier, almost impish, as I reach into my breast coat pocket for a folded slip of notepaper, and pass it to her.

She laughs. So does the entire crowd.

They know our story, how we began.

How she brought us closer and closer together with every little note that worked its way under my skin and inked its letters on my heart. And she has her own note, too, pulled from inside her bouquet, and she's even gone through the trouble of crumpling it up just like she used to, making the laughter start again.

Including my own.

And my chest is warm, tight with emotion, as I uncrumple it, smoothing the paper, reading it out loud for the benefit of our gathered friends.

"'My dearest James,'" I read. "'You drive me crazy. You make me see red.'" I stop, arching a brow. "This is hardly flattering," I whisper over to her.

The assembly laughs again. Faye's own giggle is the brightest, warm and sweet. Even the priest is chuckling. "Keep reading," she says.

Amused, I cock my head and continue, following the bold, handwritten strokes in blue ink. "'But every time I want to strangle you –" more laughter, "'I remember the most important thing. Red is the color of my heart. Red is the color of love, and I love you more than anything. There's not enough ink in this pen to tell you how much I love you...or how happy I am to be starting our life together. I'm proud to call you my husband. I'm proud to become your wife.'" On the last word, everyone sighs blissfully, while I can only smile. Smile in ways that I never let anyone see, and yet she brings it out in me, all of this emotion. Lifting my head from the note, I meet her eyes, feeling my heart turn hot as flame. "A bit more verbose than a wink and a 'made you look.'"

I wink at her then, remembering our days at Quantico, where this strange, beautiful thing began.

While another smattering of laughter erupts from the crowd, Faye sticks her tongue out, eyes scrunching up. "It *did* make you look."

"And I've never been able to look away since."

Her breath catches, and she makes a soft, embarrassed sound, her cheeks flushing. She lowers her eyes, unfolding my note. There are significantly fewer lines than hers, but as her eyes scan back and forth, she sucks in a sharp breath, her blush deepening, her smile fading as she reads out loud softly.

"'You are everything to me, Faye,'" she reads. "'You're my sun, and my world rises and sets with you. Where my life was cold, you brought warmth. Where my heart was dark, you brought light. I'm who I am thanks to you. And I'll cherish you always, my love.'" Her lips tremble as the crowd descends into sighs again. Her eyes swell. *"James."*

I can't help but smile, to see her so overcome with emotion as she reaches for my hand, squeezing tight. I squeeze back, drawing her a step closer. "Does that mean I don't need to guess the answer to the most important question of all?"

"You never had to," she whispers, then laughs, fully overwhelmed. "But we should probably let the priest do his job."

"That would be appreciated," the priest says, dryly but warmly, before laughing. "If we can continue?"

All that's left is a simple question.

Do you, Faye? and *Do you, James?*

And then she's saying "I do" and I'm saying "I do" and just like that, two simple words and Riker stealing the ring box from baby Joannie so we can slip them on each other's fingers – it's done.

We're suddenly husband and wife.

Then there's flowers in my hair from her bouquet as she throws her arms around my neck and kisses me before the priest can even say *kiss the bride*.

My throat goes tight and my fucking heart might pound out of my chest

I can't remember the last time I was this alive, this animated, this real.

Not even for my mother, when the pain of her death wrung everything out of me, left me broken and hollow. It's like Faye's kiss fills me up again forever.

I can't contain these feelings, so they must come out somehow. I'm hardly the only one going to pieces when Faye's clinging to me and crying and laughing at the same time...and fuck, so am I.

But I thank Faye every day for bringing back the light.

Breathlessly, we break apart. That's when I remember there are other people here, clapping, laughing, cheering us on, and there are a few more damp eyes in the crowd.

With everybody here, celebrating us becoming one, it just hits me. I feel something massive.

I feel like I'm *part* of something for the first time in so long.

That I belong among these people, instead of invisible, haunting the edges.

And they envelop me, envelop *us*, as the wedding turns into a flash reception.

Drinks materialize on the back patio in massive tubs of ice, everyone milling around, wanting to congratulate us, hug us, take pictures together that I'll never live down.

Not when I can't seem to stop smiling. Oh, everyone at Enguard will remember this the next time they catch me brooding over something.

Not that I think I'll be brooding much anymore, considering I'll get to spend every day at the office with my lovely new wife.

Still. A man has to have some dignity.

But for now, I throw dignity aside to enjoy the warm summer day, the sun shining down like its banishing the last memories of those frozen days of us in hell.

Those days at the lodge tested the strength of our relationship. Tested how bad we wanted forever. Saw us through to the other side only because we could trust each other.

The bond between us, and the silent language of warmth and love that seems to say so many things without words every time we look at each other.

And another of those looks tells us when it's time to leave, though Grandpa will likely be hosting festivities late into the night.

This is our day, though, and it's time for us to celebrate it our way.

Alone. Just the two of us, riding high on this euphoria between us like electricity.

It's the same energy moving us forward as we steal away while everyone's distracted, clasp hands, and run.

STILL NOT LOVE

By the time anyone spots us, we're almost to the car, Faye clutching her skirts and laughing, and everyone calling out well-wishes after us, teasing, friendly, egging us on.

Even I'm laughing by the time we dive into the open-top convertible, nearly slamming the door on Faye's skirt, and take off.

As we sail down the road, some of the flowers in Faye's hair fly away, bright petals lifting up into the sky, rising toward the heavens.

Maybe they're taking a few little love notes up to my mother, just to let her know.

Just to let her know I'm going to be okay.

And that I'll do a proper tribute to her dream.

I'll write every bit of love I feel right now into her book.

That love carries me forward during a long drive down the coast, the sunset to our right, Faye a vision in white in the passenger seat.

We never even decided what we'd do for our honeymoon. I'm such a planner that it's liberating to just have our bags packed and *go* with no destination in sight.

We'll stop when something catches our eye and come back when we're ready.

For now, we're runaways.

Castaways in love, driving down the California coastline like we're flying.

We finally stop in Morro Bay. It's a place where the water glows so blue that the night turns it luminescent.

A huge stone cliff presides over the picturesque little town like some ancient watcher.

The tiny bed and breakfast we find hangs over the water, with private cottages whose floor-to-ceiling glass windows open wide. Then they become open-air spaces, letting in the salty night air, gauzy curtains fluttering beneath the stars, cool wood beneath our feet.

In the little blue pond behind our cottage, candles float against the water, glimmering like fireflies in the night. This quiet, this moment where we clasp hands and step inside what'll be our wedding boudoir? It's damn beautiful.

It's everything to me, and I look down at Faye with a wonder reflected in her eyes, shining like twin stars in the dark.

I'm not sure who reaches for who first.

Only that our bags hit the floor and we're in each other's arms.

This kiss tastes like forever as we tangle, tumbling together on the bed, her dress a flow of white all around us. Like it's dragging me down into the undertow of a love so deep, I'll gladly let it drown me.

Faye's lips are ripe, perfect, plush.

She's so delicate right now, so perfect, the fire in her simmering down to a steady flickering glow like hearth-fire blended into every sweetness in the world.

I know this sex will be otherworldly. What else?

As many times as we've come together, as many times as I've teased and taunted her, ruled her body, made her weep and beg for me, this time is different.

Tonight, I kiss her like she's made of smoke, and if I breathe too hard, she'll blow away.

Each time I brush my lips across hers, she lets out a sighing whisper of my name, her body molding to mine, the heat between us a slow and quiet thing.

It's timeless here. There's no urgency, nothing demanding, no countdown as we trade kiss after kiss for what feels like forever, each one slowly stoking me higher and higher until I burn with the need for her.

The satin of her dress is cool under my palms. I stroke the shape of her body again and again, taking my time to savor her, know her, relearn her again and again.

I know Faye's body, her lips, as well as I know my own.

But this is the first time she's been mine as my *wife*, and that means something incredible.

That means some delectable, insane fuckery I can't even put into words.

She tastes even sweeter than ever.

I delve into her mouth to trace, caress, explore, worship.

Her voice is a trembling thing as I slowly draw her dress up higher, skimming my fingers over the sleek, tempting stockings underneath, the lacy garter straps, the naked flesh of her quivering, plush thighs.

Shifting onto my back, I draw her on top of me until she's this glorious creature spread over me, her hair a wind-tumbled mess still half-tangled with wilted flowers. Until I see Tink, this fairy thing I want to keep for all my days.

Her eyes go dilated and dark and needy as she looks down at me through the thick fan of her lashes.

"You ready for your husband, Faye?" I whisper, running tense fingers through her hair. "You ready for me all damn night?"

"Mm. Not long enough. We'd better get a head start."

Smiling, we do.

Darting her tongue over her lips, she shifts to straddle me, and I hiss through my teeth.

I lift myself up as the soft slip of fabric guarding every sweet slick space inside her drags over my slacks, my cock.

Fuck!

I want her just like this. Still in her dress, but disarrayed.

Let the fabric be a perfect mark of this day, but the mussed hair, the faded lipstick, the skirt lifted up over delicate white lace panties and stockings just one more reminder I've made her *mine*.

And when I slip my hands down the back of her panties,

kneading my fingers over the lush curve of her ass before sliding my fingertips over her steaming cunt, I'm gone.

She steals my breath away, arching her back, bracing her hands against my stomach.

Her lips fall slack with pleasure as I stroke deeper and deeper inside her.

Just to feel her wetness around my fingers, her tight, mad heat that just makes her want it more.

Just to see how she closes her eyes so tight and makes those soft, gasping sounds.

Just to sense how she digs her nails into my shirt, her shoulders thrust up to either side of her throat, pure bliss written on her face as she rocks back into my thrusting fingers.

I need her. I crave her.

And this time I'm the one who can't wait, the one driven to the edge, as her soft flesh tightens around my fingers and I'm driven half insane, imagining that tightness around my cock.

I need to be *with* her, damn it.

One with her, and she lets out a pleading mewl as I withdraw my fingers, unzip my slacks, and shove her panties to one side.

Her pussy waits like something from a dream. Hot and slick and ready. It's as lush as her moans, eager as the steady current running through my dick.

"Knees, Faye," I whisper.

She lifts herself up at my command, bracing herself with those luscious tempting thighs spread wide, just a glimpse past her skirt of that sweet pink I ache for.

Then she sinks down as I grip her hips, pull her into me, closing my eyes with a shuddering groan as her perfection draws me in.

God, she's too perfect. Created just for me.

From the tight clench of her body around my cock as she takes me so full, to the way she arches and shudders with such wanton abandon. Just moving over me until I don't know if I'm thrusting into her or she's thrusting down on me.

Not when we're just meeting in this perfect rhythm between us, this wordless understanding that guides us as if we're one being.

Her fingers lace with mine, our hands clasped. We move together in a steady push and pull of deep, aching pleasure.

That bliss rips at my heart and pulls at my body.

Even as my flesh demands I close my eyes and give in, I can't stop myself from watching her.

From devouring her. My pleasure comes as much in seeing hers as it does in the friction and fire gliding over my cock, making it throb like mad.

It's too overwhelming in all the best ways, taking my wife like this.

I fuck her over the edge once, fist in her hair, snarling as she comes real sweet for me.

"That's it, Tink. Let it go. Give it up for me if you want mine," I whisper through her first O.

Always loving the screaming, gorgeous mess she becomes.

Always loving how she goes off like a rocket, louder with every jab of my hips.

Always loving every bit of her as she falls apart naked just for me.

Soon, I'll be doing the same. It's a miracle I've lasted this long at this pace, this rhythm, this siren temptation.

Faye's hair is a halo of fire, shining with starlight.

Her lips are ruby plushness, gleaming and parted and so erotic it hurts.

Her tits swell, nearly spilling over her loosened bodice,

swaying and moving each time she rolls her hips gracefully to bring herself back down and take me into her fully.

Her breaths come hotter, faster, and on each exhale, she cries out.

"James, James, *James!*"

I smile.

I need no other words to know she's mine. That she'll always be mine, and I draw her down to me, kiss my name from her lips and tumble her back to pin her against the bed, hold her, keep her, bury so deep that we'll feel each other always, imprinted on each other's flesh like a tattoo.

This, here, is my love note.

Written in passion, inked in flesh, forged in pleasure.

No words, but just the sounds our bodies make as they meet, again and again.

I show her I love her with each slow, drawing stroke, with each touch of our lips, each meeting of our bodies.

And her love crashes down around me as we find the stars together.

Hell, as we find each other. Again. Just like we always do.

Then we find forever.

It comes in the explosion that strikes between us with lightning force.

She's coming. I'm coming. We're coming together so hard and so deep I just know one thing.

I could never feel this with anyone besides Faye Harris – now Faye Nobel.

She's what makes my pulse move and my body burn.

And tonight as we fall, as we tangle, as we collapse in a breathless rush of manic pleasure and aching flesh and slicked sweat, it's ours.

This night is our promise.

Our oath that I'll never, ever betray, for as long as we both shall live.

"I love you, Tink. I love every wicked thing you do to me, and every little wonder," I whisper, pushing my forehead against hers.

"You're lucky I love you, too, Peter Pan. We'd never find home without each other or take down Hook, as silly as that sounds."

Her eyes are bright and wide and she's smiling so peacefully. I'm smiling, too.

Because maybe it does sound ridiculous in that way that's all Faye.

Maybe it's silly that we're stuck on these fairy tale names, and she's finally given me an obvious one in turn.

Maybe it's so insufferably playful because it's real. And we're in love. And it's the only thing that matters tonight between a thousand soft words and laughs and fiery kisses with the woman I've pledged my life to.

XXIII: EXTENDED EPILOGUE (FAYE)

Years Later

IT'S NEARLY three in the morning by the time I'm done reading.

It's the final draft of *the* book, the one started by James' mother and finished by her son.

I'd transcribed it to digital and then printed it out and tossed it in a binder so I could curl up with it and read through every page. Hoping to savor every last painstaking word scrawled out a decade ago.

But I suppose it's truly James' book, now, isn't it?

It's totally his touch in the revisions he's been working on for the year since we returned from our honeymoon. But I can also feel the touch of a woman I've never met.

A woman I'd like to think would smile to see her very pregnant daughter-in-law binge-reading until predawn because it's just *that good*.

And so's the ending James gave it.

STILL NOT LOVE

Sweet perfection.

In it, the hero proposes to the heroine like any good romance book.

But just as he does, from overhead the thousand love notes he wrote her come showering down. Whether they were written on paper or in flower petals, on paper cups or in sparks of light, they fall down in a rain.

Either the notes themselves or their symbols, becoming this mad, pretty shower of love that pours down on them, littering everywhere until it's like seeing the cherry blossoms in Japan.

This beautiful expression of adoration and devotion and the work a man was willing to do to show how much he really loved his woman.

All with a thousand little love notes.

Sure, it's a little ridiculous.

Sure, it's a lot sappy.

Abso-freaking-lutely sure, it's heavy on the *awww*. Because I know who breathed life into those words, those moments, those last little pieces of a dead woman's swan song to love on planet Earth.

James thought he couldn't finish this book. He denied it so many long nights, practically ripping out his short ice blond hair. Telling me he was done when he'd come home from a long day at the office with a pounding chaos of writer's block.

That's where I came in. His last little nudge.

I wouldn't let him quit because he never quit on me. I'd throw my arms over his strong, wide shoulders, urging him on to rearrange just a few more words. Or add another sentence. Or cut himself just a little deeper and bleed into the manuscript.

I'm not an unbiased critic, and it's not just the writing I'm in a total swoon for.

This book, this masterpiece, is more than just one last goodbye between the veil for a mother and her son. It's a living, breathing testament to our love in the here and now.

I think he finished it just right. Any publisher would be insane not to snap it up.

Apparently, our unborn son agrees, because just as I close the back cover with a smile, a hearty kick rattles my belly, making me grunt out an *oof*.

"Calm down there," I whisper. "You like Daddy's book too, huh?"

James is awake in an instant.

He's back in ninja-robot mode, bolting to full alertness in a heartbeat. It's been that way ever since he found out I was pregnant. It's equal parts adorable and frustrating.

I could make the smallest whimper in the middle of the night, and he'd be up before the sound was fully out of my mouth, rearranging the bed, calling an all-night mattress company for a replacement when really, all I'd needed was a little help rolling over.

He's the most ridiculously, over-the-top, overprotective father and husband ever. The *definition* of extra.

And I love him for it.

Just as I love him for the concerned way he watches me as he pushes himself up, the blanket falling down from his bare shoulders until sculptured muscle gleams in the faint moonlight, drifting through the window of our bedroom.

"Faye?" he asks, voice dark with worry. "Is the baby all right?"

I smile, shifting to lean over and tuck myself against his side. "He's fine. We just stayed up reading your book and he wanted to add a little colorful commentary."

James makes an amused snort, slipping an arm around my shoulders and gathering me close, keeping me safe in the shelter of his arms.

"Lovely. Not even born yet and already a literary critic." There's a pause – one of his stony silences that I've learned now is hesitation, uncertainty, before he asks softly, "And? How was it?"

It's such a simple question, but there's so much more in it. I know what he's really asking.

Is it good enough?

Is it good enough for her memory?

I smile, nuzzling his shoulder, wrapping my arms around him and squeezing so tight.

"It's a beautiful tribute, James," I murmur. "To your memory of her, and to love in general." I hug the bound manuscript to my chest. "I felt like...in a way I got to meet her. And to see the parts of her in you."

"I'm really nothing like my mother."

"But you are." I tilt my head up to look at him, taking in the sleep-mussed tangle of blond hair, the new softness that never seems to leave those silvery-blue eyes when he looks at me.

"This book tells me she was a woman who loved hard and deep, with everything in her." I lean into him enough to push him lightly. "Seems to me like that's something her son inherited."

For a second, he's staring blankly at the wall. It's like I can see everything ticking away behind his bright eyes, all the pain and strife and years we had to sacrifice to bring us here.

Homer, eat your heart out. Even your Odysseus didn't suffer a fraction of the hellish monsters we did on his way back to love.

Then James shifts next to me, staring longingly into my eyes.

"It's hard for me to see myself that way, I suppose. Until I see myself through your eyes." He leans down, breathing gently into my hair, inhaling my scent. "You make me a better man, Faye."

"Nah. I just remind you there's one hiding under that asshole façade."

He laughs softly, squeezing me tighter. "So then. Are we up for the day, or going back to sleep?"

"Ask *him*." I pat my belly, but the baby doesn't kick again. "I don't think he's hungry, and I'm a little sleepy, so..."

Gently, James tumbles me backward, spilling me down on the bed so he can hover over me, his gloriously chiseled frame blocking the light as he leans down to brush his lips on mine. "Then try to sleep, Tink," he murmurs. "You have the baby shower tomorrow."

"Ugh. Thanks for reminding me." I don't really mind.

It's with all of the other Enguard girls, Kenna and Skylar and Liv and even Em showing up, but I have no idea how to handle this kind of thing.

I'm going to be wrung out by the end even if I wind up enjoying myself. "I never understood the point of baby showers."

"I believe it's so everyone can spoil you rotten into forgetting why being pregnant is nine months of torturing your body."

I laugh. "And eighteen years raising a child who's just going to hate you for it."

"They always grow out of it. Any child we raise will eventually realize the truth." He touches his nose to mine.

"Yeah? What truth is that?"

"That we love them more than anything and would do anything for them. Because I can't imagine it any other way, Tink."

Neither can I. Not when James is so loving, so attentive, and I can't picture him being anything but perfect with our child.

Children, plural, if I have my way. Kenna's already got a head start on me with her baby last year, Skylar's got her a second one coming, and I need to catch up.

With James and the other men of Enguard so busy with the business growing and each one of them finding their niche, the expression of their strengths and talent makes them as happy as my job makes me. It's a freaking miracle any of us have time for kids.

But we *make* time.

Just like we make time for each other. In all my time with Enguard, I've learned it's worth it.

It's more than just a company.

It's a family.

It's our family now, just as much as James and our unborn son and I are a family all our own.

It feels right. It feels perfect.

It feels like home.

And I find that feeling again and again as I draw James down and kiss him, wrapping my arms around his neck, pressing my body into him, inviting him to show me how I ended up with this swollen belly in the first place.

And as he whispers "Faye," his hands firm on my body yet his lips so gentle on mine, I know.

I know there could never, ever be another man made for me.

James Nobel is the only man I could ever love, and I'm going to cherish many more love notes with our little family.

Months Later (James)

"Okay. You're taking the fall this time, Peter Pan." Skylar slams a small stack of papers down on my desk.

I turn, looking up, searching her eyes with mine to ask, *what the hell now?*

At least she's smiling in her own devious, sharpening-her-claws-on-the-world way. "Gabe. That's what. Gabe...freaking Gabe...is writing me love letters. No thanks to you."

I smile as she rolls her eyes, moving her hand off the papers. "Hell, I don't even know why I'm sharing this but take a look, Mr. New York Times Bestseller. This is what you did."

Adjusting my glasses, I stare at a few lines on the first page. It's hard to keep my jaw from falling clean to the floor.

Definitely his style. Definitely over the top. Definitely heartwarming in his own huge, gentle giant way.

S*unbeam*,

S*omething's all different today.*

I think I woke up loving you even more.

It ain't just James' silly book or us sharing the same breathing space or the way you rocked my world something fierce for the ten thousandth time last night. It's that I realized something I already knew every day but hadn't ever said this way.

I love you for being you, Sky.

For loving me.

For putting a family, a life, and a smile in this crazy old brain.

"T*ouching*," I say. I'll admit it's a little hard not to burst out laughing or just stand up and hug the woman while she's standing there, looking too much like a wet cat that's just doubled its woes by biting into a lemon.

"Oh, that isn't even half of it," she whispers, shoving aside Gabe's letter and tucking it back in her hand. "Read the next one."

The next? What the –

Oh. I see Riker's handwriting on a fresh page and almost choke on my tongue. Well, this should be entertaining.

Liv,

You'll always be *the big writer in the family and I don't have a thousand and one love notes like my buddy with his book.*

But I was up last night, worrying over how Em will take her graduate level astrophysics class next Fall and still have time for evening taekwondo lessons with that Ryan kid and...screw it. Here goes.

I love you like nothing else, baby girl.
I tell you every day and it's still not enough.
Not by half.
You need it in the word and in the flesh and in the tongue.
I love it all.

Love every word, every laugh, every night I get with you. Love every moment you're mine. And the only thing I hate about it is how it took James' loud-ass boasting about his hit novel for damn near a month to pull it out of me.

I stand, straightening my tie, squeezing her shoulder. I hear the keyboard clicking away a few paces away, which tells me Riker hasn't left for the day.

He has no clue how hard I'm going to bust his balls just as soon as Sky lets me –

"Wait. There's more, jackass," she whispers, sniffing back the wetness in her eyes. "Don't ever let him see this. I need to put it back on his desk when we're done, but..."

She pushes a third page into my hand, this time with the stylized header of his famous romance author wife at the top.

FROM THE DESK OF MRS. KENNA STRAUSS:

Reb,

I lost you for too long one time because you read something I couldn't stand you seeing.

Now I've had you back in love and marriage and maybe I'm crazy for wanting to write you a letter...but there's no better way I can show you my soul.

You're the best wife and mom a man, a baby boy, and two blue furballs could ever hope for.

You're the best fire any man could ever have between the sheets.

You're a bestseller to the world, but to me, you're just one thing and always one.

The best.

Period.

Now that we've got the corny stuff out of the way, how about dinner?

Landon

"Oh. Oh, fuck," I whisper, unsure whether I want to beam like the sun or throw myself off the rooftop. "You'd better get this back to his desk before he catches you, I suppose. I certainly never set out to inspire the boss."

"Yeah, well, you kinda did. Congratulations. We'd might as well change our name to Enguard Romance at the rate it's going. *Ugh.*" The last rough sound leaving her throat is so strained in its denial, I laugh.

"Don't tell me. You're wondering how you can repay the favor?"

"Huh? What, no, I just came by to show you, um..." Skylar sucks her bottom lip, her cheeks turning crimson. "Oh, okay, damn it. But not a *word* about this to anyone. I don't know a thing about writing sappy love notes. That's more you and Faye."

I nod solemnly, guilty as charged, then lean in to whisper. "Mum's the word. Listen, Sky, if there's one thing I learned from revising this beast of a book, it's that there's an infinite number of ways to tell someone you're in love. My mother just captured a thousand and one of them. Even if you think they've heard it before, even if you think you're repeating yourself, even if you think they won't understand...reach down. Find it. Pull it up, sure as your own heart. Give your love on the page, give it true, and always give everything."

"Awesome, Nobel. So now you're a writing professor, too?"

I grin. I hardly ever imagined myself teaching, but who the hell knows what I'll do when I retire. Whenever chasing psychopaths and terrorist kingpins gets boring.

"Seriously, I'll work on it. Thanks. I know your head's already the size of Golden Gate Bridge around here, but I figured you deserved to know. People *love* your book. Not just the editors and all the book clubs who keep buying it...but your friends, too."

"Thank you. Again. Take care of yourself, Skylar," I say, standing as I watch her turn the corner sharply to Landon's office, rubbing at her eye.

For the next sixty seconds, I'm stunned. Bewildered.

Standing in awestruck wonder, glued to the floor by questions, wondering how the hell a closed off man like me could work this kind of black magic on an entire crew of busy, hardened, scarred people I'm lucky enough to have as friends.

Briefly, I consider storming up behind Riker and quoting his own lines back at him just to see how red his face can get under his beard.

Then I think better of it.

Because I know I have something better to do.

I know why I finished mother's huge tome about love.

I know why it became a bestseller in twelve different languages.

And I know she's waiting for me at home, about to lay our little boy down for a nap, before she hops on her laptop to study a few more white papers in advanced bomb detection for the company presentation in Seattle next week.

I'm going to see Faye.

But first, I have this terrible urge to one up my own book by writing her a love note to end them all.

ABOUT NICOLE SNOW

Nicole Snow is a *Wall Street Journal* and *USA Today* bestselling author. She found her love of writing by hashing out love scenes on lunch breaks and plotting her great escape from boardrooms. Her work roared onto the indie romance scene in 2014 with her Grizzlies MC series.

Since then Snow aims for the very best in growly, heart-of-gold alpha heroes, unbelievable suspense, and swoon storms aplenty.

Already hooked on her stuff? Visit nicolesnowbooks.com to sign up for her newsletter and connect on social media.

Got a question or comment on her work? Reach her anytime at nicole@nicolesnowbooks.com

Thanks for reading. And please remember to leave an honest review! Nothing helps an author more.

MORE BOOKS BY NICOLE

Stand Alone Novels

Accidental Hero
Accidental Protector
Accidental Romeo
Cinderella Undone
Man Enough
Surprise Daddy
Prince With Benefits
Marry Me Again
Love Scars
Recklessly His
Stepbrother UnSEALed
Stepbrother Charming

Enguard Protectors Books

Still Not Over You
Still Not Into You
Still Not Yours
Still Not Love

Baby Fever Books

Baby Fever Bride
Baby Fever Promise

Baby Fever Secrets

Only Pretend Books

Fiance on Paper
One Night Bride

Grizzlies MC Books

Outlaw's Kiss
Outlaw's Obsession
Outlaw's Bride
Outlaw's Vow

Deadly Pistols MC Books

Never Love an Outlaw
Never Kiss an Outlaw
Never Have an Outlaw's Baby
Never Wed an Outlaw

Prairie Devils MC Books

Outlaw Kind of Love
Nomad Kind of Love
Savage Kind of Love
Wicked Kind of Love
Bitter Kind of Love

Printed in Dunstable, United Kingdom